CHILLING ADVENTURES OF

SABRINA

Daughter of Chaos

BY SARAH REES BRENNAN

Scholastic Inc.

For Tasha and Dave, with love and congratulations
and thanks for the witchy pickup lines.
I only have eye of newt for you two!

© 2020 Archie Comics Publications, Inc.

All rights reserved. Published by Scholastic Inc., *Publishers since 1920*. SCHOLASTIC and associated
logos are trademarks and/or registered trademarks of Scholastic Inc.

The publisher does not have any control over and does not assume any responsibility for author or
third-party websites or their content.

No part of this publication may be reproduced, stored in a retrieval system, or transmitted in any
form or by any means, electronic, mechanical, photocopying, recording, or otherwise, without
written permission of the publisher. For information regarding permission, write to Scholastic
Inc., Attention: Permissions Department, 557 Broadway, New York, NY 10012.

This book is a work of fiction. Names, characters, places, and incidents are either the product of the
author's imagination or are used fictitiously, and any resemblance to actual persons, living or dead,
business establishments, events, or locales is entirely coincidental.

Edna St. Vincent Millay, excerpt from "Dirge Without Music" from Collected Poems. Copyright
1928, © 1955 by Edna St. Vincent Millay and Norma Millay Ellis. Reprinted with the permission of
The Permissions Company, LLC on behalf of Holly Peppe, Literary Executor, The Edna St. Vincent
Millay Society. www.millay.org.

ISBN 978-1-338-32606-2

10 9 8 7 6 5 4 3 2 1   20 21 22 23 24

Printed in the U.S.A.   23

First printing 2020

Book design by Katie Fitch

This year may we renew the earth.
Let it begin with each step we take.
Let it begin with each change we make.
Let it begin with each chain we break.
Let it begin when we awake.

—Traditional witches' chant

ALL THE WITCHES IN YOUR TOWN

December 10, the Night of the Greendale Thirteen
SABRINA

Never get caught crying in school. It shows weakness.

This is especially true in a school for witches. Yet on the night ghosts came to destroy my town, there I was in the Academy of Unseen Arts, sitting on the balcony that overlooked the statue of Satan and fighting back tears.

I couldn't let myself fall apart. I had a plan. My family and I intended to protect the mortals of Greendale. We had a place to keep them safe.

Except the mortal I loved best wouldn't come. And I didn't blame him.

I'd loved Harvey ever since he and I and our best friends Roz and Susie met on our first day of mortal school. He was the tallest, sweetest boy in class, and I was the smallest, bossiest girl.

1

But my whole life, I'd kept a secret from him. I'd never told him that I was a witch. My family were all witches. And one day I was expected to sign my soul away to Satan and leave Harvey forever.

When is the best time to tell the boy you love that you're a witch?

The best time is definitely *not* after you've brought his brother back from the dead as a soulless husk. Harvey had laid Tommy to rest himself. He'd broken up with me. Now he wouldn't even let me protect him.

I'd thought I could bring Tommy back to life for Harvey. I'd meant my love and my magic to be a gift. Maybe I'd thought it was a good way to show Harvey how wonderful magic could be. See? No mortal could do this. See how a witch loves you.

I'd shown Harvey all right.

I'd shown him a witch's love is disaster. A witch's love is ruin.

I was scared of what might happen to Harvey. I was scared he'd never forgive me. And I was scared of what I might have to do to protect the town that was my home. I sat on the stone balcony and hugged my knees, curled up in a tight ball to stop myself from shaking. I couldn't let myself tremble or falter.

I was here on a mission.

Just then, the red lanterns in the hall fell on the dark hair of the boy running up the steps to the balcony. He saw me on the floor and dropped the book under his arm.

The book was bound in human skin, with a single eyeball set in the cover. The eyeball rolled mournfully up at Nick from the dust, but Nick ignored it. "Sabrina! What are you doing here?"

I swallowed. Nick's dark gaze flickered, tracking the movement. He had a striking face, but it was frequently difficult to read. He'd once offered to be my shoulder to cry on. I wasn't sure how he would react if I actually took him up on that.

"I was looking for you."

"On the floor?" Nick asked. "Did you think someone dropped me and I'd rolled away under the furnishings?"

Quietly, I said: "I'm having a hard time."

I didn't know how to tell Nick about heartbreak. Nick Scratch was the one friend I'd made in the Academy of Unseen Arts. He'd also asked me out practically as soon as we met. When I said I had a boyfriend, he'd suggested I could have two boyfriends.

That was obviously out of the question, and Nick was clearly a playboy. If he thought a girl could have two boyfriends, who knew how many girlfriends he had? Maybe Nick had twenty girlfriends. Maybe he had a hundred.

He'd taken rejection with an easy grace that made me like him. I figured Nick Scratch wasn't the type to break his heart over a girl. He might be a playboy, but he was a playboy interested in the same spells and books I was fascinated by, and he listened when I had problems, offered advice, and risked getting into trouble for me.

So he was my new, oddly flirty, unsettlingly handsome friend. But I hadn't known him that long, and I didn't know if I could trust him. Now I sat on the edge of the balcony, hugging my knees and feeling desperate. I didn't know if it was safe to be desperate around Nick.

I heard Nick walk toward me. His steps rang on the stone, echoing up to the shadowed ceiling of our school. The whole Academy was made of pentagram shapes, stretching on in the shadows. Sounds were different here, with strange depths to them. Light was different here, catching red in the students' eyes. I was different here.

"What's this about, Sabrina?" Nick murmured.

"I need help," I whispered. "I don't know who to ask."

When I looked up, Nick was kneeling beside me. We sat in the scarlet-drenched light on the edge of the stone balcony together. Nick's gaze was intent, as though I were a riddle he was trying to work out.

"Ask me," said Nick Scratch. "See what I do."

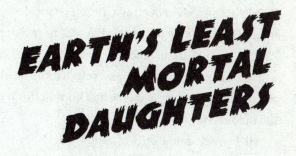

EARTH'S LEAST MORTAL DAUGHTERS

December 10, the Night of the Greendale Thirteen
HARVEY

Sabrina told him death was coming, but someone else came instead.

The insistent knocking on the frosted glass of Harvey's front door made him flinch, but he wouldn't be a coward anymore. He had to stay in this house and protect his passed-out dad, who couldn't stop drinking because the wrong son died.

Harvey wanted desperately to be brave, like his brother would've been. He walked to the door, the pulse at his throat hammering harder than the fist against the glass, and opened it wide.

"Hey, Harvey," said the dark stranger on his doorstep. After a barely perceptible pause, he said: "Right?"

It didn't sound like a question. He sounded sure. Even though Harvey'd never laid eyes on this boy before.

"Yeah," Harvey faltered. "Who're you?"

The boy was moving even before he answered, striding into Harvey's house without invitation. Harvey'd never been as self-assured in his whole life as this boy was in two steps.

"I'm Nick Scratch," the boy tossed over his shoulder. "Sabrina sent me. I'm a friend of hers, and your backup for the night. I'll need you to show me every window and door in this house, so I can seal and bind them for you."

All Harvey could do was follow Nick's lead through Harvey's own home, demanding: "What *kind* of friend?"

But Harvey already knew.

In *A Christmas Carol*, Scrooge was visited by the Ghosts of Christmas Past, Christmas Present, and Christmas Yet to Come. Nick Scratch was the Prospect of Sabrina's Boyfriend Upgrade Yet to Come.

Harvey'd always known Sabrina could do better than him.

Sabrina was so smart and beautiful, and sometimes so strange. All their lives, she'd seemed off in her own little world where Harvey couldn't reach her. He'd had a lurking fear someone might show up who was worthy of her. Someone clever and good-looking and sophisticated and cool. Someone who could connect with her on a level Harvey wasn't able to. Here he was, and he had *magic powers*.

A guy like Nick had been Harvey's worst nightmare for years. Now Harvey had far worse nightmares.

Harvey still wasn't thrilled about Nick.

But Nick hadn't come to mock Harvey. Nick said he'd come to help with this mysterious danger threatening their town.

Harvey wanted to believe that he wasn't afraid and he didn't need magic to save him. Once the sun sank into the black and the wind through the leaves sounded like whispering ghosts, he'd begun to doubt.

Maybe Harvey was just as useless and helpless as Sabrina believed.

"What's happening, exactly?"

"The spirits of thirteen dead witches are trying to kill everyone in town," Nick announced, as though that was a normal and reasonable thing to say. "Sealed doors and banishing spells might hold them off for a while."

"How long?"

"Probably not long enough," Nick said coolly.

"Great," Harvey murmured.

He was annoyed and jealous that night, but he was also deeply relieved to see Nick. He trailed after Nick, showing him the entrances to the house. The sealing spells took a while. They sniped at each other, and Tommy was dead and Sabrina was gone, but Harvey finally had someone to talk to again.

Then silhouettes flickered behind the mist-gray glass of the door, women with snarled hair. Every door, every pane of glass in the windows, rattled like bones in a box.

Harvey aimed his rifle at the front door. "You going to do something here?"

"I'm doing it, farm boy," Nick sneered. "Not that you deserve it. You're a witch-hunter, aren't you?"

Harvey didn't know what to say. Sabrina'd told him he was a witch-hunter, and a lot of things had fallen into place. Did he have a choice about whether he was a witch-hunter? Did Sabrina have a choice about whether she was a witch?

Maybe not.

Nick's hands were crossed before him, in an attitude almost resembling prayer. He was murmuring what Harvey presumed was a banishing spell. Harvey couldn't make out the words, but every syllable made the hair on the back of Harvey's neck stand up.

Something was emanating from Nick, like heat or light issuing from a fire, but it wasn't bright or warm.

It was magic.

Once Nick's spells were cast, quiet fell between them. In the silence, Harvey could hear evil draw near. The winds rose, from a mutter outside the windowpanes to a faraway scream that was growing closer. The deep shadows cast against the pale porch light loomed large.

And none of this was Nick's problem. This boy hadn't come to make Harvey feel better. This boy hadn't come for him at all.

Trying not to show how scared he was, Harvey said: "You sealed the place, right? You kept your promise to Sabrina. You can go."

When he managed to tear his gaze away from the windows brimming with darkness, he saw Nick watching him. Nick's eyes were almost as dark and opaque as the night beyond the glass.

Almost.

"No," Nick answered slowly. "I'll stay."

Nick helped Harvey stack more furniture up against his front door and sat beside him on the floor, shoulder to shoulder, their backs set against that frail barricade as the doorknobs and windows rattled and the wind shrieked and the dead came. It was pathetic, but Harvey was painfully glad Nick was there.

At the moment Harvey thought the ghosts would break through, the rattling ceased. The world and the dead went quiet. Harvey and Nick exchanged a look and began to take down the barricade. Once the door was clear, Nick moved toward it, but Harvey pushed in front of him. He wouldn't allow Nick to go first. He couldn't watch anyone else die.

Nick wore a disconcerted expression.

"What?" Harvey snapped.

Nick sneered. "Nothing. You're a funny kind of witch-hunter, aren't you?"

He let Harvey go ahead. Harvey opened the door, Nick peering over his shoulder, and aimed his gun at empty night. The ghosts were gone, and Nick said Sabrina had saved the town somehow, in a way Nick understood but Harvey didn't.

Standing on the threshold of his home, Harvey asked Nick awkwardly: "Why'd you show up here?"

Nick looked outside as if the answer was lost in the whispering darkness. "She asked me. So I came."

There was something bleak in the way he spoke. Harvey felt bad for Nick suddenly, the way he did for hurt animals and strays, even though that made no sense.

"No, but…" Harvey bit his lip and forced his voice to be gentle, because everything about this night was harsh and chilling. There must be some gentleness left in the world, even if he had to make it himself. "Why?"

Nick's head turned. He stared up at Harvey, face briefly puzzled as if a soft voice was a foreign language to him. Harvey swallowed.

"Are you—are you guys…?"

He couldn't finish the sentence. *Just tell me the worst*, he wanted to say. Put a seal on my misery, the way you sealed the windows and doors. I knew as soon as I saw you. I knew as soon as you said why you'd come.

Nick said: "She loves *you*, mortal."

Sabrina had told Harvey she loved him, but she'd been lying to him their whole lives. Maybe she'd never meant any of it. Magic was real and his brother was dead and the whole world was broken. The idea of Sabrina's love, the most fragile and beautiful thing in Harvey's life, had been shattered too. Hearing this strange boy say Sabrina loved him made Harvey feel as if it was true.

She loves you. Nick's voice was steady and sure. Harvey repeated those words to himself in the hollows of his sleepless, lightless nights, when he felt utterly alone.

There was one person alive who loved him.

Nick hadn't needed to say it, any more than Nick had to stay. But he had.

ONE READS OF A WITCH

December 27, After Hunt the Wren Day, Morning
SABRINA

It's a question of luck, Sabrina," my aunt Zelda told me, on an icy morning two days after Yule. "More specifically, I feel—and I hope we can all agree—that this family had more than their share of bad luck in the past year. What with the constant home invasions by demons, the truly embarrassing dinner parties, and the evil ghosts who tried to kill everyone in town. Several of us also made deeply irresponsible decisions, but I'm not pointing any fingers."

I lifted my eyes to the ceiling. "You are actually pointing right at me."

Aunt Zelda was pointing her cigarette holder at me, the wickedly sharp prongs glittering. I gestured to it.

"But not with a finger," Aunt Zelda said dismissively. "Of course

I was pointing at you. Has anyone else in the family attempted forbidden necromancy in the last year?"

She swept the turquoise cabinets of the kitchen, and the faces of our family gathering, with a ferocious glare. The kitchen cabinets were innocent of necromancy. So was my aunt Hilda, who was standing at the stove and stirring rosemary and lavender into a potion as she sang a little song to herself.

I was less sure about my cousin Ambrose, who was sitting sideways on a bench and stuffing his face with cereal. He gave us a cheerful smile.

"Don't look at me," he said between mouthfuls. "I'm innocent as Cain."

Aunt Zelda's face suggested her last nerve was fraying. My aunt had taken the baby she was looking after to a witch in the woods yesterday. I was sure that was why she was sitting so stiffly, her back broomstick-straight.

I got up and put my arms around Aunt Zelda's neck, hugging her from behind. Aunt Zelda touched my arm lightly, affectionately. With the cigarette holder.

"I don't see what the big deal about New Year's is," I told her. "You say it's a mortal holiday."

"The membrane between the worlds is thin during the time between Yule and Epiphany," said Aunt Zelda. "The spirits are listening, and the weight of so many mortals believing that their luck will turn with the turn of the year exerts a certain pressure on the world. At this time of year, bad luck can be caught like an infection. I have big plans for our future. It's vital for our family's fortunes that we all perform the correct rituals, and none of us make any mistakes in the next few days. We might attract a bad-luck spirit to follow us through the whole year like a starving wolf on our heels."

Her voice cut through the warm potion-laced mist of the kitchen like a prophecy of doom.

"It's your relentless optimism I love most, Aunt Z," said Ambrose at last.

"Membrane's a horrible word," I remarked. "Let's not say membrane."

Aunt Zelda gave Aunt Hilda an accusing look. She blamed Hilda for me and Ambrose growing up irreverent and impossible.

"The traditions for luck are fun, my love," Aunt Hilda told me coaxingly. "If you leave coins on the windowsill on New Year's Eve, you'll have good luck all year round. If you hang lemons in the doorway, that'll ward off bad luck and evil spirits. Don't break mirrors or glass, lest your year be a wreck. Keep an acorn in your pocket always. Don't say goodbye to a friend on a bridge, or you'll never see them again. 'Ware a cat's cry, and hope a frog hops over your threshold. And they say that the new year is the best time to begin a new love."

Aunt Hilda went faint pink. She'd been talking a lot about Dr. Cerberus, the guy who owned the bookstore she worked at. I was sure Aunt Zelda disapproved. She believed mortals and witches should never mingle, but my mother was a mortal and my father was a warlock. Even though Harvey and I had broken up, I was certain love between a mortal and a witch was possible.

Aunt Hilda deserved to be happy and loved more than anyone. I gave her an encouraging smile, and she beamed back.

"They say calling on Anne Boleyn on New Year's Day will bring a witch a lover. You stand with your eyes to the horizon on the new morning, and you give your wish to the wind. You say, *'Lady Anne, Lady Anne, send me a man as fast as you can...'*"

"I've got a man." Ambrose threw a piece of cereal into his mouth like a performing seal catching a fish in midair. "But if Lady Anne insists on sending me another man, or a lovely lady, I welcome them."

"I've always wondered why we call on Anne Boleyn," I said. "I know she was a pioneer in brewing love potions, but she wasn't exactly lucky in the romantic area."

"She was lucky enough. She married a king," said Zelda. "What does anyone marry for, if not power?"

The mention of power made me shiver. I'd signed the Book of the Beast, signed away my soul to Satan, so I could get the power I needed to defeat the Greendale Thirteen. I'd seen no alternative, yet I still didn't know if I'd done the right thing.

"Love?" I suggested. "Also, Henry the Eighth cut Anne Boleyn's head off."

"So he did. Men all love witches, until they don't. Mortal men can't be trusted, any more than love." Aunt Zelda shook her head, the stiff waves of her hair unmoving. "Power's the thing. You have to learn from Lady Anne's mistake and make sure no man has power over you."

I drummed my fingers against the back of Zelda's chair and tried not to think of my broken heart.

"Such as the power to cut your head off?"

"Lavender's blue, rosemary's green," Aunt Hilda murmured happily to

her potion, ignoring our decapitation discussion. *"When you are king, I shall be queen."*

"Exactly," said Zelda. "Let's make a New Year's resolution right now. If you lot can stop stumbling into disasters, I'll make the Spellmans magical royalty. Do we have a bargain?"

"I don't know about that. I *do* have a coffee date before the Academy," I told her. "A new tea shop has opened in the center of Greendale. I'm meeting Roz there."

She'd called and asked me to meet. I'd been so happy to hear her voice. Witches and wicked spirits hadn't scared Roz off. She was still my best friend. Roz and Susie were standing by me, even if Harvey didn't love me enough.

Aunt Zelda wasn't wrong. The last months of this dying year had been very hard, but through darkness and danger I'd learned who truly cared for me, and how to appreciate them.

This bright space with my family around me was like a warm golden hollow carved into the ice of winter. It was difficult to leave this cozy kitchen, but snow had turned the world clean and bright, and my friend was waiting for me. When I opened my front door, I saw the frost on the path through the woods shining as though my way was strewn with diamonds.

I was entirely a witch now, my name in Satan's book and my soul in Satan's keeping. I was afraid that meant I was evil, but perhaps there was still a way to walk a path of light. I didn't want to let down anybody, not ever again.

"Just stay out of trouble until New Year's Day has passed!" Aunt Zelda called after me. "Even you should be able to manage that."

LORD, WHAT FOOLS THESE MORTALS BE

December 27, Morning
HARVEY

The bridge was a white curve over the frozen river, as though some witch queen had passed her pale hand over living waters and transformed them to ice.

Harvey felt as frozen as the river. However much he told his feet to move, they wouldn't. He couldn't make himself go over that bridge.

He'd asked Roz to walk with him, not saying where he wanted to go, but she had plans with Sabrina. Then in desperation he'd asked his dad to come with him over the Sweetwater. His dad told Harvey to stop moping, and suggested they play basketball.

"I know you were never a football man," he'd said. "But you like to shoot hoops in the summer, right? I was thinking it would be a good idea for you to try out for the basketball team."

"Um, I don't think I can," said Harvey. "I have WICCA meetings after school. It's this organization for women's rights with Roz and Susie and—"

He couldn't say Sabrina's name. His dad regarded him with narrowed eyes and total incomprehension. But then, his dad never understood Harvey. "You need to go to meetings of your group of lady friends, who you see every day, so that you can talk about the stuff you always talk about?"

His dad did have a point.

"There's AP art classes—"

Dad snorted. "What do you want people to see when they look at you?"

"Just me," said Harvey.

His father snorted again. "That's it?"

Harvey knew what people *wouldn't* see when they looked at him. They wouldn't see Tommy, the captain of the football team, the apple of his father's eye. Tommy was gone, and suddenly his dad wanted Harvey to take up sports. As though Harvey being a bad copy of Tommy was preferable to Harvey being himself.

Harvey was tempted to play basketball and please his dad. His girlfriend was lost. His friends were Sabrina's friends. His brother was gone forever. His dad was all he had left.

He almost wanted to do it. But he couldn't play ball, any more than he could cross the bridge.

At Christmastime, Sabrina had cast a spell on his dad so his dad would stop drinking. His dad wasn't drinking anymore, and it infuriated Harvey. If magic could stop his dad, why couldn't his dad have stopped on his own? Why had he given up booze for magic, but not for his family? It would've made Tommy so happy if their dad had quit. It seemed like a bad joke, that Tommy was dead and now his dad was done drinking.

He was so angry with his father. He was so angry at Sabrina.

Harvey's hands curled into tight fists, jammed deep in his pockets. The slender white lines of the bridge wavered in his vision. He imagined them transforming into a fragile structure of bones suspended over the ice. He had the sudden nightmarish thought that if he tried to cross the bridge, the bones would crack.

He couldn't. Not today. He turned around, and he saw some of the jerks from his class shambling up the icy road toward him. Their dull eyes brightened as they caught sight of him alone.

"Hey, Kinkle," said Billy Marlin. "But where's the rest of the girl gang?"

"Hey, Billy," said Harvey. "Wow, seeing you here reminds me… I have to be somewhere else."

Living in a town as small as Greendale, your fate was set when you were five years old. Billy and his crew would always regard Harvey as the weird, arty guy whose friends were all girls, who flinched whenever Susie got a nosebleed, and who'd once said the word *chiarascuro* in class. Even though Harvey had filled out some from the string bean he used to be, these guys were certain Harvey couldn't and wouldn't defend himself.

They were right. Susie and Sabrina were the fighters in their friend group. Sabrina launched into cutting arguments. Susie lost her cool and threw herself at people. Harvey'd always figured he and Roz grew up tall so they could hold back their small, enraged friends.

"Seeing you always reminds me what a total loser you are," contributed Billy's friend Carl.

"Yeah, I gotta run," said Harvey. "Got an urgent appointment."

"With who?" Billy sneered. "Heard Spellman finally dumped you."

"Got an urgent appointment with loneliness."

"Tragic," said Carl.

"Still better than hanging out with you." Harvey shrugged. "Bye."

He pushed past the boys, but Billy caught hold of the bulky sleeve of Harvey's fleece-lined winter coat, battered and tight across the shoulders and passed down to him from his brother.

The realization pulled Harvey up short. The guys in school had never liked him, but they hadn't messed with him much. He'd always been under the protection of his big brother. Tommy the football hero, beloved by the whole town.

Tommy couldn't protect him anymore.

Through his teeth, Harvey said: "Let go."

Billy hung on. For a moment, Harvey thought he'd have to hit Billy.

For a moment, Harvey wanted to.

Then a voice rang out from the bridge. "Hey, mortal!"

Harvey jerked away from Billy and turned to the river of ice. Standing against the snow with his dark hair and black clothes, Nick Scratch looked like a single ink blot fallen on a white page.

Harvey closed his eyes in horror. "Oh, holy God."

He'd sincerely hoped he would never have to see Nick again.

When he opened his eyes, Nick had made his way across the bridge and was strolling toward them. Billy and the guys were bristling at his approach, clearly regarding Nick as some smooth out-of-towner in fancy clothes. Billy advanced on Nick, squaring his shoulders.

Harvey stepped hastily in between.

"Don't hurt them!" he told Nick.

"Sorry, what?" Billy's voice was totally confounded.

Billy and the others were idiots, but he wouldn't let them face a magical attack. It wasn't fair. They couldn't defend themselves.

Nick tilted his head, snowflakes settling like lace in his dark hair. He appeared to notice Billy and the others for the first time.

"Go away, other mortals," Nick commanded.

"And who are *you*?" Billy spat.

Nick's next-door-to-midnight eyes narrowed. "I'm the guy telling you to go away. Now."

Billy was a bully, so confidence always knocked him back. He glanced at his friends, dismissively at Harvey, and finally sneered at Nick.

"Or you'll do what, city boy?"

Nick smiled like a bad angel. "Oh, I'll—"

"No!" said Harvey.

He put himself physically in front of Billy, so Billy was blocked from Nick's view. Billy made a low growling sound. Clearly, Billy's big day of harassing citizens was not going according to plan.

"I'll tell you a secret," Nick suggested at last.

He met Harvey's eyes and nodded. Harvey stepped aside. Billy shifted his weight from foot to foot, smart enough to be uneasy.

Nick stepped in, grabbed the collar of Billy's jacket in one hand, and whispered in the other boy's ear. It sounded like only one word. Harvey watched as Billy's face drained of color.

Billy stumbled backward, almost falling, then began to run. He staggered as he went, as if the snow was deeper than it was. He left his friends behind.

Nick spread his hands like a stage magician calling attention to a trick. "Who else wants to know a secret?"

The other boys fled. In a matter of seconds, it was just Harvey and the warlock and footprints in the snow.

"Friends of yours?" Nick asked lazily.

"Uh, no. Do people in your school often threaten their friends?"

Nick's smug smile stayed in place. "Only my closest. They were bothering you?"

"It's their way."

"So why not let me deal with them?"

In some ways, it was as if Nick really was a stranger in town. Someone who spoke a different language. No matter what he and Harvey said to each other, neither of them would understand.

"Billy and his friends don't know what you are," Harvey tried to explain. "I couldn't let them get hurt."

Nick's face remained puzzled, but he shrugged, clearly dismissing hurt mortals as unimportant. "Do you remember me? Nick Scratch."

"No, I've totally forgotten the night my house was besieged by murder ghosts," Harvey muttered, then louder: "Hi, Nick."

He would've said *Nice to see you again*, but it wasn't.

Harvey had never thought of himself as the jealous type. But he was aware there wasn't much competition for Sabrina's attention in their school. Sabrina had once described Baxter High students as jocks with beef jerky for brains, then added that she was being harsh on beef jerky.

This was competition. Actually, this was the knowledge Harvey couldn't compete.

It didn't matter. Sabrina was a witch. The world was suddenly a terrifying place. Harvey badly wanted to go home and have someone there waiting for him.

Nick seemed amused. "Hi, mortal."

"I have no idea how witches keep themselves secret from the world if they go around calling ordinary people 'mortal' all the time," said Harvey. "I don't think it's very sneaky. You know my name."

"You're so right, Harry."

Harvey was beginning to get a headache. He'd heard about witches being evil, but nobody mentioned how annoying they were. "What do you want, Nick?"

Nick said: "Sabrina."

Harvey wasn't sure why the answer shocked him. Maybe it was the surprise of hearing Nick be so straightforward.

He took a deep breath. "Okay. Well, Sabrina and I are broken up. Who she does or doesn't date has nothing to do with me."

"Exactly," said Nick disapprovingly. "You're still broken up? Get it together, mortal."

He felt a snap in his brain like a crack appearing in ice.

"Excuse me?"

"Your behavior is ridiculous," said Nick.

"*My* behavior is ridiculous?"

"I told you Sabrina loves you."

"You . . . did do that," Harvey admitted.

"So I thought by the time I returned from vacation in the Unholy

Land, you'd be back together. But my friend says you're not, and you wouldn't keep Sabrina's Yule gift. Can you explain to me why you are so stupid?"

"I asked Sabrina to get back together!" Harvey shouted. "After what you told me, I asked her to start again with no secrets between us. She wouldn't. She said it was too dangerous for me."

He didn't even know why he was telling Nick this. Maybe because he had no one else to tell. Maybe because he *was* stupid.

"So she still loves you," said Nick. "And you still love her."

"Sorry," interrupted Harvey. "How is any of this your business?"

Nick appeared startled. It was unbelievable that this stranger had descended from the sky to ask questions about Harvey's personal life. Harvey'd lost everything, Nick had the gall to rub it in, and now Nick was the one acting surprised.

"Right," said Nick. "I see the problem. I didn't make myself clear. I'm down to share."

"Share?" Harvey echoed. "Share what?"

They hadn't been talking about anything it was possible to share. In fact, they'd only been talking about one thing, and she wasn't a thing.

Nick looked puzzled by Harvey's confusion. Harvey stared at him with growing outrage.

"You can't mean . . . you don't mean . . . share *Sabrina?*"

Harvey's voice rose in a shout. He looked around hastily to see if the guys from the football team might be within earshot. He didn't see a single human soul, which was reassuring until Harvey remembered magic was real. Maybe animals could talk.

Innocent baby squirrels might be listening to Nick Scratch

right now. The baby squirrels must be horrified.

Nick seemed pleased by Harvey's comprehension. "Yes!"

"Yeah, so…" Harvey shouldered his bag. "Never talk to me again. Thanks. Bye forever."

He shook his head as he walked off. What a weird joke. He'd thought Sabrina's aunts were eccentric, but he'd had no idea.

Night was falling, turning the snow gray as dust, by the time Harvey reached home. The house was chilly and dark when Harvey let himself in. His father hadn't come back. Harvey doubted he would. When his dad was angry, he always gave Harvey the cold shoulder. Maybe he wouldn't go to the bar, but he'd go out shooting or take an extra shift at the mines.

When their mom died, he and Tommy had agreed they would bring each other up well, because Dad wouldn't look after them. They had to be a team now. They learned how to make a bed and clean a bathroom, and how to make themselves dinner. Eleven-year-old Tommy agreed with six-year-old Harvey that they wouldn't learn to cook broccoli or any other disgusting thing, so they'd never have to eat their vegetables. Mrs. Link next door warned it would stunt their growth. Years later, Tommy reminded her of that, laughing in the way that made other people laugh with him. Harvey and Tommy were both a head taller than their dad by then, and Tommy told her: "I think we grew up all right."

Since his dad had poured his booze down the sink, Harvey'd made a lasagna, but he guessed they weren't having dinner together. Harvey hung around in the gathering dark waiting for a while, just in case. Then he couldn't stand waiting any longer. He decided he'd slink off to his bedroom as he usually did when his father was mad, and try to draw.

Harvey called out, "Good night, Tommy," to his brother as he had every night for sixteen years. Then he remembered Tommy was dead, sat down at the kitchen table, and put his head in his arms.

His dad sneered that Harvey cried too easily, that he was a baby, that he was a sissy girl. He'd cried for an overwhelmingly beautiful sunset, cried for missing Sabrina when they were seven and her aunts took her away on a three-day trip, cried for an injured baby bird he'd rescued that hadn't lived, cried for his great-aunt who liked mints more than children when she passed away. He'd cried into his big brother's shoulder when his mother died, miserable beyond words but safe in the circle of his brother's arm.

He hadn't cried for this.

Harvey hadn't cried for Tommy. Not since he'd picked up the gun and gone into Tommy's room, where the shell of his brother slept. The relief of tears seemed impossible.

ONCE WITCHCRAFT GETS STARTED

December 27, Afternoon
SABRINA

The new café in town was quaint, in a totally different way than the kitschy interior of Dr. Cerberus's bookstore and diner. The Bishop's Daughter Coffee and Teas was an old-fashioned tea shop, with Victorian blue-patterned willow ware and scones served along with cakes on gleaming brass tiered trays. Even the residents of Greendale, often suspicious of novelty, were lining up. I spotted such unlikely people as jocks from school, including Billy Marlin, and Mr. Kinkle with his miner friends.

The woman who ran the tea shop, a Welsh widow named Mrs. Ferch-Geg, wore a polka-dotted red apron and had her blond hair done in a beehive so high it was tilting to one side like the Leaning Tower of Pisa. She said she'd made the hundreds of éclairs in the display cases herself. The whole café was humming with the sound of conversation.

I wished the meet-up with Roz was going as smoothly as the new business. We usually couldn't stop talking, but today our table was the only circle of silence in the whole place. Roz was staring at me apprehensively, as though at any moment I might enchant my croissant.

"So, um, how's the baby?" Roz asked at last.

My aunt Zelda had stolen our High Priest's baby daughter on the night of the Greendale Thirteen. Roz was called in to do emergency babysitting on the eve of Yule. December hadn't been a restful month.

"We gave Leticia to a woods witch," I said. "For her own safety."

Roz boggled. "Does witch adoption usually work like that?"

"This was a bit of a special case."

"I didn't mean to sound judgmental," said Roz hastily. "I'm sure you made the right decision. I was visiting Susie earlier. She's still shaken up by the whole business with the…"

Roz seemed to have difficulty saying the words. She turned her empty teacup around in its saucer, as if searching for inspiration in its dainty china depths.

"Yule demon," I filled in.

The Yule demon had kidnapped our friend Susie. It'd been a whole thing.

"Yeah. That." Roz gave a small, uncomfortable laugh. "She said you and your aunts really helped her out. That was good."

"If you've seen Susie…" I said. "Have you heard from Harvey? Do you know how he's doing?"

There was a pause. Roz frowned at her teacup. She looked intensely uncomfortable.

I guessed it was rough for everyone, when two people in a friend group broke up. I hoped that Roz wasn't trying to think of a way to say, "Harvey and I get together all the time! We talk about how much he hates you. And witchcraft. And witches. And you."

"I haven't seen Harvey," Roz answered finally. "He called and asked me to go on a walk with him, but I was already seeing you. I told him we should meet up tomorrow."

I tried not to be jealous. I would've given anything for Harvey to call me.

"How did he sound on the phone?"

Roz looked up from the gilt rim of her teacup. Her eyes behind her big glasses, the amber of tea without milk, were always a little unfocused and usually warm. Not today.

"Sad. Harvey sounded really sad."

I coughed, painfully. "How are you? How's your sight?"

"It's not great," Roz answered, her voice clipped. "Listen, Sabrina, hearing I'm losing my vision because a witch cursed an ancestor of mine was—a lot. I don't know that I can talk about it with you."

I blinked. "But we're best friends. We should be able to talk about anything."

Roz made a small impatient gesture. Perhaps she misjudged the movement, or perhaps her vision was too blurred to see exactly where things were. Her cup and saucer chimed together and then almost fell over the rim of the table. I murmured a spell, and the cup and saucer righted themselves. Roz jumped as if hearing the breaking sound that hadn't happened.

Mrs. Ferch-Geg bustled over to us, rescuing her cups and saucers.

"Another cuppa?" she asked in her musical Welsh accent. "Some éclairs? I can see you two are having a lovely chat."

Roz's mouth worked nervously, then went flat. "Actually, I have to get going."

The tea shop lady nodded, her elaborate hairstyle wobbling, and went to bring our check. I reached out across the glass-topped table and grabbed Roz's wrist.

"The curse isn't my fault."

"I know it's not," Roz whispered.

"I'll find a way to lift the curse and help you. Roz, I swear I will."

Roz was already grabbing her stuff. "Give me time, Sabrina."

I watched her hands, fumbling as she tried to pick up her hat and scarf, and my heart broke.

Once we were outside the café, Roz tried and failed to smile at me. It felt as though our friendship had fallen and broken on the floor.

I'd already lost Harvey. I didn't want to lose my mortal friends. I knew I shouldn't push, but that was who I was. Either I pushed my friends, or I left them alone. I couldn't work out a middle way, and I didn't want to be without them.

"Let me at least walk you home."

"No, Sabrina. I really have to go."

I watched as Roz scurried across the main street, worried because she was walking so quickly on the icy surface. Maybe my friends would rather be without me.

She looked both ways before she crossed, but on the other side of the street was a white van. I watched Roz step out in front of the van and realized she hadn't seen it against the snow.

There was only a split second for terror. The van was going too fast. The roads were covered in ice. Teleporting wouldn't be fast enough. I shouted the spell without even thinking.

"This is not something she should face. Give me leave to take her place!"

There was a whirl like snowflakes in a sharp breeze, and I found myself in the middle of the road with the van bearing down upon me. Roz was safe on the other side of the street. My face broke into a small, relieved grin.

"I don't like the scene I'm in. Let's give it a little spin," I murmured. The wheels of the van spun in the ice. The vehicle pirouetted, so I saw the black letters reading CAPITAL GLASSWARE on the side, then saw the van drive straight into a fire hydrant.

The doors at the back of the van burst open, and the contents exploded outward. It was like being caught in a storm of glass. Sparkling shards cascaded through the air, clustering at my feet in bright heaps. It was finding myself in the center of a vast chandelier. It was a hundred windows breaking around me, all at once.

I wasn't afraid of being hurt. I was a witch, and Aunt Hilda and Aunt Zelda never let me leave the house without casting protection spells. But I could hear my aunt's voice, ringing like a bell in my memory as the glass shards descended.

Don't break mirrors or glass, lest your year be a wreck.

Roz rushed across the road to me, and half the occupants of the tea shop spilled out into the street. I gave Roz a hug and said I was so glad she was safe, and then hurried off before anyone could ask me questions.

In my haste to get away, I ran into my old elementary school principal.

"Watch where you're going," Mr. Poole muttered. "You little witch."

I hesitated, not sure I'd heard him right. I stood frozen, alone amid the ice and shattered glass, as he disappeared into the crowd.

I was still shaken up when I got to the Academy for Unseen Arts. The sound of breaking glass, first a crash and then a sweet tinkling melody as the pieces fell, haunted me even as I ran down the corridor. My footsteps echoed against the stone as though someone was chasing at my heels.

There was no time to worry about bad luck or grumpy old men. I didn't want to be late for class.

Witch school didn't close as long as mortal school did for the holidays, though the official first assembly wasn't for a few days. *No rest for the wicked*, Father Blackwood said, sternly and often. We had several lectures to attend, even though we didn't have classes, and we'd been given several assignments to do over Yule. One assignment was due to be handed in today. Sister Jackson, my most noxious teacher, had given us a huge project and then suggested we work on the assignment in pairs. Of course, nobody had volunteered to collaborate with the half mortal. I'd spent a couple of sleepless nights over Yule getting the work done on my own.

Sister Jackson's mouth twisted like a wire with too much weight on it as I whirled in the door.

"Ah, Sabrina," she said. "Here at last. I presume you have brought your detailed treatise on the scandal of Anti-Pope Joan, and its causes and effects?"

I gave her a defiant smile as I unzipped my bag. "Would I dare show my face if I hadn't?"

"Who knows," said Sister Jackson. "I've noticed you make many unwise decisions. You and the rest of the unruly Spellman brood."

I flicked through my books, searching for the bound essay. I thought I'd left the project at the very top of my bag, but I couldn't see it anywhere.

Joy spread across Sister Jackson's face. She gloated over me like a vulture over a dying donkey while I knelt on the stone flags of the classroom and searched desperately for my project. I even tipped the bag upside down. The project wasn't there.

I looked up from my books, tumbled on the floor, to the crowded rows of students before me. Students from the year above mine came to these lectures too, and I noticed three in particular. Once, I would've suspected Prudence Night and her Weird Sisters of playing a trick and hiding my homework, but the trio of magical mean girls and I were getting on better lately. My eyes found Prudence, her queenly head held high and her dark eyes observing the spectacle with faint interest, but I didn't see the pleased malice I would've expected if she'd done it.

I didn't think this was a trick of Prudence's. That didn't change the fact my project had disappeared, Sister Jackson was leering at me with hungry menace, and there was no help to be found.

Until a voice called out from the door behind me.

"Sabrina and I did the assignment together," claimed Nick Scratch, lying through his teeth.

I twisted around from my undignified seat on the floor to see Nick bare said teeth in a smile that was both disarming and alarming. He produced a sheaf of pages, bound in scarlet embossed leather, presenting them to Sister Jackson with a flourish.

Thwarted, Sister Jackson muttered that Nick and I were both late for class.

"Sin is one thing, Nicholas. Tardiness is another. You may take your seats."

"I was so busy sinning, I lost track of time," murmured Nick, gesturing me to a seat beside him.

He was unwrapping a long black scarf from his neck and shrugging out of his jacket. There were snowflakes half melted in his ebony hair and on his shoulders, glinting like stars disappearing in the morning. I took my seat beside him.

Apparently I'd also forgotten my pens, but a pallid boy across the way loaned me a pencil.

When Sister Jackson's lecture was over, I stood up quickly and told Nick out of the corner of my mouth: "You didn't have to do that."

"I wanted to," he said.

The other students were filtering out of the room. I hugged my bag to my chest in distress, while Nick shouldered his bag and walked with me out into the corridor. He lingered as though he had nowhere better to be.

"Let me assure you, Nick, I did that assignment."

"I'm sure you did. You don't strike me as the type to neglect your schoolwork."

"Of course, I'm not a *delinquent*," I told him, and he smiled.

This wasn't Nick's blinding smile for the teacher. It was smaller, warm and private between us.

"Sure. No petty rule-breaking for you, right, Spellman? You're a rebel on a grand scale. Only stealing forbidden books and necromancy is worth your time. Go big or go do your homework. Your new hair is sexy, by the way."

"Oh," I said.

I hadn't considered my new hair as being sexy or not. I didn't really know whether *I* was sexy or not. On the whole, I hoped I was.

Nick certainly was. Not that I would ever say so.

I smiled cautiously. "Thanks, I guess. I'm not sure I'll keep it. I thought I might dye it back the way it was before."

I'd signed away my soul, and my hair had turned white as the snow on the ground. I didn't hate how it looked, but it made me uneasy. I'd always loved how my hair was the same shade as my mother's in the pictures I had of her. At Yule, I'd summoned the ghost of my mother. She'd been a lovely golden-haired girl, mortal and sweet. Nothing like me.

I'd tried dressing like the Weird Sisters to suit my new hair, but that hadn't felt right. I'd tried calling my mother to me, and that hadn't felt right either. I wished I could work out who this new me was supposed to be like.

I remembered how Harvey's eyes widened when he saw my new look. He'd drawn a hundred lovingly detailed pictures of me with golden hair. He probably wouldn't want to draw me looking like this.

I raised an eyebrow at Nick, who was apparently a fan of the hair. "Would you be disappointed?"

He shook his head. "You're sexy either way."

There was that word again. I might want to be sexy, but I didn't know how to talk about it. I coughed instead.

"I can't believe I left my project at home," I muttered. "I'm not usually forgetful."

Maybe I'd put it down in the tea shop, but I could've sworn I hadn't even opened my bag. Maybe I'd left the assignment at home. I frowned, trying to recall. It wasn't like me not to have my work in order.

"That kind of thing happens to everyone. It's just bad luck."

Bad luck. I stared up at Nick, stricken, and saw the shine of broken glass in his black eyes.

"Something wrong?"

I pulled myself together. "No! Of course not. Everything's fine. Great. Peachy keen, jelly bean, as my aunt Hilda would say. Hey, welcome back from your Yule vacation in the Unholy Land."

Nick leaned against the wall, his voice sinking caressingly low. "Did you miss me?"

I hesitated. "Of course. Was the Unholy Land fun? I've never been, but I've heard there are mermaids in the Red Dead Sea. I'd love to see a mermaid. I think they're fascinating. I've read so many books about them. '*I have heard the mermaids singing, each to each. I do not think they will sing to me.*'"

I finished the quotation with another cough. I didn't think mortal poetry was welcome in the unhallowed halls of the Academy.

"The mermaids did sing to me, actually," Nick claimed. "All it takes is a little charm."

"More than a little, I'm sure."

Nick was far too charming for my peace of mind. He was more charming devil than Prince Charming, though. I knew it didn't mean anything.

"If you want to see mermaids in the Unholy Land, I'll teleport you there right now." Nick offered me a hand, palm up. "Come with me, Sabrina."

I scoffed. "Seriously?"

"Sure," said Nick. "I want our first date to be memorable."

"Um..."

His smile was invitation in motion, mouth curving, eyes dancing. If I laid my hand in his, he might whirl me off in a flurry of crimson sparks and fireworks. I was tempted, but giving in to temptation can be dangerous.

All I knew of romantic love was Harvey's hands, rough from work outdoors and calloused where he held his pencils and charcoals, but always touching me with infinite gentleness. With reverence, as though I were sacred and precious to him. I never doubted I was. Harvey wasn't an exciting stranger, but I was more than willing to trade any possibility of thrills for the certainty of true love. Even now when I was troubled or scared, I wanted to run headlong into the warm safety of Harvey's arms. The witches at the Academy couldn't understand.

Nothing was sacred to Nick Scratch.

And I'd been wrong about Harvey. I'd grown up believing true love meant withstanding everything, meant never giving up on each other. If he really loved me, he wouldn't have broken up with me. True love hadn't been true after all.

That didn't mean I'd stopped loving him. I didn't even know who I'd be if I gave up on loving Harvey. If all your life you thought you'd have one love, and that wasn't true, then what was true?

On the night of the Greendale Thirteen, I'd pledged my soul to Satan. In return, I'd received enough power to call hellfire up from the earth. Only three other witches had ever been able to do that. Harvey might have suggested getting back together, but how could I go to Harvey with hellfire burning in my hands? This would be too much for him, and I didn't want to watch Harvey turn away from me again.

I didn't know who I was anymore, but I would have to figure it out.

Nick had come through for me when Harvey hadn't. Maybe I'd gotten him wrong. He was a good friend. Maybe he could be more.

My hand wavered at my side, about to lift. Nick's eyes tracked the movement. His wicked little smile illuminated with sudden new brightness, like someone expecting a present.

"We could go skinny-dipping in the Red Dead Sea," he added coaxingly.

My hand dropped.

Nick wasn't even capable of something resembling mortal love. He'd told me as much. I was this week's sexy challenge to him, nothing more. There was no point trying to gather up the shattered pieces of my heart and give them to him. Harvey had hurt me enough. I didn't want to be destroyed.

I laughed lightly, though the laugh sounded forced, and hit Nick on the arm, the same way I would've hit Susie or Roz, a gesture that said: good buddy, old pal.

"Quit kidding around, Nick."

For a moment the calm on Nick's face flickered. But the next moment he was smiling with his usual nonchalance, and I knew I was right.

There was no time to think about Nick, or Harvey either. I hadn't left my school project at home. I'd broken glass close to New Year's.

"Rain check on the Red Dead Sea," I told Nick. "I need to find my cousin."

I had to learn how much trouble a bad-luck spirit might be.

LIFE IS A WITCH, AND THEN

December 27, Evening
PRUDENCE

Prudence Night's life was filled with fools to ensorcel and challenges to overcome. This year alone she'd found out she wasn't actually an orphan, but the illegitimate daughter of their High Priest, who'd never bothered to claim her. She'd been betrayed by her sisters of the heart, who dared kill a bunch of mortals without consulting Prudence. She'd almost been the victim of a cannibalistic murder plot.

She still found time to enjoy the simple pleasures of life, such as watching her swaggering ex-boyfriend Nick get shot down by the half mortal when he asked her out on a date. Shot down? More like obliterated. It was akin to watching a broomstick sail through the night, then get abruptly reduced to a heap of falling splinters.

"Dear Satan," Prudence told Nick. "That must have been sad for you. But on the plus side, it was very amusing for me."

Nick was leaning against the wall with his arms crossed, watching as Sabrina made her hasty exit. Sabrina was cute enough, with her little skirts and her new bone-white hairdo, but Prudence didn't understand the fixation.

Still, Nick's enormous crush was proving very convenient. Prudence and Nick were partners in fencing class. Prudence always chose Nick as a partner, since she wouldn't risk her sisters going near a man with a sword. During their last class before Yule, Nick had asked for Prudence's help. Prudence agreed to keep Nick updated on Sabrina's doings and to talk up Nick to Sabrina. In exchange, Nick was doing all Prudence's homework until summer. Nick believed they were friends. Prudence believed they were business partners.

Watching Nick get rejected was a hilarious added bonus to their business arrangement. Prudence loved winning.

"I'm doing something wrong," Nick murmured to himself. "I need to figure out what."

Actually, Prudence had no idea what was going wrong. Sabrina was obviously attracted to Nick, and Nick's seduction techniques were excellent. They'd even worked on Prudence.

She thought the matter over. "Perhaps you're being too subtle? Maybe she doesn't know you're romantically interested."

"That could be it," Nick said slowly. "I did invite her to join the good time in Ambrose's attic with us. Don't you think that might have given her a hint?"

"That was only polite," Prudence argued. "And very subtle. You were still wearing your underwear."

Nick frowned. "I suppose that's true."

"What you should do is astrally project to her bedroom tonight," Prudence suggested. "Naked."

She began to stroll down the corridor. Nick walked with her. The red flames affixed to the stone walls, held aloft by withered Hands of Ingloriousness, cast brief illumination on the pin-scratch mark between his brows.

"It's a classic move," he admitted. "Simple, yet elegant. I'm not sure it's the right move in this particular case."

"In these uncertain times, we can't lose sight of unholy truths. Nothing says romance like naked astral projection."

Prudence reflected on many memories that proved her point. Some mortal boys had tried to worship her as a goddess. Many tried to touch her and fell to their knees howling in misery when their hands passed through the vision that was her body. Naked astral projection never failed.

Even though she'd solved his problems, Nick was still frowning.

"Stop dragging your feet, Nick!" Prudence told him severely. "You need to come on much stronger than this. Sabrina and her mortal have been broken up for weeks. Her quaint notions about fidelity kept the other boys at bay while they were together, but as I told you earlier, the time has come to act. Now she's fresh meat up for grabs and the sharks are circling. Plutonius Pan is making a play for your princess." Prudence shuddered. "Try saying that three times fast, or thinking about it for more than three seconds."

Nick appeared on the verge of being physically ill.

"Plutonius Pan? Sabrina would never let him touch her."

"Let's not pretend Sabrina's standards are high, shall we?" asked Prudence. "Consider the evidence. Not only a mortal, but a witch-hunter! Only maniacs are in for witch-hunters."

"She didn't know he was a witch-hunter!" Nick defended Sabrina loyally. "Nobody knew."

Prudence shrugged. "Doesn't change the fact any warlock would look good after years with a mortal. Even Plutonius."

"The mortal *is* an annoying idiot," muttered Nick. "Who is ruining his life, but more importantly, *my* life. Plutonius Pan. The Dark Lord is testing me."

"Have you noticed how some people begin to look like their familiars?" Prudence asked.

Every witch was given a familiar, a goblin to be the other half of their soul. Plutonius's faithful goblin companion was an albino weasel. The resemblance was pronounced.

Nick didn't respond to this observation. Nobody had ever seen Nick's familiar. Nick had familiar trauma he refused to discuss and was clearly brooding over this new information.

"I won't share Sabrina with Plutonius Pan," Nick announced. "I don't have an open-door policy."

"The witches' bathroom wall says different, Nicholas."

Nick sneered. Prudence beamed saucily.

"Not for Plutonius Pan, I don't. I hate him. I hate everything about him. I hate his whole face. This is a disaster."

"Ha ha," said Prudence.

"What are you laughing at?"

"At your pain," Prudence explained cheerfully.

Nick rolled his eyes. "Aren't you just sweet as cyanide."

They turned a corner and saw Sabrina approaching a bunch of Prudence's father's most prized warlock students. The members of the club Father Blackwood wouldn't let girls join and Nick refused to join. Luke Chalmers was a member of this noxious brotherhood. Prudence could see his smooth blond head leaning against Ambrose Spellman's dark one.

"Ugh, there's Luke," murmured Nick.

Prudence shook her head. "We hate Luke."

She and Nick exchanged a fist bump. Nothing brought witches together like mutual hatred.

Prudence was pleased to note Luke's face darkening when Ambrose caught sight of his cousin and immediately broke away from the Judas Society.

The whole Academy knew Father Blackwood had given Ambrose the choice to stand with him when the ghosts came, and Ambrose declined. He chose to stand with his family instead. Father Blackwood was still enraged that Ambrose had picked a bunch of renegade Spellman women over the High Priest.

The witches of the Academy felt differently about Ambrose's show of loyalty. Imagine having a man who valued women above power, who believed keeping faith with women was worth punishment. Many of the witches were in the midst of a full-blown Ambrose Spellman Situation.

Sabrina hurried toward her cousin. Ambrose's smile welcomed her, a fire spell set to a dry torch that created a sudden blaze in the shadows. Prudence wondered sometimes what it would be like to be smiled at that way.

The Spellmans were weirdos. Prudence had watched Hilda

Spellman smooth wrinkles in Ambrose's shirt, or fix the hairband in Sabrina's hair, little gestures that served no real purpose except being close. Now Ambrose was allowed to spend time at the Academy, he and Sabrina were constantly doing totally puzzling things right in front of the other students. They would say "Just checking in on you" to each other and go out of their way to walk together.

A few days ago, Prudence had seen Sabrina lying on a stone bench with her head in Ambrose's lap. They'd been chatting idly. Occasionally Ambrose brushed Sabrina's hair back and sang a brief line of song to her, then returned to the conversation. Prudence lingered, along with many other students, to look at them. It was like watching a strange play, a performance that made no sense but was oddly fascinating.

The Spellmans obviously thought this kind of behavior was normal.

Prudence had made it clear to every witch having an Ambrose Spellman Situation that if Ambrose was open to being with witches as well as warlocks, *she*, Prudence, was first in line.

Ambrose studied Sabrina's face, the arched wings of his eyebrows flying up. "Something wrong, cousin?"

He called Sabrina "cousin" all the time. Prudence thought she understood why. It was the same way she called Dorcas and Agatha "sisters." It was both a claim and a proclamation made. *You're mine, my very own. I'll take care of you.*

Sabrina shook her head, bob flying about like a cloud in a too-strong wind. "No," she said unconvincingly. "But can we talk?"

Ambrose gave her a little kiss on the forehead. "Sure. Let's go home."

As they turned and walked off, Ambrose moved away slightly, but Sabrina put her arms around his waist and hugged him. That wasn't an efficient way of getting where they were going, to their stupid home.

Once Prudence had believed Nick Scratch was the best it was going to get when it came to warlocks.

She remembered Nick's existence and tore her eyes off the Spellmans, only to find Nick still watching them. Prudence hoped to Satan that she wasn't half as obvious as Nick was being about his Sabrina Spellman Situation. She'd caught him watching Sabrina with a look of open longing that lasted almost three whole seconds. Pathetic.

She poked him in the side with a wine-red fingernail. "Naked astral projection is the answer!"

Nick's gaze moved to her. "No. I have a different idea." He turned and stalked off.

"It's your sexless funeral," Prudence called after him.

Prudence wouldn't normally waste her time advising Nick. Except things were strained between her and her sisters because of the stupid mine-collapsing spell they'd done without her. Usually the Weird Sisters stuck together. They were stronger that way. They were a unit, the power of each amplifying the other, the three in one.

But now Agatha and Dorcas were hanging back from Prudence. Maybe they hated her for finally having a father when they were still orphans. Maybe they'd decided to leave her out from now on. Prudence certainly wasn't going to make the first move to reconcile. But sometimes she found herself wondering why she had nobody to talk to.

"Hi, Prudence," said Mania Brown, passing by with Elspeth and Melvin. "You look beautiful and mystical today."

"As I always do," said Prudence. "No need to comment on it. How dare you speak to me."

Prudence swept on, hurrying. She'd stayed too long after class. Judas must be waking from his nap.

She entered the High Priest's private chambers to find the baby already screeching in his elaborately carved ebony crib under his inverted cross ornament. Prudence cursed, threw down her book bag, and picked him up. His small brown face was screwed up in distress, his little fists flying everywhere as if he wanted to fight.

"Be quiet," Prudence murmured. "I know your mother's dead. So's mine. You don't catch me wailing about it, do you? There is no need to show off like this."

Baby Judas kept screaming despite Prudence's words of comfort. He was constantly crying. Prudence didn't know how to make him stop.

He was the son of Father Blackwood—her father, she reminded herself; he wasn't only her High Priest but really her father—and his late wife, so Baby Judas was her brother. She'd never had a brother before. She was used to sisters.

She had a baby sister now too, but Zelda Spellman had taken her away to keep her safe. Prudence sometimes thought her baby sister wouldn't cry at her like this.

"Shut up," Prudence told the baby.

She fed him and changed him and gave him the skull of a ferret with teeth rattling inside it. Baby Judas possessed every luxury. She didn't see what else he wanted.

The door to Father Blackwood's study slammed open. The baby's crying intensified.

"Prudence, make Judas cease that blessed racket *at once*!"

Prudence glared daggers at her father. He studied her with ice-blue eyes that always found her wanting.

"I'm trying."

"Try harder," he bit out. "Stop constantly disappointing me."

Prudence had believed, when Father Blackwood told her to care for the babe, that now Lady Blackwood was dead, her father wanted to claim her at last. She'd thought they would be a family. But over Yule, Father Blackwood had presented Judas to his relatives. He hadn't presented Prudence to anyone. She was an illegitimate girl, no use to him except as a skivvy.

Men didn't care about daughters, unless they had wives to make them. Prudence had heard someone say once that the right woman could rule any man at home. Lady Blackwood had hated Prudence like poison, no matter what Prudence did to please her. But now Father Blackwood was in need of a new wife to preside over his infernal affairs.

Everybody knew Father Blackwood and Zelda Spellman regularly engaged in revels of dark carnality. The orders of whips to the Academy had doubled over the last few months. The Spellmans were trouble, but they were undeniably high class. Zelda Spellman was the former High Priest's sister, and a much-feared witch in her own right. Hilda Spellman was a joke, but nobody dared laugh at Zelda.

When the babies were born, Prudence helped Zelda deliver them. Zelda hadn't indulged in even a moment of sentimentality about Father Blackwood, despite their carnal acts.

"He's not a man who should have daughters," she'd said crisply. "Agreed?"

"Agreed," Prudence answered.

"I will take her," Zelda said.

She'd rocked the little girl in her arms and told Prudence to feed Baby Judas with the milk of a Judas goat to keep him thriving. Prudence crushed down the urge to say: *Take us with you.*

That would've been silly. Prudence wasn't Ambrose Spellman, impulsive enough to throw away her advantages. He'd made an adorable decision, but ultimately a foolish one. She'd spent her whole life as an orphan, but now she could be the High Priest's acknowledged child. Prudence wouldn't lose her chance at power.

Father Blackwood must choose another wife. Surely his choice would land on a beautiful, magical, well-connected woman of spirit. Surely his choice would be none other than Zelda Spellman.

Sister Jackson, a woman bitter as winter apples fallen from a tree and rotting, had recently found out about Zelda and Father Blackwood's affair and begun talking loudly about how much she pitied Zelda. "Poor woman. You know why she became a Night Mother, don't you? Wishes she was a real mother. She *lives* for babies."

That sounded fine to Prudence. If Prudence's mother had lived for babies, she wouldn't have thrown herself in the river when Father Blackwood didn't marry her. She would have lived for Prudence. They would be together now.

If Zelda wanted children, Prudence decided, she could have the Blackwood children.

When Sabrina got herself into trouble over her mortal boyfriend,

Father Blackwood wanted to destroy her. Zelda stood in his way. *Her transgression is mine*, Zelda said in the choir room before the eyes of everyone. Prudence saw and understood. Zelda meant: Every part of her is mine. Sins and all, soul and all. Nobody, not even Satan, will touch her.

Zelda fought for Sabrina fiercely as a lioness. If she liked a niece that much, surely she would like a daughter more.

Prudence could imagine it now. The grand wedding, the beautiful infernal ceremony. Maybe the anti-pope would attend, since it was a union between two important families. Zelda, Lady Blackwood, would wear a black satin gown encrusted with bloodred rubies and crows' feathers. Father Blackwood's eyes would follow her with pride, delighted enough with his new bride to follow her wishes in domestic matters.

"These are my babies, Judas and Leticia," Zelda would say, then lay her hands upon Prudence's shoulders. "And this is my eldest daughter, Prudence Blackwood. Allow me to present her to you, Your Unholiness. One day we will dance at her infernal bridal, but not for a century or so, I hope. The family would collapse without Prudence."

Prudence's sisters would be so jealous. She'd make sure they were taken care of, though. In the end her sisters would see this was for the best.

If Zelda absolutely insisted, even if it would be a little embarrassing, Prudence was prepared to call her "Mother." She'd practiced saying it a few times.

Her father would come to value her. She'd be able to talk to him about taking the Blackwood name. She wasn't an orphan. She never had been. She walked the dark floor, rocked the crying child, and didn't understand why nothing reassured him.

"Will you hush, brat," she told Baby Judas. "Don't worry. I have a plan."

A new year was coming. All Prudence needed was a little luck.

NO MORTAL MAN IS WISE

December 27, Evening
HARVEY

When the knock on the door came, Harvey thought his dad had forgotten his keys. He bolted up from the table and flung open the door.

Then he stared in dismay at Nick Scratch, standing on his threshold in a whirl of black night and white snow.

"You again?" Harvey shook his head. "I can't deal with any more witch garbage right now."

Harvey made to shut the door, but the other boy threw himself bodily against it. Harvey fought to get the door closed and keep his voice steady. Neither worked.

"Seriously, I can't do this. If you could leave, and stop reminding me of all the ways in which my life is completely screwed up, that'd be great."

"Wait!" said Nick Scratch. "Help me."

It was the last thing he'd expected Nick to say.

Harvey stopped trying to shove the door closed. "What do you mean?"

"I helped you on the night the ghosts came. You owe me, mortal."

Harvey bit his lip. "I know. But how could someone like me help someone like you? I can't do any magic."

"The way you looked at me earlier, before you turned away," Nick said. "It's the same way Sabrina looks at me, as if she can't believe what I just said. Witches have always liked what I had to say before now. I'm not a fool. I can tell I'm doing something wrong, but I have no idea what it is."

There was a silence, in which Harvey leaned against the door and weighed Nick's words. It was a strange revelation, that Nick Scratch might be sincere.

"So you ... really don't know what you're saying is horrifying?"

Nick frowned. "Why would it be horrifying?"

"Huh," said Harvey. "Okay."

Roz had explained to Harvey that misunderstanding other people's cultures was hurtful. It was like when you stepped on somebody's foot. You should apologize and stop doing it before you did anything else.

Witches weren't the same as persecuted minorities, but if Harvey was misunderstanding Nick, he felt bad.

"I'm sorry," said Harvey. "I think we're having communication issues. The way you talk about Sabrina is normal for witches?"

"I have a friend who thinks I'm not coming on strong enough," said Nick. "Do you think that's the problem?"

"I do *not* think that's the problem!"

The words burst from Harvey without his permission, but with extreme conviction. He saw Nick smirk.

"See. I knew it. Tell me what I should do."

"Witches must do things really differently from mortals," Harvey said, still shaken. "Maybe you're flirting with Sabrina in a witch way, but—but Sabrina went to school with mortals. She's used to being friends with mortals."

Nick caught on fast. "And dating mortals."

"Dating me," said Harvey. "Yeah."

The words were heavy as stones in his mouth. Harvey used to dream they would be together always.

Now always was over.

For Sabrina, there was bound to be someone else.

That didn't mean Harvey had to be involved. He looked at his own hand, fingers curled tight around the edge of the door. He could close the door and pretend none of this was happening.

Nick reached out and laid a hand on his arm.

"Listen," Nick said in his oddly low voice. "I know you hate witches for killing that boy, your brother. But I didn't have anything to do with it. And you and Sabrina, you love each other, the way mortals do. Right? I'm worth keeping. I'm smart, I'm strong, and I'll do anything she asks. Having me by her side will help her. Give me a chance."

Harvey almost didn't hear him over the roaring in his ears. *Witches killed that boy. Your brother.*

Oh, he'd known magic was evil. He'd always sensed something strange lurking beneath the surface of Greendale. He'd seen what he now knew was a demon in the mines, long ago.

Harvey had spent years trying to make sense of what he'd seen, trying to turn horror into art. Then horror came to his home and took his brother. He was so scared of magic, and Sabrina was living in a world of magic now.

He was terrified of what might happen to her there.

He wanted to hide from magic forever, but he couldn't let anyone else he loved get hurt.

Nick was one of the witches, and kind of a jackass, but he'd come to their house to protect Harvey and his father. From what Harvey gathered, when the evil ghosts came, the other witches had holed up somewhere safe. Nick had put himself in real danger to do as Sabrina asked.

There was a chance Nick might be a good guy. Harvey was certain there must be a lot of magic boys at Sabrina's other school who liked Sabrina. They might not be good guys. Harvey didn't know what was happening at that Academy, and he couldn't be there to support Sabrina. Nick could.

Harvey hated the idea of Sabrina with someone else. The mere thought made his stomach tip and roll as if he were on the sea in a storm, made him actually want to throw up.

But he hated the thought of her alone and in danger even more. If there was any way for him to help Sabrina, he wanted to do whatever he could.

He hesitated. "Do you really like Sabrina?"

Nick said: "Yes."

"I'm not promising anything. And I don't want you making fun of me with any more weird jokes. But I guess I could teach you about the mortal way to court someone. If you want to learn." The words almost stuck in his throat, but he forced them out. "Sabrina deserves to be treated right."

Harvey was a pretty quiet guy, always afraid he'd say something dumb and be embarrassed, or say something mean and be ashamed, but Nick *wanted* Harvey to tell him what to do.

"I'm a quick study," Nick said, moving to come inside.

Harvey rolled his eyes. "Could the first thing you study be boundaries?"

Nick appeared genuinely bewildered. "What about boundaries?"

"Well," said Harvey, "it would be nice if you had some. You do realize you keep trying to barge into my house without an invitation."

This seemed to startle Nick. The wind howled, as though outraged a witch might be denied entry into a mortal's home.

"If a witch didn't want someone to come in, they'd lay protection spells on their threshold."

"Okay," said Harvey. "But I can't do that. What would you say to a witch with, uh, protection spells on their threshold?"

"I'd ask if I was welcome," Nick answered slowly. "If I was, the witch would say, 'Come in out of the cold.'"

There was a long pause. Harvey made a gesture for Nick to continue.

Nick hesitated, his brows pulling together for a dark moment. Harvey got the impression witches didn't get told what to do by mortals often. It was possible Nick might storm off.

Instead, Nick began to smile. He tapped his knuckles lightly against the open door.

"So, farm boy," he drawled. "Am I welcome?"

Harvey sighed, nodded, and began to open the door all the way, before a terrible thought occurred to him.

"Wait! One last thing." Harvey held up a hand. "You're not, like...actually the devil, are you?"

Nick's eyes went wide. "I'm very flattered you would think that."

"Wow, don't be," Harvey advised. "I just wondered, because... your name is Nick Scratch, as in 'Old Nick' or 'Old Scratch,' and those are names for Satan, aren't they? No offense, but if you're Satan you can't come in."

There was a moment in which Nick seemed torn between amazement and anger. Then he shook his head.

"I'm not Satan. It's considered good luck among the old traditional witch families to have an infernally-inflected name. Don't mortals have names associated with their saints and false gods?"

Harvey blinked. "Totally. Mom and Dad almost named me False God Kinkle."

Nick laughed, which was a bit of a shock.

"At the Academy there are two guys named Apollyon and Diabolus," Nick offered. "We call them Polly and Bolly."

That surprised a laugh out of Harvey. "I don't believe you."

"It's true, though. And there's a guy named Plutonius Pan." Nick stared broodingly out into the middle distance. "He's the worst."

"Sure he is." Harvey came to a decision and held the door open for Nick. "All right, Satan Junior McLucifer the Third, or whatever your name is. Come in out of the cold."

It was a terrible mistake. But Harvey didn't realize that until later.

DEATH IS ALWAYS DUE TO WITCHCRAFT

December 27, Night
SABRINA

My cousin and I sneaked past my aunts and up the stairs to Ambrose's room. I sat cross-legged on silk cushions under the British flag he had hanging up. The skylight let the stars peep in. Ambrose paced the floor as I talked, his scarlet-embroidered black silk robe flaring as if he were a very fancy judge.

"So hypothetically, Aunt Zelda told me to stay out of trouble and take especial care to avoid attracting any bad-luck spirits, and instead within an hour I broke glass. Like, a house's worth of window glass. A lifetime's supply of mirrors. Seven hundred years' bad luck."

Ambrose stopped pacing. He stood staring down at me. "You broke your word . . . and all the glass . . . in under an hour."

"Maybe so." I gazed up at Ambrose apprehensively. "How bad is it? Hypothetically. I already lost a school project."

His face stayed attentive and solemn for another handful of moments. Then his lips split into a wide, incredulous grin.

"Cousin, you are hypothetically *screwed*!"

Typically, Ambrose couldn't stay serious for more than five minutes at a time. Usually, I didn't mind. I could be serious enough for both of us.

Ambrose snapped his beringed fingers and fleecy white softness appeared, curling around his hand. He made a circular motion, then deftly wove the white cloud around my middle. I squawked. He grasped my hand and pulled me to my feet, then spun me around the attic as I laughed and flailed.

"What are you doing?"

"Wrapping you in cotton wool," Ambrose replied. "You need it! I think you might be a bigger troublemaker than me, Sabrina. It makes me very proud."

He gave the cotton wool a gentle shake. I stopped giggling, looking up at his face through the haze of protective cotton wool. Ambrose was always the one who laughed, advised me, and made everything seem all right when I got into trouble.

Even Ambrose hadn't laughed when I'd brought Tommy back from the dead. Even my wild wayward cousin thought I'd gone too far then.

"I didn't mean to," I told him. "I couldn't let Roz get hurt. I was only trying to do the right thing."

Ambrose snapped his fingers again, and the cotton wool evaporated in the air like cotton candy in a child's mouth. I could see clearly without the cotton wool veil, and I saw my cousin's brilliant smile dim.

"I know," Ambrose murmured. "You always do." The brief tenderness passed from his face, and he tugged my hair. "Then you always land in the most spectacular messes. Well, at least you never commit the only unforgivable sin."

"What's that?"

"Being boring," Ambrose replied.

"Be serious!"

Ambrose winked. "Nah."

"Look, I know I've caused our aunts a lot of trouble lately," I said. "Aunt Zelda looked really unhappy about giving up the baby this morning. I don't want her to worry about me."

"The aunts love worrying about us," said Ambrose. "It's their hobby. Cheer up, Sabrina mine. Forgetting your school project might be a tragedy to you, but when I was at Hell Harrow, hellhounds ate my homework every day for a year. It's not a disaster. Bad-luck spirits are generally minor imps, easy to banish and not worth fretting about."

I collapsed back on the cushions, feeling much more cheerful. "So I shouldn't tell Aunt Zelda and Aunt Hilda."

Ambrose circled the heap of cushions.

"Why worry them with a little thing like this? That would be unkind. And we're a kind, considerate niece and nephew. No, but keep an eye out for any signs of bad luck that seem excessive happening to you or anyone close to you. When bad luck spreads, that's when it gets really ugly. If you did attract a bad-luck spirit, we'll find out its name and banish it. Luck's mainly in your head, anyway.

The worst disasters come when you let magic mess with your mind, so stay positive and guard yourself with good-luck charms, like a rabbit's foot. Simple."

I thought of the necklace I still wore. Not a rabbit's foot. Harvey'd given me the necklace for my sixteenth birthday and told me he loved me for the first time. I'd told him I loved him back and believed this love would be forever.

That was October, and now we were in cold December. Forever hadn't lasted.

"Cousin?" Ambrose regarded me with a raised eyebrow. "Is this meltdown entirely about hypothetical bad-luck spirits?"

I sighed. "Maybe not. Coffee with Roz didn't go smoothly, and—I miss Harvey all the time."

Ambrose threw himself down on the cushions, drawing his leg up to his chest and flinging his arm around my shoulders. "May I offer you some romantic advice? The best way to get over one man is to climb onto another."

There was a pause.

"Thanks," I said dryly. "That's very romantic."

Ambrose made a sweeping gesture. "I try. And I think it's worth considering. What about the sexy one, from that time in my room?"

"From that terrible sexy party you had in your room that I walked in on?" I gave Ambrose a look indicating he should be ashamed.

Ambrose, born shameless, beamed and pointed at me. "Exactly."

"Next time could you hang up a sign on your door?" I asked. "A sign that says SEXY PARTY IN PROGRESS, so people know not to come in."

"Seems against the spirit of free love, which means all are welcome," said Ambrose. "Anyway, what about that one?"

"The sexy one?" I asked. "Do you mean Prudence? I got the vibe you thought *she* was the sexy one."

"I did and she is," said Ambrose. "And if you think you can handle Prudence, cousin, I urge you to go ahead."

I laughed and shook my head.

"I meant the boy," said Ambrose. "Nick, right? Nick Claw, Nick Scratch, Nick Sex Kitten, whatever his name is. You know the one. Sultry and Spanish around the edges. Don't you like the look of him? He likes *you*. I remember he offered to go to your room for some alone time."

"How will I ever be able to handle all this romance?"

I didn't say no. I saw Ambrose noticing. I'd never actually said no to Nick when he made his outrageous suggestions.

"Try him out," suggested Ambrose. "As I recall, he's got moves."

"You'd know better than I would!"

"Find out for yourself," Ambrose urged. "Forget about Harvey. He threw your Yule present in your face! Throw the whole man away. Let Nick Whatever bang the color back into your hair."

I'd once believed Ambrose was unusually free-spirited, but it turned out most witches were that way. It took some getting used to.

"Nick's my friend," I said. "But I don't think he's the commitment type."

Prudence had said as much about Nick, more than once. Prudence would know.

Ambrose blinked. "Who's talking about commitment? Whoa, no,

no, not that one. There's boyfriend material, and there's sexy party fabric. Nick's the second."

I shrugged. "Then I'm not interested. No judgment, I love you! It's just not my thing."

Ambrose mirrored the shrug. "Then don't do it. I only want you to be happy." He hesitated. "But if you're looking for love among witches, you might be looking a long time. We're not built for that."

"I'm not looking for anything," I told him. "But didn't Luke say he loved you?"

It was new, Ambrose having a boyfriend, but he deserved someone great. I didn't know Luke well, but if he loved Ambrose, I was prepared to like him.

Ambrose drummed his fingers against his knee, his only tell of discomfort. "I'm sure he was only trying to get out of trouble for summoning me away from my family when the ghosts came. Which he remained in trouble for. I like him, of course, but—am I really the romantic love type?"

I leaned my cheek against his shoulder. "I think you could be any type you wanted to be."

"And I think you can find whatever it is you're, ah, not looking for," said Ambrose. "New year, new man, new luck."

I pulled myself together. "You're right. I'll chill out. I just broke some glass. I didn't try to blow up the Vatican."

Ambrose grinned. "I only did that one time."

That settled, we went down to the kitchen for a midnight snack—midnight snacks are part of a balanced diet for witches—and passed under the lemons Aunt Hilda had already fixed in the doorway. Then I went to bed.

My familiar was frequently gone on business of his own. Aunt Zelda said it served me right, adopting a goblin familiar from the wild woods, but I was pretty independent myself. I liked that Salem walked free and fierce down strange paths through the trees, waving his tail on his wild lone, then returned to me.

Still, he usually went to bed when I did. Even if he was nowhere to be seen during the day, at night Salem would filter through some door or window like a thread of black smoke and settle in a warm purring heap at the foot of my bed.

Not tonight. From the time I hopped into my bed until the sun turned the ice on the tree branches to brief gold, Salem stayed on the porch steps and sang a wailing, mournful song to the moon.

I remembered Aunt Hilda's advice on how to gain good luck and avoid bad. *'Ware a cat's cry.*

A cat's cry was an omen of trouble to come.

I shivered under my covers as I heard him. I didn't get much sleep. Usually when I felt unsteady, I called Harvey. It made everything better to hear his voice, warm whenever he said my name. Roz described Harvey as sad, but he always sounded happy when he was talking to me.

Even though I couldn't sleep, I didn't call Harvey. He couldn't accept me for the witch I was, and I couldn't accept him being in danger because of magic. How much worse could my luck get?

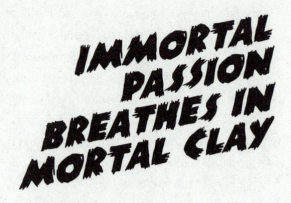

IMMORTAL PASSION BREATHES IN MORTAL CLAY

HARVEY

Nick prowling through Harvey's home was as unsettling as it had been the first time. Harvey didn't have many people over to his house. He was always afraid of what his dad might do, but he was pretty sure the host was meant to make the guest comfortable. He wasn't sure what to do when the weird magic guest was making the *host* super uncomfortable.

Nick rapped on one of the windows with a professional air. "Sealing spell's holding up."

Harvey shrugged uneasily, putting his hands in his pockets. "Couldn't tell you."

"Can I ask you something?"

"Sure," said Harvey. "Yeah."

"My friend suggested that I astrally project naked to

64

Sabrina's bedroom," said Nick. "Is that a good idea?"

"That is the worst idea I've ever heard in my life," said Harvey flatly.

He wasn't sure what the words *astrally project* even meant. He thought he'd read them in comics before, and he figured he'd look it up later. But he was very sure about his answer.

"Here's the first thing you should know about mortals. From what I can see, when it comes to romance, we go a *lot* slower than witches."

Nick frowned. "Why would you take longer to do things when you don't live as long as we do?"

Well, there was another shock. At this point Harvey was stumbling through a landscape entirely composed of weirdness, trying to deal.

"Maybe—maybe it's because we know we won't live. We want to take our time so we can make something that will last, whether that's painting a picture, or building a castle, or falling in love."

That probably sounded dumb. But he didn't know how to talk about love any other way. Nick was nodding with a scrunched-up, frowning expression of concentration that reminded Harvey of Sabrina, and the way she looked when she wanted to take notes but didn't have a pen and paper.

"Doing things the mortal way means going gradually," Harvey continued, encouraged. "That's how you get someone to believe you mean it. Do you understand?"

Nick's face smoothed into a smile. "I do."

"So absolutely no"—Harvey tried and failed to utter the words *naked astral projection*—"what you just said. None of that."

"I got it, mortal," said Nick. "What should I do instead?"

Harvey offered cautiously: "I have an idea."

He led the way to Tommy's bedroom. He hadn't ventured there since he went in with the gun in his hands. He almost chickened out now, but Nick was right behind him, and he didn't want to be useless again.

Before it was Tommy's bedroom, his dad had fixed up this room to be his mom's library. Tommy had never let his dad take the shelves down.

Harvey's mother had loved books. She'd gone to college for a year, doing social studies and women's studies—some women's nonsense, his dad always called it—before she had to drop out for the usual reason. She'd died when Harvey was too young to remember much about her, but he had a distant recollection of lying on patchwork blankets with her at bedtime. The memory was fuzzy and soft and warm, of being wrapped up in one blanket so it became a patchwork world and he was a quilt burrito, her voice reading to him the only sound he could hear. She'd read everything, books about love and poetry and celebrities from the golden age of Hollywood, and dictionaries and encyclopedias. She'd picked out the diamond panes of their living room windows, sunshine yellow and burnt orange, amethyst and teal. If she'd lived, Harvey might have grown up in a house with somebody who was like him.

Sabrina and Roz read a lot too. Harvey enjoyed sitting in the library with them. He sketched and listened to music and flipped through comics, or novels they recommended, while Sabrina made intense notes on the reading or Roz got lost in her book. Tommy was never much of a reader, but his steady girl in high school had been. Harvey suspected Tommy was drawn to her because of that. Because of their mother. Tommy told Harvey their mom used to say: *Stories teach us to live better.*

Harvey crushed down thoughts of Tommy. He had a task to perform, and he didn't want to mess it up. He opened the doors hiding the shelves from view and combed through his mother's dusty volumes to find the books on psychology and relationships. There were a lot of books all called *The Hite Report*: on female sexuality, male sexuality, and growing up under patriarchy. Whoever Hite was, they'd reported a lot of things.

"Oh, *books*."

Nick sounded pleased.

Harvey glanced at him. "Um, I was thinking you could read these." He hesitated. "You can stay here and read them. I can't let you take them away. They were my mom's."

"That's fine," said Nick. "If Father Blackwood saw me with mortal books, he'd burn them."

"Who's Father Blackwood?"

"He's the head of our coven, and the principal of the Academy of Unseen Arts."

"He *burns books*?"

Their own principal had banned some books in the school library. Maybe it wasn't so different. Harvey didn't get why people in charge of teaching you wouldn't want you to learn.

"He does a lot of things," said Nick, a trifle grimly, then cheered up. "Give me the books."

Nick continued to seem happy, rather than smug or amused,

which was new. They carried the stacks of books into the kitchen, and Nick laid out the books in a careful pattern, then requested notepaper, highlighters, and several pens. Harvey had to go empty out his schoolbag.

"Do you—like books?" Harvey asked when Nick was set up with his studies.

"Yes," said Nick absently. "When I started going to school, I wasn't used to being around people. The books in the library at the Academy made sense of a lot of things. And they were interesting."

Clearly, Nick was fond of studying, like Sabrina. Harvey'd never been much good at studying. Maybe he should go to his room and sketch and leave Nick to it.

"Stay where you are," said Nick, without looking up from his book. "In case I have questions."

"Um, okay. I don't want any sex questions," Harvey warned.

Nick was beginning to look amused again.

"Think I might know more than you on that particular topic, mortal. I'm aware you were primarily romantically committed to Sabrina, and of course she had to stay pure for Satan until she was sixteen."

"She what!" exclaimed Harvey.

Nick shrugged. He acted as if everything he said was totally reasonable. It was one of the most upsetting things about Nick.

"Whoa," said Harvey. "When we went out, her aunt Zelda used to yell at her from the window to keep the unholy temple of her body locked to unbelievers. I did wonder about that. I mean, I didn't think she was a witch. I just thought her aunt Zelda was very weird."

"No," said Nick. "It's standard."

"Does everyone do that?" Harvey demanded. "Did *you* stay pure for Satan?"

A strange expression crossed Nick's face. Harvey realized, with a burst of delight at this unexpected justice from the universe, that Nick Scratch was scandalized.

"Of course I did! What kind of boy do you take me for?"

Harvey couldn't answer because he was laughing too hard. Even when Nick huffed and glared, he couldn't stop.

"Yes, well, anyway—stop laughing, farm boy—that means I'm aware that you can't have much experience," said Nick. "What has it been? Like fifty people in your entire life?"

Nick glanced at Harvey inquiringly. Though it had seemed impossible to stop laughing a moment ago, Harvey wasn't laughing now.

"Was that too few people?" asked Nick. "Was that insulting? Obviously, I know mortals don't have to save themselves for Satan."

"I don't want to talk about this!" Harvey said loudly.

"Actually, the Dark Lord doesn't specify men must stay pure, but I figured it was only fair."

"Satan shouldn't tell women what to do," Harvey snapped, then worried he might be disrespecting Nick's culture.

He didn't know what else to do, so he took out the math homework they'd been assigned over the vacation. Usually Harvey left his math homework until the day before it was due, like a normal person. Susie did the same, no matter how often Sabrina and Roz told them it was better to accomplish their work on their first free evening.

Sabrina probably really appreciated that Nick was smart. She'd told Harvey he wasn't stupid, but she'd been lying to him for years and he hadn't caught on.

Harvey tried to concentrate on his math homework. It was difficult, but Harvey wasn't sure if that was because math was hard, because Harvey hadn't been sleeping well lately, or because there was a warlock at Harvey's elbow making extensive notes about mortal courtship.

Also, he was starving.

Harvey looked up from the equations he was trying to balance with no luck. "Nick?"

Nick didn't look up from his book. "Hmm?"

"Want something to eat?"

Nick did look up then. "What?"

His face didn't show much, and the single word came out devoid of expression. Harvey wasn't sure how he was receiving the impression Nick found this tricky to answer.

"Something to eat?" Harvey asked, slightly freaked out. It was a simple question.

Nick seemed to come to a conclusion. "I could eat."

He was still holding his pen, but he had his chin propped on his fist now, studying Harvey with the same focus that he'd trained on the books, as though he was trying to puzzle something out.

Harvey tried to ignore the bizarre-warlock-in-the-kitchen stuff happening to him. He heated up the lasagna and set the table around the papers.

When Harvey turned back to the table, Nick was filling out the equations in Harvey's math book.

"What are you doing?" Harvey asked.

"Playing the game," Nick answered.

"What?"

"Isn't it a children's game?" Nick inquired. "With numbers? It's so simple."

Harvey glared and pulled the homework away. Nick cackled like a real witch.

When dinner was ready, Nick took a purple vial from somewhere inside his dark clothes and tipped a tiny violet trickle onto his plate.

"Dude," Harvey said. "Why?"

"The potion will tell me if this is poisoned," Nick explained.

"What is wrong with witches? I'm not *poisoning you.*"

"It's a precaution," said Nick. "Alerts you to poison, truth potions, potions that make you miscarry children—not a huge concern, I admit—anything your enemies might put in your food."

Harvey rolled his eyes and began to eat. "Gosh, I wonder why you might have enemies."

"Every witch has a few," murmured Nick, and forked up some lasagna. His eyes flickered shut, then open again, and he drew the plate toward him and began to eat rapidly, as if he thought someone might try to take it away from him.

The lasagna wasn't even good. It was mostly stuff from jars. That was all Harvey and Tommy had ever really been able to work out how to do, and often it was TV dinners or chicken nuggets, especially when Tommy came home tired from working in the mines. Any special effort for family dinners usually went to waste. When Dad came in drunk, you felt like a fool for trying.

Harvey had his eyes on his own plate for literally a second, then glanced up and saw Nick had finished his entire portion and was sticking his fork in the lasagna dish.

"Hey, put it on your plate! Were you raised by wolves?"

Nick blinked. "How did you know?"

Truly, Nick thought he was a comedian. Harvey sighed and pushed the lasagna dish toward him.

"You can have the whole thing. If you put it on your plate. Do they not feed you at Invisible Academy?"

"The Academy of Unseen Arts," corrected Nick. "They feed us. It's slightly better than eating live rabbits."

Harvey was leaving that one alone. Frankly, he didn't want to know.

"While we're eating," said Nick, which was a polite word for "watching a man decimate a lasagna within minutes," "these books talk a lot about consent. I know what the word means, obviously, but does it have a different connotation among mortals? Why does it get brought up so often? Is it very important?"

Harvey's vision went hazy with horror. He wished Roz were here. She was wonderful generally, and especially at explaining things. Then he was even more horrified by the thought of Roz being in contact with magic.

It was a hideous thing to ask somebody, but he tried. "It's very important. Are you sure...the women you've been intimate with, uh, wanted to do it?"

Nick's expression turned quizzical. "I mean, people usually leap on me and rip off my—"

"Great, nonverbal consent!" Harvey said. "Let's stop talking about this. Right now. Immediately."

Because nothing about Harvey's life made sense, Nick continued to eat lasagna and muse aloud on this issue. Nick could eat at the speed of light, but with perfect table manners. Harvey suspected witchcraft.

"Is consent like ... when you sell your soul?"

"No!"

Nick looked faintly appalled. "Farm boy, it's wrong to just take souls. People have to agree before the devil can have their souls. I thought it was a good analogy."

It didn't sound right, but Harvey didn't feel he had grounds to make an argument.

"I don't know enough about how selling your soul works to say," Harvey said eventually. "Do you guys really worship Satan?"

"Yes, we do," said Nick in a placid voice, as if telling Harvey about the weather. "We sign our names in the Book of the Beast, so Satan has a claim on our souls. Why, what do mortals do with their souls?"

"Uh. Mortals keep our souls."

"Why?" asked Nick. "What are you using them for?"

"Well," said Harvey. "We just keep them."

"That seems wasteful. You could be trading them for immortal youth and beauty, and magic powers."

When put that way, it sounded almost reasonable. Nick talked about signing his soul away in the same manner kids at school who went to church a few times a year talked about Easter service.

Roz was very clear about everyone being tolerant of different religions. Harvey wasn't sure if this applied to Satan.

Roz believed. Her dad was the minister, so maybe she had to, but Harvey didn't feel entirely comfortable with Roz's dad or at his church.

Tommy believed. He'd always worn their mother's cross around his neck. The funeral director in Riverdale had given Harvey Tommy's cross, and Harvey didn't know what to do with it. He carried it around in the pocket of his jeans, always aware of the weight. Wearing the cross seemed wrong, but so did putting it away somewhere to gather dust.

Harvey didn't know what to think about a world where monsters were allowed to terrify little kids in the mines, or people like Tommy were murdered by witches. It was hard to have faith in anything these days, but he knew when something felt wrong.

"I think..." he said at last. "I'd rather keep my soul and figure out what I want to do with it."

Nick shrugged, as if to say: *Suit yourself.* The lasagna was by now totally demolished. "Sabrina didn't want to sign the Book either. But she did."

Harvey tensed. "Did someone make her?"

"Sabrina signed the Book on the night the Greendale Thirteen came," said Nick. Harvey was starting to understand that when Nick's already-low voice went lower, it meant he was troubled. "So she'd have the power to save the town. And you."

She'd appeared in his bedroom that night and told him it was dangerous to be together ever again. That was the night her hair turned white as starlight. When he'd taken her in his arms and kissed her, he tasted ozone, and midnight, and bitter sweetness. He'd known something had happened, but not what.

"You don't seem thrilled about her doing it," Harvey said. "You don't think signing away your soul is messed up at all. So why aren't you pleased?"

Silence followed. Apparently, Nick hadn't thought to ask himself this question.

"I liked her the way she was," Nick answered eventually. "I thought it was a pity to change her. And an even greater pity to make her do anything she didn't want. She said she didn't want to, so I didn't want her to either."

"So, uh," said Harvey. "That's actually a good working definition of consent."

Nick brightened. "Is it?"

"Well done."

Nick glowed. "Doing things the mortal way is a snap."

That was when they both heard the creak of the front door opening. Harvey's blood was trained to run chill at the sound, as if a certain footstep turned on the cold tap in his soul.

"That's my dad. You have to leave."

It was already too late.

"It's all right, mortal," Nick murmured. "Relax."

Harvey didn't know how he was supposed to relax when Nick kept saying things like "mortal." His dad was bound to notice.

"Harv, I'm home!" his dad bellowed from the hall. "Had a hell of a day. Two mine shafts collapsed, of all the rotten luck, and that part-timer Jones broke his leg..."

His dad's voice trailed away when he saw Nick at the kitchen table.

"Who's this?" his dad barked. He poured himself a glass of water, his hands shaking slightly. He drank a lot of water these days, reaching for a drink even though it wasn't alcohol.

"Uh...this is Nick," said Harvey. "We're working on a project together."

If his dad looked at Nick's notes, he would see Nick had written *Wooing Mortals?* in beautiful calligraphy at the top of one page, and he would have questions. His eyes were boring through Harvey instead, seeing right through Harvey's feeble excuses. He always looked at Harvey with the same expression, that of a man who didn't like what he saw.

Quick as an animal moving through the trees at night, Nick produced another vial. This one glistened green, and Nick tipped it into the water glass while Harvey's dad was watching Harvey.

"Dad—" Harvey began, warning, but even as he spoke, his dad took a deep draft.

He lowered the glass. Harvey winced.

"Nick," his dad said, and started to smile. It was a broad smile, a little foolish, and it fit badly on his dad's face. "Well, you're welcome, of course. Come by anytime."

"I will," Nick answered calmly.

"The *captain* of the football team," said Harvey's dad. "That's pretty impressive."

"Sure," said Nick. "Whatever football is."

Dad was obviously hearing different things from what Nick was actually saying. Harvey's gaze traveled from Nick to the glass to his father. Dad clapped Nick on the back.

"Nice to see the boy finally hang around with someone normal."

Nick bared his teeth. "Hilarious you would say that."

"Maybe you could have a talk with him about not wasting his

life," Harvey's dad continued. "Always drawing his freaky pictures and talking stupid nonsense with the weirdest girls in town. Don't know where he gets it from."

Harvey stared fixedly at the kitchen table.

"Not you," said Nick. "Clearly."

"He'll never amount to much," said Dad. "No spine. Can you imagine Harv playing football? Ha! He'd burst into tears at the first touchdown. But he could try basketball. Something worthwhile to occupy himself with, for a change. Have a word with him, eh?"

"Great talk. Shame you have to go to your room and not come out until morning."

Nick gave the command very casually. In response Harvey's dad yawned and stretched, as though he was a puppet and Nick could pull his strings.

"I'm worn out, boys. Gonna turn in." His dad glanced over at him. "You'd know the feeling, Harv, if you ever did an honest day's work in your life. Nice to meet you, Nick."

The door of his dad's bedroom slamming closed echoed through the house. Harvey kept staring at the knots in the kitchen table. One discolored knot of wood looked almost like a screaming face. He knew his own face had fallen into its usual sullen lines.

"You shouldn't have done that," he said at last. "Magic. On my dad."

"Would you have preferred me to kill him?" Nick asked.

Harvey was speechless.

"Would you?" Nick pursued. "Because I could do that."

"No!" Harvey snarled. "I don't want you to kill *my dad*. He's my dad! Why would I— What kind of question is that?"

When he looked up, Nick was watching him.

"Do you . . . love him?"

"Yeah," mumbled Harvey.

Nick made a face. "Why? Do you just love anybody?"

"No, I don't," Harvey said curtly.

He could count the people he loved on one hand. There was Sabrina and Tommy, always. There was Roz and Susie. Then there was his father, who he loved with a resentful, uneasy love that had no liking in it.

And now Tommy was dead. Sabrina was lost to Nick's world of shadows and blood. Magic had taken so much he loved away.

Harvey hadn't wanted Sabrina enchanting his father, and he didn't want Nick doing it either. It was awful he was glad his dad wasn't drinking any longer, and awful he was glad his dad was in his room and not coming out. It was awful that Harvey was happy to have company.

"Does your father always talk to you like that?"

"Yeah," said Harvey bleakly. "Can we stop discussing this? Get back to your books. That's what you're here for."

Nick shrugged and complied. Harvey cleared up the dishes and finished his math homework, trying to ignore the answers Nick had written, which were irritatingly correct and made sense of a few things Harvey hadn't understood before.

Then he was done. Nick was still leafing through the books, making copious notes. It was late, but Harvey knew what it looked like when Sabrina or Roz was absorbed in a problem. So he did what he usually did during late-night study sessions when his own brain had turned off, which was sketch stuff and make the beverages.

Harvey had drawn a thousand pictures of every detail of his home long ago, trying to practice every way he knew how. Nothing much changed in Greendale, but he'd never had a warlock studying at his kitchen table before.

Harvey put a steaming mug at Nick's elbow and went back to drawing until Nick gave a soft murmur of realization five minutes later when he discovered the mug was there.

"What…" said Nick, squinting at it as if he wasn't familiar with mugs.

"For you," said Harvey.

Nick kept squinting at the mug. Eventually, he muttered: "I want coffee."

"No," Harvey told him. "It's too late. You won't sleep. This is herbal tea. It's soothing. You should know this. I'm sure witches know about herbs."

Nick made a face at him. Then he made a face at the herbal tea and whispered a few spells into his cup, which Harvey found rude. Eventually, he returned to swearing quiet eldritch curses as he made more notes, pulled at his own hair while lost in thought, and drank his tea. The header on Nick's new page read *The Battle between the Sexes? Actual Weapons Seldom Involved.*

Harvey kept sketching. When Harvey was making another cup of tea, he glanced over his shoulder and saw Nick swivel the sketch across the table toward him with a fingertip. Nick, who was unruffled by discussions about sex and dark magic, seemed taken aback.

"That's me."

"You're the only new thing I have to draw," Harvey explained. "Do you mind?"

"No," Nick answered. "I don't mind."

Nick tapped his pen against the sketch and smiled briefly to himself. Harvey thought the picture had turned out well too.

Then the drawing burst into flames. The paper curled up at the edges, black as a dead rose, and within moments the sketch was only a cinder on the table and red lights reflected in Nick's dark eyes.

"What are you *doing?*"

"Can't leave any images of myself lying around for people to enchant," Nick told him briskly. "It's fine to draw them, though. I'll destroy them later."

"Oh my God," said Harvey. "I can't believe you."

Nick yawned. "Could you not talk about the false god so much? Hey, I have another question."

Harvey braced himself.

"Sometimes I go out into the world to watch mortals. What does it mean when mortals give you a piece of paper with numbers on it? Is it a code?"

"You don't know what a phone number is?"

He wasn't sure how to explain phones. He didn't remember who had invented phones. Maybe Edison. Wait, no, that was light bulbs.

"If a girl gives you her phone number…" Harvey said. "That means she likes you."

"I see," Nick said.

"Does that happen to you a lot?"

Nick smirked. "Every time I go out among the mortals."

Harvey rolled his eyes. "How nice for you."

"I thought the numbers just meant they wanted to sleep with me," Nick mused.

Harvey coughed. "Um. Well, some people only want to sleep with people they like. Uh, and some people wait to be in love."

"Witches don't do that," Nick told him cheerfully. "Witches can't love anybody. Satan forbids it."

Harvey stared. Nick seemed to mean what he was saying.

"You think you can't love people?" Harvey asked. Just to be clear.

"Sabrina's the only witch who can," Nick explained.

That fit right in with Harvey's nightmares of witches, murderous, heartless creatures who laid waste to the world.

But now someone else said it, that made no sense. Harvey remembered a sunny day in his childhood, sitting on a gravestone in the Spellman cemetery and watching Hilda cover Sabrina with handfuls of daisies.

"So many flowers," Hilda had said. "But where's my flower? Wait, I see her! I see her little nose."

The Spellman house was such a bright place. Her home made Sabrina who she was.

"Nick," said Harvey. "You claim you're smart, so stop talking like an idiot. Witches love people. The Spellmans love Sabrina. It's in everything they do."

Nick seemed stunned into silence. Possibly he was stunned Harvey had called him an idiot.

At last, he asked: "Do you really think I could?"

How was Harvey supposed to know? He barely knew Nick.

But Nick had come when Sabrina asked. He'd noticed Sabrina loved people. He talked about watching mortals. That made Harvey think of watching Hilda and Sabrina. He knew how it felt to long for a home.

"Sure," said Harvey gently. "Of course I do."

Nick still seemed doubtful. "I don't think I would be very good at it."

"The important part is trying," said Harvey.

Nick let out a deep breath, shook his head, and retreated to his books.

By the time Harvey found himself nodding off at the kitchen table, he decided this was ridiculous and he was going to bed. He went off to brush his teeth. When he came out of the bathroom, Nick was sleeping with his head in his arms, protectively cradling the latest book. Harvey sighed in annoyance and went to get a blanket and a pillow from the closet in his room.

He turned and found Nick at the door, yawning again and still clutching the book. "Where'd you go?"

"It's very late."

Maybe it wasn't late for witches? Did witches stay up all night, every night? When did Sabrina go to her other school, exactly? Harvey felt too tired to contemplate the insomniac habits of witches.

He offered the blanket and pillow to Nick, who accepted them and wandered over to the desk where Harvey usually sketched, sat, and continued to read. Harvey gave up on being a polite host and went to bed.

He woke to find the morning gray behind the fir trees outside his window, the blanket folded on the desk, and Nick finally gone.

Harvey climbed out of bed and picked up the last book, left on the desk beside the blanket. He turned the book over in his hands, holding on to it the way Nick had, as though books comforted him.

Nick was weird as hell, but he wasn't terrifying, not the way witches were in Harvey's nightmares. And he'd asked Harvey for help. Harvey's own grandfather didn't even come by the house anymore. Grandpa was proud of Tommy, but he always said Harvey was useless.

It was nice not to feel useless for a change.

It had been a truly bizarre night, but the night was over. He'd get to see Roz soon.

With any luck, he'd never see Nick Scratch again.

BELIEVE IN WITCHCRAFT AND SORCERY

December 28, Feast of the Holy Innocents, Morning
SABRINA

I didn't have many classes with Nick and the Weird Sisters, who were more advanced than I was, but lectures were different. When I entered the gray cavern of the lecture hall, carrying my charms and incantations project in my hands for fear of more mistakes, they were all there.

Prudence, Agatha, and Dorcas usually sat together, but not today. Prudence was sitting alone in one row, and her sisters in the row behind her. Nick was across the way. He was reading through a pile of notes, but he looked up when I came in, and beckoned.

I remembered what Ambrose had said about him. I shook my head and smiled, and then I went over to Prudence.

"Can I sit with you?"

Prudence gave a disdainful sigh. "Do what you must."

I figure this was the closest thing to a welcome Prudence was capable of and hopped into the seat beside her. Set in the rough stone wall over our heads, there was a massive fossilized hand holding a flaming torch. I read over my charms project one last time by its orange glow.

"I did my project on protection charms," I said. "Swallowing a pearl to save yourself from drowning, that kind of thing. How about you?"

"Luck charms," Prudence answered.

The mention of luck caught my attention. I glanced nervously over at Prudence, but her eyes were on our lecturer—unfortunately Sister Jackson again—and she appeared superbly indifferent as usual.

"Oh, really?" I asked. "I mean, I shouldn't be surprised. You do have a lot of luck with guys."

"No luck needed there," murmured Prudence. "They're lining up to have their hearts crushed to powder."

I coughed. "Right. Awesome."

That was enough girl talk for me. I turned over another page, then watched as a fat orange spark from the torch floated through the dusty air and landed right on my homework. Before I could whisper a guarding spell, the pages went up in a blaze.

Several people turned around in their chairs to watch my project burning.

"Oh, bad luck, Sabrina," murmured the boy sitting in front of me.

I stared at the pile of cinders. "Yeah," I said weakly.

"Your family simply *burns* to get into trouble, don't they?" was Sister Jackson's contribution.

"Thank you, Sister Jackson," I said under my breath. "Sick burn, Sister Jackson."

"I heard that, Sabrina Spellman!" Sister Jackson threw over her shoulder. "Zero points on this assignment. See me after class."

Prudence flicked a speck of ash off the lace collar of her dress and didn't comment.

"I've been a bit worried that I might have attracted a bad-luck spirit," I confided to her.

"At the turn of the year? You mean, the worst possible time to attract a bad-luck spirit?" Prudence gave a brief laugh. "Typical Sabrina."

"Maybe I didn't. Maybe everything's fine."

Prudence didn't offer me any help, but the boy in front of us helpfully offered me parchment and a pen. I accepted with thanks. He was the same boy who'd loaned me a pencil yesterday. He must be running through office supplies fast because of me. He seemed nice. I thought his name was Peter Pan. Something like that.

I caught Nick looking his way. Maybe he and Peter Pan were friends.

Once the lecture was over, Nick rose and approached the desk where Prudence and I were sitting.

"Hey. Can I have a word, Sabrina?"

"About what?"

Nick glanced from Prudence to the boy sitting in front of me and down at the notes in his hands. If it had been anyone but Nick Scratch, I would've said he was nervous.

Then he looked up from his notes. "Will you give me your phone number?"

I stared. "Do you own a phone?"

Nick shook his head.

"Then why do you want my number?"

"I wish you'd give it to me." Nick's voice sounded almost wistful. "But you don't have to. No pressure."

"When boys ask for my number, I tell them I don't have a phone," Prudence remarked. "I enjoy cruel truths."

I chewed on my lip and thought of Roz saying she needed time before she was ready to deal with me. I thought of wanting to call Harvey so badly and knowing I couldn't. I wasn't part of the mortal world any longer. The mortals didn't want me there. Nick was only asking for a way to reach me.

I wrote my number down on the edge of parchment Peter Pan had loaned me, tore it off, and handed the number to Nick with a smile. "Here you go."

Nick took the scrap of paper with an awed air, as though I'd given him a jewel. He consulted his notes again.

"Sorry if I've been coming on too strong," he said. "I just wanted you to know I like you. I didn't mean to make you uncomfortable."

I sat paralyzed with surprise. That was the last thing I'd ever expected him to say. I had no idea what to say back. I wished fervently that we could be interrupted.

That was the moment when, with a shower of dust and sliding pebbles, the giant fossilized hand stuck in the wall came loose and crashed down upon us. Prudence, the Weird Sisters, and the boy sitting up front dived for cover.

Nick Scratch dived for me. He knocked me off my stool, and we landed on the stone floor with rocks raining down on us. Everyone was shouting out spells to quench fire and hold the walls, me included. Nick's back was arched protectively over my body, his hand cupping my head. His low voice was close to my ear as he whispered shielding incantations, and I felt oddly safe, in a way I wouldn't have expected to feel among the witches of the Academy.

The rockslide ceased, shards of stone halting in midair. Nick lifted his head. There was gray dust in his dark hair and a graze on his cheek.

"Are you all right?" he asked.

I gazed up at him.

Then Dorcas and Agatha pulled Nick off and away. Dorcas seemed deeply concerned that Nick had been hurt, though he was violently protesting that he was fine. Apparently, Dorcas was determined to remove his shirt and check for herself.

I sighed and sat up. Sure. I knew what Nick was like.

Prudence crouched down in the fallen debris of the wall, smoothing her dark purple skirt over her knees. Not a speck of dust had dared to land on her immaculately bleached and shingled hair. An amused smile played along her raspberry-painted lips.

"You know what, Sabrina? I think you might have attracted a bad-luck spirit."

"Thanks, Prudence. Thanks for that insight." I stood, dusting myself off and trying to formulate a plan.

Ambrose said bad-luck spirits were easy to banish. You only needed to find out their names. I didn't have to go running to my family. I could do this by myself.

Well. Perhaps I could use a little help.

I turned to Prudence. "Luck charms are your specialty. Could we go to the library together? I need to find out the bad-luck spirit's name."

There was a pause. I waited apprehensively. It was possible this was too much to ask. Everyone knew Prudence had her hands full with her baby brother.

"Will you put in a good word for me with Zelda?" Prudence asked abruptly.

I stared. "With my aunt Zelda? Why? Oh, because she's going to be the choir mistress?"

Prudence paused for the briefest of moments. "Naturally. I want a solo."

I nodded eagerly. "Of course I will."

"Then...yes," Prudence agreed. "We have a bargain. I'll help you banish your bad-luck spirit."

MORTAL EYES CANNOT DISTINGUISH

December 28, Morning
ROZ

Rosalind Walker sat in the new tea shop with Harvey across the table from her. To someone who didn't know them, this might look like a date.

As soon as the thought occurred to Roz, she poured the contents of her little flowered teapot directly onto her éclair.

"Whoa, Roz," said Harvey. "Hey."

He was abruptly out of his chintzy armchair and on his knees at her feet, mopping up the tea with the paper napkins.

Roz made an agonized face. "Sorry, sorry…"

"It's okay. You didn't get burned?"

"No."

Harvey smiled up at her, his singularly sweet and distracting smile. "Then it's all okay."

From another guy it might've seemed like a line, but that wasn't Harvey. You could rely on Harvey to mean what he said.

Once the mess was cleaned up, Harvey paused and switched the plates, giving Roz the éclair that wasn't soaked in tea.

"Come on, Harv," Roz protested. "Don't."

Harvey shook his head. "Hey, teenage guys eat everything, haven't you heard? Anyway, I love coffee-flavored éclairs. This tea-flavored éclair is probably going to become the latest trend. It's mine now. Don't think you're getting it back."

Roz stifled a laugh. "Thanks."

Roz gave a lot of thought to words and what they meant. The words *nice* or *good* weren't specific enough. The words covered so much that they didn't actually mean much. The people in Roz's church were—mostly—nice and good. Harvey was *considerate*. He didn't consider what might be virtuous or sinful. He considered other people, and he put them first.

Harvey hesitated. "Are your eyes bothering you?"

Roz shrugged, feeling bad blaming her vision for her clumsiness. "Yeah."

It was true, though it wasn't the whole truth. Her eyes were always bothering her these days. She looked over at Harvey. They were sitting at the table set in the big front window of the Bishop's Daughter Coffee and Teas. Behind Harvey and the glass, the main street outside was a glittering stretch of snow, but Roz couldn't make out the curve of fire hydrants or the lines of tree branches anymore. She could barely discern Harvey's face, but she knew it so well she could fill in the lost details: the sharp nose and crooked vulnerable line of his mouth, his eyes always a little hollow from lack of sleep as he stayed up sketching. Right now she knew that dark gaze was soft with concern for her.

She knew, but she wanted to *see*. Magic was taking that away from her, the sight of all she loved.

"I'm sorry," Harvey told her, very quietly.

"It's not your fault."

It was the witches' fault, but Roz didn't say that. Instead she ate her éclair, the smooth cream and rich chocolate slightly bitter in her mouth. Maybe the éclair was going off. The blond who ran the shop, Mrs. Ferch-Geg, made so many that the glass cabinets were crowded with pastries. She must have dozens left over and spoiling by evening.

She told Harvey about the book she was reading. He always asked.

"Not everybody knows this, but the same guy wrote *Rosemary's Baby* and *The Stepford Wives*."

Harvey sounded like he was frowning—not in a bad way, but in concentration. "That would be the book about having Satan's baby and the book about robots, right?"

"Technically, yes," said Roz. "But actually, both those books are about the patriarchy!"

"Is that right? I don't know how having Satan's baby is about the patriarchy."

"I'll prove it to you."

"I believe you already, Roz," said Harvey. "But tell me. I'll try to follow."

Roz was silent, overcome with a rush of affection. Then she felt like a traitor and said: "Sabrina!"

Harvey started. "Where?"

"Oh, no," said Roz. "She's not here. I think she's at her, uh, other school. Which must be a weird place, right?"

"I bet it is a weird place," mused Harvey. "Full of weirdos."

Roz laughed nervously. "I met up with Sabrina yesterday. I almost got into an accident, but she saved me. With magic."

She used the words as a shield. Sabrina might be a witch, and witches might've hurt Roz, but Sabrina wouldn't hurt Roz. Sabrina was Roz's best friend, and that meant her boyfriend—even her ex—was off-limits.

"Is she all right?" Harvey demanded. "Are you all right?"

He sounded terrified. She hated that she'd scared him, and hated magic for scaring him first.

Roz tried to be soothing. "Everybody's fine. The biggest casualty was a bunch of broken glass. So, seven years of bad luck for us, I guess. Like we'd notice in this town." She chewed her lip. "How are you feeling... about Sabrina?"

Harvey answered, low as if the words made his throat ache: "Pretty miserable."

He must have seen her expression change, because he leaned forward and touched her wrist.

"Hey, Roz. It's okay. We can't all be as accomplished at romance as you."

"Me?" Roz laughed. "How do you mean?"

"Yeah, you," said Harvey, teasing. "Whenever you go off to summer camp—nerd camp or Christian camp—you always get a boyfriend. Then he writes sad postcards to you after you come back. You're a total heartbreaker, Roz."

"Not really," mumbled Roz.

She'd had a few boyfriends, at a few camps. She'd slept with someone for the first time last summer, and her dad would die if he knew. But as soon as she came home, she lost interest in dating.

She didn't want to date any boy in Greendale until she found a boy in Greendale she liked better than Harvey. And she never had.

She didn't think about it in terms of liking Harvey *that way*. She didn't let herself. He was the property of her best friend, and even if *nice* and *good* were unspecific words, Roz always tried to be a nice girl and a good friend.

They'd grown up together, the four of them, friends even when the thought of girls being with boys, or boys being with girls, was gross. Then one day, Catie Murphy asked their group who had a crush on who. Roz glanced shyly over at Harvey and found him already looking at Sabrina.

He was always looking at Sabrina. That never changed. Roz wouldn't even want it to. That was part of why Harvey was such a great guy, his wholehearted and unwavering devotion.

But now Harvey and Sabrina were broken up, and though Harvey was clearly heartbroken about it, Roz couldn't help having new intrusive thoughts. Like: *Hey, Sabrina. What do you say, bestie, if I tell you not to worry that a magic curse is turning me blind? I promise I won't hate magic. In exchange, can I have your man?*

"Harvey," Roz said suddenly. "I'm sorry for bringing up Sabrina. I shouldn't have."

"I'm sorry you were in an accident," said Harvey. "I'm glad she was there, and you're okay. I only want you and Sabrina and Susie to be safe."

Roz's grandma had died on the night the ghosts descended on

their town. She'd told Harvey he didn't have to come to the funeral, not so soon after Tommy. But of course Harvey came, wearing the same suit he'd buried his brother in twice, and stood loyally by her side. Susie and Sabrina and Harvey took turns holding Roz's hand.

Roz cried over her grandma until her eyes ached, but it wasn't the same as losing someone young, losing your brother.

She opened her mouth to reassure him, when Harvey said: "I know why you brought up Sabrina. It's because this feels wrong, right? Being here with me."

Roz's teaspoon fell out of her nerveless fingers. She didn't see where it went, and she didn't care.

Harvey retrieved her spoon. Her dimmed vision caught the glint of silver as he laid it carefully by her saucer. Then he reached for her.

She thought of another specific way to describe him: *gentleman.* Harvey was one, in the best sense of the word. She'd never seen him even touch someone roughly. Her grandma said once that it was dangerous, in this cruel world, to be gentle.

He touched her gently now, his fingers curling around her hand.

"You're all stiff. You've barely looked at me this whole time. I can tell what's going on. It's too awkward, now that Sabrina and I have split. One person usually gets the friends in the breakup, right? You're Sabrina's best friend, and—you guys feel like you can't be friends with both of us."

"No, Harvey!" Roz exclaimed. "That's not it."

"Then what is it, Roz?" Harvey asked. "Don't say it's nothing. I know you better than that."

She wished she could reach out and trace the lines of his face where they blurred in her vision, so she knew he looked exactly the way she remembered. She told herself the sudden intensity of this crush was because she was scared of magic, of the curse stealing her vision. It wasn't a real crush. She was clinging to someone she knew was safe.

She said nothing.

Harvey's voice stayed quiet and tender. "That's what I thought. I—I get it. I won't bother you anymore. And I don't blame you. Take care of yourself, Roz. Please."

Harvey stood, leaned down, and gently kissed her cheek. Roz was struck mute.

By the time she could speak he'd left the tea shop, the little bell jangling softly in his wake. She couldn't see much, but she saw him brace his shoulders against the cold.

Roz got up, but it was socially irresponsible to leave without paying. She ran over to Mrs. Ferch-Geg and tried to shove money at her, but the woman wouldn't take it.

"Your boyfriend paid while you were in the bathroom," she said cheerfully. "Isn't he a sweetie!"

"He's not her boyfriend," said a sneering voice. "Doesn't he go with that Spellman girl?"

Roz turned to see who'd spoken, but her eyes betrayed her, as they did so often these days. She saw only the shadow of Mrs. Ferch-Geg's piled-up hair, turned long and almost sinister as it stretched across the teacups and pastries.

There was dark muttering all around Roz. She stumbled out of the tea shop, into the cold clear air, but she could still hear the last murmur ringing in her ears.

Someone said: "I heard a whisper the Spellmans are witches."

THOU MORTAL WRETCH

December 28, Afternoon
HARVEY

Harvey hadn't driven the truck much since the day the mine caved in. Tommy had saved to buy the red pickup when he was in high school. Harvey'd thought getting rides from his older brother was the coolest thing ever, back then. Tommy had taught Harvey to drive in this truck, playing country music loud and laughing at him from the passenger seat. On the night after the mine shaft collapsed, Sabrina had slept next to Harvey in the bed of the truck, cuddled up with him under his jacket.

He didn't know why Sabrina hadn't understood that was what he needed. Not necromancy, not magic that was supposed to make everything better but instead made it worse. Only for her to stay with him, so they could hold on to each other.

He'd been looking forward to seeing Roz. Susie wasn't answering his texts or calls, and he missed them both. Roz was so warm and sure of herself, she usually made him feel better about everything, but not today.

Roz always threw a big party on New Year's Eve. All the church kids would come. Last year Harvey had kissed Sabrina on the stroke of midnight in the light of fireworks over the mountains. Then he and Susie high-fived.

He'd gone over to Susie's house yesterday with snacks, but her dad said she wasn't seeing anybody. Harvey guessed he wasn't invited to the New Year's party this year.

Roz and Sabrina were best friends. Of course Roz would take Sabrina's side. Harvey had to stop being such a wimp. He drove home. If he played country music loud and didn't glance over at the passenger seat, it was almost like Tommy was there.

He was singing quietly along to lyrics describing someone as "small-town kind of pretty" when a tire blew out and he almost went off the road. Only wrenching the wheel around desperately saved the truck from plowing right into a tree.

Harvey wasn't far from home and didn't want to block the narrow, icy road, so he decided to drive on carefully and patch up the tire in the garage. Dad always told Harvey and Tommy they should repair a blown-out tire rather than waste his money on a new one. He was still shaken as he drove the rest of the way home and parked. So he was incredibly startled by the loud rap on the roof of his truck.

"*She's cheer captain, and I'm* . . . constantly harassed by minions of Satan," Harvey finished, under his breath.

He hastily switched off the country music as Nick Scratch's jackass face appeared at his side window.

"This is how you get around?" Nick asked. "How odd. It looks lopsided."

"Yeah, a tire blew out," said Harvey. "The tires are new too. Bad luck on winter roads, I guess."

Nick seemed uncomprehending. "I mostly fly."

Harvey blinked. "You have—a private jet?"

"No," said Nick, clearly entertained by the notion.

Harvey recalled: *witches*. "Oh, right."

"Wicked practitioner of the dark arts, remember?"

Harvey climbed out of the pickup, stuffing his keys into his down jacket. The snow crunched under his boots. Fresh snow had fallen in the night, so when the darkness ebbed away, it left the whole world white. Nick was dressed inappropriately for winter, holding a bundle that looked like sticks wrapped up in a rag. It was probably intended for a scary spell, and he was a jerk who seemed constantly amused at Harvey's expense. He was also the only person in the world seeking Harvey's company.

Harvey smiled at him. "I do. Hey, Nick."

Nick appeared vaguely surprised, but after a moment he smiled back.

"Hi, mortal."

"What's up? Do you—want to hang out?" Harvey asked. "And what have you got there?"

"It's a baby," Nick answered, and shoved the baby unceremoniously into Harvey's arms. "Hold, please."

It really was a baby. Harvey stared in terror at the little scrunched-up face. The baby blinked open round dark eyes and gazed up at Harvey. The baby looked as stunned as Harvey felt.

"Oh, Nick," said Harvey tragically. "Oh, no."

He blamed himself for being even a tiny bit pleased to see Nick. No, he didn't. He blamed Nick for everything.

"I can't hang out right now," said Nick. "I think Sabrina's in trouble with a bad-luck spirit, and I should help her, so will you watch this baby for us?"

A chill went through Harvey that had nothing to do with the winds of winter. "Why do you think Sabrina's in trouble?"

"Little signs," said Nick. "Subtle hints. A wall fell on her."

"A wall fell on her!" Harvey shouted.

"At the Academy," elaborated Nick, as if Harvey was concerned about the specific wall location.

"Is she all right?"

"Of course. I made sure to shield her."

"From the wall?" said Harvey, appalled. "Are *you* all right?"

There was another moment where Nick appeared oddly taken aback, and then he smirked. "Witches aren't fragile like mortals, Harry."

Harvey didn't know why he'd bothered to ask. He sighed and gave the baby a look to indicate "Can you believe this guy?" The baby seemed dubious about Nick as well.

"What's going on with Sabrina?"

"I'll find out," said Nick.

"Do walls fall on people a lot at Invisible Academy?"

"The Academy of Unseen Arts," Nick corrected.

"All I know is, it's not Boundaries Academy," said Harvey. "Because nobody ever taught you any! I have an important question, and it is—"

"Harvey Kinkle, is that a *baby*?"

Their neighbor Mrs. Link often cut through their property, her bright red rubber boots moving in a blur across the mud as she went on her merry way elsewhere. Now she'd stopped dead, arrested by the sight before her.

"Oh God," Harvey whispered.

"Don't say that in front of the baby," Nick hissed.

"Shut up," said Harvey. "I hate you. Uh, hi, Miz Link? Hi."

Mrs. Link clearly had no time for mundane greetings. "Whose is that baby?" Her red kerchief went askew on her white hair as she darted a look at Nick. "Young man, is this your baby?"

"Yeah, Nick, *is* this your baby?" Harvey demanded.

Nick shook his head with what seemed to be unfeigned dismay. Harvey was relieved they weren't coping with a teen dad situation.

"No. No, no, no. It's not my baby," said Nick. "It's Father Blackwood's baby."

Strangely, that appeared to be the exact right thing to say. Mrs. Link relaxed considerably.

"Oh, your minister's baby? Where's his mama?"

"She's dead," said Nick.

"And there's a community effort to care for the poor orphaned child," cooed Mrs. Link. "I understand everything now. I haven't heard of the church before. It must be small. Are you very involved?"

"Well," said Nick, "I'm a choirboy."

Mrs. Link pressed a hand against her breast. "Lovely. Harvey, introduce me to your sweet friend."

Harvey swallowed his outrage at this turn of events.

"This is Nick."

"Evangeline Link," said Mrs. Link. "Delighted."

She extended her hand. Nick kissed it. Mrs. Link giggled. Harvey thought he understood how the olden-day witch-hunters must have felt.

"Well, I have to get going," Nick announced.

"You can't go! I don't know what to do with a baby!"

"Well, heavens, Harvey," said Mrs. Link, and Harvey watched Nick control a flinch. "You only have to ask me for advice. I did raise seven."

"A wise woman, I perceive," said Nick, and winked at Mrs. Link.

She hit Nick on the arm. "Oh, you! Get along, you two."

Nick walked backward, giving Mrs. Link a wave. Harvey interrupted their horrifying lovefest by darting in between them and grasping Nick's sleeve. The baby, jolted by the sudden movement, began to scream.

Nick regarded the baby with distaste. "He does that all the time. Best of luck, mortal!"

Harvey whispered, though considering the volume of the baby's screeching, he would've had to shout for Mrs. Link to hear them. "They say witches are evil and it's true. You cannot be doing this to me. I don't even know the baby's name!"

Nick whispered back: "His name's Judas."

This information was too much.

Harvey closed his eyes. "Oh Jesus."

"Not in front of the baby!" Nick reminded him in reproachful tones. He hesitated. "What did you say was bad luck?"

"The tire blowing out?" Harvey asked. "It's no big deal—"

Nick gave the pickup truck a suspicious look. "Stay out of that thing. I'll be in touch. Please watch your filthy mouth around the baby, farm boy."

With a swirl of his impractical black coat, he departed into the snowy trees.

"Your nice friend is right," said Mrs. Link. "You shouldn't take the Lord's name in vain in front of the baby. Or in front of your friend, if it comes to that! He's obviously very religious."

"You have no idea," said Harvey.

Mrs. Link patted her hair, so the kerchief went back into place over the rigid perm. "He certainly has a way about him, doesn't he! I like to see a young man with good manners and that glint in his eye. What a charmer."

"You have no idea," Harvey repeated.

He didn't think Nick had had time to enchant Mrs. Link. Usually he believed Mrs. Link was a good judge of character. A few days ago he'd been helping her hang up her laundry, and Ambrose Spellman ran past whooping at the sky for some reason. They'd both watched as Ambrose raced for the horizon and out of sight, arms stretched wide, as if possessed by the sheer joy of being alive and free.

Mrs. Link had clicked her tongue against her teeth. "There goes a wild bird."

Harvey had only nodded, and bit his lip, and thought of Sabrina. Perhaps witches were all wild birds, their homes the wide, strange sky. Perhaps a witch would always be impossible to keep.

Mrs. Link whisked Harvey over to her house, where she talked about Nick's sensitive soul—which was truly horrible—and gave Harvey some baby formula she kept for her youngest grandchild— which was truly helpful.

"You can pack the tins of formula and bring them with you," she added.

Harvey gazed at her beseechingly. "Can't the baby and I stay with you?"

"Gracious, Harvey, no," said Mrs. Link. "I'm already late for my book club. We're meeting at that new tea shop, and after that it's quiz night. Some of us have active social lives, dear."

She patted Harvey on the shoulder. Harvey tried to recover from being verbally wrecked by a seventy-something quiz addict.

"Nice for you to have another friend," she told him encouragingly. "I heard about you and Sabrina."

A hollow space opened up in Harvey's stomach. "How?"

"Whispers spread like a virus in Greendale. You two were always an odd pair, weren't you? But it must be hard. I remember you both when you were this high, her with her little nose in the air thinking she knew it all, and you scared of your own shadow. You couldn't follow her your whole life."

"No," whispered Harvey. Sabrina was always meant to fly.

"Ask that Nick boy to introduce you to some girls at his church," suggested Mrs. Link.

"I don't think that would be a good idea."

"Why not?" asked Mrs. Link. "Trust me, Harvey. I'm certain young Nick has *no* trouble with the ladies. It's written all over him."

"Great," said Harvey. "Judas and I are leaving now."

Mrs. Link frowned. "Who?"

Harvey left, with the baby formula and the baby. Judas had screamed the whole time they were at Mrs. Link's house, and he kept screaming when Harvey brought him back to the Kinkles'.

Harvey understood his attitude. If he were the baby, he wouldn't want to be stuck with Harvey either.

He didn't have a crib or anything, so he pulled out his drawer of winter sweaters and made a nest for the baby. He made the formula the way Mrs. Link taught him, testing the milk on the inside of his wrist. After multiple wrist tests, Harvey smelled like yogurt, but that was better than burning the baby.

"I can't call a baby Judas," Harvey told the baby. "Would Jude be okay?"

Baby Jude paused in his yelling, his small fists clenched tight, so Harvey took that as permission. Jude took the bottle and drank up the formula, then threw up some of it. On Harvey.

He wanted to murder Nick. Except that Nick was helping Sabrina. She was in trouble. Harvey'd been certain, down to the pit of his stomach where nightmares lived, that her new world was dangerous.

If Nick could help her, Harvey had to help Nick. Though when he'd agreed to help Nick, he hadn't imagined it would mean baby-sitting a tiny warlock. He wished the baby would stop crying. They liked rattles, didn't they? He went through the kitchen cabinets and found everything in there that might rattle.

Baby Jude stopped screaming and stared when Harvey rattled sunflower seeds at him. His eyes went very round, as if to say "*What are you doing, mortal?*"

"I'm desperate," Harvey informed him, and shook a packet of macaroni in the baby's direction.

Baby Jude chortled and wriggled in his nest of sweaters. His small face was still sticky with snot and tears, but he smiled gummily.

Harvey began to grin. "See? We can get along." He rattled

packets for the baby until Jude started yawning, then carried the baby's drawer to his own bed, where Harvey could approximate rocking a cradle.

Jude fell asleep with his hand clasped around Harvey's finger. Since Harvey didn't wish to wake him, he stayed sitting cross-legged on the bed, fished out his sketchbook, and drew a few pencil sketches of the sleeping baby as Jude snorted and smacked his little lips.

"My mom's dead too," Harvey told the baby. "It's rough, right?"

There were so many lost mothers in Greendale, like they were trapped in the wicked beginnings of a fairy tale. But Jude slept, serene as if he were in a cradle under his mother's watchful eye.

Eventually he woke up and started to scream again, his cry lifting to the ceiling as he shook his tiny fists.

"Wow, witches are a lot of trouble," Harvey mumbled, then scooped the baby up.

Jude subsided, whimpering and gumming at the collar of Harvey's flannel shirt, so Harvey kept hold of him. He sang "Hey Jude" to the baby, because it was appropriate, and walked with him from his bedroom to the kitchen. Mrs. Link said you were supposed to walk the floor with babies, and hold them, and rock them.

There was a song Harvey's mom used to sing. She'd taken it from the title of a book and turned it into her own version of a lullaby. Harvey could remember her singing, the sound of her laughter and the fall of her long hair as she watched over him, though in the memory he couldn't make out her face. Tommy'd sung the song to him a few times after she died, his own boyish voice rough with tears.

The sweetness of those songs stayed with Harvey. Music was almost as beautiful as art, he thought. He'd always wished he could sing and taught himself to play the guitar when his dad said he couldn't have lessons. He'd serenaded Sabrina once, in a burst of courage, and attempted singing the old song of their childhood to bring Tommy back to himself, in desperation. It was no use. Whenever he tried to sing in front of other people, Harvey got self-conscious and his voice cracked. But Jude was a baby, unlikely to be a harsh music critic.

"Twinkle, twinkle, little star,
Don't get drunk or steal a car.
Like a diamond in the sky,
Except please don't get high.
Twinkle, twinkle, little star,
Don't make me wonder where you are."

Harvey had to wonder where they were now, that musical laughing mother and his kind brother.

The baby laughed. Harvey kissed the side of his head.

"That's right, don't do socially irresponsible things. Except I guess you're supposed to worship Satan. Let's leave that one alone, Jude. Up for an encore? *Twinkle, twinkle—*"

The front door stood ajar, cold night air creeping in. The door hadn't been open before.

It was Nick, leaning in the doorway with his arms crossed and that odd surprised look on his face. Harvey stopped singing and glared.

"How long have you—"

That was when a bolt of lightning streaked past Nick, screaming a thin terrible scream, and pounced on Harvey with white teeth bared and wild eyes blazing.

BEST WITCHCRAFT IS GEOMETRY

December 28, Afternoon
SABRINA

Prudence and I spent the day in the library looking up bad-luck spirits. Mortals think magic is all waving your hands and whiz-bang. Nobody talks about the research hours witches put in.

"I don't think it's Ardad, the demon who makes people lose their keys," I said, rubbing my eyes. "But I hate Ardad on general principle."

Prudence made a contemptuous sound suggesting mortal concerns like forgetting keys were beneath her, but I was very grateful she was there. The library was a massive room with mazes made of pages and a librarian who stalked the stacks, hunched and glowering like a discontented vulture. Prudence had steered me deftly through the rows of shelves toward the section on demons who turned luck sour, and spirits of ill fortune.

"Thanks again," I told her. "I'd already be the prey of Ardad if it wasn't for you. Which is my way of saying I'd be lost without you."

"Was that meant to be a joke, Sabrina?" Prudence shuddered. "That was tragic. Don't do that again."

Being friends with Prudence was uphill work sometimes, but I thought it would be worth it in the end. Prudence wasn't totally heartless, whatever she tried to pretend. She obviously cared about Dorcas and Agatha. She'd taken a break from reading earlier to visit Nick in the Infernal Infirmary. I'd gone to visit Nick after she came back, but he'd already been released. Apparently witches believed that when walls fell on someone, they should walk it off. It was nice of Prudence to be concerned for him.

Of course, Nick and Prudence used to date.

I cleared my throat. "Hey, do you—still like Nick?"

"Bold of you to assume I ever liked Nick," sneered Prudence. "He had the bad taste to ditch me. And my sisters. The man's a raving imbecile. Do I have time for raving imbeciles? Clearly, no."

"Aw, Prudence," said Nick, strolling up to our table. "Enough sweet-talking. Tell me how you really feel."

He was wearing a sleek black coat, so apparently he'd gone for a walk. I wondered where he'd gone. He looked entirely recovered and, I had to admit, rather elegant in his coat. I smiled at the sight of him.

Prudence's eyes narrowed. "Why are you here? I told you to watch Judas."

"I left him with two trustworthy caretakers," said Nick.

I watched Prudence brighten slightly at the mention of—I assumed—her sisters, then resume scowling at Nick.

"Nevertheless, I told *you* to watch him. You are a severe disappointment to me on every level. Personal. Sexual. Sartorial."

Okay, maybe Prudence wasn't into Nick.

"Please, Prudence, I blush and grow giddy," said Nick, fanning himself with a book. "We are in a public place."

Nick might be into her, though. Who wouldn't be?

I laughed uneasily. "We've got a lot of books to get through. Flirt later, guys."

Prudence sniffed. "I wouldn't lower myself."

"I wasn't flirting," said Nick, sounding unexpectedly serious.

"You're always flirting," Prudence scoffed. "You flirt your way out of all your problems."

"And it works," murmured Nick. "But—"

"You were dirty talking to Dorcas at breakfast."

Nick squawked, then coughed and resumed his usual low tones. "Sabrina, I really wasn't."

I turned the page of a spellbook without looking up. "Do whatever you want."

"Prudence, tell her I wasn't!"

"You were," Prudence insisted. "You talked about something called lasagna in pornographic detail for forty minutes. I'm not even convinced lasagna is a real thing."

"It's a real thing," I said, startled. "Aunt Hilda makes lasagna all the time."

Nick caught my eye and smiled as if we were in on a lasagna secret together. "It's good, right?"

Whenever I had lunch at the Academy of Unseen Arts, it was vile. I'd hoped that was a light form of hazing for the half-mortal student, but apparently breakfast and dinner were no better. I remembered how eagerly Prudence ate when she was staying at my house. Maybe I should invite Prudence and Nick over for dinner.

Nick might read more into that than I meant, though. I wondered who he was eating lasagna with. Someone pretty, probably. Prudence was right. He was always flirting. I was an idiot for thinking, even for a split second, that he might be serious.

I returned to my book. "It's not great when Aunt Hilda adds eyeballs."

Prudence sounded shocked. "I can't believe you get eyeballs."

"I know, right?"

"The teachers at the Academy always selfishly hog the eyeballs for themselves. You are so spoiled and lucky." Prudence gave a longing sigh. "Mmm, eyeballs."

When I refused to eat eyeball lasagna, Aunt Zelda would tell me to think of the starving witch children. I hadn't thought she meant at the Academy.

"You're making me hungry," Nick told Prudence as I gagged. "And none of this is helping Sabrina. Let me take a guess. Did you accidentally conjure a bad-luck spirit?"

"How'd you know?"

Nick shrugged. "Conjuring's my specialty. It's the time of year for luck spells to go very wrong, or very right. And I actually did Prudence's project on luck spells."

"Why are you doing Prudence's homework?"

"I like homework," said Nick. "Other people don't do it right."

I rolled my eyes, but in an indulgent way. That was Nick, all confidence. I'd always hated the cocky jerks at Baxter High, but that was because their swagger was empty.

Nick selected a book from my and Prudence's pile, then flipped it open. "Where do you think the summoning happened?"

"In the main street in town. I had to save my friend from getting run over. I broke some glass. Uh, a lot of glass."

"Smashing." Nick smirked in that way he had, both calming and infuriating, as though nothing was ever too big a deal. "So this happened among the mortals."

"Does that matter?"

Prudence spoke up. "A bad-luck spirit will usually stay among mortals, if they can. It's much easier for them to play their tricks on mortals. Sometimes they'll take human form, to meddle with the mortals' minds more effectively."

"Maybe you only attracted bad luck from a spirit who was already around," Nick said thoughtfully. "The broken glass would give the spirit a chance to latch onto a witch, but they might be interfering with mortals already."

I remembered Ambrose saying: *When bad luck spreads, that's when it gets really ugly.*

"If there's a bad-luck spirit in Greendale, what effect would it have on the mortals?"

"Oh, I don't know. Mine shafts collapsing. Tires blowing out on the roads. Your friend almost getting run down in the first place." Nick looked grim. "Does anyone come to mind when you think of the physical manifestation of a bad-luck spirit?"

I immediately thought of the principal of my elementary school and what he'd called me.

"Mr. Poole can be so annoying. But I don't think he's an evil spirit; I've known him for years."

"This would be someone new in town."

I considered. "A new tea shop opened in town. It's called the Bishop's Daughter Coffee and Teas."

Prudence and Nick gave a collective shudder.

"Ill-omened name," said Prudence.

"It's not ill-omened for mortals. And the lady who runs the tea shop seems nice. She's Welsh, she makes a ton of pastries by hand, and she's a widow. Doesn't exactly spell 'evil spirit.'"

"Depends on what happened to her husband," said Prudence. "I intend to be a widow myself."

I stared at her serene and perfect profile outlined against the clouded stained-glass windows as she turned the pages of her book.

"What's going to happen to your husband?"

"He'll be the victim of a mysterious tragedy."

"Will he?" I said dryly. "How do you already know that?"

Prudence's mouth curled like a tiger's tail. "Mysterious, isn't it?"

"Well, I don't know if Mrs. Ferch-Geg mysteriously disposed of her husband or not."

Nick's voice was sharp. "What did you say her name was?"

"Mrs. Ferch-Geg?"

Nick strode off toward the stacks, disappearing into the maze of books and reemerging with a book of Welsh lore that he'd already opened on an illuminated illustration.

"The Dwy Ferch Geg," he read aloud. "Handmaiden of hell and daughter of a long-dead bishop called Osbeth, she was a witch-hunter cursed by a witch she killed. After her own death, she became a dark spirit. She waits until food is rotten to consume it with her second mouth, she grows strong through mortal misfortune, and she poisons mortal souls. Once a soul is thoroughly corrupt, she can eat it."

He shut the book, his face glowing with triumph. He seemed to expect I'd be pleased.

"Oh no," I said. "That's terrible."

"But excellently researched?"

"Everyone in Greendale is going to that stupid tea shop over the holidays! The mortals are in danger. We have to stop her."

Prudence covered her yawn with one hand. "The mortals are in danger? Oh, how shocking. Are you deeply concerned, Nick? I for one am deeply concerned."

"If she's the spirit who laid bad luck on Sabrina, we should stop her," said Nick.

"I'm not the important thing here!"

"You are to me," said Nick.

I glanced up. He was leaning against the elaborately carved chair beside mine with his hands in his pockets, as though he hadn't said anything remarkable. Maybe he hadn't. We were friends, after all. He cared about me, and I cared about him. Maybe it could be as simple as that.

Thinking of friends made my hand fly to my throat. "I brought a friend to that tea shop yesterday!"

"Which friend?" Nick demanded. "Your mortal?"

There was an alarmed note in his voice. I wondered if he might be jealous, but it was difficult to imagine Nick Scratch jealous.

"No," I said, and watched Nick relax. "My best friend Roz. If that spirit tried to corrupt her—"

"Is she very corruptible?" Prudence asked lazily.

"No, Roz is rock solid. She can't be corrupted."

"I'm sure the dark spirit who used to be a bishop's daughter believed she couldn't be corrupted either," murmured Prudence.

The thought of Reverend Walker, Roz's father, flitted across my mind. I didn't say anything. I clawed through the books instead, looking up banishment spells. The books agreed the start of a new day was the best time to open or close a door between worlds.

At some point during our studies, Nick left a cup of coffee at my elbow. When I noticed the cup, it was still warm, and I gulped it down gratefully. It made me think of Harvey, who always made me cups of coffee—or tea, if he thought it was too late for coffee—when we were studying. It made me remember glancing up from a page to find his eyes on me.

I looked up to find dark eyes on me. Nick's were sharp and bright when Harvey's were tender and dreamy, but the focused attention was the same.

The smile I gave Nick was half for Harvey. But half, I had to admit, was for Nick himself.

Nick smiled back.

"By the way, I figured I should mention. Even when I'm thinking about you in a nonsexual context, I find you very beautiful."

"Oh."

Once again, I found myself somewhat at a loss regarding how to respond.

Nick dropped me a wink. "Thought you should know."

"Thanks."

"Of course, I do think of you in a sexual context frequently."

"I was almost touched for a minute there," I admitted. "But now it's gone."

Nick leaned back in his carved wooden chair, managing to lounge despite the fact that the furniture was extremely uncomfortable and carved with devils and tiny pitchforks.

"It'll come back." He spoke with his usual effortless confidence. "I'm in training."

We studied until the light died through the dim windows, and eventually Nick excused himself. As soon as he had, I leaned over the table and spoke to Prudence in an urgent voice.

"Meet me at the tea shop and let's try to banish this demon first thing tomorrow." I hesitated. "There's no need to tell Nick."

Prudence arched a brow. "Why not? It's better for witches to be three. Nick seems very eager... to help."

I ignored her significant pause. "He's very kind."

"Oh, Sabrina." Prudence laughed. "A real witch doesn't know how to be kind. And Nick's a man. Whenever a man is helpful, he expects you to return it tenfold."

"I don't think Nick's like that, but if—if he is hoping for something more than friendship from me, I don't know whether I can give it to him. I still love Harvey."

"That must be painful."

For a moment I thought Prudence was being a sympathetic friend.

Then she added: "And embarrassing. Like a lingering rash."

I accepted Prudence was going to Prudence, and leaned forward across the table toward her. "Can we go, you and me?"

Prudence rose from her chair and stretched. "I could use some mayhem in the morning. Why not? For now, you must excuse me." She wiggled her fingers. "I have dark suspicions to explore and vengeance to take."

"So a pretty average evening for you, then."

Prudence grinned nastily and departed.

We would banish the dark spirit at dawn, but that still left me some time. Ms. Wardwell always gave me good advice.

Last time the mortals of Greendale were under threat, I'd signed away my soul. I'd signed away my name, and now I didn't know who Sabrina Spellman was anymore. I was full of doubts these days.

I would protect my friends whenever they needed me, but I hoped this time was easier than the last. I didn't have another soul to sell.

WITCHES ESCAPE ALL THAT

December 28, Evening
PRUDENCE

Prudence tracked Nick Scratch from the library, flew into the witch-hunter's home, and wrenched her brother out of the witch-hunter's arms. The witch-hunter didn't fight her, so she let him live. She clutched Judas tight to her chest for a moment, hearing his startled whimper in her ear. She palmed the fuzz of black hair on his head, then whirled and dumped him on Nick so she could range herself between her little brother and danger. Nick gave a dismayed exclamation. She fixed him with a glare that promised death and torments even beyond the grave.

"Nicholas Scratch, you dumb slut," Prudence hissed. "In a lifetime of dumb-slut decisions, this one takes the cauldron. What in Satan's name made you think it was a good idea to hand over babies to witch-hunters?"

Nick opened his mouth, but the witch-hunter got there first.

"Um," he said. "It's not okay to slut-shame people."

Prudence looked at him over her shoulder. "Is it okay to rip out your tongue?"

The witch-hunter continued quietly: "And I didn't hurt the baby."

The fury that passed through Prudence felt like a lightning strike. She whirled on the witch-hunter, who blinked down at her with his stupid cow's eyes and his total lack of a survival instinct and parted his lips to no doubt say more fool things. She launched herself at him, uncapping a vial, and forced the liquid between his teeth as she held his scruffy hair in one clawed hand, yanking his head back and holding him even though he tried to struggle.

It wasn't Hilda Spellman's truth cake, but even the most unsophisticated truth potions would do in a pinch.

"What was *that*?" demanded the witch-hunter, white-faced. "It tastes terrible!"

He looked terrified, and she was glad. He should know the consequences if he messed with what was hers.

"Now you have no choice but to tell me the truth," she snarled. "What did you do to my brother?"

"My neighbor advised me how to look after babies," said the witch-hunter. "Then I gave him a bottle, rattled things to amuse him, and walked the floor with him, and I sang him a song. Which Nick caught me doing, so I stopped."

"Why?" Nick asked.

"Because I was very embarrassed, Nick," the witch-hunter snapped. "God."

Prudence gave a shriek of rage. "Do not use language like that in front of the baby!"

"Oh, right," said the witch-hunter. "Sorry."

He'd probably been talking like that in front of Judas all day. It was as if Nick had delivered the baby to hellhounds who'd given him hellfleas. She had to admit Judas seemed unharmed, but that didn't allay Prudence's suspicions for an instant.

"What were you *planning* to do with him?"

"I was hoping to get him down for a second nap?" the witch-hunter offered.

Even through the blood roaring in her ears, he sounded helpless. Nick gave a pointed cough. Prudence threw a menacing look over her shoulder. Nick was holding the baby very awkwardly. Judas was crying, and Prudence didn't blame him one bit.

"Did you say he was your brother?" the witch-hunter asked unexpectedly.

Prudence bristled. "So what if I did?"

When she faced him again, the witch-hunter's eyes had gone soft in a hideous way, like someone was melting feelings right there on his face. He still looked frightened, but as though he'd found a reason to ignore fear.

"I understand," he told her.

"You don't understand anything about me, witch-hunter, and you never will."

"The baby liked being with him," Nick contributed.

Prudence spat in Nick's direction: "If one of his witch-hunter relatives walked through this door and decided to drown a warlock baby, who'd stop them?"

Nick looked chastened for the first time. Nick Scratch always did think he could get away with doing whatever he wanted. He never expected real consequences.

The witch-hunter said, "I would stop them."

She'd noticed the first time they'd met that the witch-hunter tried to make himself look smaller than he was, hunching his shoulders and ducking his head. He wasn't doing that now. There were weapons of cold iron in the room, and the witch-hunter looked ready to fight. This wasn't a bunny rabbit. This was a snake in the grass. Even if he didn't know it himself, Prudence knew. He was dangerous.

"You have to believe me," the witch-hunter told her, with a slight crooked smile. "Because of the truth spell."

"Oh, I don't have to do what any man tells me, mortal," she sneered, but she felt her anger slipping away.

He was doing it on purpose, she realized, saying words to calm her, in the same soothing the way he'd rocked the baby. She couldn't work out his game, but she wouldn't be lulled into a false sense of security. There was no security to be found in the world, and least of all in a hunter's house.

Prudence held on to anger. That felt safer.

"I didn't mean to upset you, Prudence." Nick winked at her, a little conciliatory and a lot flirty. "I didn't actually plan for you to find out about this."

Anger suddenly came very easy.

"Oh, I will kill you, Nick Scratch!"

"I thought it would be a good thing to do," Nick continued, suicidally. "I figured the mortal would be kind to the baby. Babies need kindness."

The witch-hunter gave Nick a strange look. "Everyone needs kindness, Nick."

There was a horrible, lost silence. Nick gazed at Prudence beseechingly, as if she knew how to respond to such a bizarre statement any more than he did. Nick gave up, bit his lip, and stared at the floor.

"So, scary nose ring Prudence is a witch too?" the witch-hunter asked, like what he'd said before was normal. "That makes sense, I guess."

Nick laughed.

"Stay out of this, Nicholas!" The force of Prudence's glare sent Nick retreating discreetly to the porch.

He didn't go far. Prudence could still see him in the doorway with the whimpering baby bundled in his arms. Hesitantly, and very softly, Nick attempted a howl for the baby. Prudence suspected it was the closest thing to a lullaby Nick knew. Judas kept whining.

"Don't try to sweet-talk me," Prudence ordered the witch-hunter. "I know what you are. I remember visiting your stupid mortal school, and hearing you talk about your family's history of murdering my people as '*kind of messed up.*'"

She sneered. The witch-hunter's face flushed. It made Prudence sick to look at him, fumbling for words as he blazed out his terrible emotions for anyone to see.

"I didn't—I didn't know how else to talk about it. Reading about it made me feel—uncomfortable, and guilty, even though I didn't do anything. I'm not great with words. Maybe I didn't put it the right way."

"Imagine how I feel about witch-hunters. Imagine how I feel about you," hissed Prudence. "Imagine how my sisters felt, when they saw you and your brother in the grove of familiars, with guns in your hands."

"My brother?" The soft voice and soft eyes were gone. The witch-hunter's voice went sharp. "Did you have something to do with what happened to my brother?"

He caught Prudence's arm and shook her. She recognized the storm passing over his face, darkness with a glint of fire. Lightning, born in a black cloud. This was wrath. She knew how to deal with wrath.

She grabbed his absurd flannel shirt in both fists, pulling him in threateningly close. "No," she said between her teeth. "I didn't."

The witch-hunter's voice was cold as well as sharp, like the blades of his ancestors.

"But witches killed him. Imagine how I feel about witches. Imagine how I feel about you."

Prudence didn't flinch. He might have weapons in the room, but she had magic in her. She could kill him and paint the walls with his blood.

"Hey," said Nick from the doorway. "If you guys are going to make out, could I put down the baby and join in?"

Prudence and the witch-hunter let go of each other abruptly. Prudence gave him a shove across the room for good measure.

"I find you physically repulsive," Prudence informed the witch-hunter.

"Well, you terrify me to the point where I'm pretty sure I couldn't, uh, perform," he said, then added hastily: "Truth spell!

Remember I'm under a truth spell. I wouldn't normally talk this way in front of a baby."

"I'm just saying," said Prudence. "It's probably what you expect of witches at this point, but *I* won't fall tragically in love with you."

The witch-hunter swallowed a laugh. "Sabrina's over me. Every other witch I meet hates my guts, except maybe her aunt Hilda. Zelda never liked me. Ambrose always looked down on me."

This information was distracting.

"Did he?"

"Uh, yeah. He constantly made fun of me."

"Oh," Prudence breathed.

Ambrose Spellman. Such a dreamboat.

"Now you understand," said the witch-hunter. "I'm pathetic. Everybody knows. There's no need to be afraid."

He spoke easily, not fighting the truth spell, as though he was only telling her the bare facts. She hadn't realized mortals could be as lonely as that.

The witch-hunter's name was Harvey, Prudence recalled. She didn't have any special reason to remember it. She wished she could forget his stupid name, actually, but Sabrina said it so often that was impossible: Harvey, Harvey, Harvey, I love him, his feelings matter, blah, blah, blah, Harvey.

"Stop saying I'm afraid," she bit out. "I'm not afraid of anything."

"I can see *you're* not under a truth spell." When Prudence snarled, Harvey put his hands up in a gesture of surrender. "But I am. Don't kill me."

"I might kill you," said Prudence. "I might kill anybody."

Her gaze traveled from the hideous sight of Harvey the

witch-hunter, all flannel shirts and feelings, to Nick Scratch being smug in a black sweater. Prudence despaired, she truly did. Men were the false god's worst mistake.

She sighed and leaned against the kitchen cabinets. "I'll get you, Nick Scratch. You won't know when, and you won't know where. Sometime when you least expect it, you will pay for this."

"You shouldn't have given the baby to me without telling her," Harvey told Nick earnestly.

"Don't be on my side," Prudence grumbled. "I don't like you."

"I don't like you either," said Harvey. "You're very beautiful, but I hate magic, you horrify me to the marrow of my bones, and I've never seen you be nice to anyone. Your only redeeming quality is your cool eye makeup."

Prudence and Nick both stared at him. Harvey appeared to be trying to stare at his own mouth.

"Unholy hell, I like truth spells," Nick murmured.

"But that doesn't change what's right and wrong," Harvey said. "You also shouldn't have hit on Prudence when she was clearly upset."

Nick exchanged a baffled look with Prudence, but Prudence shook her head. She had no idea what the witch-hunter was talking about either.

"Didn't mean anything by it, Prudence. Just a reflex. I used to date her and the rest of the Weird Sisters," Nick explained helpfully.

It was the witch-hunter's turn to seem staggered.

"At the same time?"

Nick nodded in a cautious fashion, as though he feared this might go wrong for him but he couldn't yet see how.

"How many girlfriends do you have at once?" Harvey demanded.

"Well." Nick frowned. "It varies."

The witch-hunter was getting agitated. "How many girlfriends do you currently have? Are you planning to add Sabrina to your girlfriend *stable*?"

"I don't have any girlfriends right now," said Nick. "Would Sabrina want it to be just us?"

Surely not, thought Prudence.

"Of course!" said the witch-hunter.

Nick shrugged. "Then that's fine."

"Does Sabrina know about the girlfriend stable?" Harvey asked.

Nick nodded. Harvey shook his head with conviction. Slowly, Nick began to copy the head shaking. Prudence thought they both appeared ridiculous. Baby Judas wailed judgmentally at them.

"You might want to clarify this issue for Sabrina," advised the witch-hunter. "She might think—I don't know *what* she would think."

Prudence had no idea what was going on, or why Nick believed any of it was a good idea. Possibly Nick had been dropped on his head as a child. Possibly he'd been dropped right off a mountain as a child.

To cover her uncertainty, she strode menacingly over to Nick and snatched her brother away from him. Nick seemed pleased to be relieved of the burden. Prudence shot him a venomous glance and whisked away from the door.

This brought her into unfortunate proximity with the witch-hunter, at which point Prudence was cruelly betrayed by her own flesh and blood. Baby Judas cooed and made grabby hands in the witch-hunter's direction.

Prudence recoiled. "Is he brainwashed? What have you done with him?"

"Nothing! God, you are so weird," said the witch-hunter. "You're almost as weird as Nick."

"Language!" thundered Prudence.

The witch-hunter, with reckless disregard for his own safety, actually dared to lean against Prudence's shoulder and curl his fingers around Baby Judas's tiny hand.

"Hey, Jude." He smiled a little smile and gave the baby's hand a little shake.

His voice had gone stupid and soft again, and his unkempt hair fell into his eyes as he stooped over the baby. Prudence wished to visit extreme violence upon him, but she had her hands full.

Harvey glanced up at her through his awful hair. "He looks like you."

"Does he?" Prudence studied her baby brother's small face. "Well. Perhaps he does."

Her father didn't look like her. Nobody who belonged to Prudence had ever looked like her before.

"Doesn't have the cool eye makeup," Nick contributed sardonically. "But give him time."

The witch-hunter laughed. Surprising herself, Prudence laughed too. She and the witch-hunter gave each other a mutually disconcerted look.

"The Weird Sisters," the witch-hunter said, after a pause. "Is that a band?"

They *were* a band of sinners. Prudence nodded.

"Cool," said the witch-hunter shyly. "Are you the singer?"

"I do sing," Prudence admitted.

The witch-hunter seemed to be weighing something. "Do you guys . . . want to stay for dinner?"

"Yes," said Nick instantly.

"Aha!" exclaimed Prudence. "*You* were the lasagna dealer!"

"Um," said Harvey. "I don't know what you're talking about."

Prudence shoved him. "Weren't you ever taught not to feed strays!"

She'd heard of a honey trap. Possibly the mortals did lasagna traps too. Possibly they used many foods to trap people.

Prudence could see how that might work. At the Academy of Unseen Arts, they kept the students' rations low, to make sure the students stayed keen and sharp. Witches were born hungry, ravenous for power, for sustenance, for immortality and dark glory. Prudence sometimes thought Satan forbade witches to love because if witches loved at all, they would love with the same consuming ferocity that they hungered.

Satan's command saved them from the weakness that destroyed mortals. Imagine the shame, groveling for scraps of affection like a beggar at a feast. Better to turn away from love forever.

Witches were meant to be starving creatures. She found herself wondering what they might have for dinner if they stayed, and grew even more furious because she'd actually considered it.

"What are you trying to do?" Prudence demanded of the witch-hunter. "You want to make friends with witches? Don't make me laugh. You must hate witches. I'm sure you hate Nick."

Both of their gazes went to Nick. He had his hands in his pockets and an unreadable look on his face.

The mortal swallowed. "Sometimes."

Prudence threw a triumphant smile at Nick. "Of course you do. He's better-looking and more sexually charismatic than you—though it wouldn't be hard to be more sexually charismatic than *you*—"

"Thanks," the witch-hunter said flatly.

"He can do magic. He can understand Sabrina. He can do everything for Sabrina, better than you could dream. Doesn't it burn you up inside? You have nothing a witch needs. You'll spend the rest of your miserable mortal life knowing you touched magic and you can never get it back."

As soon as she said *Sabrina*, the mortal flinched. He might as well put up a sign pointing out his weakness. He might as well show Prudence where to slide in the knife.

"Is that why you asked us to stay?" she asked. "Are you desperate for magic? Or are you desperate for company? How sad."

The witch-hunter looked at her with his stricken, sorrowful eyes. "Wow. Who hurt you?"

Prudence wasn't under a truth spell. She didn't have to answer: *A lot of people hurt me.*

Instead she said: "Anyone who hurts me gets hurt back. I'm not staying for dinner."

"Understood," said Harvey.

Prudence sailed toward the door, before she could hesitate or weaken. She grabbed hold of Nick's sleeve as she went. He resisted, then glanced at the mortal's bowed head and let her pull him away.

Prudence aimed a parting shot at the witch-hunter from the

porch before the three witches disappeared into the night and out of his life.

"Don't you know witches are dangerous by now? Do you need another lesson? Remember this. I *could* kill you. Someday, I think I will."

SATAN'S HANDMAIDEN, THE LEGENDARY WITCH

December 28, Evening
SABRINA

A witch never feared to walk through the woods alone at night. A witch in the woods was at home. Moonlight made the icy path a silver ribbon that guided my feet to the door of Ms. Wardwell's cottage.

I knocked. As I did, I recalled she used to have a horseshoe hanging up over her door. It must have fallen off.

Ms. Wardwell threw the door wide open. Light burned behind her as though her cottage was home to a falling star, and the tail of her emerald satin dressing gown followed her like a snake.

"Is it you, my beloved?" she cried in a voice of thunder. Then her wide green eyes blinked and focused on my face.

The echo of her ringing voice faded away. The light behind her flickered.

"Oh," she said. "Sabrina. Well. Forgive my outburst."

She waved her hand, nails painted brilliant red, and the blaze of light behind her dimmed further. I saw now it was only the fire in her grate, sparks flying upward into the dark recess of her chimney. There was a stain on the floor near her armchair. She must have spilled some red wine.

Or, knowing witches, something else.

"I totally understand," I told her.

I'd heard the rumor that Ms. Wardwell had a boyfriend who was a globe-trotter. Some people said that he couldn't be much of a boyfriend, constantly leaving her on her own.

She must be waiting for him, hoping every knock on the door and footstep on the path might be him. I felt terrible for her. I knew how lonely it felt, to have love fail you. I hoped Ms. Wardwell's boyfriend came back soon.

"Is this a bad time? Or can I come in?"

Ms. Wardwell swept a look over her shoulder at the emptiness of her cottage, then lifted the same shoulder in a graceful shrug.

"Why not come in? Sad to say, I am doing nothing at all. Life is a barren desert, and one wanders within it."

The holidays must be lonely for people with no family. Ms. Wardwell was an excommunicated witch. She didn't even have a coven to turn to. Perhaps she had no friends, witch or mortal.

I'd been feeling so sorry for myself about my mortal friends, but I still had the witches in my life. I should appreciate them more.

"Are you looking forward to going back to school?" I asked sympathetically.

There was a pause.

"Yes," Ms. Wardwell said distantly. "Education is my passion."

She twitched the ties of her dressing gown closer together, then swept across the floor and threw herself into the winged armchair. The green satin snake of her hemline hid the dark stain at her feet.

"But naturally your education is the most important to me, Sabrina. How, as your indispensable mentor in the dark arts, may I expand your knowledge of unholiness today?"

I sat down in the chair across from her, folding my hands in my lap. "Well, I accidentally attracted a bad-luck spirit called the Dwy Ferch Geg."

Ms. Wardwell clicked her tongue against her teeth. "Oh, Sabrina. You do hurl yourself into the oddest situations. I suppose it's inevitable. What girl of spirit can stay away from demons? I know of the Dwy Ferch Geg. It's amusing for witches to see a former witch-hunter as a hell-bound spirit. As I remember—from my extensive readings, you understand—she became the handmaiden of a prince of hell."

"A prince of hell! Which one?"

I wanted to conjure, banish, and defeat Satan one day so I wouldn't have to do his bidding. Yet ever since I signed the Book of the Beast, it was as though I could always feel power brimming within me, as if I was nothing but a vessel full of dark liquid.

Whose could the power be but the Dark Lord's? I wasn't ready to face him. I didn't think I could face down a prince of hell either.

I was full of doubt these days. Sometimes I even found myself doubting Ms. Wardwell, which was terrible. She'd been so kind to me. She was my father's disciple. My father would want me to listen to her.

Ms. Wardwell was silent. She seemed to be thinking. The dancing sparks and shadows of the hearth fire fell across her dramatic bone structure, making her face look skull-like for a moment.

"I . . . don't recall. No doubt she's left her lord to meddle with the affairs of mortals." She sounded unutterably weary. "We all grow tired of being a handmaiden at times."

The shadows ebbed away, the light warm on her face. It'd been a shock for the entirety of Baxter High when Ms. Wardwell showed up one day, living the fantasy of the mousy secretary who takes off her spectacles and lets down her hair to some va-va-voom music, and becomes a total bombshell. Many football jerks had got a single look at her tailored skirt-suit-with-dominatrix-flair fashion, and her newly loosed wild tumble of dark hair, and instantly began discussing how they wanted an authority figure to take advantage of them.

Her new look was amazing, but it hadn't occurred to me before now that it meant she was unhappy.

Maybe she'd transformed herself so the man she was waiting for would be dazzled.

Who was I to judge a woman in love? Changing up your style was a lot less extreme than bringing your boyfriend's brother back from the dead.

Ms. Wardwell studied me. "What are you thinking of, Sabrina?"

I hoped she didn't think I was judging her.

"Nothing, really. Your hair looks nice tonight," I said awkwardly.

Ms. Wardwell twirled a glowing chestnut curl carelessly around her finger. "One of Satan's greatest gifts to me. I rather like your new 'do. Since you signed the Book, it seems as though your halo of gold became a crown of bones."

Someone had described me as wearing a bone crown once. A dark spirit. Ms. Wardwell couldn't know that, but I still found myself shivering.

"Who knew Satan does great blowouts? But I doubt the Dark Lord wanted to give me a makeover," I said. "I wish I knew what he had planned for me."

The shadows were dark on Ms. Wardwell's face again, but her voice was light.

"Who can know his mind? To address the issue at hand, the Dwy Ferch Geg is a spirit whose power depends on malicious words, so when banishing her, you mustn't listen to her. Whatever she says, you must complete the ritual."

"I thought she was a bad-luck spirit."

The crackling of the fire sounded like a muttered warning, not quite heard.

"What is bad luck but the wind turning against you and blowing ill your way? A whisper can be the most destructive thing in the world. If everyone believes the worst of you, doesn't it become true?"

"No," I whispered.

Ms. Wardwell smiled warmly at me, though her eyes were distant. "You're young, Sabrina. When you're old enough to wear your story like a shadow behind you, we'll see how you feel. I'm sure you think you're powerful enough to banish the dark spirit by yourself, but the Dwy Ferch Geg's connection to a prince of hell makes her dangerous. You should tell your family. Even though I know you hate to worry them, even though they will be so disappointed in you, you shouldn't risk defeat and death."

"Thanks," I told her as I got up.

I didn't promise anything. She didn't ask me to.

Ms. Wardwell turned her head to watch me go. In the firelight her cascade of brown hair burned gold, as though she was the one wearing a crown.

"For what?"

"For your help," I said. "Not just with the dark spirit. I know you meant it for the best, having me sign the Book of the Beast. I know you're looking after me, because it's what my father would have wanted. My family is great, but you always help me do what I want."

It wasn't Ms. Wardwell's fault if I'd gone too far.

"Your family loves you," said Ms. Wardwell. "They want to protect you." She paused for the barest second. "And of course, so do I. But I have a duty to encourage you to become the independent witch I know you can be. Your father would want you to be strong."

Sometimes I thought I liked Ms. Wardwell better before I knew she was a witch, when she was my lonely and timid teacher. She seemed kinder then. But I guess that's part of growing up: learning people can be cruel, and love can betray you.

I want to grow up. I want to be strong. My new world is exciting, and beautiful, and I chose to be here.

It's only that the whole world seemed kinder before I signed the Book. Sometimes I miss the old world so much.

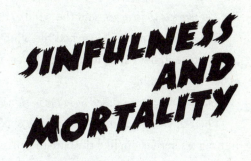

SINFULNESS AND MORTALITY

The whispers were loose on the wind, and Rosalind Walker was dreaming her cunning dreams that told the future. She walked in the woods on a summer's day, by the side of a crystal-clear pool that reflected a bright blue sky.

In the sky was not a single cloud. Instead there was a flock of black birds, all burning, yet somehow still flying. In the pool was a rock, and a frog sitting upon the rock as though it were a throne. As Roz and the frog watched, a black feather enveloped by flame tumbled through the air. The feather twisted in the breeze, then fluttered down into the pool and was swallowed by its waters.

My prince will come! cried the frog, very suddenly.

Roz peered through the trees. Her vision was sharp, every detail of every leaf on every tree clearly defined, but she couldn't see anybody coming. She was all alone, the wind sighing words into her ears.

The witches, the witches, said the wind. *The Spellmans are witches.*

Roz turned, and as she turned the wind changed and spoke with a new voice in her ears. Her father's voice, ringing as it did when he spoke from a pulpit.

You know they are witches! Soon the world will know.

The tall trees hemmed Roz in, the shadow of every tree a dark line across her vision, like the bars in a prison window. The feathers fell like black snow, burning and drowning.

If the witch banishes the handmaiden, the frog sang out, *then the prophecy will be fulfilled. The river will run red with blood when my prince comes to me!*

Roz sat bolt upright in bed. She reached for her phone to call Sabrina, but she misjudged the distance and knocked both her phone and her glasses on the floor. She cursed with the sheer frustration of her own body betraying her, hitting her knee with her fist. Then she searched for her phone among the scattered clothing on the floor.

She was going to spend her whole life fumbling in the dark. Because of magic. She could accept it if her blindness was natural, but this was happening because an evil witch wanted to spite her family.

She couldn't accept this. She shouldn't have to.

A dark thought unfurled within Roz, like a worm turning in the apple of knowledge, rot born in the heart of a rose. She swayed slightly, as though she was straining to hear a secret whispered in her ear.

If the whole world found out about witches, would that be so bad?

Roz bit her lip. If she did call Sabrina, what could she even say? The cunning had sent her a dream with a whispering wind and a talking frog. The dream made no sense. Was she supposed to call Sabrina and say, "Hey, whatever you do, don't banish a handmaiden?"

If her grandmother were alive, Roz could consult her about what the cunning meant, but her grandmother was gone. Roz felt lost.

Roz didn't call Sabrina. She was tempted for a moment, but she didn't call Harvey either.

Roz texted Susie, asking if Susie wanted to hang out tomorrow. Then she went back to sleep.

ONE WIZARD TO A HUNDRED WITCHES

December 28, Night
PRUDENCE

On the way back to the Academy of Unseen Arts, Prudence made Nick explain himself. Then she made him explain again, because her ears couldn't comprehend that level of stupidity the first time around.

When they entered the Academy, Prudence paused to lean against the stone statue of the Dark Lord. She felt she needed support.

"So you went against the High Priest's order and left unholy sanctuary to *risk your own life* by protecting a *witch-hunter* from harm. Because Sabrina Spellman asked you to."

"Yeah," said Nick.

He was carrying a sheaf of notes in a black leather folder under his arm, his expression indifferent and his tone faintly superior. He seemed like the boy she knew.

"Then you approached the witch-hunter for relationship advice."

Nick nodded.

Prudence sucked in a deep, fortifying breath. "Oh, Satan's red high heels."

Nick raised an eyebrow. "Does Satan have red high heels?"

"He might," said Prudence. "You don't know. You don't know anything! This whole mess is happening because you weren't raised properly."

She'd grown up in these woods, between these walls. She remembered the day Nick arrived at the Academy. She was sitting on a high stone wall with her sisters, watching from above as the strange boy came stumbling down from the mountains and through the woods. The boy was covered in blood and snow, his clothes rent by claws.

From high up on their perch, Agatha whistled. "Wow. Clean him up, then bring him to my bed."

In those days, before Prudence talked Dorcas into truly believing they were the fiercest witches of all, Dorcas stammered when she was nervous. She'd said: "He is d-d-dishy, but what do you think happened to him?"

The boy turned out to be Nick Scratch, who'd been presumed dead for years. Perished with his parents whose bodies were found, long ago and long dead. Nobody searched for Nick. Everyone believed the child's corpse was eaten by animals.

Nick never talked about what had happened to him. He got right into the swing of things at the Academy. A week after he arrived, he'd read half the books in the library and laid half the witches in school.

Father Blackwood said the Weird Sisters should be grateful to the Academy for setting their feet on the correct cursed paths. Prudence hated when he said that, but perhaps he was right. Without early training, witches went astray. There was clearly something badly wrong with Nick Scratch.

Nick strolled away and up the stairs. She followed him, clutching the baby.

"That's where you've been getting the bizarre notions about *liking her* and thinking she's *beautiful*," Prudence sneered. "People can hear you when you say these things! Aren't you embarrassed?"

"No," said Nick.

"Well, you should be! Have some self-respect, Nicholas. Watch me."

At this opportune moment, Ambrose Spellman was passing by, running lightly down the steps as they climbed them.

"Hey, sexy," Prudence called out. "I don't care if you live or die."

"Evening," drawled Ambrose, with a hint of a smile.

Nick's lip curled. "I'm not saying that to Sabrina."

"That line is a surefire winner," Prudence murmured absently.

She was watching Ambrose leave. Ambrose was wearing a red silk waistcoat with no shirt underneath. It was almost unbearable.

Having a crush on someone was like being buried alive and swallowing a vast quantity of grave worms, then feeling them wriggle around in your stomach all day long.

When she wrenched her gaze away, she found Nick watching her with a measured amount of sympathy. "Maybe you should tell him how you feel."

"How dare you, Nick Scratch," said Prudence. "I have never felt anything in my whole life! I'm not the one who's gone 'round the twist on a broomstick and is dining out at a mortal's house. Tell me you at least test the food before you eat it!"

Nick sighed. "I didn't fly up with the last shower of sparks. I'm being careful."

They reached Father Blackwood's chambers. Prudence unlocked the carved oak door and went into Judas's chamber, laying the baby down in his ebony cradle. Prudence slept on a settee close by the cradle, waking when he did. Usually Judas slept fretfully, but as she covered him with blankets embroidered with pentagrams and stars, he barely stirred. He was exhausted from his day out. Prudence knelt on the red velvet hassock with its upside-down crucifix that she'd placed beside the cradle, remembering her own terror when she saw her baby brother in a witch-hunter's arms.

"You're being so reckless." She whispered so she wouldn't disturb Judas's peaceful slumber. "Have you ever even spoken to a mortal boy before, Nick?"

She turned and found Nick standing under the stuffed alligator that swung from the ceiling. His face was calm, his hands in his pockets, and above his head were jagged gleaming teeth.

"Three of them."

She was beginning to think she had more chance of reasonable conversation with the alligator.

"Three," Prudence repeated. "Terrific. While you were getting traumatized in the snowy mountains, *I* became an expert in mortal boys. Let me share my expertise with you. This is how things work with mortals. First, they fall in love with you and bring you flowers."

Nick blinked several times in rapid succession. "Why? For spells?"

"No. Mortals put flowers in containers called vases and watch the flowers slowly die in their homes."

"Whoa," said Nick. "Morbid. Are you sure?"

"I swear by Satan's hoofprint in a burning field. After the flowers, mortals give you compliments. They say, 'You're pure evil.' When you reply, 'Thanks!' they get angry. This is funny if it's a normal mortal, but dangerous if it's a witch-hunter. Because witch-hunters kill us."

"They can try," Nick scoffed.

Prudence explained, slowly and carefully: "Witch-hunters were born to hurt us."

From the adjoining room in Father Blackwood's suite came the boom of Satanic chanting, and the shrill cackling of several witches at once. Prudence rocked the baby's cradle.

"Please." Nick sneered. "I realize being a witch-hunter isn't ideal, but this one likes to draw little pictures and sing little songs. Oh no, soon I shall be slain."

"Here's another fun fact about mortal boys," said Prudence. "Whenever you think, 'Oh, this one's different . . .' This one's *not* different. Witch-hunters are all the same. They aren't safe."

Nick smiled because he didn't understand. "Nor am I."

Talking about witch-hunters made Prudence's flesh creep. Even an orphan knew the stories. Children murmured tales of horror under the covers in the Academy. You lived your life sheltered in the shadow of the Dark Lord, then one day you were blinded by terrible lights. Witch-hunters, with their blazing torches. If you were lucky, someone might scream a warning. She and her sisters had run witch-hunter drills a hundred times, planning to combine their power to bring the witch-hunters down.

Prudence understood it was difficult to imagine Harvey organizing a mass slaughter, since Harvey couldn't organize a haircut. She tried a different approach.

"What happens at the end of your master plan? Let's say this works out. You and Sabrina get married. What if she wishes to move the mortal in with you? You can't keep one of those in the house! They age and crumble apart all over the place. It's unsanitary."

Nick frowned. "About when do they die?"

"When they're seventy or eighty."

Nick recoiled. "That can't be right."

"Pathetic, isn't it? They're basically people-shaped goldfish."

He seemed to be mulling this over. "I read if you build a foundation of trust and affection, the ravages of time won't matter."

"That's drivel," Prudence told him.

"Quite right, Prudence," said Father Blackwood. "Stop reading trashy books, Nick."

Her father stood framed in the doorway between their rooms. His robes were slightly askew. Over his shoulder, Prudence saw several witches dancing around naked but for black feather boas and entrails. It was a pretty standard Wednesday night.

"So sorry to interrupt the seduction in progress," Father Blackwood added. "I only wanted to look in on my darling child."

He walked past Prudence as though she wasn't there, robes swishing, and ran the sharp points of his nails along the carvings of Judas's cradle. Judas opened his eyes and began to scream at the top of his lungs.

"I hear you, Judas," Nick murmured. He raised his voice. "I was only talking to Prudence. I wasn't planning seduction."

"Then why bother talking to her?" Father Blackwood winked. "Oh, Nicholas. You can't fool me. We're crows of a feather, my boy. Will you come to the next meeting of my little society, on the mortal New Year's Eve?"

Nick wandered over to the settee where Prudence slept, then lay down with his face on the pillow. In muffled tones, he said: "Can't. Busy. A woman to woo, a mortal to annoy, a to-be-read pile I have to keep in the bell tower. You know how it is."

Father Blackwood frowned, chucked the screaming Judas under the chin, and as he departed flung over his shoulder: "Silence the child, Prudence!"

She could silence his precious son and heir by putting a pillow over the baby's face. Better yet, she could silence *her father* by knifing him repeatedly.

When she pulled her gaze away from his closed door, she saw Nick watching her.

"You sure you want him for a father?" Nick drawled.

"Who else do I have?" Prudence snapped. "Like you're any better. You're chasing after a dead man. You read everything Edward Spellman ever wrote. You never stop boring me and my sisters with tedious facts from his books. Now you're obsessed with his daughter. You think corpses and books will teach you how to be a man?"

"What else do I have?" Nick asked, copying Prudence's snapped question with a mocking lilt to his voice. "But I'm not only interested in Sabrina because of Edward Spellman."

"What's this fascination with Sabrina about, then?"

"Satan ordered me to seduce her," Nick said flippantly.

Prudence rolled her eyes at the sarcasm.

"It doesn't matter how it started," said Nick. "You and I witnessed everything Sabrina did for the mortal. She performed a forbidden ritual. She picked up a knife and cut a throat. She walked into the land of the dead. What did you think when you saw her do it?"

Prudence grimaced. "I thought, *She's a madwoman who has gone too far!*"

Nick's voice was very soft. "I thought, *I want someone who will go that far for me.*"

"So . . . she's a witch who won't devote her heart to the Dark Lord. She's a witch who loves people," said Prudence slowly. "And . . . you want her . . . to love you?"

There was a long silence as she waited for him to deny this horrible accusation.

Then Nick gave a very tiny nod. Prudence saw lights go on and off behind her eyes.

So he'd had a traumatic childhood. Who hadn't? That was no excuse.

"You want her to *love* you?" Prudence repeated. "Nick, you kinky freak. Settle for whips and devil worship like everybody else. If you want her love so badly, shouldn't you make sure she and the witch-hunter don't get back together?"

Nick frowned. "Why? I told him to forgive her."

"You did what?"

"I want Sabrina to be happy," Nick said simply.

Witches sharing partners was nothing new. She was prepared to share Ambrose with Luke Chalmers, Satan help her, but the ways of most mortals were different.

Nick was romanticizing the idea of mortal love, but Prudence knew better. Desire was crueler with mortals than it was with witches. She'd seen how ugly mortal boys could be when they were jealous. True love was for fools. The only thing you could trust was family.

"Won't the mortal get jealous?"

"Up to him," said Nick.

"Aren't *you* jealous?"

There was a sudden flicker of darkness in the room, as if Prudence had blinked. But she hadn't blinked.

When she could see again, Nick's eyes were hollows in his face, pits with horror hidden in their depths. "Jealousy is a wolf that eats happiness. I'll never be jealous of anybody." He shrugged off the seriousness and threw a wicked, sparkling glance her way. "Honestly, Prudence. Me, jealous of *him*? It could never happen. He's only mortal."

Nick might think he was ready for love, but he didn't look it when he laughed with his head thrown back, proud as the angel who fell to rule hell, a witch's child every inch of him.

Prudence was abruptly exhausted. "Remember I warned you, Nick Scratch. Now leave."

Nick could slight Father Blackwood and get away with it. He could presume he was welcome wherever he went, including a girl's heart. He'd suffered plenty, but he'd always been a man, so he assumed things would go his way in the end.

If Nick was Father Blackwood's son, Father Blackwood would've claimed him, and proclaimed him to heaven and hell.

Prudence had to make her own way, and her own luck. She certainly couldn't trust Nick to watch the baby as she did so. Judas's howling hurt her head, but she picked him up and carried him to the dormitory where she used to sleep with her sisters. The baby's wail chased her down the corridor.

"Be quiet or I'll give you back to the witch-hunter," Prudence whispered. "Do you want that? Ugh, maybe you do. Satan in a sun hat. Listen to your big sister, Judas. Masochism is a fine thing, but it can be taken too far."

Dorcas and Agatha were sitting on a narrow white bed together, Dorcas painting Agatha's toenails black. When she saw Prudence, Agatha jumped up.

"Prudence. You're here!"

Did they not want her to be?

When they were small, Prudence worried about them constantly. Agatha, who became overly enthused and ran headlong into trouble. Dorcas, who got her tongue tangled in front of strangers. She'd drilled the lessons of witchcraft into them. They were orphans. Nobody was looking out for them. They had to be the wickedest witches to be found in all four corners of the world.

Was it Prudence's fault her sisters had cast the spell to collapse that mine, killing those mortals—the witch-hunter's brother—as thoughtlessly as if they were playing a game of cat's cradle? Was it her fault they'd decided to leave her out, because they didn't need her any longer?

The Dark Lord had taken their souls, but she had taught them to be heartless.

Prudence didn't tell her sisters: *I miss you*. She wasn't Nick Scratch. She knew longing to be wanted got you torn to shreds.

"Don't fret," she told Agatha. "You two keep on whispering secrets without me. I'm not interested. I have places to be and horror to unleash. Watch this baby for me, or else."

She turned away from her sisters and her little brother. She went into town to help Sabrina Spellman banish a luck demon.

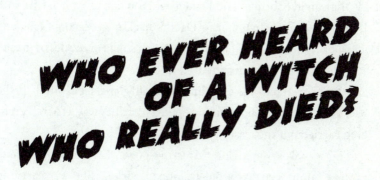

WHO EVER HEARD OF A WITCH WHO REALLY DIED?

December 29, Feast of David the Conqueror, Morning
SABRINA

t hadn't snowed last night, but it had rained. Some of the old ice and snow had washed away. The world beneath was showing through, slimy dark stone appearing in patches where the snow had grown thin and gray as an old man's hair.

Maybe I was viewing the world through jaundiced eyes because I was looking at it from behind a trash can.

"Let me make myself perfectly clear," said Prudence from behind the trash can next to mine. "I'm here to banish a minor bad-luck spirit. If this turns into anything more difficult or dangerous, you're on your own."

I nodded absently, trying to keep a lookout.

The shop was shut up, with no sign of the owner. So we were lurking behind the café, hoping for a chance to jump a demon in an alley.

"I got it."

"I mean it, Sabrina," said Prudence. "You don't so much flirt with Death as slip your number in Death's back pocket, cop a feel, and whisper, 'Call me, lover.' If you do anything stupid or reckless, I'm out."

"I understand," I whispered. "Shut up!"

Prudence fixed me with an outraged glare. I gestured to the back door of the tea shop, sliding open in the alleyway as Mrs. Ferch-Geg carried out the trash.

She was wearing a floral dressing gown, her blond hair done up in a rainbow array of old-fashioned curlers. She was carrying a basket of sad-looking éclairs and squashed cream cakes. She looked so normal that I thought for a moment we'd gotten everything wrong.

The Welsh woman walked over to the trash cans, her worn house slippers sliding in the melting snow. I braced for her to discover us. When she pulled the lid off a different trash can, I gave a small sigh of relief.

Then the breath froze, like an ice cube of horror lodged in my throat.

In the trash can were the wet, rotting remnants of a dozen tea parties. The smell of old, stewed tea bags and sour cream drifted toward us, and Mrs. Ferch-Geg turned around to face the brick wall and let her hair down.

Curlers tumbled onto the snow, lying in the ice like a dozen snakes. Through the sparse golden strands at the back of the pleasant widow's head was a second mouth, lips twisted and withered. The maw yawned wide, seeking and hungry as a baby bird's beak lifted for its mother's worm.

She waits until food is rotten to consume it with her second mouth, Nick said in my memory. I clung to the remembered sound of his voice, calm and amused, as though nothing was a big deal.

Mrs. Ferch-Geg fumbled, clumsy with her hands behind her back. She snatched up handfuls of reeking garbage and stuffed them into that gaping mouth. The mouth chewed noisily, toothlessly, giving a guttural moaning sound of mingled satiation and demand. Crumbs spewed from its slack lips, smeared with cream turned clotted and black. I had the sense that no matter how she fed that ravenous mouth, it would never be satisfied.

Prudence was making a face of extreme distaste. I stuck my tongue out and gagged in grossed-out solidarity, then pointed to Mrs. Ferch-Geg, held up three fingers, and folded them down one by one. Prudence nodded and we sprang, sending the trash cans clattering and rolling to the mouth of the alley.

"Dwy Ferch Geg!" My voice rang out confidently. *"Dragon be my guide and hellfire my light. Satan give me the power to banish this spirit. Lucifer shield me in my fight, Beelzebub lend me glory. Spirit, begone!"*

The Dwy Ferch Geg shrank before my upraised hands, staggering back, but Prudence slipped between her and escape.

"Deliver me into delicious temptation," purred Prudence. *"Evil be thou my good, might my right, and my voice heard in hell. Spirit, begone!"*

The spirit spun in a circle. I glimpsed the pleasantly smiling face of the tea shop lady, the golden-haired bishop's daughter who had lived hundreds of years ago. Every feature was still as a mask, her blue eyes glazed as a doll's. When she spoke, it was the mouth at the back of her head that moved, as if this was the mouth that was truly hers. Rotted food slid from her lips with every word.

"Gossip stains worse than the soot from hellfire. Do you think you can cleanse this place by banishing *me?*"

"Ms. Wardwell told me that we mustn't listen to her, no matter what she says," I told Prudence. "We must complete the ritual."

Prudence rolled her eyes. "This is hardly Baby Prudence's first demon summoning. Unlike you, I don't need advice from some random outcast witch."

I let the insult to Ms. Wardwell slide, since Prudence was helping me out.

"Unleash the snakes upon my enemy," I yelled. *"Turn away the ill luck and the evil eye from this place. Spirit, begone."*

"Satan give me the strength to banish this misbegotten imp," said Prudence. *"Spirit, begone."*

There seemed to be a tiny localized storm in the alleyway. I felt a gust of wind stir my white hair as the air turned electric. The figure before me, in her floral wrap, seemed to blur. For an instant I saw a smaller woman, ashen and ghastly, her body emaciated and her hands held out in appeal.

"Live by the words, die by the words. What's a spell but a string of words," murmured the demon. "A whip of words, to lash a demon. A rope of words, to hang a witch. You won't be able to utter spells when they have you by the neck. The ill luck is already here. The witch-hunters will rise. The prince will come. Like every spirit in the Pit, I heard the bells ring through hell the day you came into this world. It was evil fortune that you were ever born, Sabrina Spellman."

I wanted to ask what she meant by that, but I remembered Ms. Wardwell's warning. Demons lied. I didn't want to make any more mistakes. I couldn't let myself weaken or get distracted.

Prudence was looking at me through shrewd narrowed eyes beneath her sweep of violet eye shadow and wing of eyeliner. She wore the colors of a tropical night bird, even in a mundane alley on a gray winter's morning.

"Prudence Night!" called out the spirit, her voice shrill. "Do you think you can afford to be rash when you have so much at risk? I was the child of a man of the church too. Look what happened to me. All the voices of the congregation told me I was doing my duty when I named the women to be drowned and hanged and burned. They said I would receive my reward. Then I died and woke to torment in hell."

"Sounds to me like you received the reward you deserved," I spat.

Prudence wheeled on me. "Satan in a miniskirt, Sabrina, you just told me to ignore her!"

I blinked. "Oh. Sorry. *Spirit, begone!*"

"Overcome by the compulsion to be righteous?" Prudence sighed. "I never feel that urge myself. *Spirit, begone!*"

On the rising wind, I heard shrieks and whispers right on the cusp of hearing. Some of them sounded like people I loved calling out to me. I was certain down to the marrow of my bones that if I could make out what they were saying, it would be important.

"So many voices," sighed the Dwy Ferch Geg. "So many voices in our heads, ringing like the bells of the church by my father's house and the bells that herald the prince's coming. I could scarcely hear the voice in my head, telling me what I did was wrong. How can you be sure, little lost daughter, that you are listening to the right voice?"

I didn't even know which of us she was talking to. I wanted to stop, to ask her, but I knew I couldn't. Instead I lifted my hands above my head and saw faint phosphorescence outline my fingers, the color of dawn light touching frost.

"By the power of Satan and his rebellious angels, I cast you out," I said. *"Spirit, begone!"*

Prudence nodded, taking a deep breath. *"By the will of Satan, this place is washed clean. Spirit, begone!"*

The Dwy Ferch Geg turned in a full circle, so I saw both her mouth and her mask. She dwindled away into a shrunken pallid ghost, every feature lost save the gaping darkness of her mouth.

Her starving lips moved once more. She said: "You can't kill a whisper."

Then she was gone. Prudence and I stood staring at each other amid the demon's discarded clothes and the old pastries.

"Huh," said Prudence. "Well, start the day with a bang or a banishment, I always say. You'll sing my praises to your aunt Zelda?"

"Already did," I said cheerfully. "She said she's planning on giving you a solo. Said you were capable on many levels. I think you impressed her, the night—well, the night Judas was born."

Prudence's smile was swift and unguarded with joy. I guessed she really wanted a solo.

Her smile twisted and hastily became a sneer, as if she feared she'd betrayed herself too much by showing a moment of happiness. "Why would you do that before I helped you?"

"Because I believed you'd come through," I said. "And you did."

I reached out across the remnants of the Dwy Ferch Geg and linked my little finger with Prudence's, the way she and the Weird

Sisters often did. Prudence raised her eyebrows, but she didn't pull away.

"We did it," I told her. "We're awesome. Come on, I'll buy you a morning coffee at Dr. Cerberus's."

Prudence didn't say yes or no, but when I tugged her along, she followed me out of the alleyway and down the main street of Greendale.

"To be clear, I will not date you, Sabrina," said Prudence. "You are far too much trouble."

"I'm not actually interested."

Prudence sniffed. "Please, I've seen myself. Everybody's a little interested."

She seemed mildly intrigued by the orange-painted storefront of Cerberus Books, complete with paintings of flames, hellhounds, and monkey demons, each window outlined in red. Prudence clearly liked her decor infernally inflected.

When we walked in, Aunt Hilda bounced up and down as if she hadn't just seen me half an hour ago. She gave me a hug, and then she eyed Prudence with slight suspicion. Aunt Hilda knew we hadn't always been on the best terms.

"Did you bring me my lunch?" she asked. "I forgot it, but I thought Zelda was getting it for me."

"Sorry, I didn't know. Just thought I'd drop by."

"And I'm glad you're here, love," Aunt Hilda told me. "Business hasn't been booming lately, what with that new tea shop."

"You know, Aunt Hilda, I don't think you need to worry about that café anymore."

Aunt Hilda blinked interrogatively, and I shrugged.

"I just have a feeling." I sank my voice down to a whisper. "Those pop-up demons never last."

Prudence snickered against the rim of her coffee cup. Then she wandered away, cup in hand, to browse the shelves. Several of Greendale's jocks, crowded around a table, followed her with their gaze. Prudence didn't seem to notice. I guessed she was used to boys staring wherever she went.

She reached up for a book on a high shelf, and her purple-painted nails only managed to brush the spine. She shrugged and clicked her fingers. I saw the book begin to sail off the shelf.

Prudence was doing magic right in front of mortals.

I started forward. At the same time, a hand reached up and snagged the book from the shelf.

"Here you go, Prudence," said Harvey.

I took a hasty step back and exchanged a panicked glance with Aunt Hilda. I wasn't ready to see Harvey. Certainly not with Prudence. She'd laugh at me, at him, and at any pain I betrayed.

I wanted to hide behind the counter and Aunt Hilda's skirts. At the same time, I wanted to run to Harvey. Even the back of his battered jacket, the overlong curl of his brown hair over his shirt collar, was familiar and dear to me. I missed being able to touch him as I used to, as easily as if his body were an extension of my own. I'd toy with his hair, or turn his face to me with my palm against his jaw and kiss him anytime I wanted. I wished I could tell him about banishing the demon, and hear him say, "Well done, 'Brina."

But he'd be horrified if I told him. I used to believe he'd always think everything I did was wonderful. I'd been wrong.

It was for the best that he didn't trust witches. It meant he'd stay away from them. I had to protect him from the dangers of my world.

Prudence gestured the book away. "Now that you've touched the book, I don't want it."

Harvey moved to put it back. "Okay."

"Oh, give it here," Prudence snapped, snatching it from his hand. "Why are you following me around?"

"I'm in the only bookstore in Greendale," said Harvey. "Buying books."

He sounded amused. It had been too long since I'd seen Harvey smile. I inched forward, hiding behind one of the bookcases.

His grin was faint, but it was there. When he smiled his shy smile, gold lights woke in his hazel eyes. They made me think of the golden lights at a festival, on the last golden day of summer. We went to a fair together months ago, and Harvey painted the faces of all the little kids.

I remembered one kid in particular. A little boy had wanted stars drawn on his face, and the boy's dad said that was too girly. The boy changed his answer to a mean robot. When the dad wasn't looking, Harvey painted a star in the hollow of the boy's palm, for him to hold in his hand like a secret.

Harvey had closed the little boy's fingers over the star and glanced up to catch me watching. For an instant his face was guilty and afraid, as though I might punish him. Then his gaze rested on me, the tension easing out of his shoulders, the gold creeping into his eyes. He didn't smile often, but whenever he did, it was so sweet. That day, Harvey smiled like summer starlight. I smiled back, helplessly in love.

My aunt Hilda told me a fairy tale about Selene, the witch queen of the moon. Selene loved a mortal and enchanted him to eternal sleep so she could always watch him, and he would never die.

But he would never smile either.

Harvey was holding up two books for Prudence's inspection.

"What is *Rosemary's Baby* about?" Prudence asked suspiciously.

"A lady named Rosemary has Satan's baby," said Harvey. "I think."

"What an honor for her," Prudence murmured.

Harvey shrugged. "Depends on your point of view, I guess."

I'd taken Prudence to school with me one day. She discovered Harvey's ancestors were witch-hunters. Prudence's sisters killed Tommy for that. Harvey hadn't smiled the way he used to, boyish and summer sweet, since then. The dangers of my world from which I must protect Harvey definitely included Prudence. I swallowed, steeled myself, and darted up to Prudence, seizing her by the elbow and dragging her backward.

"Come on, Prudence, we'll be late for class! Uh, hello, Harvey."

His smile died, the color draining from his face. "Hi, Sabrina."

I realized, with a sinking feeling, that he'd sounded far more relaxed talking to Prudence than he did speaking to me.

"She's a witch," I said, glancing in Prudence's direction. I couldn't keep staring at him.

"Yeah, I did somehow figure that out," said Harvey. "I'm not stupid."

There was a cold, miserable edge to his voice on the last word.

I bit my lip, hard enough that the ache stayed. "I didn't mean that you were. Uh, Harvey, I'd love to stay and chat, but we've gotta go."

"Yeah, I'm sure you have better places to be."

"Well, this social interaction should teach you never to approach me again," Prudence remarked brightly. "It really couldn't have gone any worse, could it?"

Harvey elevated an eyebrow in her direction. "I don't know. You didn't kill me."

I didn't know why Harvey was giving Prudence ideas. I dragged her to the door as she called back: "Next time, I probably will!"

The jocks were already at the door, in a huddle. As we passed, one of them muttered: "Witch."

The word followed us like a shadow into the bright street. I wished, with a force that shocked me, that Nick were here to make me laugh. I was tired of feeling miserable.

But Nick wasn't here.

"Did you hear what they called us?" I asked uneasily.

Prudence didn't turn a hair. "I hear that word all the time."

"You sure it's that word you hear, and not, uh, a slightly different one?"

Prudence shrugged. "I hear that one too. I like hearing both. They're just words, and I'm a witch. I decide what they mean."

She strode in the direction of the Academy, book in hand. I'd have to give Aunt Hilda the money for it later. I shrugged off my misgivings and followed Prudence. She was right. It was just a word. We'd banished the demon.

"I'm not ashamed either."

"Could've fooled me, back there."

"I just don't want . . . someone I love to think the worst of me," I whispered. "I'm a witch, but I don't want him to think I'm awful, or irredeemably bad."

She was silent as we entered the woods. Then, with morning

birdsong in the bare trees, she reached out her hand and linked her little finger with mine. When I caught her eye, she smiled.

"I *am* a bad witch," said Prudence. "Why not try being one too, Sabrina?"

We went through the doors of the Academy laughing. Nick approached, his face brightening at the sight of us. The whole situation was strange and different, but it felt as good as it did to be in Baxter High with my mortal friends. We'd succeeded, and now we could be happy.

I lifted my hand for a high five. Nick gave me one, then caught his lip between his teeth and linked his fingers with mine.

I paused. He winked. I let him hold my hand.

"What's going on, Spellman?"

"We banished the bad-luck spirit!"

"Congratulations, ladies," said Nick easily.

He didn't ask why he hadn't been invited, or act sulky. He sounded genuinely admiring. It wasn't "Well done, 'Brina," but... I had to admit, I liked this too. I beamed up at Nick.

He smiled and looked away, running his free hand along the base of the statue of Satan. He made his fingers walk along the stone, then back again.

"By the way." His voice sank, hushed and intimate. "I wanted to tell you ... I don't have any girlfriends right now."

"Oh," I said. "Uh. How many are you looking for?"

Nick looked up. For a moment I felt like I was falling into his dark, dark eyes.

"Just one," he murmured.

"Well," I said. "That's, uh. That's good to know."

The sparks of another smile were kindling on Nick's mouth. This one didn't look like a smirk at all. "Is it? Since you banished the luck demon, I guess you're free after class. Can we cash in that rain check and go see the mermaids?'

Right. I'd forgotten the brilliant skinny-dipping idea Nick had mentioned the other day.

I pulled my hand out of his. "Honestly, I'm kind of tired. I was planning to go home after class. I'll see you tomorrow. Bye, guys. Thanks again, Prudence."

I fled the halls of the Academy.

Honestly, the luck demon had been a good distraction from my romantic woes and the new doubts weighing on me lately. I'd only seen Harvey for an instant today, but the sight of his stricken face wouldn't leave my mind. How could I long to laugh with Nick? What kind of person would I be, to turn away from true love and go for some wicked fling?

I didn't want to make any more mistakes this year. I didn't even know who I was any longer.

Maybe I didn't need a luck spirit to curse me. I'd been born with the bad luck to be torn between worlds. Being torn hurt. I'd always miss one world, even if I had the other.

CAN A MORTAL ASK

December 29, Afternoon
HARVEY

The bells rang in Harvey's head, jangling as the shop doors closed behind Sabrina and Prudence. He looked at the place where she'd stood, so bright with her red coat the color of a robin's breast. He'd forgotten how small she was, though she never seemed fragile. She used to tease him about being so much taller than her.

"Stay safe; I worry about you up there," she'd say, fiddling with his shirt buttons, then tugging him toward her. "Better yet, come down here and kiss me."

He sighed, turned away, and went to buy the books. Roz had talked about *The Stepford Wives* and *Rosemary's Baby*. Even if she didn't want to be his friend anymore, he wanted to read them. Every time he read a book Roz recommended, the world reshaped itself in his mind.

Hilda Spellman gave him a staff discount on the books. He'd always thought she was the sweetest lady.

"I still think you're the one for her, love." She patted his hand. "I'm rooting for you two."

Sabrina had barely spoken to him, she was in such a hurry to get to her Invisible Academy. It was pretty pointless to root for Harvey when he'd been outclassed by actual classes, but he tugged a hand through his hair so Hilda wouldn't see his face, and mumbled a thanks.

The morning had started out sunny, but he saw through the window that there were storm clouds gathering in the sky, gray and seething. There was the feeling of a storm fermenting inside the café. Billy and his friends were standing in the doorway, apparently having a conference. When Harvey passed them, he heard the whisper "Everyone's saying…"

Harvey didn't care what everyone was saying. He wished he could leave that creeping darkness behind him in the bookstore. But he felt like he carried the dark with him, a storm cloud in his chest, its gray tendrils wrapping around his heart.

He headed out of town, toward Sweetwater River, but no matter how long he stood by the riverside, he couldn't make himself cross the bridge.

When he turned away from the bridge, Billy had followed him. This time he was alone.

"What?" Harvey snarled. "Come here to pick on me again?"

"Maybe we don't have to beat you," suggested Billy. "Maybe you can join us. We're gathering up a bunch of guys against the threat."

Harvey shook his head. "I have no idea what you're talking about."

He pushed past Billy, following his own footsteps in the snow. He was literally walking in circles.

"Come on, Kinkle," said Billy. "You want to be a loser your whole life? Pick the right side. You're not a freak like Susie Putnam—"

He didn't finish his sentence. Harvey finished it for him. He whirled around and hit Billy Marlin in the face, so hard Billy staggered and fell into a snowdrift. Billy sputtered, indignant and amazed, one hand clapped over his nose. Blood was spurting between his fingers, a crimson splash against the white snow.

Harvey breathed hard, dizzy with rage and shock. "I don't like to fight. But I will."

Billy gurgled what seemed to be a protest. The sight of him bleeding made Harvey feel sick. But the shadowy knot of emotions in his chest said to keep hitting Billy, until Billy was sorry, until Harvey felt better.

He didn't get sick or hit Billy. He took a step so he was towering over Billy, and watched Billy scramble away.

"Say what you want about me," Harvey said contemptuously. "Leave Susie alone. Or I'll knock you on your ass again."

When he got home, he sat on his porch steps in the cold, letting out huge puffs of air that looked like smoke, as though Harvey were a dragon having a panic attack. What was he *doing*? He didn't hit people.

He hoped he wouldn't actually have a panic attack. Those happened occasionally. The other kids at school always laughed, except for Sabrina, Susie, and Roz.

Harvey sat there trying not to freak out until he heard the sound of Mrs. Link scurrying across the snow and lifted his head.

"I wasn't fighting!" he exclaimed.

Harvey wasn't a skilled deceiver.

Mrs. Link was wearing no scarf today. Her hair blew in the wind like a huge cloud over her head. "It'd be good for you to get into a brawl."

"Huh," said Harvey.

She seemed distracted, eyes vaguely scanning the trees and mountains beyond. "Your dad's always saying what a scaredy-cat you are. You could prove him wrong, eh?"

"I'm not a coward," Harvey said sharply.

Mrs. Link nodded encouragement. "There's a big fight coming," she murmured as she turned away. "With the witches."

Harvey froze. "Did you say *witches?*"

Mrs. Link looked at him over her shoulder. Her gaze seemed to focus for the first time. "No, dear," she told Harvey. "Why would I say that?"

Harvey stayed on the steps, breathing raggedly, until he heard the cat meow.

It was Sabrina's cat, Salem, the stray she'd found in the orchard this fall. Harvey watched as the little thing climbed daintily up his porch steps.

His knuckles had split from the force of the blow, so his hand stung when he reached out to scratch between Salem's ears.

"Hi, kitty, kitty," he murmured. "Hey, buddy. What are you doing here?"

He stroked the soft black fur, mood softening as if he was the one being soothed. He'd always wanted a puppy.

When Harvey's hand briefly stilled, Salem meowed, rubbing his chin against Harvey's fingers. Harvey laughed and petted the cat some more.

"Kitty cat," murmured Harvey. "Let's be friends. You're sweet."

"I'm not," said Nick, leaning against the other side of the porch, dark eyes glinting between the wooden rails.

Harvey started, jostling the cat.

"I have something to ask you," Nick continued. "I didn't know you were entertaining a spy."

Harvey laughed. "The cat? You're kidding."

"Am I?"

Harvey had a sudden feeling of misgiving.

Nick smirked, raised an eyebrow in Salem's direction, then strolled over and took a seat on the lowest of the icy porch steps, leaning back on his elbows. Nick wasn't unlike a cat, in that he constantly turned up uninvited wishing to be fed, and seemed really happy when he was being a jerk.

Harvey decided Nick was definitely joking around.

"One of your popes, Gregory the Ninth, condemned the black cat as an incarnation of Satan," Nick observed.

Harvey stared at the cat. "Are you Satan?"

"Obviously he's not Satan," said Nick. "Why are you always accusing everyone of being Satan? I was only telling you an interesting historical fact."

Harvey relaxed. "Okay, nerd."

Nick took this as encouragement to expand. "Our anti-pope at the time, Mephistophelian the Fifth, and Pope Gregory were rivals. The anti-pope countered by cursing Europe with the Black Plague."

Nick's face lit up when he was discussing books, the same way

Sabrina's and Roz's did when they talked about justice, or Sabrina about horror movies, or Tommy about football, or Susie about Christmas and costumes. Love did that, changing faces and conversations, like sunlight turning snow to silver.

Harvey smiled. "I'm against animal cruelty, but that seems an overreaction. What happened next?"

"The anti-pope sent the plague a century after Gregory died, so nothing much," Nick answered. "That anti-pope was also historically known as the Mephistophelian the Procrastinator. Do you like history? Would you like to hear more interesting historical facts?"

Harvey was scanning the trees and mountains, the way Mrs. Link had. He could see nothing but Greendale under a cloud.

"Sure. Come inside and tell me historical facts."

When he glanced over at Nick, he found Nick already scrutinizing him. "Why do you want me to go inside?"

"My neighbor just mentioned witches. It was weird."

"Your neighbor?" Nick repeated in a condescending voice that set Harvey's teeth on edge. "You're concerned I'm in danger from an elderly lady? She must be four hundred years old."

"She's definitely not four hundred years old!"

"She looks it," said Nick. "Everything is fine. The luck demon situation is handled. You worry too much."

Harvey thought worry was an appropriate response. Nick never had appropriate responses to anything.

Salem hissed.

Nick hissed back. "I don't trust creatures like you. Shoo, spy."

Salem rose with dignity, departing for the woods with his tail in the air. Harvey supposed Nick must be more of a dog person.

"Now that you've seen off the wicked spy, let's go inside."

"If a senile neighbor threatens me, I can just teleport," Nick said casually.

Harvey's mouth fell open. "Dude, that's awesome! Like Nightcrawler? Can all witches teleport?"

"No," Nick gloated. "Only the awesome ones."

He was so smug. Harvey was only letting him get away with it because teleporting was undeniably awesome.

"I'll teleport you," Nick offered. "Where do you want to go?"

Tommy was forever encouraging Harvey to get out of Greendale. Tommy had never left himself.

"Don't do any magic," Harvey snapped.

There was a silence colder than ice and snow.

Nick sneered, showing no understanding or pity, only a witch's fury. "Sabrina's a witch. How can you love a witch and hate magic?"

Harvey licked his dry lips and shook his head. "I keep trying to work that out."

"Then work it out," said Nick, relentless. "You chose someone extraordinary to love. Did you expect loving her to be ordinary? Would Sabrina ask you not to draw in front of her?"

"No," said Harvey automatically. His heart sank. "Is it that important?"

Nick shook his head. "Magic's more important."

"I'm trying," Harvey said, low.

He didn't say: I'm so scared.

Nick's face was furious for another moment. Then he gave an irritated sigh. "You'd better get used to magic fast, mortal."

Harvey swallowed. "I know."

In Greendale, there was no other option.

"You hurt yourself," Nick remarked. "Don't be careless. Sabrina will worry. What happened?"

Harvey frowned, confused, then followed the direction of Nick's gaze. He saw his own hurt hand.

He looked across the snow-white fields into the dark woods. "I hit somebody. He was bad-mouthing my friend Susie, but I should've given him a warning."

Nick seemed puzzled. "Why?"

There was no way to talk about his dad hitting him, how Harvey's lack of surprise was worse than the blow.

"You think the world needs more people hurting each other in it?"

The answer seemed obvious, but none came. Harvey sat listening to the sound of the wind chasing itself through the ice-bound woods. When he turned his head, Nick was giving him a funny look.

"You're so weird," Nick said, but the last trace of anger had faded from his voice.

"No, you're weird," Harvey told him firmly. "What did you come to ask me?"

It was no use pushing about what Mrs. Link had said. Nick didn't take mortals seriously and he wouldn't listen, but he'd come here for help.

"I want to..." Nick began. "I saw you and Sabrina on a date once. You both looked—happy. Then I met Sabrina. She walked into our Infernal Choir in front of a dozen enemies, and she sang. Defying all of us, and Satan."

Harvey thought of Sabrina singing in the woods, sweet as a wild bird. His magic girl.

"She used to sing for me," he murmured.

Not anymore.

"When I got to know Sabrina," continued Nick, "I thought...I want to be happy too."

Nick said the word *happy* as though it was in a strange language. Harvey couldn't believe he was feeling sorry for a guy determined to steal his girl. Harvey really was stupid.

Since he was stupid anyway, he asked: "Are you...not happy? Is there anyone at Invisible Academy to talk to?"

He was pretty sure witch school didn't have guidance counselors. Even though it was becoming clear witch school needed guidance counselors.

"There's Prudence," said Nick.

Harvey nodded. "Prudence seems cool."

She'd scared him, but that didn't matter compared to the way Prudence's face changed when she gazed down at her baby brother. For a moment Harvey'd thought they could all be friends. Then he'd go to Sabrina and say he understood, and he wasn't scared anymore.

Nick seemed surprised. "You enjoy getting force-fed truth potions?"

"I wish Sabrina had told *me* the truth."

Sabrina had made him forget the truth, once. He wished she hadn't. He wished she'd made him believe. Maybe before magic hurt him, he would've loved it, as he loved everything else about her.

"Seems like telling the truth screwed everything up," Nick remarked. "Best if you never found out."

Harvey shook his head. "Telling the truth is the only way to have something real. Is there anyone besides Prudence?"

Nick blinked. "There's Dorian. He's a bartender."

"Oh, a *bartender* friend?"

His dad also had a bartender friend. By the time your bartender was your best friend, things were very bad.

"When the Academy is too much, I go to his bar to forget."

"Maybe you could just talk to someone about your feelings!"

Nick looked like he might throw up.

Harvey bit his lip. "If you want... you could come here."

It was a dumb suggestion. His dad hadn't ever chosen to go home instead of the bar, and his dad actually lived here.

"All right," Nick said quietly.

Harvey knew he shouldn't show how surprised he was, so he nodded. He wasn't sure if mortals and witches could be friends, but everybody needed someone they could talk to.

"So..." said Harvey. "Witches talk about weird sex stuff all day long, but everybody pretends they don't have feelings?"

"Of course!"

Harvey was speechless.

Sadly, Nick was not. "The way mortals and witches do things is so different. What would you think if someone hit you with the line 'Hey, sexy, I don't care if you live or die'?"

"I would think the person speaking to me was a sociopath who might steal my skin," said Harvey.

"And then you wouldn't go out with them, probably!"

"Definitely not! Is that a typical witch pickup line? *Are* there typical witch pickup lines?"

Nick nodded. Against his better judgement, Harvey made a gesture for him to continue. Nick began to smile his devil smile.

"Divination is my specialty, and I see a date with me in your future."

Harvey shook his head. "That's really bad."

"Wreck me like a broom you flew into a hurricane," said Nick brightly.

Harvey put his face in his hands. "Oh my God."

"An ye harm none, do with me as thou wilt."

"No to all of this." Harvey shook his head and laughed and shook his head some more. "No to everything."

Nick winked. "I've only got eye of newt for you."

"This might be the worst thing that's ever happened to me," said Harvey.

Nick seemed highly amused by Harvey's horror.

"Did the false god hurl you from heaven? Because you are hot as hell."

"Stop now."

"I haven't even told you the one where I say, 'This is where the magic happens' and point to my pants."

Harvey snorted. "If you tried anything like that on Sabrina, of course it isn't working."

"Please don't insult me, Harry. I did *not* use any of those lines on Sabrina. I actually have game."

"Do you, though?" Harvey asked. "Because I don't have any, yet here you are asking for advice. What did you do with your, uh, several girlfriends?"

He still couldn't believe Nick had dated the whole band.

"It was more sexual sorcery in the woods than actual dating. You know, striptease with vanishing spells, the black arts with bondage."

There was a pause.

"I'd strongly suggest a movie first," said Harvey.

"How does it go for you two?" Nick asked. "Walk me through this. Look, I'll be Sabrina."

"Nick! I don't like this game."

Nick proceeded without missing a beat: "So Sabrina says to you, 'Hey, little mortal love—'"

"Do you seriously imagine that is how Sabrina talks to me?" Harvey demanded.

"Why not? She suggests going to a movie—in one of those mortal movie theaters?"

"Um," said Harvey. "Yeah. Have you never been to one?"

Nick shook his head. "Have I got this down? She says, 'Come with me' and you say, 'Yes, I will.' There isn't something I'm missing here?"

Bondage and the black arts, but no movies. Witches led strange lives.

Harvey remembered the shocking naked astral projection suggestion Nick had once made, and added: "I hope you were crystal clear that the activity would involve clothing."

"Oh," said Nick.

"Nicholas *Scratch*!" said Harvey. "You have to be clear!"

"Actually, now you mention it, she might've thought…Maybe that was the problem."

"Yeah, maybe!"

Nick shook his head as if stunned. "This dating business has pitfalls at every turn. Can we go to the movies?"

"What?" Harvey asked blankly.

"I don't want to mess this up, so I need a trial run. Why, do you not want to? Should I ensorcel some mortal girl to go with me?"

"No you should not!" Harvey yelped.

"So you'll come."

It would be an act of civic responsibility to stop a warlock from running amok enchanting the populace. And it wasn't as if Harvey had any plans.

Harvey sighed. "Yeah, I will."

How bad could it be? He'd been to the movies in Greendale literally hundreds of times. Sabrina loved horror movies, Susie loved action movies, and Roz loved depressing movies with subtitles, so there was always something to see. Harvey used to go to the movie theater with his friends almost every weekend. He missed it, as he missed a lot about the old life he'd thought was ordinary and boring at the time.

Unless they had the worst luck in the world, Harvey didn't see how watching a movie could go wrong.

WITCHES ARE ALL HUNG

December 29, Evening
PRUDENCE

When Sabrina turned Nick down for the five hundredth time, he waited until she was gone. Then he covered his face with his hands and surrendered to despair.

"I'm going to die alone. Well. Probably at a bacchanal with sexy dryads, but alone in a meaningful way." He raked a hand through his hair. Now it was a total mess, much like him.

Prudence slapped him on the back. "Nick, listen to yourself, you're raving."

"I have to go," said Nick, with sudden resolve.

"You idiot harlot. Sure, take romantic advice from a witch-hunter who can barely dress himself," Prudence called after Nick. "Enjoy having your head cut off and your mouth filled with salt when it's buried at the crossroads."

The door slammed. Nick's idiot harlot decisions were his own. Prudence had other livers to fry.

Hilda Spellman had mentioned Zelda was visiting her at work, so Prudence intended to drop by the café and verify Sabrina was praising Prudence as promised. Zelda hadn't been to the Academy since before Yule, and Prudence hadn't been able to think up a pretext to drop by the Spellman house. The silly mortal café was a public place. Prudence could go there if she wished. She could leave Judas with her sisters for a while longer. He'd thank her later, once she'd secured him a suitable candidate for a mother.

Prudence hurried out of the Academy and headed toward the town and the bookstore within it. She wasn't Nick Scratch, who wanted to marry books and raise little baby novellas, but she'd noted there were several interesting volumes on demonology in that shop. She could peruse the shelves until Zelda arrived.

She was busy thinking up the perfect way to engineer their accidental encounter, sailing down the icy main road and past the alleyway where she and Sabrina had banished the demon. A sudden impulse stayed her step. She decided to look in on the scene of their victory. It felt like that might bring her luck.

She walked down toward the upturned trash cans. Someone had gotten rid of the fallen woman's clothes, but the garbage was still on the ground. The tea shop was shut up and silent. They'd really banished a demon, she and Sabrina. She wondered whether her father would be impressed if he knew.

Mortal affairs were none of her concern. Prudence didn't pay any attention to the bustle of mortals on the street.

Not until she was hit by the blow from behind.

Something struck the back of her head, heavy and sharp-edged, hard enough to bring her to her knees. Prudence staggered and caught herself, hand braced against the wall of the alley for support. Darkness veiled her eyes for a moment, but even before the blackness receded, she spun around.

There was a small band of mortals before her. As she turned, she had to dodge another missile. It glanced off the side of her head rather than between her eyes, where it was aimed. Prudence touched the gash she could feel opening on her forehead. Blood trickled hot into one eye, obscuring her vision further, but she was able to make out a few faces and a few words.

"...saw her and two evil hags in the woods..."

"...tricked me, ensnared me with illusions..."

"Witch!"

"...told lies..."

"Witch!"

She thought she recalled a boy who she'd tormented in the mines...and another man who she believed was a miner. A guy she didn't recognize stepped forward, eyes narrowing, a brick in his fist.

They were throwing bricks at her. She was already dazed and bleeding. It might be time to try sweet-talking the mortals.

"Burn slow, witch," he yelled, hurling his brick.

Prudence caught the brick in her blood-slick hand, murmured a spell, and made the brick turn to red dust in her palm.

"Die screaming, mortal."

She'd never been that good at sweet-talking. She should let go of the wall and run at them, but she wasn't sure she could stand without support. She'd have to try an illusion spell, she thought, and tried to piece together, in her scrambled brain, the words for any spell at all.

The mouth of the alley went dark, as though someone had drawn a black curtain across it. Against the sudden midnight, like a singer taking center stage, stood Zelda Spellman.

"Hello, boys," she said, and put her cigarette out against the wall.

Her hair curled bright beneath a small black hat adorned by a tasteful raven feather. She wore a black trench coat cinched by a sharkskin belt, and on the belt was a row of shark teeth.

"I know a witch who would make you run scared by telling you she knows the deepest secrets of your own filthy hearts."

The men stared at her.

Zelda's own teeth showed as she smiled. "But she's the nice sister. I'm not. I'd rather cut out your hearts and eat them between two slices of bread. Then I'd spit them out, because no matter how long it's been since I had long pig, I still wouldn't sully myself by touching any of you."

A fool raised a brick and then dropped it with a howl. There was a sound like a bough breaking. Prudence realized it was the bone of his arm snapping.

"You have one chance to run," said Zelda. "Or you're sandwiches."

They ran, disappearing into the dark. Zelda strode forward, laying a hand against Prudence's forehead as though she was taking her temperature. Prudence felt magic rush over her skin, cooling and healing, and she let herself collapse into Zelda's waiting arms.

She woke up on her settee in the Academy, but the settee had been enchanted wider than her bed, and it was piled high with deliciously soft velvet cushions. A brocade blanket had been drawn over her, and she lay in a plush nest.

Over her head came the sounds of Zelda and Father Blackwood—no, Prudence reminded herself, *her father*—talking.

"Occasionally a mortal does get suspicious," said Zelda. "All it takes is a memory charm to sort them out. If that isn't effective, I'll break their nasty little necks and use their innards for spell ingredients."

"I do admire an efficient woman," murmured Prudence's father.

Quickly, Prudence scribbled a warning to Nick. No sooner was she done than someone pulled her blanket back.

"Prudence, you're awake," said Zelda. "How are you feeling?"

She couldn't show weakness in front of her father. "Infernally well."

She tried to sit up. Zelda pushed her back flat against the velvet cushions. "If you have the sense Satan gave a toad, you won't even dream of stirring before morning."

"Who will see to the babe?" demanded Prudence's father.

Prudence's eyes went to the cradle, where Judas lay. Zelda must have retrieved him from her sisters.

Zelda gave a shrug. "Why, Faustus, I shall handle everything in your rooms that requires handling. Be sure of that."

Faustus Blackwood swallowed slightly, tugging his high anti-clerical collar with a sharpened nail.

"First let me arrange some food better than the usual slop served at the Academy," Zelda said briskly. "Then I shall settle the children, and then we may explore … parish business in your chamber."

"Ah," said Father Blackwood. "Excellent."

Zelda left the room, her every decisive step a thunderclap. Prudence's father turned around. She thought his blue gaze would go instantly to the cradle, but his eyes held on her instead.

"Sister Zelda says that you were rather magnificent wishing death on the mortals," he remarked. "Bravely done, Prudence. There are times I think you might not be a disgrace to the family name."

The family name she didn't carry. Not yet.

Prudence wanted to ask if she could bear the name now, but she bit her tongue. She didn't want to spoil his rare good mood.

"I am happy to serve," she murmured instead.

"As Lilith served Satan, so witches must serve warlocks," her father murmured. "Well said."

She wanted to stab him, and she wanted him to pat her head and tell her he was proud of her. Which made her want to stab him even more.

"Yes, Father," she answered. "May I say, it pleases me to see a man of your Satanic magnificence attended by a worthy handmaiden."

"Ah yes," he said. "Sister Zelda is rather special."

Prudence smiled. Her father left the room with a skip in his step, no doubt to prepare the whips.

Soon after he went, Zelda came back. She laid out a meal for Prudence that tasted like Hilda Spellman's cooking, and as Prudence ate, Zelda rocked the baby's cradle.

"How is—" Prudence lowered her voice. "How is the girl child?"

She didn't say *my little sister*. It seemed a betrayal of weakness. She couldn't trust Zelda, not yet.

Her eyes fixed on the crib, Zelda murmured: "I named her Leticia."

Prudence knew that much. The night Sabrina invited her and her sisters to perform a séance at her house, Prudence came early and peeped through the windows, trying to catch a glimpse of the baby. She'd seen Zelda, usually so stern, playing peekaboo with the tiny girl and heard Leticia laughing in the warm safety of the

Spellman house. She'd never heard Judas laugh like that.

Prudence's smile was stillborn when Zelda continued: "I had to send Leticia to a witch in the woods, for her own safety."

Because Prudence's father was a man who couldn't be trusted with daughters. Prudence nodded, hardly daring to speak.

"I understand," she said at last, very low. "But my father esteems you greatly. Perhaps you might persuade him to treat a daughter well."

Zelda glanced up from the cradle, her red lips curling. "Which daughter?"

Prudence smiled back. It was every witch for herself, in the end. Zelda must know Prudence wouldn't act selflessly.

"Perhaps both," Prudence answered. "After all, I *am* the only one who knows what you did, hiding the baby. I could be a great threat to you. Then again, I might be very useful."

"We shall see, won't we?" Zelda asked, her voice dry.

She took the tray of food away and settled Prudence back down against the cushions. Her velvet nest was like a decadent cloud. Prudence hardly noticed her headache.

If she was useful, Zelda would wish to keep her close.

"If Nick Scratch comes by," Prudence whispered, "tell him what happened to me."

"Nice name for a nice boy," said Zelda. "In the choir and skilled with conjuring, isn't he? Your beau?"

Actually, I can't get your ward Ambrose off my mind, she wanted to say. But Prudence couldn't show weakness of any kind.

She tried distraction instead. "Nick seems heavenbent on Sabrina."

She saw Zelda take this in, and the satisfied curve of Zelda's mouth as she did so. There were still many coven members who gossiped about the unfortunate mortal side of Sabrina's heritage. Not to mention the fuss over the mortal boyfriend. A boy from an old respectable witch family, especially a boy with notable magical talent, must be the answer to Zelda Spellman's prayers to the Dark Lord.

"Is that so?" Zelda asked lightly. "I'll take a proper look at him if he drops by, and I'll tell him you're doing well. Attend to the black arts and blackmail tomorrow, Prudence. Sleep now."

Prudence usually had trouble getting to sleep, but not tonight. On this night she slid instantly into slumber, wrapped in her blanket and deaf to knocks and voices. There was no need to lie sleepless and worrying. Everything was taken care of, including her.

Only when Judas woke crying did Prudence stir. Before she'd even flicked back the blanket, the door of Father Blackwood's chamber opened. Zelda came out in one of Father Blackwood's gold-embroidered robes, hair streaming loose around her shoulders and falling down into Judas's crib as she bent over, murmuring sweetness.

Judas stopped crying and started giggling as he grabbed at Zelda's hair, and she laughed down at him. She picked him up and rocked him until he was quiet. Prudence closed her eyes to the sound of the satin robe swishing against their brocade carpet.

When Zelda laid Judas down in his cradle, she paused by Prudence's bed. Prudence lay very still.

Zelda sighed to herself. "She isn't much older than my Sabrina. Sleep well, child. Flights of fallen angels sing you to your rest."

Zelda passed a hand over Prudence's shorn hair. Once the door shut behind Zelda, Prudence opened her eyes, sighed blissfully, and wriggled her toes luxuriously in the velvet.

This was how being a family felt. Now she knew.

NO MORTAL WORD CAN FRAME

December 29, Evening
HARVEY

Nick Scratch appeared transfixed by the slushie machine.

"Do you want to drink a slushie?" Harvey asked at last.

Nick turned an inquiring gaze upon him. "Is it a drink? I thought it was an art installation that went around and around."

"Uh...no," said Harvey.

"I would like to try one," said Nick. "I didn't know drinks came in blue."

It was freezing outside, and everyone must be bored on Christmas vacation. There were a lot more people in the movie theater than Harvey had expected. He stared apprehensively around at the milling citizens of Greendale, wondering what weird witch thing Nick would do in front of everybody.

There were already many people giving Nick sidelong glances.

Possibly because he was a stranger in town. Possibly because he'd been staring at the slushie machine for five minutes.

"Before you go," said Harvey, "pick. What movie do you want to see?"

Nick shrugged. "I don't know. I've never gone to the movies before. Which one is the best movie?"

They scrutinized the variety of posters on the opposite wall. Tragically, there were no posters of superheroes. One poster was a cartoon, featuring a large bee in a dress and a toy soldier who were maybe in love. Harvey hoped it worked out for them. One was a portrait of shadowy woods, with a watching eye and a too-vivid splash of blood spray across the whole scene. There always seemed to be a horror movie playing in his town.

There was also a poster of a movie with people on a swing in the sunlight. They even had a fluffy dog. They looked happy.

"Well—" Harvey began, when Nick interrupted him and pointed.

"I like that picture with the blood. Let's go watch the movie with the blood."

Harvey sighed. Nick noticed.

"Is that wrong? Is that not the one Sabrina would choose?"

"No," Harvey admitted. "That's the one Sabrina would pick."

It was more crushing evidence of what Harvey knew already: Nick and Sabrina were going to be happy together.

Sabrina always used to smile and laugh in obvious enjoyment during the scary moments. He'd thought it was a cute quirk. Now he realized what she'd always known. She was the supernatural and awe-inspiring creature, not the awestruck audience, and never the victim. It never occurred to Sabrina to be afraid.

"Go get your slushie," Harvey told Nick. "Don't talk to anyone else in line. People are already staring."

Nick looked curiously around at the milling crowd of movie-goers. Harvey saw a woman he knew from the grocery store with her eyes fixed on the back of Nick's black jacket. Nick winked.

"They just want to sleep with me."

"Keep telling yourself that, Satan's gift to women," said Harvey, turning Nick around by the shoulders and pushing him toward the slushie machine.

This was a very stressful trip to the movies, but it beat staying home. As he bought popcorn, Harvey wondered what Roz and Susie were doing. It seemed like everyone in Greendale was here.

No sooner had he thought that than he turned and came face-to-face with Ambrose Spellman. Harvey almost spilled his popcorn.

He'd never actually seen Ambrose outside the Spellman house before. Ambrose was usually lounging around in dressing gowns being *louche*, which was a word Harvey had read but didn't actually know how to say. Still, he was pretty sure Ambrose was it. Ambrose never seemed to take anything seriously. Least of all Harvey himself.

Now Ambrose was out in the world. There was a strange guy with him. The stranger was blond-haired and wearing black high-collared clothes that made Harvey think of a priest.

"I don't know if you've met my boyfriend, Luke?" asked Ambrose. "Luke, this is Harvey. Sabrina's ex."

Greendale was a small town. Guys didn't openly have boyfriends all over the place.

"Nice to meet you, Luke," Harvey said awkwardly, trying to make clear he meant it.

They didn't return the sentiment. Usually Ambrose smiled at people, though not in a terribly sincere way. He wasn't smiling now. The look on his boyfriend's face was worse. His pale eyes regarded Harvey as if he were a bug. From the look alone, Harvey knew Luke must be a warlock.

"Out on the town?" Ambrose's lip curled. "Good luck trying to find anyone as special as the girl you threw away."

"That's not fair," Harvey mumbled.

He remembered turning up at the Spellmans' door in a miner's costume and having Ambrose make a crack about dressing as his future. Ambrose always acted as though he expected Sabrina to ditch Harvey and move on to better things.

Ambrose shrugged. "Life's not fair. You made my cousin cry. Now she's home alone and you're at the movies, as though some mortal girl could replace Sabrina."

Harvey was rendered speechless by the idea of Sabrina crying. She'd fallen in the playground once, when they were eight. There'd been blood. She'd smiled and patiently waited for her aunts to come while Harvey sat with her in the nurse's office. He cried, but she never did.

Their bubble of cold silence in the noisy crowd was pierced by Nick sauntering back to Harvey's side.

"This drink is delicious," he announced. "It tastes like blue."

Ambrose's mouth fell open.

Nick noticed his presence and waved his large cup. "Ambrose. Are you here to see a movie too?"

Ambrose made a wild spinning gesture with both hands, his rings catching the light. Harvey had never seen Ambrose taken aback before.

"It's Nick Scratch," Nick reminded him helpfully.

"Oh, I remember," murmured Ambrose. Nick smiled and resumed drinking his slushie.

Ambrose's expression of shock had transformed to fascination.

"Harvey Kinkle," he said slowly. "Do you have irresistible charisma I've just never noticed?"

"Um," said Harvey. "I don't think so. Nick, could you explain to him..."

Nick nodded. "We're practicing dating."

Ambrose's usual grin was beginning to creep back, wide and bright. "What happens after you practice? Do you get really good at it?"

Harvey gave Nick a reproachful look. "You're bad at explaining."

"I have no idea what's happening," said Ambrose. "Harvey, you want to try explaining?"

Harvey blinked hard twice, hoping maybe the next time he opened his eyes he wouldn't be in this situation.

He still was.

"Well..." he said. "Nick doesn't know how to date someone in a mortal way. It's like... I watch a lot of shows late at night."

"Same," said Ambrose.

"Like travel and nature documentaries."

"Nope, very different," said Ambrose. "Go on."

When Harvey was home alone and his dad was at the bar, the TV shows were company.

"I once saw a documentary about dolphins. They flirt by tapping each other with their tails. But humans sometimes pat dolphins, like, Hi, nice to meet you, dolphin. Then the dolphins go, Whoa, is this flirting? Okay, unexpected, but I guess life is a rich tapestry. And they tap the humans with their tails and the humans are like, Oh no, my spine. Not similar ways of flirting, humans and dolphins."

"Do you understand any of what he's saying?" Ambrose asked Nick in a stage whisper.

Nick grinned. "It comes and goes."

Ambrose studied Harvey in a wondering and slightly offensive manner. "He's not ensorceled, is he?"

"I prefer not to mess with people's minds, generally," said Nick. "Also I have no idea how to ensorcel someone to call me a dolphin. What even *is* a dolphin?"

Harvey didn't like this conversation.

"My point is, Sabrina and Nick were having communication issues, because even though she's . . . half dolphin . . . she hasn't flirted the dolphin way before."

Harvey surveyed the group. Ambrose and Nick were both smiling, but in a mocking fashion. Luke was staring as if he thought Harvey was a particularly stupid bug.

"The dolphin stuff is a metaphor," Harvey concluded.

"Ah, this is about *Sabrina*," Ambrose remarked.

"Yeah," said Harvey. "Obviously?"

Ambrose held out a hand. "Luke, popcorn!"

The boyfriend offered Ambrose his carton of popcorn. Ambrose took a handful and began to toss the pieces into his mouth, still grinning. He was watching Nick and Harvey as though they were his entertainment for the evening.

Nick's attention went from Ambrose, to the popcorn, to the boyfriend. His eyes narrowed. His teeth showed in a snarl.

"Nick!" Harvey was horrified. "A word."

He grabbed Nick's jacket and tugged him aside. Nick tossed a sneer over his shoulder.

"You can't act that way," Harvey whispered urgently. "It's okay for them to date!"

Years ago—when Harvey was eleven and Ambrose still looked the same age he was now, oh God, the witches really were immortal—Tommy was sixteen and had just started driving. Tommy dropped Harvey off at Sabrina's house so they could play in the woods. They'd seen Ambrose kissing a guy in the Spellmans' pet cemetery. Harvey thought both he and his brother were a little surprised, but Tommy pulled the truck over to the side of the road and spoke seriously.

"He's cool," Tommy assured Harvey. "It's cool. Don't let anyone tell you different."

Later, Roz explained further about sexuality and Kinsey scales, and the guys at school made nasty jokes about Harvey being into art, but Harvey remembered what his brother had told him.

Nick was staring blankly. "What?"

"We're, um, all God's children," said Harvey.

Nick looked aghast. "Not me!"

"Right," said Harvey. "Sorry, bad way to put it. What I'm trying to say is—"

He was distracted by the sound of someone munching popcorn. Ambrose had followed them, boyfriend in tow.

"I'm shamelessly eavesdropping," Ambrose informed them. "What Harvey is trying to say—and huzzah for being an ally, I guess, not that I need your inept help—is that some followers of the false god look unfavorably upon romance between people of the same sex."

"Really?" said Nick.

He looked at Harvey for confirmation of this astonishing news. Harvey sighed and nodded.

"I thought the big advantage of the false god was that he lets people love each other?" Nick shook his head. "Those followers are only making their own god look bad."

"I agree with you," said Harvey, "but do you always have to call him the false god? Like, I don't call Satan the false satan."

"Some mortals call Satan the Prince of Lies," argued Nick. "I've read about it."

"I guess that's true."

Harvey glanced uneasily over at Ambrose and his stone-faced boyfriend, regarding them as if they were an exhibit at the zoo.

"Don't mind us!" said Ambrose.

Harvey hunched his shoulders. He hated when people stared. "Let's go buy the tickets."

"I already got the tickets," Nick said.

Harvey noticed the difference between the word *buy* and the word *got*.

"Did you enchant the ticket sales lady? Taking tickets is stealing. Roz says capitalism is an imperfect system, but it's the one we've got. Enchanting people is wrong—"

"Who cares," Nick muttered.

"And *I don't like it*. Nor will Sabrina. Go back and pay her!"

Nick sighed. "Fine."

"Is that mortal talking like a prim governess to Nick Scratch?"

Ambrose's boyfriend wondered aloud. "*Nick Scratch*, necromancy expert and infernally skilled conjurer, keeps his pens in a pirate's skull, the guy who bound three other students in a devil's snare that was on fire? Did we fall into a demonic pocket universe? Is any of this really happening?"

Ambrose's boyfriend took a sudden sharp step forward. When Harvey lifted a hand to ward him off, Luke grabbed Harvey's wrist.

"And he's not even ensorceled?" Luke asked. "Enchanting mortals is a basic precaution."

Harvey lost patience. "Hey, jerk, could you stop talking about me as if I'm not here?"

"I wish you weren't. Someone should teach you to keep a civil tongue in your head," said Luke. "Witch-hunter."

So that was what this was about. Harvey tried to yank free of Luke's hold on his arm, but Luke's grip was tight. Harvey felt that cold, creeping feeling of magic, making every sense revolt, telling him that these were *enemies*, that—

Nick glanced at Luke's hand and gave a casual whistle. Luke removed his hand.

"Let the mortal be, Luke," said Ambrose.

Luke wheeled on his boyfriend. "Whose side are you on?"

Ambrose smiled. "Sabrina's. I thought I'd made that clear."

"Ugh, Sabrina," muttered Luke.

He seemed surprised to be glared at from three different directions.

"Not sure this is the right crowd for complaints about my cousin," Ambrose said, a note of steel in his voice.

"I mean…" said Luke. "I like Sabrina, of course. She's a lot of trouble for such a tiny person, but Father Blackwood says she'd have promise if she learned her place."

"He sounds like an idiot," said Harvey.

Nick and Ambrose looked amused. Luke looked offended.

"You insolent mortal—" Luke began.

"Farm boy," Nick interrupted. "Hold my blue drink."

Harvey blinked at him. "Why?"

"I don't want to risk spilling my blue drink. You hold on to it. You, *come here.*"

He growled the command at Luke, snapped his fingers, and stalked away. Luke followed him as though pulled by an invisible but inescapable leash.

"Please return my boyfriend mostly unharmed," Ambrose called after them. He didn't sound unduly concerned. Indeed, he was still grinning. "I like that Nick boy. He's got big witch energy."

"Sorry?" asked Harvey.

Luke and Nick were now standing at the doors of the theater. Nick was making several gestures, one of which was a graphic throat-cutting gesture.

"While they're having their little chat," said Ambrose blithely, "I've always thought you were a nice boy."

"Have you?" Harvey was startled. "I never thought you liked me much."

"I don't," said Ambrose. "I find nice boys basically uninteresting. Nevertheless, I can't help but wonder what a nice boy is doing hanging around Mister Tall, Dark, and Feral."

"He's not that tall," said Harvey.

Ambrose laughed. "You take my point."

Harvey shrugged uncomfortably. "He asked for my help. He wants to—get to know Sabrina better."

"I'm sure he does," said Ambrose. "Word on the Academy bathroom wall says Nick's running out of students."

"Yeah, it, um, sounds like witches are very adventurous in that area," said Harvey.

"Not my auntie Hilda," said Ambrose. "Satan preserve her sweet soul. Think she's a bit shy. Most of us are intrepid sexual explorers, yes. Myself most definitely included. Nick's a special case, though. From what Luke says, one has to wonder when he sleeps."

Prudence had made similar remarks. The whole situation seemed slightly concerning to Harvey, but it wasn't as if he was an expert.

"Maybe he was—looking for a connection," said Harvey. "Nick told me he really likes Sabrina."

"Why would you believe him? Here's the thing about witches," murmured Ambrose. "We are a good-looking but not a trustworthy people."

It wasn't easy to articulate, but he felt Sabrina's cousin should know.

"On the night of the ghosts, Sabrina sent him to me," Harvey said, in a halting voice. "He said, 'She asked. So I came.' Then he looked for me, to tell him how *she'd* want him to behave. He's yelling at Luke now because Luke was insulting Sabrina. Nick doesn't act as if all of Sabrina's experiences so far—the things that make her who she is—don't matter. I've loved Sabrina since I was five years old. It's the one thing I can do really well. I know when someone likes Sabrina. He does."

Ambrose crossed his arms, leaving his popcorn floating in the air beside him. Harvey tried to shield the popcorn from the view of the populace.

"That's oddly convincing," Ambrose remarked. "Even if Nick does like Sabrina with a like that is pure and true, though, why commit an act of romantic self-sabotage and help him? You do realize this behavior is insane."

"Yeah," Harvey admitted. "I hate the thought of Sabrina finding out about it."

"So why do this, then? What's in it for you?"

"My brother is *dead*."

Harvey's voice cracked. People were looking at them. He'd thought Nick was the one who would make a scene, but apparently not.

"Witches did it," Harvey continued, forcing himself to speak more quietly. "Now that I know about Sabrina, I've been able to put some pieces together. She called me once, and her voice was shaking. She was really upset. Bad things were happening to her at the Academy, right?"

Ambrose nodded. He'd stopped smiling entirely.

"I don't know how bad things are at the Academy. I don't know what signing this Book did to her. All I know is, she's in danger, and I can't bear the idea of anything happening to another person I love. I can't do anything for her. He can. All I want is for her to be okay."

That was a lie. All he wanted was to be able to help her. Ambrose leaned back against the poster of the cartoon bee. "Maybe you could do something for her."

Harvey shook his head. "I'm not going to be with her. She made that clear. If she's going to be with someone else, it should be someone who respects her and cares about her."

She'd said it was dangerous to be together, but Harvey couldn't help thinking if she really wanted him, she would have taken him back. Maybe she wanted somebody else. Someone better, smarter, more exciting than he was. There was something between her and Nick. Maybe Sabrina had seized the excuse to stay broken up.

Ambrose's voice was light. "Even if it breaks your heart?"

Harvey swallowed past the painful lump in his throat. "It does break my heart. That doesn't matter. Sabrina is what matters. And what do *you* care about my heart? You never thought I was good enough for her."

There was a silence.

"No," Ambrose agreed. "I never did. I still don't. But maybe you're a little better than I thought."

Harvey wasn't sure why Ambrose would say that. Maybe he only felt sorry for Harvey. It was still nice.

Ambrose reached out and took hold of Harvey's shoulder in a brief warm grasp.

"I'm sorry about your brother, Harvey."

Harvey cleared his throat and managed to offer: "Tommy always said you were a cool guy."

"Did he?" Ambrose's smile was pleased but puzzled. "I never really knew him. I suppose I don't know you that well either. Witches keep our distance from mortals. They don't last."

Harvey eyed Ambrose apprehensively. "How old are you?"

"Older than you," said Ambrose. "The wages of sin are life practically eternal. But we still lose people. Neither love nor magic can save them. My father was killed by witch-hunters."

Harvey gazed at Ambrose in utter dismay. Harvey'd thought of his family's horrible past as ancient history. Not something that came this close.

Ambrose's smile stayed in place. "Luke has his reasons for how he behaves. The witches have their reasons for steering clear of mortals, and the hunters above all. We have something in common. I want Sabrina to be safe more than anything."

Harvey looked at the floor. "I'm sorry about your dad."

"It was a long time ago," Ambrose said, then nodded at something behind Harvey. "Hark, my date has returned to me through various terrible dangers. Hey, honey. Hey, various terrible dangers."

Nick smirked, taking his slushie back. "Hey."

Luke looked extremely fed up with life. When Ambrose laced their fingers together and led him toward the cinema doors, he seemed relieved to escape. Nick was drinking his blue drink and looking even more self-satisfied than usual.

"Luke goes to Invisible Academy, I guess?" Harvey said.

Nick nodded. "We hate Luke."

Harvey thought of Ambrose saying Luke had his reasons. "I don't know Luke."

"He belongs to an organization run by Father Blackwood. It's dedicated to the idea that warlocks are better than witches."

"Wow, we *do* hate Luke," said Harvey.

He glared after Luke, who caught the glare and looked even more outraged by the night's events.

"Sorry," Harvey added. "I thought you might have a problem with who Luke was dating."

Nick seemed bewildered. "Why? Ambrose is the best thing about Luke, and even dating someone for long isn't like Luke. If I didn't know better, I'd think Luke had taken a love potion, but even Luke isn't dumb enough to not test his food and drink."

Harvey snorted. "I'm sure Ambrose doesn't need to give anyone love potions. Come on. We've already missed the previews."

"What are previews?" Nick asked.

"Not one of the better mortal inventions," said Harvey, heading for the theater.

It occurred to Harvey that he should mention Sabrina liked seeing trailers so she could plan for future viewing experiences. But he wasn't Nick and Sabrina's social secretary. This whole situation was humiliating and heartbreaking enough. Sabrina could tell Nick herself.

The theater was already pretty packed, and they had to negotiate their way in through the filled seats. They ended up sitting next to Linda Tapper and her mom. Harvey was sure Linda was too young to see this movie.

Nick gazed around at the audience with an air of anthropological interest.

"That mortal is yawning elaborately even though he doesn't look tired."

"Keep your voice down."

Nick lowered his voice. "Now he's stretching, and he's put his arm on the back of the chair next to him. There's a girl in it. Oh, I see what's going on."

It was extremely obvious what was going on, but maybe not to someone who'd never been in a movie theater before.

"Yeah, that's kind of—a mortal dating thing. Like, especially if you're teenagers or you haven't been dating that long. Or both, I guess."

Nick surveyed the theater with a critical eye.

"Ambrose is doing it," Nick reported.

"Yeah, he's doing it ironically," Harvey explained. "Because he's cool."

"Did you used to do it with Sabrina?"

The memory hit like a truck. How nervous he'd been, the first time he tried, and how happy when she snuggled against him.

"Yeah," Harvey admitted. "Not ironically. I'm not really cool."

Sabrina never seemed to mind.

Ambrose had his arm around Luke, but he was still looking over at them and grinning. Ambrose seemed eternally amused by the world.

"So you hate Luke," said Harvey. "But you get along with Ambrose, right?"

"I like Ambrose," said Nick. "I like everything that belongs to Sabrina. I don't know him very well, but Ambrose does seem cool."

"I guess you ran into him at Sabrina's house."

Sabrina's family were never welcoming to Harvey, but he bet a red carpet would be laid out for a warlock boy. Nick had probably been invited to dinner.

"Yes," Nick agreed. "We had a group encounter in Ambrose's room."

"Okay," said Harvey slowly. "You might want to clarify that. It almost sounds as if you mean..."

Nick raised an eyebrow.

Harvey choked on his popcorn.

"Mortal? You all right?"

Harvey didn't answer, because he was choking on his popcorn. He couldn't breathe. He heard Nick murmuring a quick spell. He felt a chill of fear, the hair standing up at the back of his neck. Magic put the world ever so slightly out of joint. Suddenly Harvey's airway was clear, though his eyes were still streaming.

Harvey didn't have time to dwell on his own brush with popcorn-induced death.

"I just want to know," he said in a low, reproachful voice, "why are you always like this?"

"Why am I in trouble? I was being careful of your delicate mortal sensibilities! It wasn't even that big a group. There were only six people."

"That is *so many people!*"

Harvey glared. Nick held his hands up in surrender. Then he said brightly: "Actually, I have a few questions about that night."

"Oh my God," Harvey said, his voice hollow.

"It was fairly standard group activity, but when Sabrina walked in, she seemed startled."

Harvey's vision blurred with horror.

"Sabrina walked in?"

Nick nodded. "I invited Sabrina to join us, of course," he added, as if that was a reassuring statement.

"You did what? When her *cousin* was involved?"

Nick was starting to look worried. "Which part of that was wrong?"

"It's all wrong!" exclaimed Harvey. "It's all so, so wrong! Were her aunts involved?"

"Was it rude not to invite her aunts? The whole thing was Prudence's idea. She likes Ambrose, you see."

"Um. But Ambrose has a boyfriend?"

"She's willing to put up with him," Nick said casually. "If she has to."

Harvey made a face. He felt he now understood how witches operated, and it was horrifying.

Nick continued, even more horrifyingly: "We let Prudence have her way, because she was about to be killed."

"Killed?" Harvey repeated.

"In a . . . witch ritual where the community is meant to consume the flesh of— You've gone a strange color, did you know that? I wouldn't worry. Sabrina put a stop to the whole ceremony."

That calmed Harvey. It made him think of Sabrina starting her club for women's rights and arranging her protest about the cafeteria food last year. Even though she was part of a nightmare world, she was still his girl.

Except she wasn't. Not anymore.

Mrs. Tapper leaned over her daughter. "Harvey Kinkle," she whispered. "Could you stop talking? The movie's getting started!"

Harvey abruptly recalled where they were, and that Linda Tapper was in the seat next to them. Linda still wore braces. Linda was too young for this conversation.

Harvey felt *he* was too young for this conversation.

He shut up and watched the movie. Almost immediately, people were murdered in a variety of horrible ways. Harvey averted his gaze.

Nick whispered: "Are you looking away because the exploding eyeballs remind you of your mortality?"

"No," Harvey said. "I'm looking away because it's gross. Could you tell me when it's over?"

"It's over," Nick reported, and Harvey looked.

It was not over. Harvey made a revolted noise, and Nick cackled. You couldn't trust witches.

Then Nick gave a soft exclamation and rolled up his sleeve. On his arm, burning letters began to appear, as though someone was writing on his skin with a fountain pen dipped in fire. *Attacked by mortals. Come at once—*

"Is this Sabrina?" Harvey demanded.

The letters continued. *Come at once, idiot.*

"Oh," said Harvey. "Prudence. You should go."

"I'm going," said Nick. "This is how to act at the movies, then? I should do it like this?"

"Do everything differently," said Harvey. "I can't stress that enough. You have to think about not attracting attention—"

Nick snapped his fingers. All the lights in the theater went on. The soft buzz of the audience became much less soft. Several seats away, Ambrose Spellman was laughing hysterically. Harvey put his face in his hands.

"Who's your friend, Harvey?" asked Linda Tapper as Nick departed. "He's a total smokeshow."

Harvey looked to Mrs. Tapper for help, but Mrs. Tapper was busy watching Nick leave.

"I think he's a little old for you, Linda," said Harvey. "Are you even old enough to be watching this movie?"

"I'm not the one who looks away every time there's blood," sneered Linda. "Ya big wimp."

"Don't go near that boy, Linda," Mrs. Tapper told her daughter in a distant voice. "I think he's a witch."

"What?" said Linda.

"What?" said Harvey.

The lights went down again. The first thing they saw was blood, spattered across a bedroom wall, a crimson stain that hung like a curtain in front of Harvey's vision.

He looked away. He'd seen enough blood already.

"What did you say?" he whispered to Mrs. Tapper. She shushed him.

Harvey bolted up and ran down the aisle. He fell to his knees by Ambrose's seat.

"Get out of here," he whispered. "People are talking about witches."

White rings widened around Ambrose's dark eyes. His whole body was suddenly coiled to spring. Wincing, Harvey remembered witch-hunters had killed Ambrose's dad. Ambrose must be as terrified of this as Harvey was of magic.

"Why would they do that?" Ambrose whispered back.

He shouldn't mention Prudence getting attacked. Not when Ambrose looked scared.

"I don't know, maybe because Nick can't stop doing magic and calling me 'mortal'?" muttered Harvey. "He's an idiot."

From the seat beside Ambrose, Luke glared. "Nick's the smartest person in our whole school!"

"That can't be," said Harvey. "You guys go. I'll try to catch up with Nick and tell him what's happening."

DANGEROUS MORTAL BEAUTY

December 29, Night
ROZ

There was a strange atmosphere at the movies that night. Roz and Susie stood in line for popcorn, hearing an unsettling buzz on all sides. Roz's head was aching fiercely, as though there were whispers trapped inside her skull. There seemed to be shadows everywhere, lurking in the corners of the room and in people's eyes.

Roz was telling Susie that she wasn't in a party mood this New Year's. She tried to ignore the other people around them. Everybody was whispering, but nobody was talking to them.

Until Billy Marlin strolled over. His nose was red and twice its normal size. Understandably, he seemed to be in a bad mood. When Billy was in a bad mood, Roz knew who he took it out on.

"Growing your hair out, Susie? Thank God. Finally you'll look more like a girl."

Susie flinched. Roz bristled and searched for Harvey, who would help her hold Susie back.

Then she remembered Harvey wasn't here, and it was her own fault.

She secured a firm grip on Susie's arm and shook her head urgently to suggest that a brawl at the movies wasn't the answer.

Susie's face twisted in fury, but she nodded. Her mouth flattened into a straight line. "Can you hear a buzzing sound, Roz? Like an annoying fly."

Roz was so proud of Susie. They go low, we go high!

"I can't, Susie. But that sure does sound annoying. Let's go over there right now."

"Cool!" said Susie. "Incidentally, I'm planning to get a buzz cut. What do you think?"

Roz nodded encouragement. "I think you'll look great."

"Wait," said Billy, who was apparently determined to bother Susie whenever he saw her. He caught Susie's other arm.

Roz contemplated getting the manager.

"Billy!" exclaimed Susie, as if she'd just spotted him. "Somebody punched you in the face! Please tell me who this real-life super-hero was."

Billy scowled. "Why?"

"Because I need to shake their hand," said Susie. "And tell them I'm in love with them now."

Billy scowled harder. "I walked into a door."

"Wow," Susie remarked cheerfully. "Can't believe I'm in love with a door, but here we are."

"Could you let up, Putnam?" Billy demanded.

Susie and Roz both spoke at once.

"*Me* let up—" Susie sputtered.

"Hey, you were the one who started harassing Susie!"

"Anyway!" said Billy. "We've got to band together, even the freaks, against the real threat."

"What threat?" asked Susie. "What band? Listen, Billy, if you're in one band, let me tell you, I'm in the other band. I might even call my band Any Band but Billy's Band."

"Even if the other side are *witches*?" Billy demanded.

Roz went still.

"Absolutely. I'm with the witches!" raged Susie, who couldn't be stopped when she was in a temper. Then she blinked. "Wait, what? Explain now."

Billy opened his mouth to do so, but a woman in a brown coat elbowed him in the side. She was middle-aged and wearing pearls. Roz recognized her from her dad's church, but she couldn't remember her name.

"Shhh," the woman hushed Billy. "You heard them. They're with the witches. I know Rosalind. She's hand-in-glove with that horrible Sabrina creature." She shot Roz a glare. "Your father would be *very* disappointed in you."

A chill passed through Roz. It felt like a ghost murmuring in her ear.

She knew her father and Sabrina's aunt Zelda weren't similar people, even before Roz realized Zelda worshipped Satan. But her dad and Zelda Spellman possessed the same certainty that they were never wrong. When they were about eight, Roz and Sabrina got talking about how it felt, to have the adults in your life expecting you to become the kind of people they already were.

"I don't know what kind of person I want to be," Sabrina had said, swinging on the swing opposite Roz's. "Not yet. But I want the chance to figure out who to be. Do you know what you want to be?"

Roz considered, and said eventually: "Let's be good people."

Sabrina smiled in the dazzling way she did when she was confident she had the right answer. She reached out for Roz so they could swing with their hands linked together.

"Let's be good people," she echoed. "And best friends."

Roz could think dark thoughts about Sabrina herself. She could imagine retribution against witches, but when she heard someone else badmouthing Sabrina, she didn't feel vindicated. Her first impulse was outrage. *Not my bestie. Don't you dare!*

"She's not," Roz said now, unable to help herself.

"Not what?" the woman said. "Not a witch?"

Roz went silent. She wished she could talk to her grandmother, who made everything to do with Sabrina and witches seem so clear, but her grandmother and her grandmother's wisdom were gone. Roz had to be wise on her own. She wasn't sure how. Her head hurt so much.

The churchgoing woman and Billy moved off, heads bent together, talking intensely.

Susie's small face was screwed up in distress. "Should we warn Sabrina? Or her aunts?"

"Warn them about what?" Roz asked. "People always talk. I've heard people call the Spellmans witches before now."

"Not *Billy*," exclaimed Susie. "Not as if they meant it!"

"It doesn't mean anything will happen."

Susie still looked worried. Roz bit her lip.

"If everybody did find out about witches...would that be so bad?"

"What would happen?"

Susie sounded extremely anxious. It was different for Susie, Roz thought. Susie had no reason to be afraid of magic. No witch had cursed Susie's family. Susie thought of witches as friends. Sabrina and her aunts had helped Susie, and Susie would want to help them in return.

Don't let her tell them. The thought was almost a hiss, going through Roz's brain.

That made sense, Roz told herself. Susie was always getting into fights. She could be hurt. It was Roz's job to hold her back. The witches could take care of themselves.

"I don't know what would happen if everybody found out about witches," Roz admitted. "But maybe everybody should. People deserve the truth."

Susie flushed and nodded.

"Listen," Roz continued. "You trust me, don't you?"

Susie's eyes went wide. "Of course."

"That woman talking to Billy goes to my dad's church," Roz said. "I'll ask around and find out what's going on. There's no need to worry Sabrina or her aunts. Keep quiet for now, will you, Susie? I promise, if something bad is happening, I'll stop it."

Susie hesitated for a long time. Eventually, she nodded.

That's her dealt with, Roz thought, and shook her aching head to clear it.

They heard murmurs in the bathroom, and then again as they were taking their seats. Nothing direct, nothing addressed to them, but whispers flew through the air like leaves.

The witches.

The witch in the alleyway.

Something should be done about the witches.

Greendale always was a spooky little town.

They'd picked a rom-com because Roz felt they both needed comfort, sunshine, and unlikely hijinks right now.

The room was packed with people, frost melting off their winter coats. There was so much ice and darkness outside, it was surreal to see the movie begin with a crash of waves and a burst of sunshine. Even if it was false light, Roz enjoyed seeing it.

Until pain shot through her temples, and her vision wavered and betrayed her. All she saw was shadows, and all she felt was panic. Someday soon the shadows would close in and she'd be trapped. She'd never see anything ever again. Because of what the witches had done to her.

If everyone found out about the witches, maybe someone would stop them. Maybe someone should.

Roz tried to control her breathing. She didn't want to scare Susie. Susie had been through enough in the last few days. She should let Susie enjoy the movie.

The walls wavered and loomed in the dark. Roz couldn't stay here.

"Bathroom," she gasped, and lurched to her feet.

She made her way out, muttering frantic apologies as she stepped on and scrambled over people. Even when she pushed the door open, the gray smudges over her vision only paled and didn't vanish.

She groped for a handhold she couldn't find. She shouldn't have come out alone.

Shadows spinning about her, Roz lurched dizzily through the corridor and crashed into someone passing by.

"Sorry!" she exclaimed, clinging for sheer support. "I'm so sorry."

"Why be sorry?" a boy's voice asked. "I'm all for beautiful women throwing themselves into my arms. Right now, I'm otherwise committed and a little busy, but…"

He trailed off. Roz was trying to place his voice. As faces faded out of her sight, she'd been getting better at recognizing people by voices or gestures or certain clothes. Greendale was a small town, and the townsfolk were people of habit.

His voice was distinctive. She couldn't place the accent. She didn't recognize it at all.

Roz realized she was being embraced by a total stranger.

"Hang on," said the stranger. "Are you under a curse?"

What remained of her breath left her as if she'd been hit. She was in the arms of a *witch*.

He guided her and she stumbled, not knowing where he was taking her, until he deposited her firmly in the seats by the door. Sitting down again, Roz felt more secure, but then the stranger touched her face, hands tilting up her chin as though he might kiss her. Roz's heart felt like a caged bird, wild with panic, slamming against the bars.

"Oh, that's a curse all right," he remarked, his tone brisk. "Very strong. Ancestral, is it?"

Roz nodded, barely breathing.

"Nothing I can do about the curse, I'm afraid," he continued. "But I can ease the symptoms temporarily."

Roz sat there, trembling, her fists clenched tight. She felt the stranger come close.

"In the name of the fair," he whispered in her ear. *"Do beauty a kindness. Mercy doth her eyes repair. Help her of her blindness."*

The pain in Roz's temples eased. The shadows were fading and retreating, and her panic with them.

"Thank you," she murmured, stunned.

She still couldn't make out his face. She only heard his footsteps as he walked away. Before he did, he spoke again, his low voice slightly amused.

"Call it a random act of kindness. I've heard everyone needs kindness."

Roz shut her eyes, willing her vision to return. When she opened them, light poured in. Stark fluorescent light, but it still seemed sweet. So did the faces of Susie and, incredibly, Harvey, both emerging from different movies. Harvey was looking around wildly, but he went still when his eyes found Roz.

"Roz," Susie called out. "You didn't come back, so I was worried..."

Susie trailed off upon catching sight of Roz. She felt better, but she must look shaken, because Harvey and Susie came running. Harvey, with considerably longer legs, got there first.

"Are you all right? Roz, is it your eyes?"

He grasped her shoulder gently, studying her face. It was a far less intimate touch than the strange boy's, but the stranger's touch had felt impersonal, and this wasn't. This was Harvey.

She could see him, clearer than she'd been able to for months, the affection and concern plain on his face. Roz almost sobbed with relief.

"I'm okay," she assured them both. "I'm really fine."

Susie was frowning in Harvey's direction. "Were you watching a horror movie by yourself?"

"Uh," said Harvey, "just for a minute there."

Susie made a face. "You don't even like horror movies, Harv. Why didn't you come with us?"

Harvey exchanged an awkward glance with Roz as he climbed to his feet, letting go of her shoulder. "I didn't know if I was welcome."

Susie looked at Harvey as if he was deranged. "You're always welcome, jackass."

Susie elbowed Harvey in the ribs. Harvey grinned down into Susie's face. Roz felt supremely guilty. She didn't want to mess up anything between them. Susie and Harvey had always been total bros.

"Thanks, Sooz. Since I'm here, I'll give you guys a ride home."

"You don't have to," Roz muttered.

"I'm gonna," said Harvey. "You're not even taking one step outside this movie theater when you aren't well."

"How am I supposed to— Harvey, no!"

Harvey leaned down, slid one arm around Roz and one arm under her legs, and scooped her up out of her seat.

Susie whooped and clapped. "Harvey, yes!"

Roz made a fist and thumped Harvey's chest, alarmed both by his closeness and the immediate concern that she wasn't tiny like Sabrina or Susie.

"You can't!"

He gave her his familiar smile, crooked as though he was always torn between several feelings at once. "I can."

He started walking, carrying her easily in his arms and out

into the night. She hadn't known Harvey was this strong.

Susie trotted by Harvey's side, taking hold of Roz's dangling boot and swinging it as though it were her hand. "You heard the man, Roz. Don't worry about it. We've got you."

Hesitantly, Roz clasped her hands behind Harvey's neck.

"Susie's right," she told him in a whisper. "You're always welcome."

He ducked his head and smiled. He always looked surprised when he was happy, and astonished when he was loved. It broke her heart. Roz's dad was no picnic, but she never doubted he adored her. Harvey's dad was so awful, Harvey doubted everything: constantly worrying that he wasn't brave enough, smart enough, that nobody could really like him.

She wanted to kiss him so much. He would never guess. She could never tell him.

Because of Sabrina.

A dark voice in her head whispered: *That witch.*

LET WITCHCRAFT JOIN WITH BEAUTY

December 29, Night
SABRINA

I dreamed I was kissing Harvey on the steps of my house with autumn leaves whirling around us. My new necklace was shining around my throat and his face was shining too, lifted up to mine. My hands curled around his collar as he whirled me off my feet and told me that he loved me, loved me, loved me.

Golden leaves turned to golden lights, a Ferris wheel spinning behind us at the summer festival. Harvey looked up at me, scared for a moment, until he smiled. I promised myself that no matter what, *I* would never hurt Harvey. I would never make him feel afraid.

But you did, said my own voice, as though I'd whispered in my own ear. *He trusted you, and you hurt him worse than anyone else.*

The lights and sweetness of summer dissolved, and I was sitting

215

across from Harvey on a long, dark winter night, telling him what I'd done to Tommy. I heard Harvey's voice break as he tried to understand.

Suddenly I was weeping in the girls' bathroom, telling Roz and Susie what I was, and Roz and Susie didn't turn away as I'd always feared they might. They embraced me instead. I clung to them, my face hidden in Roz's shoulder, my arm tight around Susie's waist. I didn't know what I would do without them.

Then my friends went up in flames. They burned with hell-fire, as the Greendale Thirteen had burned, because of me. I screamed and screamed, but I couldn't change what I'd done. They were lost because I'd tried to hold on to them. They were ashes in my arms.

I woke with a jerk, flinging out a hand. Maybe to shield myself, maybe to reach out. Even I wasn't sure. I hit my hand against the barrier of the window and cringed back from the sudden sharp pain. I must have bitten my tongue because my mouth was filled with the taste of blood.

On the window, where my palm had rested, there was an icy handprint struck against the glass. I stared at the glass and tried not to imagine what would have happened if I were reaching for a mortal I loved.

I stretched and rose from the window seat where I'd fallen asleep, curled up with a book on spells to defy Satan. I paced my bedroom floor. As I passed by my mirror with its frame of white roses, I thought I saw a ghost in the glass.

It wasn't a ghost. It was only me, my face pale as my new hair. I thought again of my golden-haired mother.

I'd always known I wasn't like her. Not really. How could I be? I'd grown up in a house of witches.

I crawled onto my bed, still wearing my fluffy bunny slippers. The next moment, Ambrose whirled in. He was laughing as though some invisible imp had whispered a joke in his ear, though that might be the mouse familiar in his pocket.

"Evening, cousin."

"Not really, anymore."

Ambrose waved a hand. "I was going to talk to you in the evening."

There'd been too many emergencies lately. My stomach clenched with alarm, and my voice went sharp. "About what? Why didn't you?"

My cousin paused. "Because my life doesn't revolve around you."

I bit my lip. "I know that."

"Sometimes I wonder," Ambrose murmured, but his voice was light enough. "I have a whole wildly exciting existence independent of yours. Guess who Prudence called sexy the other day? This guy. She's right, and she should say it."

"I'm happy for you."

"Yes, well. Tonight Luke and I were occupied."

I grinned. "Playing Scrabble, no doubt."

"Let's just say I got a triple word score and leave it at that."

Ambrose swaggered forward, clasping ringed hands around the post at the foot of my bed. He was wearing a bronze silk shirt and leather pants. It was still new and wonderful to see Ambrose dressed to go outside, rather than in fancy pajamas. Father Blackwood had recently lifted his house arrest, and Ambrose was technically only meant to go to the Academy of Unseen Arts and back, but Ambrose never did play by the rules. He was taking full advantage of his new freedom. I figured he'd dragged Luke to the movies this evening. Luke hadn't seemed impressed by the idea of a mortal activity.

"How was the movie?" I asked.

"Cut short," said Ambrose.

"Why?"

His gaze traveled over my face, brows drawing together. "Don't worry about it. What's wrong with you?"

I sighed. "Sorry I was snippy. I did something cool this morning, and I thought I'd feel better about fixing a problem."

I'd done something on my own, for a change. Well, with Prudence's help, but I hadn't dragged my family into my worries this time. I was trying to do better for them. I should feel like a whole new witch, powerful and capable.

But banishing the bad-luck demon hadn't lifted my mood. I leaned against my pillows and stuffed toys and recalled how I used to lean against Harvey when I was studying, my back fitting against his chest. He'd stay like that for hours, a warm support for me, whispering occasional sweetness in my ear.

I missed him so much.

"Come now, cousin," murmured Ambrose. "Don't be sad."

He climbed onto my bed like a cat, headbutted me in the stomach, and then put his head in my lap. Salem meowed, outraged at this usurping of his place, and sprang from his seat by the window onto the pillow by my head. I was suddenly surrounded by loving company, my familiar and my cousin tumbled on my hawthorn-flower bedspread. I scritched Salem between the ears, ruffled my fingers through Ambrose's densely curly hair, and smiled down at him. He grinned at me, upside down and bright.

"Maybe this information will cheer you up. There was a boy at the door for you earlier."

I sat bolt upright. "Harvey?"

"Sorry, Sabrina sweet. Nick Scratch."

Even the sound of his name was like a slight, pleasant electric shock.

Ambrose waggled his eyebrows. "Not so bad to think of him coming calling?"

I hit Ambrose's shoulder. "Why didn't he come in?"

"Auntie Hilda wouldn't let him in," said Ambrose. "Thinks he's mad, and bad, and she doesn't want to know. Don't blame me, Sabrina. I was occupied with Luke—I didn't know our auntie was turning away prime specimens."

I tucked my bunny-slippered feet under me and pulled thought-fully on one of Ambrose's ears.

"Oh, well. It doesn't matter. Like we said before, he's not serious, so I'm not interested."

Ambrose lifted himself up, curling his arm around one knee and leaning back against the wrought-iron footboard. He was always in motion, my cousin. Nobody could pin him down.

"Maybe he's more serious than we figured."

"Why would you say that?"

Ambrose made a noncommittal sound. "Maybe I made the wrong call. Rakes can reform. They do in Auntie Hilda's romance novels all the time. Maybe the guy's looking for a connection."

"Maybe he's looking to hook up with everyone in school."

"Can't he have both?" Ambrose laughed while I belabored him with my fists. "Cousin. I'm just saying. You're worth being serious about. Maybe he is. Maybe you should give it a try."

I looked out the window, the woods black behind the gauzy white of my curtains.

"Of course, I was also thinking I'd been too hard on our little Harvey," declared Ambrose, who was considerably shorter than Harvey. "He's going through some rough stuff."

I frowned. "So you're saying I should give Nick a shot, but then again make it work with Harvey?"

"Can't *you* have both?" asked Ambrose, laughing as I picked up my pillows and began throwing them at him.

He defended himself, deflecting the pillows with little spells so they struck me from the side when I was unsuspecting. Salem gave a low, eerie growl because we were both vexing him. We left Salem's pillow alone.

"You never know," said Ambrose. "Maybe they'd get along."

I scoffed. "Oh, sure." Then I hesitated. "I do miss Harvey. Every minute. But I don't want to mess up his life again. He couldn't bear it. He insisted that he'd be the one to—to put down what was left of Tommy. I hate that he had to do that because of me. I only wanted to bring Tommy back to him."

Ambrose seemed unusually solemn. Which, for Ambrose, meant that his wild wicked smile flickered.

"I know you did, cousin. If it was me, in Tommy's place—if it was you, in Harvey's—"

He'd never talked like this, comparing us to mortals. It was almost encouraging that he could empathize with Harvey to that extent, but the idea of losing him was too horrible. Ambrose was like a hummingbird, never resting anywhere long, but I reached out across a space of moonlit blanket and grabbed hold of my cousin.

"Don't," I said into his shirt. "Don't even say it."

"This scenario does posit me being a miner," Ambrose murmured, back to joking around. "Wouldn't be caught dead in one of those hats."

I laughed, muffled into the silk. Ambrose brushed a kiss against my hair, pulled back gently, and produced a folded piece of paper from his pocket.

"Cheer up, now," he said. "Nick left a note. Auntie Hilda threw it away, but she unwisely didn't burn it and even more unwisely told me, so I rescued it for you. Sweetly trusting soul, Auntie H."

He placed the note in my hands. It was folded parchment, with flowing black script across it. I'd heard there was a way for witches and warlocks to write notes to each other that would show up on their own skin, but paper seemed more sensible. I was using my skin for other things.

"Am I the best wingman, or am I the best wingman?" asked Ambrose. He rose from the bed, tugging a piece of my hair as he did so. "Give Nick some thought, cousin. Mortals are passing sweet, but they pass, and their sweetness passes with them. I never want you hurt, and a mortal will hurt you."

"Even if he loves me?"

But Harvey didn't. Not enough.

"Especially if he loves you," said Ambrose. "Love hurts worse than anything. I'll leave you to read your letter."

A note from Nick. I wondered what he had to say. Probably not "Do you like me? Circle yes or no."

I unfolded the note, and read the words struck across the page.

Look outside your window.

I scrambled out of bed, threw open the window, and stared down into moonlit snow and dark eyes.

"Nick?" I said in amazement. "What are you doing out there?"

"I need to talk with you," Nick shouted. "It's urgent."

"Then get up here!"

I slammed the window shut and turned in a frantic circle, trying to kick off my bunny slippers before Nick could teleport into my bedroom. This left me unbalanced as I spun, came face-to-face with Nick, and almost tipped right over. He caught me, arms drawing reflexively around my waist, and studied me as though very pleased with his catch.

"Hello there, Spellman."

I was leaning against his chest, which seemed like a dangerous place to be. Hastily, I set my hand against his shoulder, then stepped back with an exclamation as I felt his skin beneath the fabric.

"You're freezing, Nick. You should have come inside."

"I was trying to respect your boundaries," Nick told me. "I have to say, I find boundaries annoying. And chilly."

I frowned. "I don't want you to get sick because of me."

Nick smiled. "I won't. You're too used to mortals, Sabrina. There isn't much that can hurt me."

I winced at the mention of mortals and took another step back from Nick. He leaned against the window and watched me retreat.

"What was so urgent you couldn't tell me tomorrow?" I asked.

"Banishing the luck spirit didn't end the spell corrupting the mortals," Nick answered, his voice suddenly all business. "Prudence was attacked outside that tea shop today."

My hand flew to my mouth. "Oh no. How is she?"

"She's fine. I went to the Academy, but your aunt Zelda was there. She wouldn't let me see Prudence. Said she was sleeping, that a pack of vicious mortals went after her."

Nick's mouth twisted, eyes going even darker as they met mine. The same rage I saw in him rose in me, hot as hellfire. I was scared I might destroy my friends, but I was eager to destroy my enemies.

"We should meet with Prudence tomorrow morning," Nick said. "I don't know what's going on, but it *must* be connected with the bad-luck spirit."

I nodded, trying to think. "When Prudence and I banished the spirit, she said a lot of things. My teacher Ms. Wardwell told me not to listen, but...the spirit said, 'The witch-hunters will rise. The prince will come.'"

"The witch-hunters," Nick repeated.

"Harvey," I whispered. "His *dad*. What if his dad attacked Prudence? Harvey might not be safe in the house with him. I have to go to Harvey."

Harvey might be in trouble again. Because of me. My head reeled as though I were on a carnival ride, the lights of the Ferris wheel blurring in my vision. Then came a touch that steadied me.

Nick had my elbow cupped in his hand. He was holding on to me. "I'll go," he said firmly. "I can teleport."

I let myself relax into the warm certainty of his grasp. "Sorry for freaking out," I whispered. "It's just—I hurt him."

"You didn't mean to."

I nodded, dragging in a breath. "You're right. I'm too used to mortals. It was so easy for Tommy to slip right out of my hands. I can't stop worrying."

"There's no need," said Nick. "I'm here now."

There was a loose strand of hair in my eyes, cutting a moonlit-white bar across his dark intent face. I tucked the hair behind my ear, then leaned forward on a sudden warm impulse and kissed his cheek.

"I'm so happy you're here, Nick."

When I drew back, I was surprised by the look on his face. It was a smile I hadn't seen before.

"I'm . . ." he said. "I'm happy too."

I smiled back at him. "Can I ask you something before you go?"

Nick nodded.

"My father," I said. "I know you've read all his books. What made you like them so much?"

There was a silence as Nick considered the question. "I came to the Academy hoping to learn a secret," he said at last.

"What secret?"

"How to make sense of the world." Nick shrugged, one-shouldered, and smirked. "Simple, right? But nothing Father Blackwood taught me helped. Then I found Edward Spellman's books. He wrote about women and mortals and the secrets of power in a way I could understand. Reading his books was like reading a language I hadn't realized anybody but me knew. His books finally made sense of the world. So I guess he changed the world for me."

"Oh," I murmured.

Quietly, Nick said: "I think you must be a lot like him."

"I always hoped I was," I whispered. "Thanks, Nick."

"Anything for you, babe."

Nick winked and teleported away. Where he'd been, there was only night waiting outside the window.

I went and sat on my rumpled bed, crunching Nick's note in my fist. Salem meowed and climbed into the crook of my arm. I dropped the note and hugged him.

"Should I tear that boy Nick's head off for you?" Salem's goblin whisper came rustling through my mind like the wind in the woods. *"I could. Easy as if he were a mouse."*

"No," I whispered back. "I like Nick's head where it is."

"That boy is rude," Salem continued disapprovingly. *"At least the mortal has nice hands. Gentle. But then he's a spectacular idiot who does not understand a word I say. Neither is worthy of you. Let us embrace splendid solitude and go live together in a hut in the forest."*

I cuddled him close. "I will take these wise words under advisement."

He indulged me and purred like the cat he wasn't, not really. The low rumbling hum acted on me the way stroking did on Salem, soothing and steadying. I nestled into my tumbled pillows, under my blanket, around the companion who'd chosen me and would never leave me.

Tomorrow I'd meet Nick and Prudence and figure out what needed to be done.

I closed my eyes. In the dark I relived the moment of terror in the moonlight, when I'd clung to my cousin at the mere idea of what had happened to Harvey happening to me.

Everything, in that silver instant, had gone clear. There was no need for me to mope around reproaching myself any longer.

If I'd lost Ambrose, if I'd lost Aunt Hilda or Aunt Zelda, I would've torn purgatory to shreds to get them back. I would have brought hell to ruin. I would have burned heaven to the ground.

Everyone told me I'd gone too far with what I'd done to bring Tommy back, but I disagreed. I hadn't gone far enough.

I wasn't like my mother; I was like my father. He wasn't scared of power. He was High Priest. He'd changed the world of witches. I could change the world too.

Maybe my mortal friends couldn't help me right now. If I was more in control of my magic, if I changed the witches' world enough so my friends would be safe there, then I could let them in.

For now, perhaps we needed some distance. I could give them that. Especially since I'd found a friend among the witches. Nick was here now.

I was done doubting myself. Whatever new danger threatened, I would handle it by facing it, and never, ever backing down.

Harvey would be horrified at the idea of me in danger, but I wasn't scared. Nothing seemed frightening compared to the idea of losing someone I loved. Whatever trouble came, I always had Spellman ground to make a stand on. If I was sorrowful or lonely, my cousin would come make me laugh, my aunt Hilda would make me a thousand treats, my aunt Zelda would hold me fiercely as I cried and never let go until I stopped. I was a Spellman witch, and I was done fearing the year to come.

I couldn't imagine being in Harvey's place, couldn't imagine being so alone. Salem purred to me, and in the attics above my cousin danced, and down the hall lined with cursed shoes, my aunts bickered. The sounds of home lulled me to sleep.

We all need company in the dark.

AIM TOO HIGH FOR ANY MORTAL LOVER

December 29, Night
HARVEY

Harvey was sketching in his room when he heard the thunderous knocking. He dropped his charcoals and ran, but his dad got there first. By the time Harvey reached the front door, Nick was already tucking an empty vial into his jacket.

"Hi, mortal," he said. "You, go away."

"What are you?" his dad muttered in a dazed voice as he began to shamble away.

Cold air blew through the open door. Harvey thought it might snow again soon. There was a tang to the freezing wind that lingered in Harvey's mouth. Like tin. Like blood.

"What did you say?" Harvey demanded. "Nick. Did you hear him?"

Nick sneered in his dad's direction. "I wasn't listening. I don't pay much attention to mortals. Certainly not that one."

Harvey stepped into his father's path. "Dad. Did you ask Nick what he was?"

"Can't you tell what he is?" his dad demanded. "Are you blind as well as stupid?"

His father's eyes focused as they fell on Harvey, narrowing with dislike.

Harvey flinched.

"Don't look at him," Nick ordered. "Go to your room and stay there."

"No, *wait*," said Harvey, but his father was already leaving. He rounded on Nick. "Stop enchanting my dad!"

"Seems a poor idea," said Nick. "A pack of mortals went after Prudence earlier. Your father's a witch-hunter. He's a problem that needs to be managed."

Harvey hesitated. "Is Prudence okay?"

"She is. Zelda Spellman's with her."

That was a relief. Harvey couldn't imagine anyone getting past Sabrina's aunt Zelda.

"Okay," said Harvey. "That's good. Back to my dad..."

"Right. Let's revisit the idea of killing your father," Nick suggested.

"Let's not!" said Harvey. "This isn't funny."

Usually there was laughter somewhere to be found in Nick's face. Not tonight. The icy calm made him seem a sinister stranger. It made Harvey repeat to himself, with horror gathering like dark clouds, his father's words: *What are you?*

What had Harvey invited into his home?

When Prudence threatened Harvey, he'd decided she was

kidding. She wore her bravado like armor, like her winged eyeliner, that much was clear. He told himself she didn't mean it.

But maybe she did.

That guy Luke wanted to hurt Harvey. Prudence said she'd kill him, and Nick hadn't cared at all. Witches killed people. Harvey knew that.

Every time he thought he could accept magic, he was reminded how dangerous magic could be.

"Nick, my dad is *all I have*," Harvey said desperately. "Please be joking."

Nick's face was cold and strange for another instant. Then he scowled. "Fine," he snapped. "Let's say I'm joking. You're annoying. I want lasagna right now."

"It's past midnight. I'm not making you a lasagna," said Harvey.

They ended up in the kitchen with Harvey pushing a plate of heated-up fajitas Nick's way.

Nick looked at the plate, took the purple vial out of his jeans pocket, and tapped the vial against the side of the table without unstoppering it. Then he met Harvey's eyes and put the vial away.

"Listen—" Harvey began, taking the chair across from him.

"Can you please take note of what I just did!" Nick protested. "It was meaningful."

Harvey sighed. "Wow, I'm so touched you trust me not to poison you when I'm *obviously* not going to poison you."

Nick was somehow eating two fajitas at once. "Earlier, you were saying you punched one of those idiot mortals?"

"Yeah," Harvey said warily.

He wondered whether it was Billy and his goons who'd targeted

Prudence. Trying to bully Prudence seemed an obvious bad idea, but Billy was no brain trust.

Nick made a thoughtful sound. "And that's not like you. Have you gone to that new tea shop in town?"

Everyone said that place was great. Harvey wasn't sure himself. Roz had spilled tea on her éclair, so Harvey'd switched desserts with her, but the tea-soaked éclair hadn't been good.

"I didn't eat much. Were you thinking of taking Sabrina there on a date?"

Nick propped his elbow on the table as he stared through the window into the dark woods. "Probably not."

"She'd prefer Dr. Cerberus's," Harvey advised. "Her aunt Hilda works there."

"Hilda will poison me," muttered Nick. "But I'll take Sabrina to Dr. Cyborg's if she wants."

Harvey scoffed. "It's not called Dr. Cyborg's."

"It's not called Invisible Academy either." Nick grinned. "How about I remember the important stuff, Harry?"

Harvey rolled his eyes. "How about you listen to me for a change, Nick? It's not only my dad talking about witches. My neighbor was too, and people at the movies. Something's going on."

"No kidding, farm boy," said Nick. "A bad-luck spirit was running the tea shop. I think she influenced the mortals who ate there."

"Why would a bad-luck spirit run a tea shop?" Harvey demanded. "Magic is so weird! Why would some luck demon want people to know about witches?"

"She was a witch-hunter before she was a demon," Nick said, his voice mild. "So I intend to keep your father under control."

A witch-hunter. Harvey felt the same guilty unease he had when Prudence looked at him, when he found out witch-hunters killed Ambrose's dad.

"It's good that you didn't eat much at that place," Nick continued. "You seem mostly unaffected. Sabrina and Prudence banished the luck demon, and that should have solved the problem, but it didn't. We're going to work out why. For now, stay home. I'll monitor your father, and we should ward your house. I'll sleep here tonight. We should put lemons in the doorways."

"Garnishing my doors will hold off the tea shop demon?" Harvey muttered. "Magic definitely isn't getting more normal."

As Nick conjured lemons into existence, and they hung them in the doorways like bright yellow mistletoe, Harvey remembered that Roz had eaten her éclair. He couldn't point a warlock Roz's way. He'd call Roz tomorrow. He'd figure out what he could do.

"Nick, I don't want to stay at home," said Harvey. "I want to help."

Nick, standing on a chair to hang up a lemon, gave him a look equal parts superior and amused. "Against a demon? You'd die, and Sabrina would be sad."

"I'm not helpless," Harvey insisted.

Nick's smile filled with evil mockery. "You're our delicate little teacup."

"Seriously," said Harvey. "If people are in trouble, I want to protect them."

Nick teleported off the chair rather than hopping down. He was suddenly standing with his hands on the chairback, meeting Harvey's eyes, his point made.

"Seriously," Nick said. "You're a mortal. What could you possibly do?"

Harvey wished that he had an answer. He didn't. He knew despair was written all over his face.

"Listen," Nick continued. "Do you have any idea how lucky you are? Sabrina sang to you. She loves you. She wants to protect you. Nobody ever came to save me. Do you know what I would give to have what you have?"

"Have it, then," Harvey snapped. "I don't want it. That's what *you* want. This works out great for you."

His brother had loved him, protected him, and died. Sabrina had lied. Harvey couldn't bear the idea of being loved that way any longer. Love like that was love for a feeble child who could never give anything in return.

There was a terrible silence. Nick seemed at a loss for words.

Arguing with Nick was pointless. Nick didn't care whether Harvey lived or died. Sabrina was the one who wanted to protect Harvey. He had to convince her he could be something more than a burden.

He didn't know how.

Even if he talked to Sabrina, it wouldn't change the fact he was mortal. *He can do everything for Sabrina, better than you could dream*, Prudence whispered in his memory. *You have nothing a witch needs.*

Frustration and misery coiled darkly in his chest, wanting to lash out, but Nick hadn't done anything wrong. Nick was doing his best, for Sabrina. Harvey didn't want to be cruel to Nick.

"You said..." Harvey cleared his throat. "You said nobody came for you."

Nick's response made Harvey remember days out hunting in the woods. Nick had the look of a wild thing, suddenly trapped.

"I don't want to talk about it!"

"For what it's worth," said Harvey, "I wish someone had come."

He went to his room and started looking through the shelves at the top of his wardrobe till he'd produced a graphic T-shirt and some sweats, along with the blanket and pillow he'd given Nick last time. He tossed the blanket and pillow on the floor by his bed, and tossed the clothes to Nick, who caught them.

"You can stay. Sleep in these. Captain America's my favorite, but I figured you're more of an Iron Man guy."

"Wow," marveled Nick. "What are you talking about?"

"There are a lot of movies," said Harvey. "It'd take too long to explain."

Harvey went to the bathroom and changed into sweats and the Nightmare on Elm Street shirt Sabrina had bought him. He wore the shirt for comfort, because it was from her, but tonight there was not much comfort to be found in the thought of creeping horror in a small town.

Among his drawings of monsters and adventures and super-heroes, there were hundreds of sketches of Sabrina, Roz, and Susie through the years. When Harvey came back, Nick was looking through them, fanning the sketches out in a sheaf in his hand.

"Sabrina's so little! Did she always wear the hairband?"

"For as long as I can remember," said Harvey. "She likes to be tidy."

Nick held up the picture Harvey had been drawing when Nick knocked on the door.

"I saw 'Brina earlier," Harvey explained. "In Dr. Cerberus's."

Drawing the picture of her, in her bright red coat with her snow-white hair, had felt as soothing as stroking her cat. Drawing her made the shadows crowding his mind dissolve.

Nick regarded the picture affectionately. "This is great."

Harvey grinned. "Thanks."

It was nice of Nick to take an interest. Harvey's grandpa had suggested burning his drawings once.

"'Brina is not a great nickname," continued Nick. "'Brina sounds like something you would call a fish."

Apparently, it would kill Nick to be nice for more than one minute.

"It's a pet name! Clearly, witches don't understand pet names."

Nick looked annoyed. "I call her Spellman sometimes."

"Her last name?" asked Harvey. "Like you're both dudes at a British boarding school?"

Nick made a face at him, and then got distracted by another picture.

"That other girl." Nick tapped a picture of Roz when she was younger and wore her hair in twists. "I saw her in the movie theater. You like her?"

"I love Roz."

Nick turned over another sketch. "She wants you."

Harvey said, "I don't understand."

"What's to understand, mortal?" Nick raised an eyebrow. "She wants you."

He couldn't fathom half the weird stuff going on in Nick's mind. "Uh . . . no, she doesn't."

"Uh..." Nick mimicked Harvey's voice, "yes she does. I saw you two from outside the theater. One look at her, looking at you, and I knew."

"She's my *friend*!"

"So? What's the problem? I think she's attractive. Don't you think she's attractive?"

He'd never thought much about anybody being attractive. He'd met Sabrina when he was five, on their first day of school. He'd been too scared to talk to the other kids. His dad said he was always saying dumb things. She'd spoken to him first, and he'd stared mutely, overcome with adoration.

It had always been Sabrina for him.

Now he tried out the idea of Roz being attractive. He was surprised to find it easier than he would've thought. The prospect of someone good-looking who he didn't know at all left him cold. But if he thought about holding Roz in the movie theater, he could appreciate the soft warmth of her in his arms, the cloud of her sweet-smelling hair against his face. Being close to Roz in whatever way, admiring her in whatever way, didn't seem impossible. He'd always loved her so much.

"Roz is beautiful," Harvey said quietly. Then he shook his head to clear out the weird thoughts. "But there's nothing like that between us!"

"Then why sweep her off her feet?" Nick asked. "That was a move."

"That was not a move! Why does everything with witches have to be sexy-weirdness city? Shut up and go to sleep, Nicholas."

Nick settled on the floor after a period of minimal grumbling. Harvey was finally able to rest.

Relentless questions about personal matters aside, it was okay to have someone else there. He hadn't been sleeping well. Night after night, he closed his eyes and he was in the mines again, watching them collapse around him. He was terrified, and Tommy was shoving him. Tommy—who'd never raised his voice to Harvey in his life—Tommy *screamed* at him to *run, Harvey, go*—

Usually he woke himself up calling for his brother.

Tonight, he was woken by something else. It was a sound of distress, but not Harvey's. He levered himself up on one elbow and blinked around the darkened room, trying to work out what was going on.

"No," Nick said from the floor. "*No.* I don't want—"

Harvey slid out of bed and onto the floor. He shook Nick. "Wake up."

Nick went from sleep to a snake-strike recoil, shuddering back with his hand thrown up to protect himself or to cast a spell, until he saw there was no threat.

"Hey," said Harvey. "What's wrong?"

Nick coughed painfully, as though there were sulfur fumes caught in his throat. "Nothing. It's an honor to be visited by Satan when you sleep."

"Oh yeah?" Harvey's voice almost failed him. "Sounds great."

In the moonlight Nick's eyes were like those of a ghost you might see through your window, scratching at the glass to be let in. He looked haunted, not honored.

Nick said, tightly controlled: "He checks up on me sometimes, about doing his bidding."

"What exactly is Satan asking you to do?"

Nick shook his head, and then pressed his forehead down against his knees. Harvey hesitated, and patted him on the back.

Nick looked up. "It was lonely in the mountains."

The expression Nick wore was awful. Harvey nodded uncertainly.

"When I dream..." Nick said. "It seems lonely in hell. I don't want to go."

Gently as he could, Harvey said: "You don't have to go, Nick."

Nick settled back down on the floor, throwing an arm over his eyes. "I want to stay here. With Sabrina."

Harvey couldn't imagine wanting to stay in Greendale, but he'd never considered hell as an alternative location.

He let Nick sleep, went to his desk, and sat looking at his drawing of Sabrina in the moonlight.

People all over town were talking about witches. Satan was telling people what to do in their dreams, and Sabrina would never let anyone tell her what to do. Every day Greendale grew more dangerous. It was as if their town was built on a volcano, and they were slowly realizing the clouds in the sky were smoke.

Something had to be done.

Nick's voice came back to Harvey, clear and cold.

You're a mortal. What could you possibly do?

EVERY TATTER IN MORTAL DRESS

December 30, Feast of the Virgin
Martyr Anysia, Morning
HARVEY

He woke the second time to morning light and knocking on the door, and thought confusedly that it must be Nick, when Nick made a sad sound from the floor. "Make the noise die."

Witches weren't great at mornings. That made sense.

Harvey climbed out of bed and went to answer the door. He found Susie on his porch, bundled up for the cold, short hair ruffled and nose bright pink from being nipped by the icy fingers of the wind.

"Oh, hey, Sooz," said Harvey.

Susie grinned up at him. "Hey, Harv. Can you come out for a bit?"

"Yeah!" Harvey said. "Of course. Uh, wait a second."

If he went to his room to get changed, Susie would follow him to chat, and be surprised by the witch on the floor. Harvey eyed his own bedroom door apprehensively.

Susie noticed.

"Harvey...do you have someone in your room?"

"Have you ever met me," said Harvey, instead of answering.

Susie nodded. "Good point. Silly question. Hey, why are lemons hanging on your doors?"

"When life gives you lemons..." said Harvey, and ducked into the bathroom, where he changed into yesterday's clothes and emerged to grab his coat. "Where did you want to go?"

"Actually, Harv..." said Susie. "I was hoping we could grab your dad's guns and shoot some cans. My dad would notice if there was a gun missing from the cabinet, he keeps them locked up, but I know you guys have them lying around loose."

It was an unusual request. Susie got pretty stern about gun safety and protocols on the farm. Harvey had relayed this information to his dad, but his grandpa and his dad were both very firm on keeping guns close at hand by the door. Harvey had never understood, not until he learned about the witches.

Susie looked awkward, which Susie didn't usually. Not around him. They'd known each other so long, they had the comfort of a favorite worn piece of clothing. Harvey remembered the first day of school when Sabrina was off "sick"—probably being taught Latin or some other witch thing—and they were all little. He was still new to school, and he'd figured that without Sabrina he wouldn't be welcome. He lurked by the bicycle shed until Susie and Roz came to find him. Roz gave him a hug around the middle and told him they'd been worried. Susie grinned up at him, monkey face mischievous, and said: "What'd you think you were doing? Wow, you're a dumbass."

When they were eight, Sabrina and Roz got matching bracelets and talked about being *best friends*. Harvey was crestfallen, since he wanted Sabrina to pick him first for everything, but he knew Roz would be a better best friend. Anyway, probably being a boy meant he was disqualified as a best friend.

Sabrina and Roz had gone up ahead on the path home to tell each other best friend secrets, and he'd stared wistfully after them. Then Susie kicked him in the ankle.

"Hey," Susie said. "Guess we'll be best friends, huh?"

Harvey'd grinned, shocked and charmed, and they fist-bumped to seal the deal. They didn't get bracelets, but they had a best-buds handshake. Sometimes they practiced shooting together, or he helped design Susie's costumes. He knew Susie wouldn't have chosen him. Susie'd got stuck with him, but Susie was a good sport about it.

"Sure," Harvey said now. "Let's go shoot some cans."

They got the guns and went out into the woods, to a fence where a lot of guys shot cans. They collected some cans, rusted and with rainwater leaking out of the bullet holes, and set them up.

Harvey let Susie shoot first. Susie was a good shot, farm-raised and bred. Susie wouldn't be appalled at the idea of shooting a deer.

Susie got a couple of cans and Harvey whistled. He almost wished he'd brought his sketchbook with him, but it was difficult to draw Susie. Susie always seemed slightly upset when he tried. Harvey'd tried several different ways, but he clearly wasn't getting it right.

Susie kept shooting, intent and intense. When Susie's gun was out of bullets, Harvey offered the one he was holding.

Susie was breathing hard. "Do you not wanna shoot?"

"I'm good," said Harvey.

When both guns were out of bullets, Susie went and kicked the fence so all the cans toppled off. Then Susie turned back to him.

"You're probably wondering where I've been the last few days."

"Oh, well, I thought…" said Harvey. "I thought since Sabrina and I are broken up, you and Roz might be putting some distance between me and the group. Which I totally understand."

Susie stared. "Wow, you're a dumbass."

The incredulous tone of Susie's voice made Harvey smile. He still had one friend.

"Remember my job as a Christmas elf?" Susie asked.

"Sure, I came to see you," said Harvey. "You looked totally cool."

Susie'd always loved costumes, for Christmas or Halloween or a party. Whenever Susie wore them, Harvey'd noticed Susie looked relieved. He guessed sometimes it was nice to have a break from being yourself.

"Yeah, my boss turned out to be a demon and tried to kill me," said Susie. "Sabrina and her aunts saved me, but Greendale's crawling with darkness, turns out! Ghosts and witches and demons and—and everything."

Susie's chin trembled. Not for the first time, Harvey was struck by absolute terror for the handful of people he loved who were still living.

"I'm so sorry, Sooz," he said. "I shouldn't have got into my own head about this. I should've been there for you."

"You have your own stuff going on," said Susie. "I know that. But, Harv…that's why I wanted to come shooting with you. Sabrina and her aunts won't always be there to protect me. I got lucky, but—I have a feeling bad things are coming. We must be able to defend ourselves. And Roz. Harvey, she can't shoot. She can't *see*."

Harvey stared at Susie's tiny form, standing firm holding an empty gun. He thought of Roz helpless in his arms. Loathing for magic swelled up in him, and the burning urge to gather them up somehow, every beloved one in danger, and protect them.

Susie was scrutinizing him anxiously. "Harv? You with me?"

Harvey cleared his throat. "I'm with you. We're in this fight together."

They did the best-buds handshake. Susie grinned and punched Harvey in the arm. He took his gun, and they walked back to the house side by side. He reloaded the guns before he put them up by the door, like his dad always said.

While he did so, Susie sat, legs tucked up, on the sofa opposite the door. When he turned, he saw Susie's fists were clenched, and he was puzzled. Susie was always ready to fight, but there was nothing to be fought right now.

"I wasn't just sitting in my house shaking because of a Yule demon," Susie said. "I've been doing a lot of thinking. I didn't get my hair cut because I was hiding under the covers, and my dad said that if my hair grew out... I'd look great, like Sabrina and Roz. He meant I'd look girly."

"You're a great girl the way you are," Harvey said instantly.

There was a pause.

"But..." Susie said, very low. "What if I wasn't?"

"Huh?" asked Harvey.

Then realization struck. Susie *was* great, there was no question about that...so it was the "girl" part Susie was having problems with.

People in school noticed that there was something different about Susie. That was why they always acted like jerks. Their group had noticed too. They hadn't been certain what those differences meant. Roz, Sabrina, and he had held a few discussions, in which Roz talked about the possibilities: being butch, being nonbinary, being several other terms Harvey hadn't understood. He'd done some reading and got worried about pronouns.

"Could we start an LGBT support group?" Roz had asked at one conference. "To let Susie know we're supportive no matter what."

Sabrina wrinkled her nose in thought. "But is there anybody out at Baxter High? We don't want Susie to feel singled out before Susie's ready to tell us anything. Statistically, some of the other students *must* be gay."

There was Carl, but Carl most definitely was not out. His eyes wandered in the locker rooms. Mostly he looked at Billy, but a few times he'd glanced at Harvey. Once Harvey accidentally caught Carl's eye, watching Harvey while he took his shirt off. Carl went white as ice and froze. He'd looked so scared. Harvey didn't like to see anyone afraid. Harvey told him quietly that it was fine, and Carl called him a freak and stormed off.

Carl wouldn't be joining a support group anytime soon.

Since Harvey wasn't a total jerk, he couldn't mention this, so he'd sunk with silent awkwardness into his chair while Roz and Sabrina discussed the matter, and decided they should wait until Susie was ready to tell them.

He'd figured it didn't matter, since Susie was his friend

regardless, but suddenly he realized what Susie had to say mattered a lot. He might get something wrong and hurt Susie—all because Susie was right and he *was* a dumbass.

"Have you…uh, talked to Roz about this?" he asked now, praying Susie had.

Whether it was that Susie wanted to be called "they" or that Susie wanted to be a guy or however it worked, Roz would know. Roz would explain it to him, so he wouldn't mess this up.

"Not yet. *You're* my best friend," said Susie.

The hard knot of misery and loneliness in his chest eased. Everything inside him went soft at the realization that perhaps he had been chosen, after all.

"I *will* tell Roz," continued Susie with gathering determination. "And Sabrina. And my dad."

"Susie!" Harvey exclaimed. "Will you be safe?"

Susie stared. Sometimes the others did that, when Harvey seemed too afraid of parents and what they might do.

"Yeah," Susie muttered at last. "Don't worry. My dad would never hurt me. I'm scared he won't understand. I don't know if I understand completely myself."

Susie was trembling. It was unbearable that Susie, fierce courageous Susie, might be afraid the way Carl was afraid. It was unbearable that Susie might be afraid in any way at all.

"I'm glad you told me," murmured Harvey. "I don't really… know what to say."

Susie sniffed. "I'm still working it out too."

Harvey walked over to where Susie sat, and then knelt on the floor. He took Susie's hands and looked up into Susie's small valiant face, framed with the gold of winter sunlight streaming in through the many-colored diamond panes. He thought he might know how to draw Susie now.

"When you do work it out, tell me. I'm sorry you can't count on me to get it right away," he said. "But you can count on me to love you."

Susie nodded jerkily. Harvey reached out, folding Susie's fragile body against his own in a careful hug. Susie's hands closed on the back of his shirt, and he ducked his head down onto Susie's shoulder, blotting out tears against the material of Susie's shirt, soft worn flannel just like his.

Soon Susie would tell Roz, and then Roz would explain what to do. For now, this felt like he hadn't messed up too much. For now, this was enough.

When Susie leaned back, Harvey rubbed his eyes surreptitiously with the edge of his sleeve.

"Are you crying?" Susie asked suspiciously. "Harv! You're such a girl."

Harvey shrugged. "Makes one of us."

And Susie laughed. Hearing Susie laugh was the first time in a long time that Harvey felt things might be okay.

When Susie went home to do farm chores, because Susie didn't laze around on the holidays like the rest of them, Harvey made some coffee and brought it to his room. Nick was awake, though barely, sitting at Harvey's desk. He didn't look upset by nightmares from Satan, but he *did* look upset about mornings.

"Good morning, beautiful," Nick said to the coffee.

"It's not really morning anymore," Harvey told him.

Nick didn't appear to be listening. He was absorbed in his coffee.

Harvey was distracted with worry over something else. If Nick was awake, there was a chance he'd heard Susie's personal business.

"Did you happen to hear anything that was going on outside?"

"Not much," Nick muttered sleepily. "Just you proclaiming your love for yet another person. You love everybody."

"I love five people."

Nick's eyes widened over the rim of his cup. "Oh Satan, that is *so many people.*"

Harvey had been thinking of five as a pathetically small number. It was all in how you looked at it.

"What time did you say it was?" Nick asked, voice sharp. "I have to leave immediately."

He was suddenly a whirlwind of panic, seizing books and black jeans and drinking his coffee the whole time. Harvey was impressed he didn't spill the coffee and wondered if Nick was using magic.

Nick pointed at Harvey with the hand not holding the coffee cup. "Don't leave the house. That's an order, mortal."

"That's funny," said Harvey. "I don't take orders from you."

"I mean it."

"So do I," Harvey told him.

Nick seemed amused. "Satan keep you."

"I'd rather Satan lose me."

Nick grinned a Cheshire-cat grin as he teleported away.

"Uh," Harvey called after him. "You stole my shirt?"

There was only silence in his home and melting snow outside. Harvey went to get his jacket. Nick Scratch couldn't tell him what to do.

THE WITCH AND THE VICTIM

December 30, Morning
PRUDENCE

Prudence arrived early at the darkened classroom where she was supposed to meet Nick and Sabrina. She glared around at the stuffed owls and maps of the underworld. She was not in a good mood.

She was no longer dazed or distracted by Zelda Spellman and hope for the future. She wanted to hunt down the mortals who'd dared touch her, and she wanted to know what the heaven kind of mess Sabrina had gotten them into this time.

She sat at a desk, studying her face in a compact mirror shaped like a black swan. Her face was flawless as usual, but it didn't cheer her.

This was not the time for Plutonius Pan to approach.

"Hi, Prudence, I was thinking..."

"Doubtful," muttered Prudence.

"I was hoping you'd put in a good word for me."

"Neither of my sisters would ever waste a moment's time on you," Prudence told him briskly.

"Oh, I wasn't thinking of your sisters," Plutonius said. "No offense, but they are orphans. Hardly the infernal connections I'm searching for."

Prudence lowered her compact very slowly.

"And of course I'd never look so high as you!" Plutonius said hastily, as though any flattery would work on Prudence after he'd insulted her sisters. "You're the daughter of the High Priest, and everyone's sure you'll be acknowledged soon! But I do think I have a chance with Sabrina Spellman."

Prudence scoffed.

"She's the daughter of the former High Priest and a Spellman, I know that," Plutonius continued, blinking his pale-fringed eyes. "But she's—well, you know, Sabrina has many disadvantages. There's the unfortunate matter of being half mortal."

As Plutonius spoke, the door opened gradually behind him. Prudence watched as Nick slipped silently into the room and observed his face as Nick heard what Plutonius was saying. She grew amused.

"Poor Sabrina," Prudence cooed.

Encouraged, Plutonius nodded. "If you look at it another way, I'd be doing her a favor. Sabrina doesn't really have the full figure a warlock looks for in a witch. And she's wayward, and not in the excellent wanton way. Needs a firm hand."

It would be hilarious to see Sabrina dispose of Plutonius, but

Prudence didn't think Sabrina would get the chance. There were cities burning in Nick's eyes.

"And do you think that hand will be yours?" Prudence asked sweetly. "Are you not aware that Nick's interested?"

"Nick *Scratch?*" Plutonius Pan's voice was awed. "What, you mean seriously interested? He could do better."

Prudence controlled her urge to laugh.

"I'd say he seems serious, yes."

"Wow," breathed Plutonius Pan. "Of course it would be an honor and a privilege to share with Nick—"

At this point, Nick grabbed Plutonius by the back of his collar, shook him like a rat, and threw him to the ground. A period of intense spell-casting and high-pitched screaming commenced. Prudence hummed cheerfully to herself.

Increasingly violent magic raged through the room, purple lightning reflecting against the darkened windows. There was a pool of blood on the floor.

Prudence grew bored and stepped outside. Several minutes later, Nick followed her. He was yawning.

"Oh Lucifer, son of the morning, it is too early for this," he muttered.

Prudence was used to being awake until dawn with her mortal boy toys, then rising to see to the baby. Warlocks were weak.

"Did you kill him?" Prudence asked, out of mild interest.

"I did not," said Nick, with a dark, disappointed glint in his eye. "Sabrina and the mortal wouldn't like it."

"How would they ever find out?"

"Honesty's important, I hear," said Nick.

"Reading those terrible books is giving you terrible ideas."

Nick was still yawning. There was blood on his cuffs, which only improved his outfit. Prudence was amazed by how hideous he looked.

"You doing all right?" He squinted at her, seeming uncomfortable about asking. As he should be.

"What?" Prudence sneered. "Obviously. Ugh, are you trying to express concern for me? How disgusting. Worry about yourself, you're the one associating with that witch-hunter. Your life's about to be hit by a second meteor."

This seemed to surprise and confuse Nick, as though he hadn't noticed their lives had descended into writhing turmoil since Sabrina started at the Academy.

"How do you mean?"

"Think about it," said Prudence. "Long-term couples usually have something in common. Sabrina and the witch-hunter are both an innocent face painted on a bag of *demented snakes*. Consider Sabrina. 'What's that, aunties? You ask only that I follow our unholy traditions? Let me defy the Dark Lord and try to bring down our whole way of life!' The witch-hunter's no different. 'What's that, Sabrina? A world of dark magic I never suspected? Guess I should shoot my zombie brother in the head!' Ordinary boys take longer to order at a drive-in than he did to jump to that one. He is *not* a normal mortal."

He camouflaged his true nature well, but she knew the strange lights in the mortal's eyes were fiery torches. Prudence still had nightmares about seeing dark blood on her sister's throat. She couldn't have hurt Agatha herself.

The baby-lamb doe-eyed witch-hunter had put his brother down within minutes.

Nick said obstinately, "He told me he wants to help—"

"Protect people?" Prudence murmured. "That's how it starts. A witch-hunter is born a sword in the hands of angels. They are holy fire, and we were made for burning. That's what Sabrina chose. She is crazy as heaven. So is he. I was attacked because of her yesterday. I don't need her other half anywhere near me. Once this mess is sorted out, I'll be keeping my distance from Sabrina."

Nick smirked. "Not me."

You could never truly know someone. You go to school with a guy for years, then he breaks out a fetish for suicide in a hairband.

Prudence was even more revolted when she saw a tiny smile start on Nick's lips. There was no mischief or malice in it at all.

"Is Sabrina coming down the hall behind me?" Prudence asked wearily. "Ugh. I can see you, thinking repulsive thoughts."

"I was considering something the mortal said to me," said Nick. "About Sabrina. I was thinking—it might be possible. It really might."

Prudence didn't know what he was talking about and she didn't want to know. That was why witches lived apart from mortals. The mortals got into your head, made you weak, then burned you at the stake.

Sabrina strolled up to them, smiling and wearing a buttoned-up sweater with a pattern of daisies on it, one thousand demented snakes in a daisy-patterned bag. "Hi, guys! Prudence, I hope you're okay."

Prudence didn't deign to respond. Sabrina glanced toward the door of the classroom they'd just exited.

"Also, I thought we were meeting in the room."

Prudence noticed that Nick Scratch, for someone who was all

about honesty, stepped in front of the door very fast.

"We were saying goodbye to a friend in there. Plutonius Pan. He's transferring schools. He's very broken up about it."

Sabrina accepted this without question. "I don't think I know him."

Nick stared down into her innocently puzzled face. "You don't? I thought you liked him."

"Me?" Sabrina asked. "No idea who he is. Honestly? I think all the guys here and their warlock supremacy schtick are awful. The only one I like is you."

She took hold of Nick's sleeve and began to pull him down the corridor, toward the library. Nick glanced at Prudence, pointed at himself and then Sabrina, and made a victorious fist. Prudence sneered and followed.

When they reached the doors of the library, Sabrina paused and gave Nick a once-over, which would have been promising if she hadn't seemed so perplexed.

"Nick, do you mind if I ask what you're wearing?"

Nick looked down at the garish and abominable shirt he was wearing. His expression became one of sheer horror.

"It's not what you think!"

Sabrina was gazing at him in fascination. "So you're a big superhero fan?"

Nick was silent for a long moment, then claimed: "Yes. My favorite is . . . Captain Iron."

"Your favorite is Captain Iron?" Sabrina repeated.

"He's the best one."

Prudence had no idea what Nick was talking about, but she could see Sabrina was desperately trying not to laugh.

"I can't argue with you. I see you know too much about superheroes."

Nick nodded with obvious relief.

Sabrina smoothed her fingers along the sleeve of Nick's jacket. "Thanks, Nick," she said. "For trying out mortal things. That side of my life is important to me. I really appreciate you taking an interest."

"I *am* trying," Nick admitted. He was giving Sabrina the revolting look again, intrigued and hopeful, as though she were a box full of mysterious treasure.

Sabrina frowned. "Is that blood on your sleeve?"

"We can't talk about my clothes all day, Sabrina," Nick said hurriedly. "We have to work out what's going on with the mortals! If Zelda wasn't there, Prudence could have been really hurt."

Prudence yawned. "Mortals hurt me? Unlikely."

"I don't know why banishing the dark spirit didn't work," said Nick. "I do believe the library will help us."

Nick pushed Sabrina inside the library. Prudence followed, and as they gathered around a low, rune-marked table, she filled Sabrina and Nick in on exactly what had happened yesterday.

"There's an excommunicated witch I know," said Sabrina, who hung about exclusively in low company. "She said the Dwy Ferch Geg was the handmaiden of a prince of hell."

There was a pause. A stone gargoyle, its eyes popping out, stared at Sabrina. Prudence couldn't blame it.

"That seems like something it would've been important to mention *yesterday*," Prudence said in a strangled voice.

"It doesn't matter," said Sabrina. "We still had to fight the dark spirit, no matter what. But perhaps if we could figure out which prince of hell, we could figure out what's happening to the mortals."

Nick leaned forward, face intent on the puzzle. Prudence knew that expression from when he wouldn't shut up about riddles or history, even when the Weird Sisters threatened him. Nick was fascinated, Sabrina was on a mission, and only Prudence was concerned by the oncoming storm of disaster.

"I think the mortals who ate in the tea shop are affected," Nick theorized. "She must've poisoned their minds through her food. Poisoned luck, minds, and food. Surely the prince of hell would be one of the princes associated with poison."

"We need every book we can get on poison," said Sabrina instantly. "And we should look into the Dwy Ferch Geg more. We need to find everything we can on poison and Welsh mythology!"

They went forth and collected all the books they could. Nick built a book tower on the table in front of him. He'd read his way through most of the library, so some of his books were already annotated. He went faster than Sabrina or Prudence could, but it was Sabrina who stopped reading first and said, in a voice laden with portent, "Oh."

Prudence did not like the sound of that "Oh."

"What?" she demanded. "What did you find?"

"Um . . . an account of a massacre," Sabrina answered slowly.

Actually, that "Oh" had been fine. The sound of the word *massacre* was much worse.

Prudence laid her hands flat on the table. *Stay calm*, she reminded herself, *and blame Sabrina Spellman for everything.*

"What does it say about the massacre?" she asked evenly.

Sabrina smoothed the vellum pages of the large tome before her and began to read.

"Long ago in the old country, a prince of hell opened a door and let his handmaid through. Poison spread across the land through food that tasted sweet as lies. It is an old, old poison, the poison of hate. Hate for the witches came to those who had eaten and then to those who had not."

"That fits. The mortals who ate in the tea shop are the first affected," said Nick. "Then all the mortals in Greendale start believing in and hating witches."

Sabrina kept reading. *"The handmaiden feeds on misfortune, and the prince feeds on strife. At the end, the whispers turned to shouts, and the poison worked fast. On the first day of the end, the memories of their ancestors returned to the mortals. The knowledge of witches returned and terrified them, and with the memory of witches came certain tricks the mortals once used against us, which they have now forgotten."*

"When's the end?" Prudence demanded.

"This is just a guess," said Nick. "But I think the end might be nigh."

"On the second day, hate came to the witches. And on the first moment of the last day, the prince came. The mortals rose and hunted us as they did long ago. Witch-hunters led with steel and fire in their hands, and we died in droves. The prince fed on the war, grew strong, and swallowed the town whole. The prince killed witches and mortals alike.

"The morning after the massacre, when dawn remade the day, the hatred of the remaining mortals passed like a dream. They forgot what they had done. They woke from a dream of hate to find their hands bloody. We knew better, we few witches with the power to resist the demon's enchantment. We held the hatred in our own hearts at bay, escaped, and remembered. We leave this warning for future witches. There is no way to kill a whisper. There is no

magic stronger than hate. When the witch-hunters rise, when the prince comes, run for your lives."

Sabrina closed the book.

Prudence rose from her chair. "I've heard enough! This is serious. We should tell my father."

"No!" snapped Sabrina.

"I realize you're allergic to authority, Sabrina—" Prudence began, exasperated.

Sabrina waved off this known fact. "It's not that. What would Father Blackwood do if he heard the mortals might transform into a witch-hunting mob? He'd kill them!"

"Oh, will somebody dispose of the mortals that might massacre us?" Prudence sneered. "What a pity."

Sabrina subjected Prudence to an appalled and judgmental stare. Prudence was tempted to slap her.

"It's not the mortals' fault! They've been poisoned. Oh no, I went with my friend Roz to that place. What if the tea affected her? I can't let anything happen to Roz!"

Sabrina's priorities were wild.

"Didn't you attract bad luck in the first place because you had to help out this friend of yours?" Prudence demanded. "You've done plenty for her. She and the other mortals can fend for themselves! My concern is for my own people. You signed the Book, Sabrina. They're your people too. You owe us your allegiance, not them."

Sabrina was wearing her spit-in-Satan's-eye expression.

Nick had been silent for some time. Now he looked up from his own book.

"I don't mind helping the mortals, if Sabrina wants," he said mildly.

"Oh, what a surprise," Prudence sneered. "Nick Scratch, thinking with his—"

"But I think you should both listen to this right now," continued Nick. "I'm reading about how exactly a prince of hell might be called to the world. If a lesser demon connected to a prince is banished, her going leaves an opening for him. When the membrane between the worlds is weakest, at the point where two elements can be crossed, the prince can step through."

Prudence pressed her fist to her mouth, smearing lipstick against her knuckles.

Even Sabrina went slightly pale. "So you're saying that by banishing the bad-luck demon, Prudence and I summoned a prince of hell? The prince might come in a matter of days?"

Not me, Prudence wanted to scream. She'd only wanted to help Sabrina with a little problem and win Zelda's favor. She'd been trying to smooth the path of her own future.

"We thought the problem was a luck demon, but now a prince of hell may consume Greendale and the enchanted townspeople may rise up and kill us all." Nick started to grin. "That escalated quickly. You're the most interesting person I know, Spellman."

Whenever Sabrina was involved, there was disaster. Prudence should've known better than to get mixed up with Sabrina's schemes. She'd been a fool.

She couldn't possibly go to her father and tell him she'd done this. Her father wasn't Zelda Spellman. He wouldn't shield her. He wouldn't forgive.

Sabrina's mouth went flat and determined.

"We have to stop the prince," she declared. "Before the mortals

rise up in hatred. I must call Roz and make sure she's okay. And—
and the book mentioned *witch-hunters*." Only then, speaking one
name, did Sabrina's lip tremble. "Harvey."

"Nobody cares!" Prudence shrieked.

From the shadows of the library came a severe shushing noise.
Prudence went quiet. Cassian the librarian could be terrifying, and
she had enough problems right now.

"Your mortal is safe," said Nick. "You asked me to take care of
him and I will."

Sabrina turned to Nick, laying her hand on his bloodstained sleeve.

"Please do," she said. "Please help him."

Nick rose, inclining his dark head toward her. "You only have to
ask." He paused. "I'm getting changed first. I can't be seen this way
in public. Not even for you."

Sabrina glowed up at him as though he was her hero. Prudence
wanted to break every arched window in the library. She was surrounded by lunatics bent on their lunatic path. Sabrina wanted to
fight a prince of hell. Nick wanted Sabrina to keep looking at him
like that, though Prudence didn't know how much of the look was
even for Nick and how much for Sabrina's precious witch-hunter.
Maybe Sabrina didn't know herself.

Prudence couldn't throw things, and she couldn't stop Nick,
and she actually had to fall in with Sabrina's latest mad scheme.
Somehow, they had to work out when the end was coming and what
to do when it did.

They had to fight a prince of hell. The alternative was telling her
father she'd messed up, and Prudence couldn't do that.

He'd never let her take the Blackwood name if he knew.

LOVE OPENED A MORTAL WOUND

HARVEY

The snow was melting, showing bare stones and earth, and the bridge before Harvey seemed less like ice and bone and more like something he could cross. Now that he'd talked to Susie, he thought he could see a path ahead.

Harvey drew in a deep breath and set foot on the bridge. Then he envisioned what lay ahead. Before he even realized, he was stumbling back, being a coward *again*.

As he stumbled he was grabbed from behind, his arm caught in a tight grip. Harvey almost dropped his flowers.

"There you are, mortal!" Nick snarled. "I've been looking for you everywhere! Where in hell's name did you go?"

"I went to town," Harvey answered shortly.

Nick wore an imperious and offended expression. "I told you to stay."

"Yeah," said Harvey. "But I'm not your dog."

There was a short pause. Nick ran a hand through his wind-blown hair, scowling. "If you keep being like this, Sabrina will worry."

"Funny thing," said Harvey. "I'm not Sabrina's dog either."

Nick sneered, as though that was an unbelievable statement instead of the simple truth. The turmoil Harvey'd felt in Dr. Cerberus's twisted like a storm beginning in his chest. That was how witches thought of mortals. Pets if they were lucky. If not, pests to be put down.

"Are you feeling—odd?" asked Nick, scrutinizing him.

No, Harvey told himself. Sabrina wasn't like that, and he was almost sure Nick wasn't either.

There was a shadow on Nick's face that seemed akin to concern, though it was hard to tell with Nick. His hair and his constantly black clothes were disheveled, as though he'd been running around.

Greendale's crawling with darkness, Susie's voice said in his mind. He remembered Nick's face, shocked open by pain and seeming younger than usual, in the shadows after dreaming of Satan. Susie was right. There was too much danger in their town, and too many people being hurt. They had to band together, not break apart.

Harvey sighed and shook his head.

"Do you want to punch somebody again?"

"Oh, you never know," Harvey joked, then saw the shadow on Nick's face deepen. "No, all right? I don't want to hurt anyone. Chill, Nick."

He wanted to protect people. He couldn't do that if he retreated whenever he was afraid.

"I'm always chill," Nick murmured, leaning back against the post where the bridge began. "I'm noted for it."

Harvey stared at the bridge, then glanced toward Nick.

"You're not afraid of anything, are you?"

"I tell myself that every day."

"Will you come with me somewhere?" Harvey asked.

Maybe Nick could help him be brave.

"Is it to your home, where you should stay and be safe like a good mortal?"

"I'll go there afterward," said Harvey. "Come with me now."

Nick seemed to notice the flowers Harvey was carrying for the first time. "Are you going to make up with Sabrina? She's not home."

Harvey shook his head. "I'm not going to see Sabrina." He looked at the river running below the bridge. The sound of the water running filled his ears like a roar.

"Are they—for me?" Nick made a face.

Harvey's eyebrows rose. "Dude. Don't be weird. They're not for you."

Nick seemed relieved. "I think it would be weird too! But Prudence says mortals do it all the time."

"Prudence, huh," said Harvey. "Another person I have no desire to give flowers to. Look, just don't be weird for five seconds and come with me. And . . . if I try to turn around, don't let me."

"Am I supposed to stop you with magic? Or violence?" Nick asked. "Either's fine." He smirked. Harvey might have smiled back, if he hadn't been so terrified.

"Try an encouraging nudge," said Harvey, his voice distant in his own ears, over the roar.

He set his hand on the steel rail of the bridge and gripped it tight. Nick glanced at him warily but didn't comment. Harvey walked across the bridge and down the path, with Nick dark and silent as a second shadow beside him, until they reached the railings and saw the spire of the church in the distance.

Nick cleared his throat. "I can't go in there. It's holy ground."

"That's okay," said Harvey. "I should do this last part by myself."

He reached out a hand to open the gate. Even now, a step away, he almost lost courage.

Nick and Ambrose were both mad at him for returning Sabrina's Christmas present. He was mad at himself too. Sabrina's gift had been magic pencils. Such a small thing, and so sweet.

Only Harvey couldn't sleep with them in the house. Whenever he thought of magic, he thought of his brother. Sabrina'd brought Tommy back wrong, and said she'd stop Tommy with her own hands. Her small hands with their ferocious grasp, the hands that had taken Harvey's on their first day of school. The hands Harvey had kissed a hundred times, the little hands he loved.

He couldn't let her do it. So he did it. He'd never loved himself the way he loved Sabrina. It didn't matter if he hated himself.

He'd loved five people, his whole life. He could count them on one hand. Every time he imagined reaching out for a magic pencil, trying to draw something beautiful, he thought of what he'd done. He gave the pencils back. He couldn't cross the bridge.

He was here now. The time to be brave was now.

He opened the gate of the churchyard and went inside. He found his way through the graves to the tombstone for the one who belonged to him. He stood there, reading the words struck deep into the stone. *Thomas Kinkle, Beloved Son and Brother. Rest in Peace.*

Perhaps he was at peace now.

"Hey, Tom," Harvey whispered. "You must have wondered why I didn't come before. I-I'm sorry. I couldn't. I'm here now."

He didn't know what else to do, so he knelt and laid the flowers down on the grave. He remained on his knees. Harvey often had to stoop to talk to people, but never Tommy before. His big brother had been taller than Harvey.

His big brother, the hero of his childhood. He was all the things Harvey wasn't. Tommy was the type of person who mattered. He never let anybody down. Just being with him made you feel better. He was brave enough to face anything. He was ready to love people and ready to fight for them. He was everything a hero should be.

Harvey covered the name on the stone with his hand, but it was still there. So he stroked the name instead, as he'd stroked Sabrina's cat, trying to comfort himself.

"I guess…I was having a tough time, Tommy," he said softly. "Like the poem you told me about, the one Mom's college friend read at her funeral. You remember."

He looked at his own hand, touching his brother's name. Five fingers, for the five people he loved. The hand he drew with, the hand that picked up the gun. These were the only hands he had. He had to use them. He had to live with what he'd done.

"'*Down, down, down into the darkness of the grave,*'" he recited, struggling with the words, with the fragment of a poem he could recall. "'*Gently they go, the beautiful, the tender, the kind…I know.*'" He leaned his forehead against the gravestone and whispered: "I know."

The winter wind, blowing cold on the hot tears running down his face, made him realize he was crying. He put his arm around the grave marker, looping it tight around the stone, as he'd fastened his arm around his brother's neck a thousand times. He pressed his forehead against the place where Tommy's name was written and howled, sobs grating in his throat, shaking his whole body so he had to cling to the stone or fall to the ground.

"I'm sorry. Oh God, Tommy, I'm so sorry. I didn't know what else to do."

He could picture what Tommy would say: *Hey, nerd. It's okay.* Tommy always told him everything would be okay, but Tommy was gone now. Harvey was what was left. He had to do something, be something, make his life worth something, or his brother had died in vain. He had to survive this on his own.

He fumbled in his pocket and took out the cross that Tommy had worn around his neck, then scrabbled for a moment in the dirt. He buried the gleaming bit of metal in a shallow grave.

He whispered, "This is yours. I'll leave it with you."

Tommy wasn't here. Harvey knew that, as he knew Tommy hadn't really been there when Sabrina sent Tommy's body shambling to Harvey's door. The last time he'd touched his brother, his real brother, was down in the mines that always terrified Harvey, as though he'd known one day that place would take away the dearest thing he had. He remembered the hell of dust and rocks, and his brother's hands on him shoving Harvey toward the world outside.

He laid his hot, wet face against the cool stone. "I bet you're worried about me, huh?" he murmured. "You always were. You can quit worrying now, do you hear? I'll be okay."

He knew one more thing, down to his bones. Tommy would've thought it was worth the sacrifice, his life for getting Harvey out. Somehow Harvey had to make that true.

He kissed the word *beloved*, graven into Tommy's tombstone, as he'd kissed Tommy's cold forehead while Tommy lay sleeping on his bed. Before Harvey aimed the gun.

Then he rose. "Bye, Tommy," he said quietly.

He turned and left the graveyard, wiping his face with his sleeve. Nick Scratch was still waiting outside, his back turned, leaning against the churchyard fence. He looked to Harvey when Harvey came out.

"You were crying," he said in a subdued voice.

"Nothing gets by you, Nick," said Harvey.

He made for home. Nick fell into step with him.

"You seemed . . . very upset."

"You sure you're the preeminent genius of Invisible Academy?" Harvey asked.

"I think it's time to stop loving your brother," said Nick, with sudden decision. "It's not doing you any good, is it? Cut it out."

Harvey scrubbed at his face roughly with the back of his sleeve. "Not really how love works. You'll see."

"I don't want this!" Nick snapped. "I'm not doing this. Look at you. Love wrecked you. Love is garbage. Why love anybody?"

Harvey shrugged, helpless. "You love someone—to just love them. Sometimes you have to let it wreck you."

Nick made an exasperated sound in the back of his throat. The bridge was easy to cross from the other side. They followed the path through the trees leading home.

Harvey remembered something. "Here, maybe this will help."

He took the book out of his jacket. Nick stared as if he didn't know what books were. That was strange, since Nick definitely knew what books were.

"What?"

He put the book in Nick's hands, since Nick hadn't taken it.

"I went to town to buy the flowers," said Harvey. "So they'd be nice. I passed the library, and I thought of you. It's a book on the typical development of social bonds in different cultures through history, and it's more recent than my mom's books. Do you not want it?"

He reached to take it back.

Nick took a step away. "Hands off, grabby mortal. I'm keeping it."

"Well, you can't keep it," said Harvey. "That's not how library books work."

He tried to get it back, but Nick waved a hand and several shadows and tree branches waved in between them. The shadows and crawling sensation of magic opened a pit of horror in his heart, but Harvey swallowed the dread down. Nick's magic wouldn't hurt him.

"I was outside your house that night," Nick said suddenly. "The night when you—dealt with your brother. The Weird Sisters were coming to finish him. I stopped them. I wanted to let Sabrina do things her way. Should I—not have stopped them?"

It hadn't occurred to Harvey that night could have been worse. At least, at the last, he'd been able to choose.

"I'm glad you stopped them. Thanks," said Harvey softly. He

meant for that night, and for coming with him today: all of it. "You're a good guy."

Nick's eyes cut away. "I'm really not."

He was. And, maybe, they were friends.

As they reached home, Harvey gathered courage to ask: "Have you found out anything more about the enchantment on Greendale?"

"Mortals don't need to know," Nick said loftily. "Mortals need to stay home where it's safe and hear about how the witches handled it later. I'll check in on your awful father, restrain him if necessary, then go."

Maybe they weren't friends.

There was a silence as Harvey regarded Nick's disdainful face, the absolute arrogance he carried himself with even when he was only leaning against a wall in Harvey's house and fussing with a book. Possibly Nick didn't know how bad he sounded. Possibly he didn't care.

"That'd be a no to everything you just said," Harvey remarked coldly. "Hang on."

He left Nick flipping through his new book and went to the bathroom, where he splashed water on his face until the fact he'd been sobbing uncontrollably was less obvious.

Then he went back out to find Nick in the kitchen, already drinking a cup of coffee.

"Thanks for making this," said Nick. "I require it at all times, but especially when I have a night of intensive study ahead."

Harvey stared. "I didn't make it."

"I did," announced Harvey's father. He moved past Harvey and into the kitchen.

His step was the heavy one Harvey always dreaded, the tread that meant he was angry.

"Nick," Harvey said urgently. "You didn't test the coffee. Did you?"

"Oh, unholy *f*—" Nick began.

He was cut off by Harvey's dad, taking a chisel out of his belt and slamming it into the side of Nick's head. Nick went down hard. Harvey stared at the uplifted chisel, the dark shine of blood on metal.

"Oh my God," he whispered. "Dad."

"He's a witch, Harvey!" his father growled.

There was something unfamiliar about his father, the shine of his eyes odd, the movements he was making uncoordinated in a different way than when he was drunk. It was as though he was sleepwalking.

He sounded very awake when he told Harvey, his voice rapid and furious: "He's a witch, like the old stories your grandpa used to tell when I was a boy. I had nightmares when I was a kid, about how the witches would come back, but today the dreams are different; they're not like dreams at all. Today I dreamed—I dreamed of how we used to fight them. The stories were true, Harvey. The witches are real, and they're here in our town. We never got rid of them."

"You never will," Nick ground out between his teeth.

He pulled himself up off the floor, knuckles white on the back of a kitchen chair. His face was pale and his eyes were black with murderous fury. He lifted a hand and snarled a spell.

Nothing happened.

Harvey's father laughed a strange frantic laugh. "I dreamed it. The herb we used to give them so they couldn't use the powers the devil sent them. I put it in his cup. They can wreak such evil, Harvey, but we can stop them."

He punched Nick in the face and then laughed again.

"There's nothing you can do, witch."

Blood was running down Nick's cheek in a vivid crimson stream. When he snarled, red stained his teeth. "I'll show you what I can do."

"Dad," Harvey breathed. "Nick—"

"Oh, stop standing there whining," his father snapped. "If you're going to be useless as usual, go to your room."

"Yeah, go to your room, mortal," Nick agreed. "You don't need to see this."

Nick, bleeding and enraged, very clearly intended to kill Harvey's father with his bare hands. His father, even more clearly, intended to murder Nick for being a witch. *They can wreak such evil*, he'd said, and Harvey knew they could.

He could see why a witch-hunter would go after a witch. He could see the temptation of the witches being the powerless ones, for a change. Nick was used to relying on his magic, and Harvey's father was strong when he was angry. Harvey's dad would win.

"If you want to be useful for once in your life, Harvey," said his dad, "get the gun."

So Harvey did.

He went to the front door and picked up the gun, its weight familiar in his hands. His mind was cold and clear as it had been the last time he'd used it, when there was absolutely no other choice.

Nick watched him, eyes narrowed, face guarded. His father gave Harvey a brief nod of approval. "Give it here."

Harvey said, "No."

His dad threw him an irritated glance. It was almost comical, how ordinary and dismissive he was being with Harvey when he was planning a murder. "What do you think you're playing at? You can't shoot a deer. Give me that gun before you hurt yourself with it."

Harvey aimed the shotgun.

"I'm a very good shot," he said. "Tommy taught me. Cup."

He shot. The coffee cup exploded into black liquid and shattered fragments, white as bone. Nick and his father sprang back in different directions, which was probably a good idea. It wasn't safe to shoot in the house.

"Hat," said Harvey, and fired again.

His father's miner's hat, hung up on its hook, spun with a bullet dead center and fell off the hook to the floor.

"What target should I pick next, Dad?" Harvey asked. "Nick, get behind me."

Nick didn't move. He was staring at Harvey with his eyes gone wide. Harvey understood this was a scary situation, but Nick wasn't helping himself.

"Are you with me, Nick?" Harvey asked.

Nick murmured: "Yes."

Nick came prowling cautiously forward. His dad tried to follow. Harvey fired again. He jerked the gun aside a crucial fraction of an inch, but not much more. The bullet passed very close by his father before it shattered the window and let in the cold air. The blood-stained chisel fell from his father's nerveless fingers.

"We're leaving," said Harvey. "Don't follow us."

Nick stopped at his side, so Harvey took a step forward, to shield him. His father was staring in baffled fury, and Harvey could see the twin desires struggling on his face. He wanted to kill Nick—and hit Harvey.

Harvey looked down at his father and shook his head.

They left. Harvey took the gun with him.

"Come on," Harvey told Nick. "You won't be able to teleport yourself to Invisible Academy. Get in the truck. I'll take you."

Nick complied. There was silence but for the purr of the engine until they came to a fork in the road and Nick said to go left. As far as Harvey was concerned, they were driving into the wild depths of the woods, but he figured Nick knew the way.

It was a strange path, barely wide enough for the pickup truck. The moon seemed caught in a prison of thorns overhead, white rays playing in wild bright flickers as though to dazzle Harvey's vision and stop him from seeing. Invisible Academy, indeed.

When he stopped the truck, he looked toward Nick, who was sitting still with white moonlight in his open eyes. It was possible Nick was in shock.

"Will you be okay from here?" Harvey asked. "You can just go inside, right, and sleep off whatever herb it was. Then you'll have your magic back."

"Yeah," said Nick. "Should be fine."

"Cool," said Harvey.

He waited for another while.

"You should test your food and drink with those spells from now on," Harvey said. "I'm sorry. I didn't understand what could happen. How do you feel? He hit you pretty hard."

"I know that, mortal," Nick drawled, the usual edge surfacing in his voice like a shark fin cutting the water. It was probably a good sign it was back. "I was there."

"Should I have taken you to the hospital?" Harvey asked. "I thought you'd want to go to the Academy."

"Yes," Nick said instantly. He still didn't get out of the truck.

"Do you need help getting inside? How's your vision?"

Nick waved off the question as though it were an irritating fly. "Harry, I've had worse than this a thousand times. Do you intend to go back to that house?"

Harvey laughed. He leaned forward against the steering wheel, resting his chin on his folded arms.

"I really doubt Invisible Academy wants a mortal scholarship kid."

Nick thought for a moment. "Sabrina—"

Harvey'd imagined taking refuge at Sabrina's sometimes. Not lately.

"No. I'm going back to my home, okay? My dad was—he was being a witch-hunter. I'm not a witch."

"He's never hurt you before?"

Harvey was silent.

Nick bared his bloody teeth. "That's what I thought."

"I'm still going back," said Harvey. "Don't act like people don't get hurt in the Academy. I know they do. You're going back to your home and I'm going back to mine. Go inside where it's safer, at least."

He gestured for Nick to go. Nick opened the door of the truck at last, and then instantly turned back around.

"When can I come back?"

"Back?" Harvey asked. "Back to—to my house? To the *murder house*? Why would you want to do that?"

Nick shrugged. "I left my book there."

Harvey raised his eyes to heaven. "My dad will be out with his friends tomorrow, nerd. You can get your book."

"All right." Nick climbed out of the truck, leaning an arm against the roof to look inside. The mocking gleam was back in his eyes. "Hey, farm boy? Prudence says you're out of your mind."

"What?" Harvey gasped. "Prudence? Force-feeds people truth potions Prudence? Death threats Prudence? She's a psychopath. I'm totally normal."

Nick tapped on the roof of the truck and smiled brilliantly at him. "Crazy as heaven. She was right."

He was gone then, a shadow in his black clothes heading for a shadowy edifice with staring windows, a building that kept trying to slip out of Harvey's sight and become a mausoleum farther off among the trees.

"What a jackass that guy is," Harvey muttered to himself, and drove home.

He opened his front door, very cautiously. When he didn't hear a roar of fury, he walked carefully to the kitchen, where the cold winds were blowing through the shattered window.

His dad was sitting at the table with his head in his hands. When Harvey came toward him, he looked up.

"Did that really happen?" he murmured, sounding half asleep. "Harv . . . ?"

"I'm here," said Harvey.

"Your grandpa used to tell me such stories," his dad muttered. "Greendale was a mountain once. Then the angel fell, and green grass grew over the scorched earth, but there was never a mountain again.

We took the land, but we didn't know what we were taking. The earth was still black under the grass. The witches were here, Satan-touched red in their eyes and red on their hands, and laughing. Laughing. I was a puny kid, before I got my growth. I used to have nightmares about them, the wicked witches. Toughen up, your grandpa used to say."

His father wrung his big hands. Black dust was ingrained in every line on his palms, from the mines. It couldn't be washed off now.

"If I had a few drinks, it stopped me thinking of the laughing. Your mom said we wouldn't tell you boys those stories. Enough horrors, she said. But the black earth of this town, it got to her. She was riddled with sickness, the doctors said. It was so fast. Like evil magic. And you were always this shivering spineless kid, the worst of me, as my Tommy was the best of me. So scared of everything, and you made me think of being scared. No matter what I did, you wouldn't toughen up. And you would look at me, the worst of me but with your mother's eyes, reproaching me for—I don't know. I kept drinking. But the laughter didn't stop, in my head. It never stops."

Harvey knelt on the floor, amid the broken glass and the shards of porcelain. His dad was almost clawing at his own hands. He'd hurt himself. Harvey held his father's shaking hands still, looked up into his father's face, and saw he was terrified.

Maybe he'd always known, deep down, that his father was scared like he was. Maybe that was why he could love his father, the way he couldn't love his flint-eyed grandpa, no matter how much he tried.

"You were always such a weakling," his dad said. "I thought this town would *eat* you. But it ate my Tommy instead. And that thing came back, and it wasn't my Tommy. It was the witches' creature, in our house, and the drink didn't help. Nothing helped. I prayed for it to go away. Someone got rid of it. Tommy didn't do that to himself. Not with the shotgun, he couldn't have. So who—who?"

Harvey went cold, staring up at his father. His dad reached out his rough hand and touched Harvey's hair.

"There was nobody in the house but you," he whispered. "But you couldn't have done it. You poor pathetic wimp. My scared baby. You'd never have the guts. Would you?"

Long ago, Harvey used to take his drawings to his dad wishing for approval, hoping his dad would praise him the way he praised Tommy.

His father's hand touched Harvey's hair almost tenderly. He'd hit Harvey in the face with that hand. He'd wished him dead instead of Tommy. It didn't matter. Harvey'd known, for years, what his father thought of him. He shook his head and thought: *Don't love me for that. For anything else, but not for that.*

"Oh God," said his father. His shoulders seemed to collapse in on themselves as he sagged forward. "I'm so scared. I've always been so scared. Where is God? I wish this was a dream. It feels almost like a dream. Is it a dream, Harv? Let it be a dream."

Harvey caught his dad as he fell forward. It was almost like a hug, though his father didn't hold him. His father's hands were shaking too much for that. Harvey rested his chin against his dad's shoulder and rubbed soothing circles onto his back until the shaking stopped.

Some things couldn't be forgiven, or forgotten, but you had to go on anyway. He didn't want to live in a world without some kindness. Harvey could understand being scared.

"Okay, Dad," Harvey told his father gently. "It can be a dream."

THE GUILT OF WITCHERY

December 30, Evening
SABRINA

Prudence and I had been searching through the books about princes of hell for hours. It was like clawing through a dating website, if all the boys' interests were dismemberment and blood rain. I didn't see how any prince of hell was more likely than another.

But we had to find the name. There was no chance of banishing any demon without a name.

"I don't think it's Caliban," I said at last.

"Word has it Caliban is sexy," Prudence drawled. "But unlikely to be our prince."

I slammed yet another book shut. Prudence glanced up inquiringly at the sound.

"I keep thinking about that one line in the book. *On the first day of the end, the memories of their ancestors returned to the mortals,*" I quoted from the passage I'd read about the massacre in Scotland. "How much time do we have? When is the first day of the end?"

Prudence didn't answer me. Nick Scratch did.

He stood outlined in the doorway. There was a dark trail of blood running from his temple down to his throat. He'd always seemed untouchable, but he wasn't. He could be hurt. I'd sent him out into a town crawling with people enchanted to be dangerous.

I hadn't realized, until that moment, how much I cared.

Nick said: "The end is now."

THE WITCH'S VOICE LURES SPIRITS FROM THE TOMBS

December 30, Night
PRUDENCE

*S*eeing Sabrina Spellman fuss over Nick Scratch was nauseating. They didn't have time for this, but Sabrina insisted on cleaning the wounds and healing him and asking him tedious questions about how he felt and was he sure he was all right.

Nick didn't appear to find the questions tedious. He answered them patiently, seeming entirely charmed to find himself in this situation.

"You should go lie down," Sabrina urged.

"I like it where I am." Nick clearly wouldn't have moved if the library was on fire.

Sabrina made another worried sound and passed a hand over Nick's hair, though the wound was already gone. Nick shot Prudence a swift inquiring glance, as if Prudence had any idea why Sabrina did the weird things Sabrina did.

Then he canted his head slightly to the side, hopeful, inviting Sabrina to stroke his hair again. She did.

"Oh, Nick," she murmured. "I feel so terrible. I shouldn't have asked you to do this."

"Don't," Nick murmured back, something soft and startled in his eyes, as though he was surprised to find himself capable of tenderness. "Don't feel bad. I'll do whatever you like."

Prudence wanted to bang her own head against the table, but if she sustained a wound and Sabrina tried to stroke *her* hair, Prudence would be forced to do murder in the library.

"Can we please focus? A witch-hunter attacked you and robbed you of your magic! If mortals know how to do that, they're too dangerous to live. We have to go after that guy and kill him immediately. Who was he?"

She watched with incredulous fury as Nick turned to her and made the visible decision to lie through his teeth.

"No idea," he said.

"Can you describe him?" Sabrina asked. "Not that I'm saying we should kill anyone, mind you."

"No," said Nick, that *liar.* "I checked on your mortal. Afterward I was coming back, and I got attacked. It was dark. I couldn't see a thing."

Like witches couldn't see in the dark. Like Nick couldn't teleport.

Sabrina, who had been raised overly trusting, nodded to herself. "It's a relief Harvey is all right," she murmured.

"Yeah," said Nick. "He seemed good."

When Sabrina eventually left to get another book on the princes of hell, Prudence stabbed Nick through the hand with her pencil.

"Harvey did this to you, didn't he?" she hissed.

Nick wrung his hand and glared. "No!"

"Yes he did," Prudence insisted. "Why else are you *lying*? Don't expect me to buy that absurd story. Sabrina would be frantic if she knew, so you're hiding what happened to protect her stupid feelings. Once a witch-hunter turns dangerous, they don't stop. I'll cut his throat."

Nick snarled, "I won't let you upset Sabrina!"

They could hear Sabrina's footsteps returning. The cold anger left Nick's face.

"He didn't do it," he said, low and rapid. "I swear by hellfire and blood. Trust me."

"Oh," whispered Prudence. "But I don't trust anybody, Nick. Least of all you."

Sabrina came back to find them staring intently at their books.

"I found a book on a demon called Murmur," she said. "That seems right, doesn't it, with the bad-luck spirit talking about whispers? He's only a great duke of hell, not a prince. How important is the hierarchy of hell? Should we be looking at dukes?"

"Maybe," said Nick thoughtfully. "But nobody below an earl."

Satan wept, that meant more books. Prudence wasn't Nick. She didn't have time for all this reading. She was busy being radiant and awe-inspiring as the dawn.

She kept reading, though her head hurt. She worried Judas was crying with nobody to hear him, but she'd fed him and she couldn't do any more.

When she reached for another book, she saw Nick watching Sabrina with that strange new look in his eyes.

"Sabrina," he said. "If a witch-hunter came for me, and you were there, what would you do?"

"I'd protect you," Sabrina answered promptly.

"Why would you do that?" Nick asked, his voice soft.

"Because you're my friend, and I care about you," said Sabrina. "I'd never abandon you. I'd die first. And because it's the right thing to do, if anyone was in trouble."

Nick waved off the last part as boring.

"Back to that first thing you were saying..." he said, beginning to smile.

"I'd leave you to die," Prudence announced icily. "Any true witch would. I hope the witch-hunter would be so busy slaughtering you that I'd get away. You have to look out for yourself first. Everyone else does. No matter what they pretend."

Sabrina's face filled with outraged virtue. Prudence couldn't read Nick's expression.

"But then, I'm not your friend, Nicholas." She saw the slight flicker in his eyes and sneered. "Did you think I was? How pathetic."

She pushed her chair back from the table and went to find a book about the earls of hell.

Through the stacks piled in the shelves, she heard Sabrina murmur to Nick: "Don't mind her. It's the worry talking. Maybe also... her personality. She should remember you were hurt and be gentle with you."

"Will you be gentle with me?" Nick sounded amused. "There's no need."

"I wish there was something I could do for you," Sabrina muttered.

There was a pause.

"Will you sing to me?" Nick asked.

Sabrina sounded almost as startled as Prudence was. "What?"

"Sing," Nick coaxed, sweet as sin. "Like when you sang for the Infernal Choir. But just for me."

Surprise was fading from Sabrina's voice, replaced by flattered pleasure. "I could do that. Do you mean—a serenade, or a lullaby? Would it have to be a witches' song, or could it be a mortal one?"

"Anything you want," said Nick. "As long as it's you. As long as it's for me."

Sabrina sounded like she was smiling. "All right."

There was the sound of a book closing, then Sabrina began to sing. It was not a song Prudence recognized, so it was presumably mortal. That was disgusting.

Prudence returned to the table, her step slow because she didn't want to see the hideous scene that was unfolding. She did, all the same. It was even more horrible than she had feared. There was Sabrina, sitting in her chair carved with devils as though it were a throne, singing in her golden fearless voice. And there was Nick Scratch, dark head propped on his arm, adoring her.

There was no saving him. He would follow her to ruin. Prudence could only save herself.

WITCHCRAFT OF HIS WIT

December 30, Night
SABRINA

We studied all night. I sang Nick to sleep and left him slumbering while I kept reading. I was starting to think it must be the demon Murmur. Nobody else fit the bill.

I yawned and left the table, wandering through the stacks searching for princes. Aunt Zelda would be so pleased I was devoting myself to my magic studies.

Not if she knew I'd unleashed a prince of hell on Greendale, admittedly.

There was a book on a high shelf, embossed spine reading *Pseudomonarchia Daemonum*. Before I could snap my fingers to summon it, Nick reached for the volume and put it in my hands. I turned to face him. His hair was falling into his face, his eyes hooded and still sleepy. The library was dim, the night so late it was early, and in the shadows, he was handsomer than ever.

Or maybe it just mattered to me a little more than before, that he was handsome.

I hugged the book to my chest. "I had it."

"You always have it, Sabrina," said Nick. "But I like helping you. That book's a good choice."

I smiled up at him. "Okay. Thanks."

Usually he smiled whenever I smiled, but now he was staring at the books on the shelves. As I watched, he ran his fingers lightly over the spines, as though to reassure himself they were there.

"I have to tell you something," he said. "Because—I should be honest."

I nodded encouragingly. "Of course."

Nick hesitated. "You might be angry. I didn't think it was a big deal at first. It was before I really knew you."

"We know each other now, right?" I said. "Whatever it is, you can tell me."

Nick opened his mouth, then shut it. He stared fixedly at a point over my shoulder, out of the great diamond-paned arched window where the night was growing pale.

"Actually, perhaps we should discuss this after you save the town from a prince of hell."

"You sure?" I asked. "What if I can't do that? This might be your only chance."

Nick laughed. "If it's you, Spellman, a prince of hell will be easy."

"Thanks for the confidence."

"Any time," said Nick.

It sounded like he meant it. Suddenly feeling shy, I nodded.

"Sabrina, can I ask you something?"

"Sure," I whispered.

"If there was someone you knew," Nick said.

"A friend, do you mean?"

"Maybe something like that," Nick admitted. "If they were crying…"

He said nothing else. That seemed to be the scenario.

"If my friend was crying, I'd feel terrible," I said. Nick nodded. "But I'd try to make them feel better by doing something nice for them. And then we'd both feel better. Does that help?"

When I glanced up, Nick was smiling at me. "Yeah."

"I'm glad, then." I glanced over my shoulder. "We should be getting back."

"Wait," Nick said hastily. "One last thing."

I looked back at him inquiringly. Nick stepped in, suddenly breathtakingly close, and slid his arm around my waist. He glanced down at me, raising a wicked eyebrow as if to ask whether that was all right. A nervous smile woke on my mouth before I realized.

Nick picked me up by the waist and whirled me around in a circle, then perched me on the sill of the great arched window. My hand flew up involuntarily, to catch at his collar. There was still a trace of blood against the black material. He gazed up at me, with the first light of morning falling on his face.

He could have kissed me. I would have kissed him back. He didn't.

"I do want to try it," Nick Scratch murmured. "Love, the mortal way. Sabrina, I really will try."

THE REIGN OF WITCHES PASS OVER

December 31, New Year's Eve, Morning
SABRINA

I slept in the library, my head pillowed in my arms, and woke to a deserted table and the realization I needed help. I knew I'd be in trouble, but I'd promised myself to stop being afraid. I had to go to Aunt Zelda.

Horribly, I thought I might know where in the Academy I could find her.

Prudence was presumably with her little brother. I didn't know where Nick was, but I found him while I was walking through the dining hall on my way to Father Blackwood's. He was sitting at a table eating breakfast with Dorcas, talking to her in his coaxing voice and brushing her red hair out of her eyes. Dorcas was lapping it up.

I rolled my eyes and tried to ignore the twinge in my chest. I should never have expected anything else. Of course Nick Scratch wanted to try love, with whoever was closest.

That wasn't my idea of love.

"I'm going to Father Blackwood's chambers," I told him curtly, stopping by his table. "Try to meet me and Prudence in the library before evening."

"Sure." Nick paused. "Something wrong, Spellman?"

"What could be wrong, Scratch?"

I didn't have time for this. I pulled out my phone and tried calling Roz again.

She didn't answer. She hadn't answered yesterday either. I'd called her home and Reverend Walker told me she was sleeping.

I stormed on, through the scarlet lights and stone halls of the Academy. I was worrying about Roz, and fuming over Nick, and I didn't notice Father Blackwood until I ran into him.

"Sorry, Father Blackwood. Have you seen my aunt Zelda?"

"She is sleeping in my chambers," said Father Blackwood, his tone hideously possessive. "I fear she is altogether worn out. You shouldn't trouble her."

I started forward. "I think Aunt Zelda would want to hear what I have to say."

I was pulled up short when Father Blackwood caught my shoulder, his grip alarmingly strong. The ends of his pointed nails dug into my skin through my sweater.

"You do insist on troubling people, don't you, Sabrina?" he asked softly.

There was a strange, sleepwalking glint in his pale eyes.

"There are many ways to be wanton," he said, tone slightly

slurred. "The right way is to walk in the red light of Satan's eyes and subjugate yourself to his dark glory. Look at Sister Zelda. She has a proud spirit, but it is all the more superb to see a proud spirit bend its will to our dark god, as Lilith did. A woman must choose either to be a Lilith or an Eve, who was ungrateful for the gift the serpent gave her. Don't you agree?"

"With you?" I said brightly. "Hardly ever."

"Tongue sharper than a serpent's tooth on you, girl," sneered Father Blackwood. "An Eve in our Academy could poison every student within its walls. Sister Zelda has changed from the magnificently heartless girl I once knew, because of you. And I see you getting your claws into Nicholas Scratch. That boy has a darkly shining future ahead of him. He is one of the touched by Satan, who stand very close to our Dark Lord. I can always tell. Nicholas does not need you to drag him off the path of unrighteousness. Why is it that everything you touch is spoiled somehow? Why did Satan want you in my school? Why is the Dark Lord so interested in you, when you're nothing—an Eve—a weak woman, who should kneel or be crushed?"

The pressure on my shoulder was inexorable. The sharpened nails bit like daggers.

"Take your hand off," I said. "If Aunt Zelda saw you touch me, she'd kill you."

Father Blackwood's blurred eyes became slightly clearer. I saw his gaze dart toward the door of his chamber. He noticed that I saw, and his mouth twisted with fury.

He was afraid of Aunt Zelda, I realized, and he hated it. He liked her because she was unconquerable, and he'd resent her for being unconquerable too. She wasn't safe with him, not in the long run.

I wasn't safe with him now. Not with the curse affecting him.

Father Blackwood dug his nails in, then removed his hand. "Let us not admit the curse of Pruflas between us, child. We are both dear to Sister Zelda and should not quarrel."

He was turning away. I relaxed for an instant, then saw him whirl back with his hand lifted to strike.

"What you should learn, little Eve, is *obedience*!" thundered Father Blackwood.

His spell never got the chance to land. I was already running at him, both hands upraised. Father Blackwood talked too much.

"Damnum absque injuria!"

Whatever damage he'd planned to do to me would be visited on him. Father Blackwood screamed and fell in a heap on the ground.

"Disobedience has always been my sin of choice," I said, fixing my hairband. Then I turned and ran back to the library.

Yesterday the mortals had recalled their ancestors' memories, of secrets used to fight witches.

Today was the second day, the day the witches turned to a dream of hate. If we could lift the curse, Father Blackwood wouldn't remember I'd struck down the head of the Academy in his own school. For now, I couldn't go to my aunts or my cousin for help. They might be affected by the spell like the High Priest was.

I was as strong as I needed to be because I stood on certain ground at home. I could always be sure of my family's love. Now I could bear anything, except seeing them changed by enchantment I'd brought down.

Now, I thought, was the time to trust the friends I'd found in the world of witches. They hadn't disappointed me yet.

Prudence was already in the library when I returned. I stared at her coolly lovely face, the proud tilt of her chin.

"Are you feeling more hateful than usual?"

"You just walked in, Sabrina," said Prudence. "So yes."

She didn't seem enchanted or unhappy. She sounded the same as ever. It was hard to tell how Prudence felt about anything. (Other than when she was annoyed, which she always made very clear.)

But Nick had talked about a friend crying, and he had to mean Prudence. He was scornful around the other guys, and he talked to Prudence often. I was almost certain he'd been hurt when she said they weren't friends.

Prudence was going above and beyond to help me. I thought she and I might be friends too.

I came up to her chair and quickly, before I could lose my nerve, I gave her a sideways hug. "If there's anything bothering you, Prudence, you can tell me."

Prudence was silent. I squeezed her rigid shoulders, wondering if she was actually touched.

Then she said: "Try to embrace me *ever again*, Sabrina Spellman, and I will hex off your arms and beat you to death with them."

I let go fast. "Not a hugger?" I nodded to myself. "Noted. Prudence, I wasn't really raised as a witch."

"Tell me something I don't know," Prudence murmured.

"Aunt Hilda didn't want me to learn to speak like a witch and freak out the mortals at school," I said. "My family didn't tell me a lot about witch holidays and customs, or even phrases, until my dark baptism. What does the phrase 'the curse of Pruflas' mean?"

Prudence's hands clenched on the edge of the table.

"It means not to give way to quarrelsomeness," she answered slowly. "Pruflas is the dark prince of discord and falsehood."

"A prince," I repeated. "Is he? Hang on."

I ran around to my side of the table and found the book Nick had taken off the shelf for me, the *Pseudomonarchia Daemonum*. I'd been so tired when I was reading it, but now I had a fuzzy recollection of reading a certain name.

"Pruflas," I read aloud. "A great prince and duke of hell, who causes men to commit quarrels, discord, and falsehood. He should never be admitted to this world. He lives outside the Tower of Babel, attended by . . ." My voice failed. "Attended by his handmaiden."

I looked up from my book, and my own fiercely triumphant gaze met Prudence's. I cradled the book in my arms as if it were a jewel. Better yet, as if it were a weapon.

"We've got him, Prudence! Where's Nick?"

WE ARE ALL MORTAL

December 31, New Year's Eve, Afternoon
ROZ

She didn't actually know where she was going. Her feet seemed to know, negotiating the melted snow on the sidewalk outside her house with more certainty than she'd felt in a long time. The whispers in her ear guided her way. She had a destination; she had a purpose. That was all she needed to know. The witches must be stopped.

"Roz!"

The sound of familiar voices broke through her reverie.

"Hey, Roz!"

The single shining path in front of Roz blurred. Harvey and Susie stood before her, blocking her way. Harvey wore his sheepskin-lined jacket and had his arm around Susie's neck like a scarf. Susie was carrying take-out boxes.

"We were bringing you snacks from Dr. Cerberus's," said Harvey.

His voice, sweet and clear, cut across the whispers. There was sudden discordance in her head.

"I'm not hungry," Roz snapped. "I don't want you to baby me."

The venom in her voice made Harvey step back, as she'd known it would. All Harvey wanted was a chance to cherish and be chosen. If she made him believe he wasn't welcome, he'd retreat.

Susie stepped forward. "We're worried about you. You're not answering anybody's calls. And you're acting really strange."

Roz's head whirled, trying to think her way around this. She could make Susie stop by insisting she wanted to keep her secrets. She could make Harvey stop by rejecting him. She didn't know how to stop them both.

And why would she want to? They were her friends.

When she thought of her friends, she remembered Sabrina. Frustrated tears sprang to her eyes. Phrases about blindness crowded her mind. *Blinded by tears, blinded by rage.* It would be the same result in the end.

"Do you ever get angry with the world?" Roz whispered.

"All the time," said Susie. "But not with my friends."

If Roz couldn't make them back down, she would go through them. She stepped forward. So did Harvey.

"Roz," said Harvey. "Rosalind."

He called her that when he wanted her to take him seriously. He reached forward, so careful, and cupped her face in his hands. Roz trembled and went still.

"I don't understand whatever enchantment is happening, but I saw it affect my dad. And Susie and I were telling each other, we feel...different too. You went to the demon's shop twice. You're more affected than we are, but you're so strong. Whatever it is, you can fight it. We can fight it together."

"Wait, the demon's shop?" asked Susie. "Demons run small businesses now? What's next, a demonic lemonade stand?"

Roz laughed, and the sound hushed the whispers.

Harvey grinned at Susie and then redirected his grin encouragingly Roz's way.

"Roll with the weird, Sooz," said Harvey. "I'm learning to. Roz? Does this feel...as if you're trapped in a dream?"

"No," said Roz. "I don't get trapped in dreams."

That gave her an idea. She saw terrible sights in dreams, felt awful foreboding, but she wasn't trapped. She didn't want to be trapped now. Maybe this bright clear path before her was a trap.

Roz nodded slowly. "You're right, guys," she said. "Thanks for coming for me."

Harvey stepped back, putting his hands in his pockets. "Anytime," he mumbled. "Always."

"What do you want to do?" Susie asked, the light of battle in her eyes.

Harvey was a head and a half taller than Susie, but Susie was the one who stood like a soldier. Their faces were dim in her vision, but somehow better than the bright path. Roz smiled for her friends.

"Sorry, but I think I have to rest."

To sleep, perchance to dream.

She wouldn't follow the whispers. She couldn't follow her grandmother's advice. Her grandmother was gone. Roz had to find her own way.

The cunning might show her how.

REMEMBER THOU ART MORTAL

December 31, New Year's Eve, Evening
HARVEY

Harvey walked up the steps of his porch slowly. After they'd visited Roz, he and Susie had gone around Greendale. There were a lot of people on the streets in town this New Year's Eve, moving like sleepwalkers, with the same slightly glazed look that had been in his father's eyes yesterday.

Susie had gone to check on Mr. Putnam. Harvey didn't know what to do except go home himself.

The moment Harvey came through his front door, he saw Nick leaning against the wall, reading his book.

"Oh, Nick," said Harvey. "Here you are. In my house. Without me letting you in. It's as if I just talk to myself about boundaries all day long."

Nick looked up from the book. "I don't like your shirt."

"You're not doing awesome on the boundaries front today at all."

"I don't think anyone else will like it either."

"Stop insulting my clothes," said Harvey. "I don't talk about your hair."

Nick scowled. "What about my hair?"

"I don't talk about it," said Harvey, walking toward the kitchen.

There was a light on in there. He was pretty sure he hadn't left a light on in there. A redhead was sitting at the table, wearing a small sulky pout on her mauve-painted mouth. He definitely hadn't left her in there.

Harvey turned around to face Nick, who was following him, and raised his eyebrows. "Friend of yours?"

"We used to date."

Harvey sighed. "Of course you did."

"Is it all right for her to be here?"

He thought of Roz's stricken and confused face today, Susie scared by the darkness of the town, Nick dreaming awful dreams about Satan. If they were going to survive Greendale, they had to stick together. He was considering introducing Nick to Roz and Susie. His friends would like Nick. Maybe Harvey *should* be getting to know more witches.

"I . . . guess," said Harvey. "I mean, sure. All my friends are girls." He hesitated, thinking of Susie. "Well. Except one."

Nick smiled. "Come meet her."

There was something odd about Nick's expressions today. Harvey couldn't work it out, but it didn't seem bad. Not like the way the people in town looked.

He didn't know how to bring up the issue of an enchanted town in front of a stranger. He was awkward with strangers at the best of times.

He hovered near Nick, eyeing the girl apprehensively, and said: "Hey."

The girl glanced up at Harvey. "I don't like his shirt."

Nick smirked. "I did tell you, farm boy."

The girl didn't seem thrilled to be here. Her hands were folded tight on the table. Harvey wondered why she'd come when she clearly hadn't wanted to. Then she threw Nick a yearning look, so that answered that.

"This is Dorcas," Nick continued.

"Dorkus?" Harvey repeated.

"Dor*cas*," corrected the red-haired girl. She sniffed. "It's an ancient and respectable witch name. Not that I'd expect you to know, w-witch-hunter."

Her tiny stammer put her stiff shoulders and her pout in a different light. Harvey thought of what his dad had done to Nick yesterday, in this very room. Maybe this girl was frightened.

He went over to her, kneeling down by her chair. "There's no need to be scared. I won't hurt you."

"Like you could," Dorcas snapped, but her shoulders eased slightly.

He smiled encouragingly up at her. After a moment, she gave him a tiny smile in return.

"He's cute," she said in surprised tones. "If he lost the flannel and fixed his hair."

She reached out, put her hands into Harvey's hair, and drew it back from his brow, ruffling it about between her fingers.

Wow, witches really had no idea about boundaries.

Harvey tried to edge away. "You can talk to me as well as Nick. I'm right here."

Dorcas seemed startled. "I've never really talked to a mortal who wasn't ensorceled." She paused. "I have slept with and tormented many of them. No witch-hunters, of course, but Nick swore you were harmless."

"Did he?" said Harvey testily. He glanced at Nick, who was lounging in the kitchen entryway and being unhelpful.

"Yes," said Dorcas, touching Harvey's hair. "And he said we could have lasagna. Can we?"

Dorcas perked up as she asked. She was very handsy, but maybe she was trying to be friendly.

"Sure?" said Harvey. "I mean, at least you're willing to stay for dinner, unlike Prudence."

Dorcas's smile immediately turned warm. "You know my sister?"

"Oh," said Harvey, liking her more when he heard the affection in her voice. "Yeah. Well, Prudence force-fed me truth potion and threatened to kill me."

Dorcas beamed. "That's typical Prue."

She seemed much happier. She took one hand out of Harvey's hair, which was nice, then smoothed her palm down his chest, which was weird again.

"I *am* excited about lasagna," she told him.

"Well, aren't you two getting along swimmingly?" said Nick. "Great! Protect him, Dorcas. Don't ensorcel him. Don't do anything he doesn't like. Later, Harry."

"Wait, Nick, where are you going?" Harvey demanded in terror. "Don't go!"

"Yeah, Nick," Dorcas agreed in a purr. "Don't go. Stay." She rubbed Harvey's shirt with what, horrifyingly, seemed to be approval. "I think you and I will get along, witch-hunter."

Harvey had no idea why she would think that. He turned to Nick, who was still leaning in the doorway, hands in his pockets and smirking.

"Oh, hey," Nick drawled. "Thanks for the thought, guys, but I have an important appointment elsewhere. There's a prince of hell."

"There's a *what?*" Harvey demanded, staring at Nick and then looking toward Dorcas to see if she knew what Nick was talking about.

When he turned to Dorcas, she leaned forward. She was inches away when he realized she was going to kiss him. Harvey made a strangled sound and pulled back so fast he tipped over. Dorcas fell out of her chair.

"We're on the floor." Dorcas shrugged. "Well, okay."

"Wait," said Harvey. "Nick, are you trying to fix me up on a *date?*"

The two witches exchanged a look Harvey couldn't interpret.

"She's more a magical bodyguard," said Nick. "But see where the night takes you."

"Oh my God," said Harvey. "I don't want a bodyguard or a date!"

"I have asked you not to call upon the false god so much," Nick complained.

"I don't mind," Dorcas informed them. "Mortal boys say it all the time during certain situations."

Nick was immediately intrigued. "Do they? He says it a lot, but I didn't know it was a general thing."

"Hey, nerd," Harvey said accusingly. "Could you not be interested in mortal linguistics right now? I *cannot* believe you would do this! You are totally inappropriate and out of your mind."

Dorcas shook her head, clearly wishing to dissociate herself from Harvey's take on the situation.

"*I* think you're totally gorgeous," she told Nick. "And you should be out of your pants."

She winked up at him. Nick, in what seemed to be pure reflex, winked back.

Harvey didn't know why witches had no chill. "Look, Dorcas, I recently had a bad breakup and I'm not interested in dating you. Maybe we could just have lasagna and a conversation about the *enchanted town* and what we can do about it?"

He scrambled off the floor and to his feet, then offered Dorcas a hand up. She took it, and he helped her stand. She regarded their joined hands with a vaguely interested air.

"I'm sorry about this mess," he told her. "It's Nick's fault."

It was shocking and embarrassing, but it'd been a long few days with Nick Scratch and he was getting used to that. Harvey honestly didn't blame Nick. He'd probably meant well. This was like when cats brought their owners mice and expected them to be pleased. From the cat's point of view, it was a nice present. So from Nick's point of view, having a witch protect Harvey and getting Harvey a date probably seemed like a win-win.

"Did I get something wrong again?" Nick sounded resigned at this point.

Harvey grinned. "Little bit, yeah."

"Can we have lasagna soon?" Dorcas asked. "I don't mind

protecting him, I realize I owe the mortal, but I don't want this night to be a total waste—"

"Wait," said Harvey. "Why would you owe me anything? I don't know you."

She flapped an impatient hand. "Because of the spell I did that collapsed the mines."

There was a silence. Harvey dropped the girl's hand, as though her touch had burned him. There was a cold feeling in the center of his chest, where the darkness was concentrated.

"You killed my brother?" said Harvey quietly. "And you, Nick. You brought her here."

He looked between them, the witch and the warlock. He'd thought of witches killing Tommy as older, distant and evil figures. This girl looked like a child, guilty because she'd been caught killing flies.

That was all mortals were, to the witches.

"She . . . wasn't supposed to talk about that," Nick murmured.

"Oh," said Harvey. "That makes it okay, then?"

Nick said, "Wait." He took his hands out of his pockets. Dorcas was edging over to him.

"I think we should ensorcel him immediately!" she suggested.

"Just another sick hilarious game with the mortal?" Harvey asked. "Tormenting them, enchanting them, murdering them. It's all the same to you, isn't it? Because you don't think we're people. God, I am so *stupid*. You're all evil. My dad was right."

His heart was thundering in his chest, darkness flickering at the edges of his vision. There were guns by the door, and he wanted to use them.

Nick's lip curled back from his teeth. "Your father who tried to kill me? He was right?"

Dorcas said, "I don't like this place. I want to leave."

"Why does my dad trying to kill you matter?" asked Harvey slowly. "If it doesn't matter that she killed my brother. Oh, right, you think that a witch's life is worth more than a mortal's."

He advanced on them, toward the door and the guns. Dorcas backed away, whispering spells under her breath that buzzed in Harvey's ears in a high insectile whine.

"You'd better run, you murderer," he told her. "Or I will kill you."

They reached the door. The witch turned and fled.

The warlock stayed.

"Calm down," said Nick. "I could've set the entire Academy on your father for what he did, but I didn't. I protected that disgusting worm, *for you*, so—"

"So what?" Harvey demanded. "I'm supposed to say thank you for not ripping my dad to pieces? Well, maybe I shouldn't have stopped my father. I did it for him, so he wouldn't be a murderer. It wasn't for you. I hate you. I hate all witches."

Oh, all but one.

I could never hate you, Sabrina.

The wild raging in his chest quieted. Harvey checked his reach for the gun.

There were red lights in Nick's eyes. Red in their eyes and red on their hands, his dad had said, as if quoting from an old, old story. Satan-touched.

Satan seemed very close.

"You are trying my patience, mortal," Nick snarled. "I've been very forbearing with you. I could tear you apart with a word."

"You really don't get it, do you? I *know* you can kill me. That's the problem. Your people live by murder and magic. You might kill us at any moment." Harvey paused, breathing hard. Darkness almost obscured his vision. "Unless we kill you first."

Nick laughed a wild witch laugh, the kind that had kept Harvey's father awake with terror for years.

"You think I'm scared of you, witch-hunter?"

Harvey picked up the gun. He stood, holding its cold weight in his hands, and said: "Maybe you should be."

No, said something that wasn't the storm and the rising dark, said his longing for some kindness in the world. *No, that's not you. That was never who you wanted to be.*

Harvey swallowed and lowered the gun. Nick's eyes registered the movement, and the fury in his face flickered.

"Mortal, you're under an enchantment," said Nick, the snarl tightly leashed in his voice. "The whole town is. So I'll overlook this."

"Just . . . get out." Harvey spoke with difficulty. "Don't ever come back."

Nick disappeared into the night. Harvey put down the gun and sank onto the floor, his head in his hands.

'TIS NOW THE VERY WITCHING TIME

December 31, New Year's Eve, Evening
PRUDENCE

t seemed as if there was no help to be found in the world.

"The spell's affecting my father?" Prudence demanded. "Are you *certain?*"

Sabrina's small face was pale under the hairband as she nodded. "I mean, I know he's generally awful, but I'm sure. It's the second day, when the witches succumb to hate. Are you feeling... any different?"

Prudence wanted to snap back *no*, but this was too serious to deceive herself. She remembered Nick tearing apart Plutonius Pan. She'd barely looked in on Judas, and before the last couple of days she'd checked on him all the time.

They were witches, children of storms and bloodshed. It was hard to tell if more hate had been added to the ocean in her. And yet... and yet...

She didn't say no.

Instead, she said: "I can keep it together."

Being violently miserable happened. She wasn't going to let any stupid curse or prince of hell tell her what to do. There was already her father and Satan. No other man should dare try to control her.

"When the membrane between the worlds is weakest, at the point where two elements can be crossed, the prince can step through," Sabrina quoted. "My aunt Zelda told me that mortal belief made the membrane between the worlds weak. At the turn of the mortal year. It's New Year's Eve now. We have to stop Pruflas from coming."

Prudence wished Zelda were here. But she didn't want Zelda to be disappointed in her, either.

"We can't win," Prudence said. "We need more than a name to stop a prince of hell. We don't know what to do."

Sabrina set her jaw. "I'll think of something. *Where* is Nick?"

Nick said, "I'm here. I was in town checking on your mortals. Your mortal friend Roz is in her house, as far as I can tell."

Sabrina and Prudence whirled around. Nick was standing in the doorway of the library. He had an air that suggested the wrath of witches had come to him. He moved restlessly, sparks seeming to travel under his skin, as though there was hellfire burning in his blood.

"And I have an idea," he added, controlling his voice with a visible effort. "The point where two elements meet and can be crossed. A bridge."

"Let's go," Sabrina said instantly.

She charged forward, but as she passed Nick she stopped, caught by a sudden thought.

"Wait. How is Harvey? Is he safe?"

"You know what, Sabrina?" Nick bit out. "I really don't care. I'm sick of even hearing his name."

Sabrina looked hurt, but after a moment's pause, she resumed her charge. Nick followed her.

"Finally, the man talks sense," murmured Prudence.

She ran after them into the gathering night and chaos.

TO LOVE WHAT IS MORTAL

December 31, New Year's Eve, Night
ROZ

Roz's head was whirling with strange dreams. Her cunning that saw the future, and the whispers of hate, seemed to combine in her mind. They made such an overwhelming din that her head felt as though it was splitting. Even her mind's eye could not see clearly any longer.

Sabrina kept calling, and Roz kept not picking up.

For now we see through a glass darkly, her father had said in a sermon once, his voice booming from the pulpit. It was one of the times when what he said caught on a hook in Roz's heart and stayed. *Now I know in part, but then shall I know.*

Roz woke from another dream with flames dancing in front of her eyes and wished she knew what to do. She knew witches were taking the light of the world from her, and she knew her best friend was a witch. She felt like she only had broken parts of knowledge that she couldn't fit together.

There were whispers in her head about stopping the witches, and she did want them stopped.

But Sabrina was a witch. When she'd told Roz what she was, Roz held her and promised herself it wouldn't change anything.

Sabrina had given her a bracelet when they were small, when she asked Roz to be her best friend. A friendship bracelet, twined with tiny flowers.

Roz was always losing things. My scatterbrain, her dad would call her, willfully ignoring the fact it was harder for her to keep track of what she couldn't see. She lost that bracelet often, but she'd always been able to find it again, as though it was returning to her hand.

Now, she reflected, the bracelet had obviously been magic.

It was the only witchcraft Sabrina had used near Roz their whole lives. And it was done to bind them together.

Roz couldn't see much, but she could see, very clearly, her own small brown child's hand wearing that bracelet, and Sabrina's hand reaching out to clasp hers.

When she thought about the witches, she wanted them stopped.

When she thought about Sabrina, or Sabrina's family, or the witch boy at the movies who'd been kind for no reason at all, it was different.

Not everything was darkness. Past strange dreams, past fear and jealousy and all the wounded longings of growing up, she loved her friend.

She knew only part, but she knew the one thing she couldn't lose.

Roz scrabbled on the floor for her phone. She searched until she found it and called for help.

"Harvey," she sobbed as soon as he picked up. "Harvey, please help her."

"Roz?" Harvey's familiar, dear voice was grounding. "Hey, what can I do? What are you saying?"

"Sabrina," said Roz. "I saw her in a dream. There was fire by the water, and a prince laughing as he turned to wind. Sabrina was there, and a girl with bleached hair, and a boy with dark hair. I could see them, more clearly than I can see anything now. I saw them by the light of burning torches. They're so tired. I can't explain how I know, but I do. Get your truck and go to them."

Harvey's voice was strange. It was his, but it didn't sound like his, and it took Roz an instant to recognize why. Then she realized that she'd never heard his voice without a drop of kindness in it before.

"Roz," he said. "Why should I? They're a bunch of witches. They don't need me."

"It's Sabrina," Roz said fiercely. "If you don't go to her, Harvey, I will."

An incredulous laugh burst from his throat. "You can't drive, Roz. And it's dark outside."

"So help her for me," Roz said. "I know you! Something's messing with our minds, but there are some things that don't change. You'd do anything for any one of us. Help her for her. Help her for me. I don't care why you do it, but *help her.*"

Harvey hung up. Roz held the phone between her hands, held her hands pressed to her lips, and prayed.

UNITE: FOR COMBINATION IS STRONGER THAN WITCHCRAFT

December 31, New Year's Eve, Night
SABRINA

Nobody was ringing in the new year tonight. The night stretched black and cold around us. Except for the light on the water.

It wasn't moonlight shining on the stream. Instead, it was a dull red glow. At first the glow was only a thin scarlet line against the dark surface, as though the river had been cut and was bleeding. Then the line grew wider, and wider still.

There was a door of hellfire opening in the river. Steam rose with a sibilant hissing sound to the stars. Somehow I knew that not all the waters in all the oceans of the world could put this fire out.

The prince of hell was coming.

"What's the plan?" Nick asked.

I glanced at him. Nick seemed the most affected by the spell of discord. He was wild-eyed, every nerve obviously thrumming with tension, but he managed to give me a nod and a tense version of his usual slow, charming smile. I almost loved him for that.

"I have his name," I said. "I'm going to recite the banishing spell."

"A terrible, suicidal plan," muttered Prudence behind us. "I don't know what else I expected. Has it occurred to you that you cannot *invoke Satan* to banish one of *Satan's princes?*"

"I can do whatever I want," I announced, and tried to believe it.

The whole river was horribly bright by now, as though lava were running from an invisible volcano. Another flame was rising from the river—a bonfire the size of a mountain.

"Well," Nick told Prudence. "Every text bears revision."

When I glanced at Nick, I saw his face bathed in orange light. His cool façade was slipping, but he was still trying to maintain that small smile, for me. Usually I thought his smile looked a bit smug, but in the blaze of hellfire that seemed brave. His thoughts followed the same path as my own: a witch's way, but not the way all the witches thought. We could go down a different dark path together.

No more hesitation. I'd promised myself that.

I gave Nick a grateful smile back and stepped forward. The towering bonfire was taking shape, a flame with the head of a vast hawk, open beak scything at the stars. The air was full of whispers, the woods rustling with the promise of discord.

"Pruflas, Prince of Hell," I shouted, and the crimson hawk's head in the sky turned to me.

Fire fell from the sky like rain. We ran, but I made sure to run forward. I stood at the river's edge and screamed defiance. No more fear of the power I wielded. For the first time since the night of the Greendale Thirteen, I embraced my magic. I spoke in a voice to command sky and water.

"Dragon be my guide and hellfire my light. I have the power to banish this spirit. Nicholas shield me in my fight, Prudence lend me glory. Demon, begone!"

I heard Prudence's whisper on the wind, sounding very far away. "Leave me out of this."

I could see the discord Pruflas spread, written on the sky. Whispers flew bright as burning leaves on the wind.

—they're not your friends, the mortals aren't your friends, your family aren't your family, you are something infinitely below them all—

The fire and the whispers stung. Cold night air and doubt ripped through me. For a moment I thought I stood alone.

Then someone stepped up and caught my hand fast in his.

"Deliver me into delicious temptation," murmured Nick. *"Evil be thou my good, might my right, and my voice heard in hell. Demon, begone!"*

I exchanged a glance with Nick, the flames reflected in his eyes and the wicked smile, the sight of him sparking joy somewhere deep in my chest. I linked our fingers tightly together.

—I am not your enemy, daughter of chaos, I come for the mortals, they will always hate you—

"Unleash my *wrath upon my enemy,"* I yelled. *"Turn away the ill luck and the evil eye from this place. Demon, begone."*

There was a sigh behind me that sounded like "Satan in a sundress." Then someone seized my free hand.

"I have the strength to banish this misbegotten imp," snapped Prudence. *"Demon, begone."*

From the burning hawk's head came a roar like a great cat. Nick and Prudence shied away, shielding their eyes with their free hands. I found myself laughing. I could see through the hellfire, clear as day, and my friends were with me, not letting go of my hands. Prudence lowered her hand to throw me a dirty look, and I almost loved *her* for that.

"Demon, begone!"

"Demon, begone!"

"Demon, begone!"

Every witch knows the power of being three in one.

Clouds parted over Greendale. Snow fell from a clear black sky, radiant and astonishing, crystals that caught starlight, diamonds that quenched fire.

I laughed and shouted: *"By my will I cast you out! By the power of every rebellious spirit I love, my town is washed clean! Demon, begone!"*

The flames were thrashing in the riverbed, the hawk's head wailing. The whispers were only noise now. Noise that no ear, witch or mortal, could make sense of.

Snow was putting out the fires burning on the ground, but flames were still falling among the snowflakes. I felt fire rake a scorching path down my right arm and heard Prudence make a sound through her teeth, too proud to scream. One last discordant note rang defiance to heaven.

The demon's crimson became silver and shadow, the door from hell changing back to a steel bridge over a black river. Pruflas Prince of Hell was banished.

But there was still flame, not falling or rising, but glowing on the horizon.

The spell was laid on the people of Greendale until daybreak. The spell throwing them back to a state of primitive fear, when hags came to them in dreams and witches were made for burning. There was a mob coming, with flaming torches.

"So," said Nick. "Have you heard the one about the mortals who were enchanted to hate magic and saw a magical light show in the sky? It is killer."

I wrenched my eyes off the line of fire on the horizon and gazed in dismay at my companions. Prudence was hunched over, an arm around her middle.

"Are you hurt?"

Prudence gave me an annoyed look. "We're about to be killed! When does the enchantment lift from the mortals?"

"When dawn remakes the day," I answered dully.

I could hear the cries of the townspeople coming closer, smell the smoke from their torches. Prudence was hurt, whatever she was saying. I was cradling my arm to my chest. I didn't think any of us had much magic left.

"Plenty of time for them to massacre us, then," Prudence said. "So help me Satan, I will murder some of them before they kill me."

"They're under an enchantment, Prudence; it's not their fault."

"I don't care, Sabrina!" Prudence said. "I'm going to rip out someone's throat with my teeth!"

"Good plan," murmured Nick, then caught my eye. "Oh, I mean . . . give them a warning before you rip their throats out."

"No!" I exclaimed.

"No?" said Nick. "Well, all right."

"We have to go," I told them.

Hiding in the woods was our only hope. If we managed to conceal ourselves, the mob might not find us. Then by daybreak, it would be a dream, and we would be safe.

That was when I heard the scream behind me.

HEAVY MORTAL HOPES

December 31, New Year's Eve, Night
HARVEY

He drove the pickup truck pell-mell down the path among the trees, taking corners too fast, until he saw the river.

The sky was alive, but not with fireworks. There was a creature, some rough beast sketched from flame, its blazing outline blotting out the stars.

Sabrina was standing before it, dwarfed by its looming awful presence. She didn't falter and she didn't retreat. She shouted a spell. Harvey felt the air shimmer around him and contract in his lungs. He knew this was the magic of his nightmares.

Her hair was the white of lightning on snow, and so was her shadow. Darkness itself turned to brilliance, because it was her.

He watched Sabrina turn, her fresh-fallen-snow hair a brilliant halo around her head. Nick stepped up to her side, black hair wild in the wind like a crown of shadows, and when Nick took her hand, Harvey saw the way she smiled.

His magic girl.

And she had a magic boy now.

Sometimes misery made it hard to breathe.

The horrible demon thing was shrieking, and Prudence was there too, her ebony-painted lips curling back from her teeth as she shouted magic into the roaring flame. Nick was using his free hand to sketch little shapes in the air, banishing sparks as though he was catching fireflies, but a jet of flame got past his guard. Harvey leaned forward, but he couldn't see who it hit.

The demon creature in the sky was so horrible he could barely focus on it, his mind trying to hide like a child running scared in the mines. The witches were a fragile line of defense, but they were magic too. They were more horrible than the demon because they seemed almost human, and he hated magic and he loved Sabrina. Darkness boiled in his heart, magic dazzled his eyes, and he wanted to kill the witches and he wanted to draw them, to make art out of hopeless beauty.

Then the demon dwindled away, but it wasn't over. Harvey saw the mob coming. He was suddenly sure his grandfather was leading this crowd, a real witch-hunter, a tough man doing what he was born to do.

He stopped the truck with a scream of brakes, as close to the river as he could get, and leaped out with a gun in his hand.

THE WITCH BURNING

December 31, New Year's Eve, Night
PRUDENCE

She didn't look down at her side. She'd muttered a few healing spells, and she didn't want to see how little they had worked. They had no magic left, and less time.

Even less time than she'd imagined, Prudence realized when she heard a mortal vehicle come to a stop behind them. They were surrounded. She might as well have let herself be torn apart by her coven, since mortals were going to tear her apart anyway. Either way, it would be for nothing.

Prudence closed her eyes against the pain and told herself: *Dorcas. Agatha. Sisters,* because she wanted them to be the last thing she thought. Then she opened her eyes.

It was the witch-hunter, with a gun in his hand.

Sabrina showed her first hesitation of the night, wavering by the riverside like a candle flame in a sudden wind. "Is that...?" she said, very faint. "Is it...?"

"Rescue," said Nick Scratch, officially a maniac, and pulled Sabrina toward the truck. Prudence fought to free herself from Sabrina's grasp, and then staggered when she succeeded.

The witch-hunter came faster than any of them, crossing to the riverbank in three strides. He shouldered his gun and went straight to Sabrina, capturing her face in his hands.

"Sabrina, are you all right?"

She gazed up at him, her eyes stars. "Harvey," she whispered. "You came. How did you find me?"

He bowed down from his absurd height to her absurd lack of same, kissing her palm when she laid a hand against his cheek, leaning his forehead against hers. "Roz told me where to go."

"Roz sent you to help me?" Sabrina glowed.

"Of course," murmured the witch-hunter. "She loves you."

The pair of them seemed unaware there was anyone else in the world. Unholy god, the witch-hunter was going to cover Sabrina's face with kisses right in front of Nick.

Eager light had died a sudden death in Nick's eyes.

Goodbye to that weird bromance, Prudence thought with distant amusement. *Nick's going to rip the mortal's head clean off.*

Then the mortal unwittingly saved his own stupid life by taking a deep breath and a step back from Sabrina. His hands fell away from framing her face.

"Nick? You all right?"

Nick cast his gaze swiftly to the ground to hide his murder eyes. "I'm all right," he answered, sounding both sullen and pleased to be asked.

The witch-hunter left Sabrina's side.

"Prudence, are you all right?" he asked, coming at her. "I don't think you are."

She was too stunned with horror to do anything as the atrocity happened, and she was swept up in the witch-hunter's arms.

"Oh no, oh no, oh no," said Prudence, staring around wildly. "Oh, Satan, Medusa, and Beelzebub. Call back the prince of hell. I want to be torn apart by imps. I'm looking forward to being burned on a pyre by the howling mob. Unhand me. Do you realize every-where you are touching will have to be washed one thousand times with unholy water?"

Nick was smirking openly. "Ah, the move."

She was glad Nick was enjoying himself. No, she wasn't; she hoped the mob drowned him.

The witch-hunter glared. "It's not a move."

"Looks like a move," Nick muttered.

The witch-hunter carried Prudence to his awful mortal vehicle and placed her in the bed of the truck. He put the gun down so he could shrug out of his coat and settle it over her.

"This smells like mortal," Prudence complained.

She could tell that the spell was affecting him too. His mouth was tight and sterner than usual, and his eyes were dark and blank, but when he smoothed the coat over her, he did so gently.

There was no working that one out. Prudence turned her face away.

The mortal helped Sabrina into the front of the truck, careful of her wounded arm, then grabbed the back of Nick's jacket and shoved him in as well. Once he had every witch aboard, he climbed in behind the wheel, and they drove through the woods.

"Should we go to a hospital?" the witch-hunter asked Sabrina. "You and Prudence are both hurt."

Sabrina shook her head. "Witches don't go to the hospital. Could you—wait and drive us around until dawn, and then bring us to my aunts?" She twisted around in her seat. "Will you be all right, Prudence?"

"No," said Prudence. "Never again. That witch-hunter manhandled me and I cannot bear the indignity, but of course I'm not weak enough to be fazed by a tiny burn. You can be a whiner if you like, Sabrina."

This whole time, the only person who'd seemed entirely un-affected by enchantment was Sabrina. That girl thought she was unconquerable.

Prudence was starting to believe it might be true.

They drove through one of the many winding paths in the woods, in looping circles. The sky was like ink diluted by water, shading from black to a gray in which the stars were lost.

"Harvey," Sabrina said in a small voice. "I banished a prince of hell."

The witch-hunter glanced over at her, and then gave her a side-long crooked grin. "Yeah? Well done, 'Brina."

Sabrina smiled. "Thanks."

"It was a team effort," contributed Nick.

Sabrina redirected her smile to him. "Yes, it was."

"Oh, right," said the witch-hunter. "Well done, Prudence."

Nick made a face at him over Sabrina's head.

"You're not permitted to speak to me," said Prudence, and closed her eyes.

By the time she opened them, the witch-hunter had parked by the edge of the trees overlooking the town. All seemed quiet in Greendale, and there were no more whispers in the wind. The horizon was no longer painted with crimson fire but touched with the first tentative brushstroke of gold.

Dawn was remaking the day.

Sabrina's head was on the witch-hunter's shoulder, Nick's arm on the back of the seat behind her. As Prudence watched, Nick poked the witch-hunter in the shoulder.

"How's the enchantment level, Harry?"

"Nick," Sabrina scolded. "It's *Harvey*."

The witch-hunter rubbed his face with a tired sigh. "I think it's getting better."

"Then let's go home," Sabrina murmured, her voice warm on the word.

She was the only one who really had a home.

The witch-hunter turned the truck around and drove down another winding path. It was easy for a mortal to get lost in these woods, but evidently he knew the way to the Spellman house. Dawn light outlined the yellow sign, the gray grave markers, and the sloping gables. All the windows were lit up.

"There's a mortal tradition that says the people you spend New Year's with are the people you will spend the rest of the year with," Sabrina remarked.

"Please, Lucifer, no," said Prudence.

When they pulled up outside, the door was flung open. Hilda and Zelda Spellman spilled out, Hilda in flowered pajamas, Zelda in a red silk wrap, both of them rushing for Sabrina.

"Where have you *been*—"

"—worried *sick*—"

"You couldn't call?" asked Zelda. "Or send a quick bat with tidings? I despair, Sabrina."

"Hello, sweet Harvey," said Hilda. "Thank you for bringing her home."

"Hi, Hilda," Nick said with his most winning smile.

Hilda pursed her mouth as if she'd tasted something rotten and shook her head.

"Nicholas," said Zelda. "Would you take her inside?"

"Be happy to," Nick murmured.

"Yeah," said the witch-hunter. "Go."

Sabrina turned to him in clear distress. They looked at each other for a moment, profiles outlined by dawn.

"This doesn't change anything," the witch-hunter said, his voice scratchy and worn. "Does it?"

Sabrina shook her head. "No," she said sadly. "I don't think so."

Zelda's eyes, now they were no longer trained exclusively on Sabrina, rested on Nick with approval, skipped over the witch-hunter, and glanced on Prudence.

"Are you injured, Prudence? Let's get both the girls inside."

Zelda reached for Prudence, and Prudence sat up, reaching back. But Sabrina was climbing down from the truck, and Zelda turned instinctively toward the light of Sabrina's hair under the moon, all else forgotten.

Prudence clenched her fists beneath the witch-hunter's coat. She was so grateful Zelda had looked away and hadn't seen Prudence embarrassing herself.

Nick offered Sabrina a hand to help her out of the truck, and Sabrina accepted it. The witch-hunter climbed out and went around to the bed of the truck where Prudence lay.

"I'll carry you inside," Harvey offered.

"I'll turn you into a toad. You'd be hotter." Prudence lowered her voice. "I *don't* want to go in."

The witch-hunter frowned.

"You think I want to go to her home and be second best?" Prudence demanded, imagining the Spellmans healing her when they wanted to be fussing over Sabrina, their eyes passing over her the way parents' eyes did when they visited the Academy, looking for their child and not some orphan girl. "Would *you?*"

After a moment, the witch-hunter shook his head. He cleared his throat. "I'll take Prudence home."

Sabrina went around to the side of the truck, almost climbing over to try and give Prudence a hug despite Prudence's stern prohibition. Evidently Sabrina thought they were friends now.

They weren't. Prudence would make that clear, one day.

Nick and Sabrina stood in front of the house, watching as the truck pulled away, while Sabrina's aunts tried to shoo them both inside. Nick's arm was around Sabrina. Prudence saw the witch-hunter noticing.

"Just drop me off in the woods," ordered Prudence.

"I know the way to the Academy," the witch-hunter said.

Prudence sighed as she surrendered to slumber. "I'm surrounded by idiots."

She woke to find the pickup parked much too close to the Academy. The witch-hunter was sitting in the bed of the truck across from her, his head hanging, hands clasped between his knees. His awful hair was in his eyes again.

"The Academy is home, right?"

"I don't have any other," said Prudence.

"I can carry you in," he said.

Prudence envisioned the reactions of the Academy if a witch-hunter came through their doors.

"If you try, you will be blasted to red powder."

The witch-hunter silently handed Prudence a few sketches. Most were of her baby brother, but the last one was of her and Nick and Sabrina standing by a river that blazed. Prudence knew she was beautiful, but she'd never seen this kind of beauty in herself or in any other witch before.

She was sorry to burn the pictures, sorry to see the ashes blow away in the night wind, but burning them felt right. That was the nature of heartbreaking beauty. Even when it shone before your eyes, you knew it was lost.

That was when Prudence realized what the witch-hunter planned to do.

She sat up, swung her legs over the side of the truck, and made herself spring lightly onto the ground.

"You can keep the coat," the witch-hunter told her.

She'd been planning on it. Hellfire had left a hole in her dress.

"I'm going to burn it."

The witch-hunter shrugged. "I figured."

He scrambled out of the bed of the truck, making for the driver seat, and Prudence turned to the Academy, its gray façade blotting out the dawn. Then she looked back.

"Hey, witch-hunter!"

His head turned.

"Stay alive," said Prudence in her nastiest voice. "And away from me forever."

Harvey smiled, startled and sweet. "Same to you."

He gave her a little wave. Prudence scoffed and made for the Academy, letting out a sigh of relief when she was within the doors, sheltered behind the stone walls.

The relief was short-lived, since then she heard the sound of raucous partying, boys' voices lifted in loud jubilation. It sounded like a pack of them, headed from the meeting of the Judas Society for that club of Dorian Gray's, no doubt.

They passed her in a crew, laughing and singing and already drinking, the sons of Judas, chosen by her father as she wasn't. She stood with her back against the wall, an expression of cool superiority fixed onto her face, and watched them walk by without even seeing her.

All but one.

Ambrose Spellman was beside his boyfriend, hand on his shoulder, one moment. He was by her side the next. He was dressed for a party, in an open gold brocade jacket with only a gold necklace beneath, no shirt, and here was Prudence looking terrible.

Well, as terrible as she could ever look, which was still hot beyond the dreams of dragons.

Ambrose gave her a single glance, eyes wide and glossy, and then scooped her up in his arms.

"Go on without me, boys!" he called over his shoulder, laughing. "I can't resist Prudence tonight!"

Prudence laughed too, throwing an arm around his neck and a leg up in the air, flinging a look of saucy triumph over at Luke.

This wasn't the stupid witch-hunter, with his dreary sorry face, making her look weak in front of other people. Ambrose knew better. This was a *witch*, slippery and deceptive, a laugh heard in the shadows. And what a witch he was.

Ambrose set her on her feet in front of her door.

Prudence raised her eyebrows at him. "This coat really doing it for you?"

"No, it's awful," said Ambrose with his easy smile. "Where'd you get it?"

Prudence shrugged. "Stole it off a mortal boy."

"Ah, well. The coat's dreadful, but stealing's fun. Lucky mortal boy."

He didn't ask what had happened to Prudence, but he didn't leave either. He leaned against the wall by her door, his eyes running over her. He shone even in the shadows of the Academy, and just a look from him felt like a caress.

He was flirty, but so were most of their kind. She still wasn't sure.

Please *like witches as well as warlocks*, Prudence willed.

"If it was any other night," Prudence drawled, "I would do unspeakable things to you."

Ambrose kicked a boot up against the wall, leaning back with an exaggerated sigh. "Oh, speak now."

Maybe she should let him in her room. A few healing spells, and she'd be fine. Trust no man, Prudence always told herself, but... maybe she could trust this one.

She licked her lips and tested him. "I ran into a spot of trouble tonight. With Sabrina."

Ambrose's graceful lounge against the wall went tense. His eyes left hers.

Prudence had known that would happen. Ambrose said nothing, and didn't move, but his whole body was straining against the urge to run and check on Sabrina.

She respected commitment to family.

The Church of Night said Father Blackwood was deserving of high honor, that he was chosen by Satan, that he was to be lauded and cherished in the dark heart of the dark god. The Church of Night said Ambrose was a disgraced criminal, allowed out of the house on sufferance, linked to incommunicates and infidels.

Father Blackwood refused to claim his own orphan child, had left her alone in the merciless world. Ambrose was ready to hurl himself between an orphan cousin and any threat.

Prudence knew which man she believed had honor. But that didn't mean he had power. She wished the world worked differently sometimes. But it didn't.

If Father Blackwood ever thought Ambrose would pick him over Ambrose's family in any meaningful way, Prudence's father was a fool. Prudence wasn't one.

Her father was her chance for a different life. And Ambrose would always side with the Spellmans. Carnal delights were one thing. Trust was another.

Ambrose would pick his family. Prudence should pick hers. She must be ready to hurt Ambrose, if she had to.

Prudence smirked at him. "Afraid I'm exhausted. Run along, would you?"

"Catch you later, Prudence," said Ambrose, walking backward

and away from her, but still giving her a last beautiful smile. "With a net."

Prudence wiggled her fingers in a sultry goodbye. "Hold you later. With a leash."

She opened her bedroom door, her heart sinking as she heard the baby starting to wail. Then she stopped dead in shock, seeing her sisters gathered around the cradle.

"Shut up, little baby," Agatha murmured, frantically rocking. "Please, please shut up, little baby."

"Sisters?" Prudence asked from the door. She meant her voice to sound arch, but it came out blank.

"Prue!" Agatha exclaimed. "Where have you been?"

"Getting into trouble," Prudence answered. "What else? What are you two doing here?"

"*Someone* had to watch Judas," said Agatha.

Prudence bristled, but Agatha was focused on the cradle and her words only sounded factual. "We know you're still angry with us about the spell on the mines, but that doesn't mean we can just leave the baby. After all, he's your brother, isn't he? So he's ours, in a way."

"Prudence, you're hurt," said Dorcas, rushing toward her with a flurry of spells, already rummaging in her herb pouch.

Prudence permitted herself to be attended to while she thought this over. So her sisters hadn't been avoiding her. They'd been treading carefully around her, fearful of her wrath. They thought she was angry with *them*.

She supposed that was acceptable.

Once Dorcas was done healing her, Dorcas gazed up at her with beseeching eyes. Prudence sneered, but not in a serious way.

"Oh, Prue, *please* stop being cross with us," said Dorcas, flinging herself into Prudence's arms.

"Well," drawled Prudence. "I might be persuaded to forgive you."

Dorcas sniffled. "I'm sorry, I'm sorry. I'll only ever kill the people you say from now on."

Prudence hesitated and then lifted a hand and laid it on Dorcas's red braids. "I will ask you to kill many men, sister. Emphasis on 'men.'"

Dorcas smiled with gratitude. "Prudence, I'm so sad. I don't really remember, but I know Nick Scratch let me down terribly."

"Of course he did," murmured Prudence. "He's a man, isn't he? They're all trash. That's why we should pile them up in heaps and burn them."

Judas wailed.

"Oh, hush," said Agatha. "Don't be so sensitive, baby. We didn't mean you. Prue, *how* do we make this baby be quiet? He cries all the time."

"I know, it's a problem," said Prudence. "Let us try singing to him. Together, sisters."

The Weird Sisters knew no lullabies, but they joined hands and danced around the cradle, chanting an eerie chant and swaying together. Dark of the moon, light of the sun, the three in one. The child stopped crying, for once.

When Prudence's father dropped in and found his son sleeping, he laid a hand on her shoulder. She ducked her head to hide how his approving touch made her smile. Perhaps she'd misjudged the situation with him, as she had with her sisters. Perhaps, once her father came to know her better, he would appreciate her.

That night, the Weird Sisters slept on Prudence's settee together, in a tangle with Prudence at the center.

She didn't need luck. She could make the family she wanted happen without it.

After all, she'd made one family already.

ENDS A MORTAL WOE

January 1, New Year's Day, Morning
HARVEY

All in all, kind of a weird night," concluded Harvey. He leaned down and patted the gravestone. "I'll come back and tell you how things are going at school. Happy New Year, Tommy."

He left the graveyard, closing the gate behind him and making for home. There were patches of scorched earth everywhere he went today, but snow was still falling through the crisp air of early morning. The blackened earth would be hidden soon.

Someone was waiting for him on the bridge, snowflakes lighting soft on his hair. It made Harvey remember that shining moment in the dark, the dazzling snow like diamonds scattering around Nick and Sabrina, the way they'd smiled at each other. How it felt, seeing Sabrina turn to someone else.

"Hi, mortal," said Nick. "I thought you might come here."

Harvey raised an eyebrow. "You also, like, know where I live."

"You told me not to go back there."

"Oh, hey, boundaries," said Harvey. "Cool." He smiled a little before he realized he was doing it.

Nick smiled back. "Thanks for the assist last night."

"All hands on deck for a prince of hell, I guess," said Harvey. "Really, a prince of hell? You could've mentioned that earlier."

"I will next time," Nick promised.

Harvey looked down at the water running under the bridge. He'd heard somewhere that you couldn't cross the same river twice. Because the river was always different, and you were different too.

"Nah," he said quietly. "Don't bother."

"I'm *sorry*," said Nick in a fast, rough voice, as though he was pulling off a bandage. "I'm not used to—considering mortals' feelings. You have so many of them. It's hard to keep track."

Best if you never found out, Nick had told him once, about all Sabrina's lies. He'd brought the girl who killed Tommy into Harvey's home, without even thinking how Harvey would feel if he discovered the truth. Mortal lives didn't matter to witches. Mortal feelings were utterly unimportant. Harvey was sick of lies.

"I get it. I think . . . I get what witches are like now," Harvey said slowly. "That's how you are. No use expecting you to do things against your nature."

"I—I could try," said Nick.

Harvey glanced up at him, hesitated, and then shook his head.

"But I said I was *sorry*," Nick argued. "And I was honest. So now it should be okay. That's in the books."

"It's not a magic spell," said Harvey. "Sorry."

"So..." said Nick. "So...bye? Been annoying knowing you?"

Harvey took a deep breath. "Actually, I was wondering if you would do me a favor."

There was a startled pause.

"Sabrina did a memory spell on me once," Harvey said. "I was so mad at her for doing it, but now...I want you to do one. I want you to get witches out of my mind."

Nick treated him to a spectacular eye roll. "I can't give you Sabrina amnesia, mortal. You've known her since you were five. You would end up even more empty-headed than you already are."

"Not Sabrina," Harvey said, appalled by the idea. That would be like taking a color away from him that he needed for every drawing. "Not the last eleven years. Jesus. Only the last five days. Those witches. Dorcas. Prudence. Jude. You. I just wish—I hadn't opened the door when you asked to come in."

He thought Nick might respond, but Nick only leaned against the rail of the bridge, listening.

Harvey swallowed. "It was dumb," he said. "*I'm* dumb. I was lonely. I—I miss my brother. But it was magic that took him away from me. And I hate that girl, Dorcas. I want to kill her, but—I don't want to be someone that angry, someone who wants to hurt someone else that much. I don't want to be reminded of magic and murder at every turn."

Witches were killers. Witches were liars. Witches didn't need him.

It was bad enough to know with inescapable certainty that he'd come running every time Sabrina needed him. Far worse to get attached to more witches, which he would—which he *was*. Far worse to smile back when Prudence's ebony-painted mouth curved on the words *Stay alive*, or worry so much about Nick dreaming of Satan. Far worse to think of witches as friends when witches didn't even think of mortals as people.

You poor pathetic wimp, his dad said in his mind. He should never have opened that door.

Harvey appealed: "Do you understand why I'm asking? How can I trust a witch not to hurt me? I can't trust my own *father* not to hurt me."

"I understand," Nick said icily. "You're a coward."

His dad had always said so. He'd insisted that he wasn't, told Sabrina that he wasn't, fought against the creeping knowledge it was true. It'd seemed so important, once.

Harvey shrugged. "I guess I am."

That didn't matter. Maybe he had to go through being a coward to become something more.

"There are people I have to protect."

"Who?" Nick asked.

"Not witches," said Harvey.

If it was only him, he supposed he'd be lonely enough to try and love witches, but it wasn't only his life and heart at risk. He had others to think of now.

He'd imagined, at the beginning of this week, that he'd lost Roz and Susie. But he hadn't. They were still his friends, infinitely beloved and infinitely fragile. Roz was cursed; Susie had been attacked. They were under threat from the magical world. Witches didn't need him, but his friends would. He had to pick their side.

He'd always wanted to get away from Greendale. Now he couldn't imagine leaving his friends in danger.

"Be a coward or a witch-hunter or whatever you like," Nick sneered. "I don't see why I should help you."

"You don't have to," said Harvey. "I can't make you. But what is there to lose?"

Nick's gaze on Harvey was bitter. "Nothing at all."

Harvey nodded. "I can't help you with Sabrina anymore. And... nobody but you thought you'd need much help to begin with."

The sneer distorting Nick's mouth faded.

"I saw her with you," said Harvey. "She's... going to really like you. You're both... you'll be great together."

His throat felt as if it might close up again, with the bleak misery he'd felt last night. He wanted this discussion to be *over*.

"Well." Nick sounded less mad. "I hope so, but—"

"I would've thought you'd be happy to push me further out of your world," he interrupted. "Sabrina's in it. What if I decided I could accept the magical world, and I went to Sabrina and begged to be her one and only again?"

The idea seemed to startle Nick. Harvey supposed Nick had never considered him a real rival. It probably hadn't occurred to Nick for an instant that Sabrina might actually pick Harvey.

"Is that what you'd do?"

"I'm *in love with her*, Nick!" Harvey snarled. "What do you think that means?"

"I don't *know yet*," Nick snarled back.

"Well, think about it," said Harvey. "I'm sure it's hard for you to imagine, but what if you were the one left out in the cold? You want that?"

"No," said Nick.

Harvey thought of Prudence in the back of his truck, refusing to go into the Spellman house where she wouldn't be loved. Nobody wanted to be left out in the cold.

"So why won't you do the spell?"

"I don't feel like it," Nick drawled.

"Please," said Harvey. "Did you only want information to help with Sabrina? Or were we—were we ever friends? Even for a minute? Sometimes—sometimes it seemed like we were. If we were, then I'm asking you to do the spell."

Nick watched him with the eyes of an animal held at bay.

Harvey nodded, accepting silence as an answer. "Guess not."

That was what he'd figured. He'd thought it would be easier to know for sure, so he could turn away from the witches and be certain they were impossibly distant from mortals. All save Sabrina.

Now he was certain.

He turned and walked away.

Before he made it off the bridge, Harvey heard the thunder of footsteps running after him. His arm was grabbed in a vise hold. For a split second of panic, he thought: *Wait, stop. I was sure you wouldn't do it.*

Nick Scratch said: "Come here."

DREAMS NO MORTAL DARED TO DREAM

January 1, New Year's Day, Morning
ROZ

She didn't dream a dream of hate, but sometimes the dreams the cunning brought were worse. Roz tossed on her bed as, in dreams, she drifted through the underworld.

There was a tower, high and burning, and the sound of the flames was a scream. *Therefore is the tower called Babel*, Roz remembered. *The Lord did there confound the language of all the earth; and from thence did the Lord scatter them.*

There was a flame with the head of a hawk, and as Roz watched, the bright terrible flame traveled through the air to a dark throne that shadowed the whole land. She couldn't see the face of the Lord in that throne, but she saw the demon of fire and discord prostrate himself at his lord's feet.

"I have done as you commanded," said Pruflas, proud prince of hell, bowing his burning head. "The seed is strong. Praise Satan! The girl is strong. I saw her robed in the light of dying stars, wielding power as both blade and scepter, with the boy you chose by her side."

"As I commanded him to be," murmured the Dark Lord on his dark throne. "Those whose hearts are touched by Satan will be kept by me forever. He has no choice but to obey. Nor will she, in the end. Now, lie to all the world, but not me. Something in our plans went awry."

"Very little, my lord," said the prince. "A trifle. The girl had the power to turn me away, and that is well. But the spell of discord I laid upon the people, which should have resulted in beautiful bloodshed... There were too many in the town who fought against it, witches and mortals alike. They should not have been able to resist the tide of hatred, but they gathered together and toward the girl. I fear—"

The Dark Lord, on his dark throne, laughed. "I fear nothing and never have. Learn from me. Of course the girl will rebel at first. Consider whose daughter she is."

"The daughter of the Great Rebel." The prince kissed his god's feet. "Praise Satan. Praise Sabrina!"

Oh my God, Roz thought, half horror and half prayer. Her mind fragmented into panic, her thoughts scattering everywhere, with only one thing clear.

Sabrina wasn't unlucky, she wasn't bringing trouble upon herself, she was a *target*. She was Rosemary's baby, all grown up and in terrible danger. This beast on his throne was after her, wanted to make her his own. Roz had to get to Sabrina and warn her.

I know what to do, she'd tell Sabrina. *We have to gather together, we have to—*

That was when he turned his head, and the throne drew in her dreaming self as though it were a black hole.

"Oh, little cunning child," the devil whispered, his face coming close to hers, beautiful and beastlike. "You can't see this."

Roz screamed as he laid a burning hand upon her eyes.

The scream woke her up, ringing against the walls of her room. She sat up in bed, blinking hard. She'd been sleeping so much these past few days. She hoped she wasn't coming down with something.

Roz checked the time on her phone and scrambled out of bed. She was late to meet Harvey and Susie.

SNEERS AT WITCHCRAFT

January 1, New Year's Day, Morning
PRUDENCE

Prudence walked down the main street of Greendale, strolling by Nick Scratch's side and licking a large blood-and-toad-flavored lollipop he'd given her as a bribe. She was spending so much time among the mortals lately. She'd have to arrange a whole impurifying spa day with her sisters.

"There," said Nick.

They brushed by the witch-hunter, who was walking with his arms around the shoulders of those two mortal friends Sabrina ceaselessly banged on about. The tiny short-haired one was telling a joke. The witch-hunter was laughing, his head tipped back, and the tall pretty one was gazing up at him.

Lucifer in a lounge chair, Roz with the great hair *liked* him. Girl, Prudence wanted to tell her, you are beautiful, you can do better. Don't waste yourself on the witch-hunter.

It was a little strange when the witch-hunter looked straight through her, and then frowned slightly in faint recognition, eyes widening as he glanced from her face to Nick's.

He said tentatively: "Hi?"

Nick gave a curt nod. "Harry."

"*What* a jackass," muttered the witch-hunter as he and his friends passed them by.

Prudence took a lick of her lollipop. Across the street, a boy became distracted and walked into traffic, but that wasn't Prudence's problem.

"Yep, looks like it worked. Well done. Nice strong spell. You have to set them really firmly, so they can't get the memories back via suggestion. I did it for one of Agatha's mortals once."

Agatha's mortal had kept hanging around. It hadn't been safe, not for the mortal and not for her sister. Agatha was upset when she thought the mortal had lost interest, but it was for the best.

Nick nodded, walking rapidly down the street. It was getting rather difficult to keep up with him.

"He looks—happy," Prudence commented.

"You were right. Witch-hunters are all the same," Nick said calmly. "I hope he chokes."

Prudence considered the matter and smirked. "That *would* be hilarious."

The snow was still falling, each flake catching daylight and winking. Maybe it would keep snowing until Sabrina wanted it to stop.

No, Prudence told herself. Witches couldn't wish the weather into being. She'd been enduring enchantment, dealing with demons, and making poor personal life choices by hanging around Sabrina and Nick. She'd been confused when she thought she saw snow burst from a clear sky last night.

She shook off the strange thoughts and glanced at Nick. He'd just cast a swift look behind him. The mortals and the witch-hunter were being shamelessly affectionate, right there on a public street where children could see.

"Aw, are we sad? Did little Nicky think he'd made a friend?"

She mimed tears with her free hand. Nick's set face turned into bared teeth and satanic eyebrow action, which was a big improvement.

"No, sweetheart," he answered. "I know I don't have any friends."

There was something in the way he said it that made her recall what she'd told him in the library. She almost protested, but she didn't, and he was continuing relentlessly.

"Don't have any, don't want any, don't need any. I'm going to be Sabrina Spellman's one and only. I'll do everything she wants, and she'll love me best of anybody. That's how it works, right?"

He flung her a demanding look.

"I never want to be asked any disgusting questions about love ever again," said Prudence firmly, "but yes, I assume so. I mean, I expect men to do everything *I* want."

Nick nodded to himself with gathering resolve. "Since we're among the mortals already, I think I'll walk Sabrina to the Academy."

"You make me feel unwell on a daily basis," said Prudence. "Have fun."

Nick set off away from her and across the street, but he stopped under a lamppost and looked back.

"Hey, Prudence," he tossed over his shoulder, with a curving smile. "We may not be friends, but you're my favorite ex-girlfriend."

She hadn't thought he'd hold a grudge long. It was a well-kept secret, but under the bravado, Nick Scratch was nice-natured. For a witch.

Prudence, who had no such personal flaw, made a swift gesture that blew snow in his eyes. "That's because you never appreciated my sisters as they deserve, you cretinous tart."

Nick saluted.

"Oh, I give up," Prudence said. "If you want Sabrina, go get her. She dumped the mortal for you, didn't she?"

"No, that's not remotely what happened," said Nick.

"Come on, Nicholas." Prudence waved a hand and made the snowflakes dance. "You're a witch. Make it true. Good luck with your disaster-area girl. You'll need it."

He laughed and left, his path leading inexorably to the Spellman house and his lady.

Sabrina, who would do anything for her friends and who expected them to do anything for her. Sabrina, who didn't even know she expected too much from people. People who'd always had too much didn't have any concept of what things really cost.

Prudence knew. Prudence wanted power and security, and she was prepared to pay the price.

Prudence saw the path before her clearly. She didn't have time to waste on Sabrina. Or Nick Scratch, with no friends left, wolf-hungry for love and headed for disaster. Or even adorable

Ambrose. They couldn't help her. Perhaps Zelda might, but Prudence couldn't make Zelda like her better than Sabrina.

Prudence had to focus on Father Blackwood. She had to make him believe she was the ideal daughter, prove to him that she was cruel and heartless and perfect. She couldn't be distracted by people who would never choose her. Prudence had to choose herself.

She made for home, and her sisters.

FIND THE MORTAL WORLD ENOUGH

January 1, New Year's Day, Morning
HARVEY

W*hat* a jackass," muttered Harvey.

"Who was that?" Roz asked, peering after the couple as they walked on.

Plenty of people were staring. Greendale didn't see a lot of glamorous strangers, but Roz was squinting at their backs with a worried look, as though not sure she would recognize people she knew. He wouldn't let anything trouble Roz, not if he could help it.

"Don't worry about it. He's some guy I met once," said Harvey. "We didn't get along."

Susie grinned. "He clearly found you memorable."

Harvey and Susie had a brief scuffle fight, which Susie won by pulling Harvey's woolly hat down over his eyes. Harvey ended up turned around and trying to fight with a lamppost.

"Oh," he said when he rolled the hat up. "I *thought* this seemed too tall to be Susie."

"Whatever, loser," said Susie. "Gotta do chores. Catch you later, Roz. Harry."

"Not going to tell us your New Year's resolutions?" asked Roz.

The impish smile faded. "I will tell you, Roz," Susie promised. "Soon."

Harvey grabbed Susie back for a three-way hug, before he let Susie run off, stepping lightly into the dancing snow. His arm was around Roz's neck. He kept it there, walking with more care than he usually did so he could unobtrusively guide her. If she needed it.

Nick Scratch, the weird warlock guy in all black, turned his head and caught Harvey's eye. It was strange he was with that girl, the one Sabrina had called Prudence. Harvey guessed Prudence must be a witch too, but he'd been very sure Nick was interested in Sabrina. Maybe witches did that kind of thing differently.

Whenever he thought of magic, his mind scrambled from panic to fear, and whenever he thought of Sabrina, he was so angry. He wished she would come back to him. He wished he knew why she'd told the lies that led him into a nightmare. If he could just under-stand, he could forgive her.

Still, there was something more important than resentment or terror. No matter what, Harvey wanted the best for Sabrina.

He might be a jerk who'd forgotten Harvey's name, but when Sabrina asked, Nick Scratch came through. Harvey wanted that for her, in the strange world she'd gone where he couldn't follow.

Roz yawned, calling his attention to her. "You didn't sleep well?"

"I slept way too much, these past few days," Roz told him. "My head's still foggy. A lot of people are stumbling around looking ashamed of themselves and asking what happened last night. Maybe that's normal the day after New Year's, but it seems like … it might be something more. Knowing our luck, something magic."

"Yeah," Harvey said softly. "I think you're right. But I guess I'm like everybody else. I don't really remember. I hope I didn't do anything to be ashamed of."

It was possible he had. He was always messing stuff up, but he thought he remembered the important things. He'd gone to pick up Sabrina when she was in trouble. He'd visited Tommy's grave at last, and he felt lighter for it. He'd been out shooting with Susie, and they'd promised to fight against magic together.

Roz laughed. "I doubt you did, Harvey."

"Thanks for believing in me."

"Anytime," she murmured, a slight flush rising on her golden-brown skin. She leaned against him, and Harvey blinked down at her.

She wants you, said a voice in his mind, but that was ridiculous. Of course she didn't.

"Sabrina!" Roz exclaimed suddenly. "I was thinking about Sabrina. I've been freaking out over this magic stuff, but I want to try and do better. I'm ready to have a real talk with her." Her eyes searched Harvey's face, unfocused and anxious. "Don't you want to talk to her?"

He wanted so much he couldn't have. *You have nothing a witch needs*, he thought, as if someone was whispering truth in his ear. It broke his heart.

"Yeah," Harvey said eventually. "I do want to talk to Sabrina."

"We're back to school soon. We'll see her then."

"Let's enjoy the last of vacation first. Want to go to the movies later?" Harvey asked.

Roz beamed. "Sure."

"Cool, I'll text Susie," said Harvey, and was startled to see Roz's smile dim.

"Great," she told him after a momentary pause, and pulled away.

He found, unexpectedly, that he missed her warmth. There hadn't been a lot of warmth for him lately. He tugged her back in for a hug and felt her burning cheek against his.

"Happy New Year, Roz," he whispered.

She stepped back, still blushing and smiling. "Same to you. Happy also."

She wants you.

Maybe.

Maybe, if it was true, he could work out whether he could possibly do something about that. For now, he was happy to be going to the movies with his friends.

He walked home whistling and found his father outside fixing up the basketball hoop around back of his house. His dad was wearing an old long-sleeved sweatshirt Harvey hadn't seen in years, not since the days when he and Tommy were kids and his dad stayed sober enough to play with them in the evenings.

"Hey there, Harv," his dad said. "I know you weren't too keen last time we spoke, but I thought you might change your mind and toss around a ball with your old dad."

He rubbed a hand through his graying hair. Harvey watched the hand warily.

"I'd like to clear some of the cobwebs out of my mind," his dad urged. "The past few days are kind of muddy. But I haven't been drinking again. I swear."

"I know that."

Sabrina had stopped him. He hadn't been able to stop himself.

But it was still good that his dad wasn't drinking. Harvey offered him a cautious smile.

"From what I do remember..." his dad said slowly. "I think you handled yourself pretty well, Harv."

First time you've ever thought that about me, thought Harvey, but he didn't say it. He'd learned a long time ago not to mouth off to his father.

His dad moved toward him, and Harvey wanted to flinch away, but he held himself still. Now he'd gone to see Tommy, he found he didn't resent his father so much for wanting Harvey to replace his eldest and favorite son. His dad had lost Tommy too.

Harvey didn't trust his father, but he did love him. He had so few people left. Maybe his father could learn to love him back. He hadn't hoped for that in a long time. It felt good to hope again.

He took off his hat and coat and said, "Let's go."

His dad's eyes gleamed. "We'll make a tough guy of you yet."

"We'll see," said Harvey.

He could be sorry for his father, who thought he had to be so tough. It was possible his father got scared like he did, underneath. It was possible there might be, not forgiveness, but less misery between them.

He'd once told Sabrina there was no flying without her, but if she was flying without him, he had to make a life for himself on the ground. Surely there was something that could be built here. He couldn't just keep missing her. He owed it to Tommy to live.

His father threw the ball in his direction too hard, but Harvey caught it. His dad smiled to see him succeed, and Harvey ran in a circle around his father on the cleared ground.

Maybe it was time to play ball.

I FIND ALL THE WITCHCRAFT WE NEED

January 1, New Year's Day, Morning
SABRINA

I woke late on New Year's Day. It had been an eventful night. I'd fielded my aunts' questions and fallen asleep on the sofa.

The last thing I remembered was Nick touching my hair as I went to sleep, the caress so light and tentative it might have been a dream and not a memory.

The first thing I heard when I woke was the sound of heels on the floor. I opened my eyes and thought for a moment I saw a snake coming toward me.

Then I realized I was seeing the snakeskin heels of my favorite teacher. I sat bolt upright. "Ms. Wardwell!"

Her cat's eyes were wide, as though she were startled to find me in my own home.

"Oh, Sabrina dear," said Ms. Wardwell. "Alive and whole, not missing any limbs or vital organs, or consumed entirely by a fiend from the deeps? I had to come check for myself. Because I was, ah, deeply worried about you. Considering the evidence that a prince of hell almost came through to Greendale, I thought surely all was lost for you. Yet here you are, and not a scratch on you! I am stunned. But, of course, relieved."

"Thank you," I said.

"I feel terribly guilty I told you to banish the bad-luck demon. Who knew it would summon a prince of hell? Certainly not me!"

"No harm done," I said.

"No," said Ms. Wardwell. "I see that."

"Since you're here, I want to ask you something," I began. "What happened last night…it made me realize I want to explore the power I have now. To go deeper into the world of witches. So I wanted to ask you a favor. Vacation's almost over, but could you get me a few more days off at Baxter High? I'm planning to devote myself to the Academy."

Ms. Wardwell's eyes gleamed. "Do you know, Sabrina, I think that's a marvelous idea. You should put some distance between yourself and your mortal friends. I will arrange it so you don't have to return to Baxter High until you desire."

That wasn't what I'd said, but perhaps Ms. Wardwell could see what I meant.

I smiled up at her. "I really appreciate this."

"*I* do not appreciate you coming into my house without an invitation and bothering my niece," said Aunt Zelda from the doorway.

It was eleven o'clock on New Year's Day, and Aunt Zelda was wearing a three-piece skirt suit embroidered with purple thread, and a matching hat with a dyed purple feather. She was also holding a lorgnette, through which she was studying Ms. Wardwell with a steely eye.

"Perhaps you feel Sabrina is in need of a role model?" Aunt Zelda inquired. "Well, she has one. And there's only room for one wicked witch in my house. Do I make myself clear?"

"As a crystal ball," murmured Ms. Wardwell. "See you at school, Sabrina. Perhaps."

She sashayed out, seeming unaffected by Aunt Zelda's menacing air. Indeed, she gave Aunt Zelda a curving crimson smile as she passed her by. Aunt Zelda raised an unimpressed eyebrow.

"Aunt Zelda," I said. "That was not very nice."

"I'm not very nice, child," murmured Aunt Zelda, wandering over to sit on the sofa beside me. "I like veils on hats, not threats, I like my home to be an accursed sanctum, and I generally like to know what is going on. Lots of confused mortals are stumbling around the town, and you came home with burn marks on you. What happened?"

I hesitated. "Do you remember everything from last night? Did you or Aunt Hilda or Ambrose—find yourself thinking strange things?"

"We were mostly thinking about you," said Aunt Zelda.

I leaned against her. The description of Pruflas's spell said *There is no magic stronger than hate.* I didn't agree.

Aunt Zelda's eyes narrowed. "Tell me, did you get yourself in trouble again?"

"Yes," I confessed. "But I got myself out of it, without asking you for help. Doesn't that count for something?"

Aunt Zelda seemed less than convinced.

"I remembered all the things you said to me," I coaxed. "About luck, and the membrane between the worlds being weak at New Year's, and everything. Even when you don't know you're helping me, you're helping me."

Aunt Zelda tapped the lorgnette affectionately against my cheek.

"Oh, very well, Sabrina, no more shameless wheedling. Consider that you got lucky. This once."

I cheered. "Thank you, Aunt Zelda!"

"And if do you get into trouble again…which you will," said Aunt Zelda. "You can ask me for help. Ask, and I come. Seek, and I find. Cry, and I kill. That's what family means."

I gave her a hug. "I'm going to make you really proud this year, Aunt Zelda. You'll see. I'll be the most powerful witch of them all."

"Don't you think that's enough sentimentality before noon, Sabrina?" Aunt Zelda asked, but she wore a small smile as she rose from the sofa.

I didn't want power that came from Satan or anybody else. If someone gave you power, he could take it away. I wanted to get power of my own. I didn't want anyone to do it for me, but I did want friends to help me.

There was help and friendship to be found in the world of witches. I knew that now.

I followed Aunt Zelda out of the room, but she headed upstairs and I went out the door to sit in one of the wicker chairs on the porch.

Dawn remade the world every day, but today the dawn had

remade a whole new year. The snow was still falling, giving the whole world a clean slate.

I closed my eyes and murmured the little spell Aunt Hilda had taught me. *"Lady Anne, Lady Anne, send me a man as fast as you can."*

When I opened my eyes, I saw the snow had stopped falling, and Ambrose was walking onto the porch toward me.

He handed me a cup of coffee in a copper mug and tossed me a grin. "You might want to be more specific, cousin. Who knows what admirer the wind might send you?"

"It's a new year," I said. "I want to be open to whatever comes my way."

He smiled against the shining rim of his own mug. "Then hell's bells, ring in the changes."

Aunt Hilda came out with her arms full of scarves, though she'd neglected to put one on herself. "Ambrose, Sabrina, why are you out catching your deaths in the snow?"

"I'm too hot to be cold, Auntie," Ambrose drawled, so Aunt Hilda chased him around the porch while I laughed.

I was the only one looking out into the woods radiant with light on frost, every tree a snow queen. Through the dazzle I saw a shadow emerge through the trees, only a boy's shape. At first I couldn't make out which boy.

Harvey? Or Nick?

Ever since I could remember, there had only been one possible boy for me. But things were changing this year.

Whichever he was, he was the one who'd come when I called.

He drew closer, up the winding path and past the yellow sign that meant home, dark gaze surveying the family scene on the porch with an almost wondering look, then fixing on my face.

It was Nick. My heart gave an odd little thump that almost hurt. I wasn't disappointed.

"Good morning, beautiful," he said as he walked up to the last step of our porch and lounged against our toad statue. "I was passing by, and I thought I might walk you to school."

"You were passing by?" Aunt Hilda asked, hand on her hip. "You live in your school."

She'd stopped chasing Ambrose in order to glare at Nick from above. Ambrose toasted Nick with his coffee cup, but he did it behind Aunt Hilda's back.

"Be nice," I whispered to Aunt Hilda. "I know you threw away his note for me."

"I see now that I was very wrong to throw away your personal correspondence," said Aunt Hilda, adding under her breath: "I should've burned it."

Nick fired a devastating smile at her. "Good morning. May I say—"

"You may not," said Aunt Hilda. "You're too slick by half. You're not charming me this morning. I'm going inside."

"I'll charm you later, then," Nick called after her.

I told him: "I'll get my bag."

I ran in to get my bag and put on my red coat, then frowned thoughtfully at my reflection. Now that I'd decided to keep my white hair, my old clothes didn't seem to fit. I considered how I thought a powerful witch should look. Maybe I needed a badass leather jacket.

When I came back out, Nick insisted on taking my book bag from me.

"I've never walked a girl to school before," he said. "I understand the carrying of books is traditional."

I shook my head and let him have it. "Don't pretend, you player. You walked me to class the first day we met."

"Ah, but that's because you're the exception to every rule, Spellman."

Nick was flirty and swaggering as ever, but there was a bruised look around his eyes. He must be tired. I'd run him pretty ragged.

"There was something you wanted to tell me," I recalled. "Something that wasn't a big deal at first, but you wanted to be honest about it now. That's what you said. What is it?"

There was a pause, the only sound our footfalls in the snow.

Then Nick shrugged. "I've forgotten. I guess it really wasn't a big deal."

"All right," I said. "If you remember, let me know. And . . . thanks, Nick. You really came through for me yesterday."

"And I'll come through for you tomorrow," said Nick. "If you're grateful, can I ask you a question?"

I wondered if he was going to ask me out again. My heart gave that strange painful thump again. *This time*, I thought, *I might say yes*.

"You said you were my friend," Nick told me, his voice very soft, as though if he said the words too loudly the air would carry them off. "And you care about me. You meant that? You won't take it away?"

"Never," I promised.

"Even if I ask you out?" A ghost of a smile touched Nick's lips. "Even if I ask you out a lot?"

I have a boyfriend, I'd told Nick once. *Harvey*, I thought yearningly, but he'd put himself in terrible danger by venturing out on New Year's Eve. I couldn't let him risk that again.

I'd been so happy when I saw Harvey last night. I'd felt made of happiness. But nothing had changed between us, and I didn't see how anything could.

Nick was watching me with those bruised-looking eyes.

Every year until this year, I'd walked the woods with another boy. I could almost see our past selves now, lost somewhere among the trees. Me with my hair gold instead of snow-white, before I signed the Book. Me with my hand in his, the boy I'd always trusted completely, thinking I would never have to let him go.

We couldn't be those people any longer. There'd been nothing wrong with those past selves, not my softhearted and sweet-natured Harvey, or me, the girl who always tried her best. But years changed, and we changed with them.

This year, I was walking the woods with Nick. Maybe I would walk with him through the woods all this year.

Right now, with him looking at me this way, it seemed possible. Whenever Nick looked at me, I felt better than strong. I felt glorious.

"I have to be honest. I'm still hung up on Harvey. Even if I could work through that, I know how witches can be, and I'm sorry to spoil your fun, but I'm not looking for just fun. I'm looking for someone special."

"What a coincidence," said Nick. "I was hoping I might be special to somebody one day. Why don't I stick around? You can decide if you like me enough to keep me."

I couldn't make any promises, but he made me smile. He always had, ever since I'd met him.

"Stick around," I told him softly.

In spite of those shadowed eyes, he smiled back. "I'm not going anywhere. My plan is to stay with you."

The white snow crunched under our feet, but a piece of darkness slipped toward me through the trees. His silent paws left behind no trace.

"This is my familiar, Salem," I told Nick proudly. "He's from the wild woods. So he's independent, like me."

Nick hesitated. "Then consider me an admirer."

He leaned over and, moving with great care as though being gentle was something difficult and complex, stroked Salem.

"Well, well, well," said Salem. *"The boy can learn."*

I had to live among the witches. Maybe I could even come to love the Path of Night with no more doubts and no more fear. Surely after all this, I was due some luck.

For now, Nick and I went running over the brilliant snow, looping around the tall trees and laughing, still in sight of home.

Perhaps the change this year brought would be good.

ABOUT THE AUTHOR

Sarah Rees Brennan is the #1 *New York Times* bestselling author of twelve books, both solo and cowritten with authors including Kelly Link and Maureen Johnson. She is the Lodestar Award and Mythopoeic Award finalist for her book *In Other Lands*. She was born in Ireland by the sea and lives there now in the shadow of a cathedral. Visit her at sarahreesbrennan.com, or follow her on Twitter at @sarahreesbrenna (they stole her last N, and she may resort to magic to recover it).